LEOPA

AN ISLAND OF SOUND

In the same series

LEOPARD I
Dissonant Voices: The New Russian Fiction

LEOPARD II
Turning the Page

LEOPARD III
Frontiers

LEOPARD IV
Bearing Witness

LEOPARD V

AN ISLAND OF SOUND

Hungarian Poetry and Fiction
before and beyond the Iron Curtain

THE HARVILL PRESS
LONDON

Published by The Harvill Press 2004
2 4 6 8 10 9 7 5 3 1

First published in Great Britain in 2004 by
The Harvill Press
Random House, 20 Vauxhall Bridge Road,
London SW1V 2SA

Random House Australia (Pty) Limited
20 Alfred Street, Milsons Point, Sydney,
New South Wales 2061, Australia

Random House New Zealand Limited
18 Poland Road, Glenfield,
Auckland 10, New Zealand

Random House South Africa (Pty) Limited
Endulini, 5A Jubilee Road, Parktown 2193, South Africa

The Random House Group Limited Reg. No. 954009
www.randomhouse.co.uk

A CIP catalogue record for this book
is available from the British Library

ISBN 1 84343 186 6

Papers used by Random House are natural,
recyclable products made from wood grown in sustainable forests;
the manufacturing processes conform to the environmental
regulations of the country of origin

Typeset by SX Composing DTP, Rayleigh, Essex
Printed and bound in Great Britain by
Mackays of Chatham plc, Chatham, Kent

CONTENTS

ACKNOWLEDGEMENTS

The Publisher would like to thank all those who gave permission for the inclusion of material in this anthology, as listed below. Every effort has been made to contact the holders of the relevant copyrights and to ensure that the information here is both accurate and complete.

ISTVÁN BAKA: "Passing Through". © István Baka 2004. Translation © George Szirtes 2004. KÁROLY BARI: "Death of a Stag"; "Winter Diary". © Károly Bari 2004. Translations © Daniel Hoffman and Eszter Molnar 2004. ATTILA BARTIS: "Engelhard, or the Story of Photography". © Attila Bartis 2004. Translation © Eszter Molnar 2004. PÁL BÉKÉS: "The Age of Discovery". © Pál Békés 2004. Translation © Pál Békés 2004. ÁDÁM BODOR: "The Sinistra District". © Ádám Bodor 2004. Translation © Paul Olchváry 2004. SÁNDOR CSOÓRI: "Barbarian Prayer". © Sándor Csoóri 2004. Translation © Edwin Morgan 2004. ISTVÁN CSUKÁS: "Albatross with Shopping Bag". © István Csukás 2004. Translation © George Szirtes 2004. LÁSZLÓ DARVASI: "Mr Stammer in São Paolo". © László Darvasi 2004. Translation © Eszter Molnar 2004. VIRÁG ERDŐS: "A Lying Tale"; "Vision (Game Over)". © Virág Erdős 2004. Translations © George Szirtes 2004. PÉTER ESTERHÁZY: "Fraighaoters". © Péter Esterházy 2004. Translation © Tim Wilkinson 2004. GYŐZŐ FERENCZ: "The Ramsay Party". © Győző Ferencz 2004. Translation © George Szirtes 2004. LÁSZLÓ GARACZI: excerpt from *Lemur, Who Are You?* © László Garaczi 2004. Translation © Ildikó Noémi Nagy 2004. ANDRÁS GEREVICH: "Mediterranean"; "Seasons". © András Gerevich 2004. Translations © George Szirtes 2004. ÁGNES GERGELY: "London". © Ágnes Gergely 2004. Translation © George Szirtes 2004. GÁBOR GÖRGEY: excerpt from *Interview.* © Gábor Görgey 2004. Translation © Jascha Kessler 2004. LAJOS GRENDEL: "The Story that Didn't Make the News". © Lajos Grendel 2004. Translation © Eszter Molnar 2004. VICTOR HATÁR: "The Shot Hare"; "Vampire"; "Identifications". © Victor Határ 2004. Translations © Georges Szirtes 2004. GYULA ILLYÉS: "A Sentence about Tyranny". © Gyula

Illyés 2004. Translation © George Szirtes 2004. FLÓRA IMRE: "Psalm"; "Snow Covers the Garden". © Flóra Imre 2004. Translations © Jascha Kessler 2004. FERENC JUHÁSZ: "The Boy Changed into a Stag Cries out at the Gate of Secrets". © Ferenc Juhász 2004. Translation © Ted Hughes 2004. PÉTER KÁNTOR: "On Liberty"; "On Truth". © Péter Kántor 2004. Translations © Michael Blumenthal 2004. SÁNDOR KÁNYÁDI: "I Shall Die"; "History Lesson". © Sándor Kányádi 2004. Translations © George Gömöri and Clive Wilmer 2004. IMRE KERTÉSZ: "The Union Jack". © Imre Kertész 2004. Translation © Tim Wilkinson 2004. GYÖRGY KONRÁD: excerpt from *The Case Worker*. © György Konrád 2004. Translation © Paul Aston 2004. MIHÁLY KORNIS: excerpt from *Lifebook: The Hero of Our Story*. © Mihály Kornis 2004. Translation © Judith Sollosy 2004. LÁSZLÓ KRASZNAHORKAI: excerpt from *War and War*. © László Krasznahorkai 2004. Translation © George Szirtes 2004. ZSOLT LÁNG: "A Transylvanian Bestiary: Birds of the Air". © Zsolt Láng 2004. Translation © Tim Wilkinson 2004. IVÁN MÁNDY: "On the Balcony"; "At the Movies with Father". © Iván Mándy 2004. Translations © Albert Tezla 2004. SÁNDOR MÁRAI: excerpt from *Land Land (Memoir of Hungary, 1944–1948)*. © Sándor Márai 2004. Translation © Albert Tezla 2004. MÓNIKA MESTERHÁZI: "Echo (I Distance Myself)". © Mónika Mesterházi 2004. Translation © George Szirtes 2004. "Sors Bona". © Mónika Mesterházi 2004. Translation © Peter Zollman 2001. MIKLÓS MÉSZÖLY: "Exact Tales on the Way". © Miklós Mészöly 2004. Translation © Eszter Molnar 2004. PÉTÉR NÁDAS: "Blown Away". © Pétér Nádas 2004. Translation © Ivan Sanders 2004. ÁDÁM NÁDASDY: "Useful Information about Angels"; "Ethology". © Ádám Nádasdy 2004. Translations © George Szirtes 2004. LÁSZLÓ NAGY: "Squared by Walls". © László Nagy 2004. Translation © Tony Connor and George Gömöri 2004. ÁGNES NEMES NAGY: excerpt from *Journal*; "Trees". © Ágnes Nemes Nagy 2004. Translations © George Szirtes 2004. OTTÓ ORBÁN: "The Father of the People"; "A Roman Considers the Christians"; "The Spirit of the Age": "A Nice Little War"; "The Witching Time". © Ottó Orbán 2004. Translations © George Szirtes 2004. ISTVÁN ÖRKÉNY: "1949 (show trial)"; "We're a Small Nation"; "Rondo"; "Ahasuerus"; "Life should be so simple"; "November". © István Örkény 2004. Translations © Judith Sollosy 2004. GÉZA OTTLIK: excerpt from *Buda*. © the estate of Géza Ottlik 2004. Translation © Eszter Molnar 2004. LÁSZLÓ PARTI NAGY: "A Swell on the Balaton".

© László Parti Nagy 2004. Translation © Tim Wilkinson 2004. GYÖRGY PETRI: "Gratitude"; "The Under-Secretary Makes a Statement"; "On the 24th Anniversary of the Little October Revolution"; "Song"; "Credit Card"; "To Be Said Over and Over Again". © György Petri 2004. Translations © George Gömöri and Clive Wilmer 2004. JÁNOS PILINSZKY: "Harbach 1944"; "On the Walls of a KZ-Lager". © János Pilinszky 2004. Translations © János Csokits and Ted Hughes 2004. SZILÁRD PODMANICZKY: "Happy Birthday to You". © Szilárd Podmaniczky 2004. Translation © Tim Wilkinson 2004. ZSUZSA RAKOVSZKY: "Decline and Fall"; "Old Women of My Childhood"; "New Life". © Zsuzsa Rakovszky 2004. Translations © George Szirtes 2004. GYÖRGY SOMLYÓ: "A Fragment from a Play". © György Somlyó 2004. Translations © Jascha Kessler 2004. GYÖRGY SPIRÓ: "Forest". © György Spiró 2004. Translation © Eszter Molnar 2004. ANNA T. SZABÓ: "Hospital Window"; "On Darkness". © Anna T. Szabó 2004. Translation © George Gömöri and Clive Wilmer 2004. FERENC SZIJJ: "Breadstickers (Sell-by date) / Monday". © Ferenc Szijj 2004. Translation © George Szirtes 2004. ZSUZSA TAKÁCS: "The Double"; "Refurbishment". © Zsuzsa Takács 2004. Translations © George Szirtes 2004. DEZSŐ TANDORI: "An Otherwise Unoccupied Swimming Pool in 1965; A String of Similes"; "1976711/b". © Dezső Tandori 2004. Translations © Bruce Berlind 2004. SÁNDOR TAR: "Special Treat". © Sándor Tar 2004. Translation © Eszter Molnar 2004. KRISZTINA TÓTH: "On the Nature of Pain"; "Metro Trains in Contrary Directions"; "File". © Krisztina Tóth 2004. Translations © David Hill 2004. SZABOLCS VÁRADY: "Quatrain". © Szabolcs Várady 2004. Translation © George Szirtes 2004. "Chairs above the Danube". © Szabolcs Várady 2004. Translation © William Jay Smith 2004. ISTVÁN VAS: "Pest Elegy". © István Vas 2004. Translation © George Szirtes 2004. "Dialogue between Strangers". © István Vas 2004. Translation © Daniel Hoffman 2004. SÁNDOR WEÖRES: "Monkeyland"; "Queen Tatavane". © Sándor Weöres 2004. Translations © Edwin Morgan 2004. "Antithin". © Sándor Weöres 2004. Translation © Richard Lourie 2004. PÁL ZÁVADA: excerpt from *Jadwiga's Pillow*. © Pál Závada 2004. Translation © Judith Sollosy 2004. PÉTER ZILAHY: "News"; "Eternity". © Péter Zilahy 2004. Translations © Tim Wilkinson 2004.

INTRODUCTION

Both Paul Tillich and W. H. Auden employ the term "Age of Anxiety" to refer to the inter-war years of the twentieth century, the latter in his long poem "A Baroque Eclogue". But for Hungary, most ages, certainly since the sixteenth century, have been anxious. The title of this anthology hints at one reason why. The Hungarian language is, in effect, an island of sound in a sea of Teutonic, Slavic and Romance languages. Its Finno-Ugric roots lie between the Volga and the Urals, and the people who first spoke it arrived in the Carpathian basin a little over a thousand years ago, the date AD 896 being the conventionally assigned one for the occupation of the land that constitutes the basis of the present state. Naturally enough, Hungarian has borrowed many words from its neighbours, but its structures, its modes and its sounds remain its own, incomprehensible to anyone else, even to the Finns to whom Hungarians are distantly related. Hungarian is, to begin with, a language without genders and dipthongs. Its consonants are flat, clear and unremitting. The mouth adopts a range of rigorous positions, as in some light military drill, and moves abruptly from one to the other. A British Council representative once described his first impression of hearing women talking at a Budapest bus stop as being like listening to the clucking of hens: short, low staccato bursts. The vowels too are more crisply defined than their English equivalents, each syllable enjoying fuller articulation. When a Hungarian gets angry, he is likely to break words up into their individual syllables in a series of blunt hammer taps. One way to distinguish a Hungarian accent through a foreign language is to listen out for that clarity of articulation, the almost equal weight given each part of each word.

This might suggest that the language is somewhat unyielding, resistant to lyrical effect, but that is not the case. Its clarity is wedded to great softness and liquidity. Hungarian poetry can be scanned by either stress or duration. Its complex and supple syntax offers a wide range of voices and moods. Like most vernacular literatures, Hungarian started with the translation of sacred works but moved quickly to classical texts and forms, forms for which the language was peculiarly well fitted. There was fluency and grace in Hungarian hexameters. Poets could draw on a tradition of song, and rhyme too came easily to a highly inflected language. Indeed, most Hungarians will tell you that it is not their music nor their visual art that they most prize but their literature.

For all that, the language remains isolated. Unlike other endangered languages such as Gaelic or Cornish, it cannot call on other more powerful members of the same family for support. And its neighbours are suspicious and frequently hostile.

So the first cause of anxiety is the Hungarian language. Is it wasting its time talking to itself? Is there anybody out there listening? Almost inevitably, Hungarians have had to go abroad to make their reputations. There is a peculiar Hungarian drive to succeed that animates scientists, entrepreneurs, photographers, film directors, musicians, composers and theatre producers, and turns them into figures of myth and joke: the man who enters revolving doors behind you but comes out in front; Nepommuck, the "important-looking young man with an astonishingly hairy face" in Shaw's *Pygmalion*, the pupil of Professor Higgins who declares: "I am interpreter. I speak 32 languages. I am indispensable at these international parties. You are great cockney specialist: you place a man anywhere in London the moment he open his mouth. I place any man in Europe." Nepommuck is, of course, vulgar. Higgins's retort is cutting: "Why don't you shave?" There is, then, also an anxiety about vulgarity. How to avoid it when speaking 32 languages?

Vulgarity is, in any case, so provincial. The anxiety of the fringes, the provinces, is articulated by Portia, Brutus' wife, who wonders, in *Julius Caesar*, whether she dwells "but in the suburbs" of her husband's good pleasure. For an artist, to be provincial is to be at the edge of events when it may seem better to attain the centre. But what has ever happened in Hungary? What can happen to arouse interest, excitement, envy, admiration in such a small, isolated country? A football team once in a while? A failed revolution or two?

The flipside of ambition and vulgarity is melancholy and withdrawal. Dürer's *Melancholia I* shows a figure brooding over compasses and globe. According to Aristotle, melancholics are earnest men with a gift for intellectual work, and this describes one aspect of Hungarian culture very well. But it is not only the isolation of the language, by extension an isolation of the spirit, that breeds anxiety. It is history itself. The deep myth of Hungarian history is that of defeat snatched from the jaws of victory, of centuries of misery following on days of joy. The nightmare is enervation, one of the vices associated with melancholy. The catastrophic defeat by Suleiman's Ottoman Turks at Mohács in 1526 ended a dynasty of thriving renaissance power when Hungary was a major European cultural centre that could draw Italian Mannerist artists to its court and compile the magnificent Biblioteca Corviniana. The very fact that such things were once possible but are no longer so actually makes the situation worse. The notion of loss is firmly embedded in the Hungarian literary imagination. The very word *melancholy*, the one-syllable word *bú* (pronounced like a long "boo"), and its adjective *bús* (booosh) recur time and again in Romantic and early twentieth-century poetry, partly as pose and garb (you can never make that "oo" sound quite long or closed enough) but partly as a sound in the very depths of the chest and the spirit.

The eighteenth-century German historian and philosopher Herder predicted the disappearance of small European nations, and some language theorists in the early twentieth looked forward to the disappearance of small irrelevant languages too. It is not surprising, then, that despair, self-pity and anxiety should underlie much of nineteenth- and twentieth-century Hungarian literature.

There is also the anxiety of geography. Where are the borders of Hungary? Where are the borders of any country in Central Europe? Some of the greatest Hungarian writers of all periods were born outside present-day Hungary. Major modern figures like Dezső Kosztolányi and Gyula Krúdy set their works in the places where they grew up, but by the time their books appeared, those places were on the other side of the border. This anthology includes a number of writers currently living in the "lost" territories.

The idea of a shifting map will seem strange to an island people. Imagine Hungary as a place in which every town is a potential Dunwich, likely to be broken off and washed away, its bells continuing to ring beneath a sea of other nations' colours. All of mainland Europe is liable to such shiftings but Hungary more than most. After Suleiman's victory the country was split first into two, then into three: the narrow, curving strip of its northern and western part became part of the Habsburg Empire, the Transylvanian Principality to the east retained some precarious independence, and the rest was under Ottoman rule. There was much toing and froing, and Transylvania looked to play the Turks off against the Austrians. Many Hungarians in the central part were enlisted as Turkish janissaries. Hungarians were likely to find themselves on various sides in the tensions generated by division. Turkish baths, tombs and mosques are still to be found in Hungary.

After the victory of John Sobiesky at Vienna in 1683, the tide rapidly turned and a much weakened Hungary was entirely absorbed by the Habsburg Empire. The country was slowly recovering its place in Europe after 150 years of absence. But the Austrian yoke was in many ways worse than the Turkish, and after the post-Napoleonic national revivals that affected all of Europe, Hungarians rose up in the revolutionary year of 1848. The revolt was defeated with Russian help in 1849, sending the country into a period of repression and trauma from which it emerged after 1867, the moment of the so-called *Ausgleich*, or unification of the Austrian and Hungarian crowns. Now Hungary was big. In fact it was huge. It comprised historical Transylvania but ran to the gates of Belgrade and included Croatia–Slavonia, with a seaport at Fiume. By the end of the nineteenth century, Hungary was a fast-developing, prosperous nation full of self-confidence, although that confidence would not have extended to the poorer peasantry, who lived in semi-feudal conditions, and continued to do so until the end of the Second World War. Budapest was the fastest-growing city in the world, amusing, wealthy, ambitious, a little dissolute perhaps, with the world's second Underground system after London. It was a cultural hothouse, too, with a wealth of eclectic architecture, Secessionist art and Symbolist literature.

By 1918 the game was up. Following defeat at the end of the First World War, the country underwent two revolutions: the so-called Autumn Roses Revolution of Count Károlyi in October 1918, which set up an administration that lasted into March the following year, and then the Soviet regime of Béla Kun, which lasted for 134 days. Throughout 1918–19 various lines of territorial demarcation were established and then moved. In August 1919 the Bolshevik regime was swept away, and a primitive Romanian army occupied Budapest. In November Rear-Admiral Miklós Horthy entered the city and established a right-wing authoritarian regime that lasted until the latter days of the next world war. He ushered in a period of savage repression which mellowed within a few years to a relatively tolerant, if reactionary, system. Indeed, the inter-war period produced some of the finest Hungarian writers, poets and novelists such as Ady, Babits, Kosztolányi, Karinthy, Móricz, József and Krúdy, who, along with many brilliant others, constitute a veritable *Pléiade* of literature. In the meantime, the treaties of Versailles and Trianon were busily cutting Hungary down to size: one-third of its territorial and half of its population size. Vast tracts of land were lost, including the Croatian seaport, much of modern Slovakia, the Novi Sad region of current

Serbia, bits of the Carpathian region (modern Ukraine) and all of Transylvania. Everything happened very quickly. The trauma was immense. The shape of contemporary Hungary was established and a hard, hot stratum of bitterness and nostalgia laid down for future generations.

This was not the end of the story, for during the Second World War parts of Transylvania were reannexed – Hitler's brief benefaction. Hungary kept out of the active war as long as it could but could not help being drawn in, and once more suffered catastrophic losses, the entire 2nd Army being destroyed at the bend of the Don. Soviet forces poured in from 1944 on and, at the end of the war, occupied all of Hungary. The borders were smartly reset at pre-war norms. After a series of manoeuvres, the Soviet-backed Hungarian Communist Party (later the Hungarian Workers' Party) took control of the country and led it through seven years of harsh Stalinism with the usual show trials, executions, tortures, internments, resettlements and internal exile – while rebuilding its infrastructure. The uprising that broke out on 23 October 1956 lasted 13 days. Although this did not redraw any borders, it did send about a quarter of a million people over them to the West.

The corollary of anxiety tends to be flight. Every major upheaval produced its own diaspora. The Turkish occupation pushed many aristocrats, landlords and scholars overseas in the seventeenth century. The defeat of the 1848 revolution created its own exiles. At the end of the nineteenth century a large landless, penniless peasantry, whose fate was unaffected by the rise of Budapest, was forced into emigration, usually to America, where its members hoped to earn enough to return and buy some land of their own. The changes of regime in 1918–19 produced political exiles who either left for good or took some time returning. The persecution of the Jews before the Second World War resulted in a wave of emigration, as did the imposition of the Soviet system in 1948. I have already mentioned 1956.

The notion of displacement and flight is deeply embedded in the Hungarian imagination. It is part of the Romantic mindset of Hungarian writers. It is of course loose talk to speak of Romanticism as such, but many of Romanticism's elements – apprehension of the sublime, the threatened sense of selfhood, the primacy of passion, the naturalising of states of crisis and loss, in tension with an idealising of that which has been lost and is always likely to be lost again – are clear enough.

Hungarian poetry for that reason has no real equivalent for Dryden, Pope or Johnson. In a country as unstable, as prone to invasion and revolutionary change, the Augustan poetry of stability has remained just out of reach. Hungarian poetry develops in adverse circumstances, in a rump state, almost as an act of survival, and survival often involves flight. The first great poet of the vernacular, Bálint Balassi, was a late sixteenth-century soldier and fugitive who died in battle. In the late eighteenth century, Csokonai, a marvellous Rococo-Romantic poet, spent much of his time on the road. The major poet of the early nineteenth century, Mihály Vörösmarty, wrote the first national epic and lived to see the revolution of 1848, after which he too became a fugitive. The great Romantic poet of the revolution itself, Sándor Petőfi, died on the battlefield at the age of 26. His great friend and fellow poet János Arany lived almost to the end of the century. Hungarian poets are in fact very much political creatures, not just in the revolutionary sense but in the everyday practical one. The twentieth-century poet Gyula Illyés wrote somewhere that people in villages tended to look to poets for advice on everything including the condition of local floodgates. Lack of political representation for the peasants and the poor lay behind this and partly accounted for the relatively late development of Hungarian literary culture.

There is an often-remarked gaiety of spirit in Hungarian literature too. When Walter Starkie, the itinerant Irish scholar and fiddler, embarked on his walk through Hungary in 1929, he was struck by the tendency of Hungarians to party, to have a wild fling of feverish, almost Dionysian merrymaking. He discovered a Hungarian word for this: *mulatni*, which, rather flatly, means simply "to have fun". But *mulatni* to Starkie carried with it a sense of furious energy: dancing, desire, danger, inspiration, exhaustion and death. It may be assuming too much, but perhaps there is a connection between the daemonic energy of this dancing, music and partying and the intellectual energy of Shaw's ridiculous Nepommuck with his 32 languages, between the excesses of amusement and those of overproduction or gigantism that are also part of the Hungarian literary imagination. Inspiration and aspiration are, after all, only attempts at different forms of flight.

There has been talk of anxiety and flight but nothing so far about density. The density of Hungarian writing resides in its mapping and layering. It has often been remarked that the literature of repressive societies takes refuge in irony, whereby the tension between hope and despair is resolved through distance, through the cultivation and application of an intelligence superior to that of your oppressors. Repression breeds an obsessive reading between the lines, the substitution of one set of images and meanings for another. It may be that the criticism apparently directed at one quarter is really directed at another, that when one jokes or sighs the cause is not altogether plain. Even the apparently simplest lyric, the most unambiguous line, is open to interpretation.

The multi-layered reading of literature in any language is usually associated with poetry. The memorability, poignancy and vigour of a good poem is partly a product of its ambiguity, each level of meaning echoing with, underscoring and modifying the other. That is why poetry rings. It is also why it is sometimes regarded as difficult. In consumer societies we want the product to do just what it says on the packet. The poetry of non-consumer societies was once articulated to me by one of the poets included in this anthology, István Vas: "When people have no shoes, they want poetry: once they have shoes, poetry is no longer so important." This is not entirely an argument about poverty or about poetic ambiguity. But the use of ambiguity in overtly repressive societies is disruptive and subversive. The contract between reader and writer is closer, more intimate.

One by-product of ambiguity in Hungary is an interest in the grotesque, in the black joke, the apparently pointless blank anecdote, the magical gone wrong. The Budapest joke of the '50s attained something of an international currency in that one would sometimes see examples of it translated and presented in the Western press as part of Cold War entertainment. As we shall see, the grotesque tradition is alive and well even now, albeit fulfilling a slightly different function. Political circumstances may change, but the mindset moves more slowly.

Another by-product of ambiguity is post-modern display: a dazzling eclecticism blending high with low, tragic with comic, the intellectual with the dumbly demotic. This is probably best embodied in the work of Péter Esterházy, who is, unlikely as it may seem, one of the most popular and highly respected Hungarian writers. But Esterházy's post-modernist technique is not a symptom of psychosis and nihilism, a draining of meaning, as Western post-modernism can sometimes be, but the expression of a humanist temperament in the conditions of late communism, as opposed to late capitalism. Esterházy may be cool in most his work, but his wit is a confirmation that, despite everything, something matters beyond wit itself.

Having said that, there is also a powerful documentary, sociographic tradition in Hungary, particularly in the work of authors such as Illyés and László Nagy, exploring the semi-feudal conditions in the countryside, a tradition impressively continued to this day in an urban and war context in film and photography. Indeed, there is a deep desire, an anxiety, to record and preserve the frailty and strangeness of life.

This anthology does not aim to give an overview of Hungarian literature as such. It concentrates on the work produced by writers since the Second World War and, more particularly, on the period leading up to and beyond 1989. Because 1989, like 1789, changed a great many things, not just in Hungary or in Europe but in the world at large. We ourselves are living its consequences which are dramatic and destabilising, still mysterious, still unknown.

Everything changed after 1989. As if by coincidence, the major poets of a period generally recognised to have been one of the richest in Hungarian history started dying off. Gyula Illyés and János Pilinszky had already gone, as had László Nagy. The most remarkable of them, Sándor Weöres, died in early January. Soon after that, the political system started rolling downhill and finally crashed. Within a couple of years two other very important poets, István Vas and Ágnes Nemes Nagy, had gone. That most laconically poetic of novelists Iván Mándy soon followed. Remarkable figures like Ferenc Juhász, author of the poem Auden referred to as one of the greatest of the century, "The Boy Transformed into a Stag Cries at the Gate of Secrets", entered a literary twilight. Political divisions blew the career of Sándor Csoóri off course (the same political divisions had swept the satirical writer István Csurka to the leadership of a neo-fascist party). My own generation (now in their late forties or early fifties) is in the process of being reassessed in the post-1989 reorientation. Reassessment is a normal part of literary life and moves with the generations, but post-1989 it has had a different edge. The reorientation goes on while the body politic is in an anxious, almost fraught state of transition.

It is early days yet. Nevertheless, this anthology would not exist without the events of 1989, for it is since then that Hungary has re-entered Western Europe, not as an observer but as a player. The pieces in the book have therefore been selected with an eye to their relevance to the historical moment. It would be good to think of the anthology, then, as a kind of temperature chart reflecting cultural, social and political change, reacting to circumstances, discovering metaphors for situations, finding languages and strategies to articulate, in overt or covert ways, the stresses, expectations and possibilities of social and individual life. In any case, like all anthologies it is a political act, only more so.

As I have already suggested, the twentieth century was a brilliant period in Hungarian literature generally. Some of the country's greatest poets and novelists emerged and sank in its spectacularly turbulent waves. It would have been unforgivable to exclude all the major figures simply because they died about 1989, nor would it have made sense to proceed without a context. So the prelude of this anthology, "Landlocked", includes a minimal selection from their work, especially where they reflect on the nature of public life, or where the private and the public sphere meet. These works do not appear in chronological order but are arranged thematically.

It is perhaps fitting that this section begins with Sándor Márai, whose novel, *Embers*, was such a posthumous international success, for Márai was indeed a product of flight. He died by suicide in San Diego, California, in the very year of change, 1989, but he had been moving around since 1948, the year he left Hungary to enter the outer dark of silence. He continued writing but as an emigré, almost into a vacuum. Márai had been a popular, much travelled writer, a playwright, journalist, novelist and poet. He loved the Hungarian language but cast himelf out of it, or rather was cast out by circumstances, being, as he himself put it, a bourgeois writer with a bourgeois audience. His journals of 1944–8, published in English under the title *Memoir of Hungary*, embody many of the qualities I have already enumerated. In fact, they provide a first-rate front-line report on the beginnings of a new world in which Márai himself was to play no part, the world introduced by the Russian soldier.

János Pilinszky's work is known through the translations and partisanship of Ted Hughes. Pilinszky's intense, ascetic, stripped-down sensibility, often more classical than it appears in Hughes's renderings, led him too to be labelled a bourgeois individualist – a common charge against some of the finest poets and novelists of the post-war period, and one that prevented their publication for a time. Pilinszky's work represented a break with the Hungarian realist tradition. The two poems included here refer to his experience of the last days of the war.

István Vas began as a modernist but soon turned away from experimental techniques to develop his humane, lyrical and discursive verse. Vas, a warm, deeply civilised man, was a survivor, a Jew who succeeded in hiding in Budapest when his close friend, the great poet Miklós Radnóti, was taken off to forced labour and eventually killed. Vas survived everything, including Stalinism, to emerge as an important public poet, anthologist, memoir writer and supporter of younger talents. "Pest Elegy" has been taken to refer to the aftermath of the war, but he has said that it actually refers to 1956.

Sándor Weöres has a good claim to be regarded as Hungary's greatest poet of the century. His oeuvre is compendious, including poems, plays and translations. His range is extraordinary. The normal thin volume could give no useful idea of it, rhapsodic and mystical at one extreme, playful, experimental and ironic at the other. The poems included here were chosen to reflect some of his circumstances rather than to hint at his range. Weöres, reputed to have been shortlisted for the Nobel Prize on some ten occasions (Illyés and Juhász were nominated at other times), makes great demands on his translators.

The novelist and short-story writer Iván Mándy is a magical fabulist of Budapest life. His love of the fabric of the city and of the films he saw in his youth is set against the harshest period of Stalinism. His characteristic short sentences are almost like lines from poems, and there is something of the poet in his writing generally.

The master of the grotesque, István Örkény, is represented by six very short pieces taken from his *Egyperces novellák* (*One-minute Stories*), tiny pieces of Budapest absurdity, menace and dark pathos told rather like jokey anecdotes. The show trial of László Rajk in 1949 was the most dramatic act of Stalinist terror enacted by the newly established Rákosi administration and indicated what was to come. The grotesque surrealism of "November" reflects the absurdity of public life. But Örkény was much more than a slick joker.

Gyula Illyés had established an international reputation before the war, and by date of birth he ought to appear earlier, but his work is placed at this point because the poem in question was first famously published in 1956, though he is thought to have written it in 1951 in the darkest days of repression. A poor village boy, his *Puszták népe* (*People of the Puszta*) describes the conditions endured by the peasantry. Illyés was clearly a major virtuosic poet (most Hungarian poets have been virtuosic one way or the other), though his star was hitched closer to the regime than those of other poets. As the regime did not touch him, he could occasionally speak up for those it did.

One of the first poets to be silenced by the state, chiefly through the agency of György Lukács, was the co-editor of a new and innovative literary journal *Újhold* (*New Moon*), the very young Ágnes Nemes Nagy. Once again the charge was bourgeois individualism, but there was little comfortable or bourgeois about her. Her spare yet monumental, sometimes epigrammatic, at other times enigmatic poetry (there isn't in fact very much of it) makes her a major European figure, her vision dwarfing her circumstances. "Trees" is about personal survival, while "Journal" meditates both on her own nature and on the nature of those who banned her work.

László Nagy emerged as a major poet after the war. Born of peasant stock, he studied painting, then worked as an editor, but always maintained his contact with his folk-culture roots, not only in his own work but also as a translator. A writer of passionate, magical love poems, he was an unwitting beneficiary of the political changes after the war, and therefore in the opposite camp to Nemes Nagy. The power of his work derives from a mixture of folk-roots and surrealism. His early death in 1978 signalled a serious loss to Hungarian letters.

The last of the writers included in this section is also remarkable for his vision in works like the already mentioned "The Boy Changed into a Stag Cries at the Gate of Secrets". Ferenc Juhász is one of the great compendious producers of Hungarian literature, his epic poems running to thousands of lines. Like Illyés, he is from a rural background, and folk legend blends with surrealism and personal vision in his poetry. He rather suffered from being lionised by the state, and his poems became longer and more rambling as time went on. "Silver" is an early work, a slice of Hungarian village life, a piece of humble folk magic opening on the starry universe. He doesn't exactly fit the brief of this book, but it was impossible to leave him out.

The anthology's main section, "Comecon Islands", takes its title from a poem by the outstanding political satirist of the late twentieth century, György Petri, the Comecon Islands being the supposed paradise administered by the Warsaw Pact countries. There are three Comecon Islands subsections, the first of them, "The Isle of Memory", referring to the period during which submerged themes came to light. Once again, the pieces here are placed by subject.

The repression and executions that followed the failed revolution on 1956 were succeeded by a longer period of slow relaxation and liberalisation under János Kádár, who had been a member of the revolutionary government before disappearing to return on the back of Soviet tanks. His story is more suited to an opera than a passing note, but some details should be mentioned. Briefly, Kádár returned in 1956 as a hated traitor-dictator but outlived everyone to become the architect of what was referred to as "goulash-communism", a mixture of severe centralism, gentle coercion and relatively benign corruption. The Russians had no intention of sending tanks in a second time, and they left Hungary on a long leash, providing it adhered to the Moscow line when it mattered – on the question of the 1968 Prague Spring for instance. In 1988 Kádár was nudged aside. His legacy was an enormous foreign debt, a vague sense of guilt, some self-loathing, inefficiency on a massive scale and a disintegrating sense of security and comfort.

Géza Ottlik was one of the modern masters of Hungarian prose, and it is from the pocket of his Gogolian overcoat that writers like Péter Esterházy emerged. In fact, Esterházy spent much time writing out by hand, in tiny script, on a single large piece of paper, the entire text of Ottlik's major work, *Iskola a határon* (*School on the Border*), a novel about life in a cadet school in the '20s. The sheet of paper is on exhibition in a small provincial gallery in Hungary. It is an extraordinary homage to a writer who was far from productive, and who was almost as interested in bridge as in literature. The excerpt here is from a later work, *Buda* (Buda being the hilly and bosky half of Budapest and quite different from urban Pest), which, like *School on the Border*, is a work of memory and irony meditating on the distant past.

The first of the submerged themes, the revolution of 1956, is referred to in a piece by the recent recipient of the Nobel Prize for Literature, Imre Kertész. Kertész is in this section because his reputation and production belong primarily in the period after that encompassed by "Landlocked". All of Kertész's work is linked to the theme of the Holocaust and what followed, he himself having been an inmate of Auschwitz as a 15-year-old. "The Union Jack" is primarily a memory of the '50s and of the revolution in particular, but the author embeds it, in typical fashion, in a longer, fragmentary anecdotal framework that reaches back to the war.

Péter Nádas is already well known through his novels, which have been widely translated. The short story included here is another memory of 1956, seen from a different angle, by a writer younger than Kertész. Nádas is of course a major figure whose work is philosophical and closely concerned with the meaning of historical events.

George (György) Konrád wrote two classic books, *A látogató* (*The Case Worker*) and *A cinkos* (translated as *The Loser*), which brought him international fame and immediately made him a focus of intellectual opposition to the system. He, like Nádas, is too well known to require introduction and has recently been active as a political and moral essayist. The short piece included in this volume is from the first ground-breaking novel about conditions in Budapest in the '60s.

The beginning of Mihály Kornis's novel, *Napkönyv* (translated here as *Lifebook*), is another slice of Budapest life, a specifically Jewish life, of the same period. The survival of a significant proportion of Budapest Jews ensured the continuation of a cultural sensibility that might relate as much to Philip Roth as to Central Europe. As Kertész has pointed out, the placing of Jewish experience in Hungarian history (and literary history) is still problematic.

Sándor Tar is primarily a short-story writer, a former factory worker whose prose is cast in the classic realist mode. László Parti Nagy began as a poet but started to publish fiction in the '90s. His voice is much more slangy, linguistically inventive and ironic than Tar's. They are both represented here by stories that recall life in the post-1956, post-repression period. László Garaczi is the youngest writer in this section, and the excerpt from his novel, *Pompásan Buszozunk* (literally "The Splendid Bus Ride", though the piece was originally published under the English title *Lemur, Where Are You*), is a memory of teenage life in the '60s.

The second subsection, "Kádár's Isle, Atoll and Mainland", begins with the atoll, that is to say the coral ring off the island coast. It includes writers who work or have worked in the parts of Hungary that were reassigned to other states after the First World War – chiefly Transylvania (now Romania) and Slovakia – but also others working outside or within the country.

The work of Victor Határ is remarkable in that it was mostly written after he left Budapest in 1956. Határ is in some respects the emigré writer *par excellence*. Resident in London since his departure, his output includes novels, plays, poems and philosophical essays in astonishing quantity. His copiousness is matched by his virtuosity and vision. He is master of his entire field, a tremendous innovator and experimenter while at the same time producing song-like rhymed verses of high-flying brilliance. His sensibility is both modernist and Victorian, a sort of Captain Nemo in his private submarine in Wimbledon. Since 1989, his collected works have appeared little by little in Hungary. Of the three poems included here, "The Shot Hare" is directly concerned with flight. Határ as a single individual bears out almost everything I said in the first part of this introduction. He is in this section as, in many senses, he is a product of the revolution recalled by Kertész and Nádas.

The poet György Somlyó is one of the major figures connecting the great wartime and post-war generation of writers to the present. A modernist by nature, particularly in his later work, he is an important translator from the French and has provided a lifeline to French thought and culture.

Miklós Mészöly was also an experimental writer, chiefly of fiction. His versatility was considerable. Like Nemes Nagy and others, he was associated with the journal *Újhold* and therefore, in the eyes of the Stalinist regime (and György Lukács), with bourgeois literature. He wrote parables, hyperrealistic fiction and a remarkable short novel, *Film*, about a walk taken by an elderly couple. The excerpt included here is from *Pontos történek, útközben* (*Exact Tales on the Way*). It describes an excursion into provincial southern Hungary. Mészöly, who died in 2001, talked of putting the obscure into plain words.

The lot of Hungarian writers living in Ceauşescu-governed Romania has been harsh. Transylvania is a territory that tends to arouse fierce passions in both countries: its history and traditions are disputed, its population has been resettled. In Ottoman times it was the stronghold of Hungarian culture. Some of the oldest Hungarian settlements are located in Transylvania. Ceauşescu proposed to flatten them, though he did not get round to doing so. Hungarians are certainly in a weak minority now, and they have faced a variety of repressive measures in the past. Even apart from that, conditions in Romania have been considerably grimmer than they were under Kádár's goulash-communism. Transylvania is a source of some of the magical elements of the Hungarian rural tradition.

Sándor Kányádi is one of the most important Hungarian poets of the period and has continued to work in Transylvania despite all difficulties. His work is mostly about rural life as affected by the region's bloody history. His long poem "All Soul's Day in Vienna", written over ten years, is his key work on the subject. The two short poems included here reflect the strains under which the two million Hungarian inhabitants of Romanian Transylvania have lived.

Ádám Bodor was born in the capital city of Transylvania, Cluj-Napoca or, as the Hungarians have it, Kolozsvár. His dark, fantastic, unforgettable short stories pick up elements of Örkény's grotesque but are far from funny. They are nightmares based on real conditions.

His work has appeared in English in book form. The passage included here is from *Sinistra körzet* (*The Sinistra District*), a fragmentary novel.

Zsolt Láng belongs to the next generation of Transylvanian writers and explores the miraculous and fantastical in his fiction. His novel, *Bestiarium Transylvaniae: Az ég madarai* (*A Transylvanian Bestiary: Birds of the Air*), from which an excerpt is included in this anthology, provides a way of dealing with folklore and history by mixing real and imaginary animals. Combining dislocation and fantasy is one of the strategies employed by Transylvanian writers to manage the harsh realities of life under Ceauşescu. Sándor Csoóri was one of the important dissident figures of the 1980s. His work is in the line of László Nagy and Ferenc Juhász but not unrelated to that of the Transylvanian writers. Like Nagy and Juhász he is from a peasant background, and, like them, he draws on the tradition of the magic ballad, informed by modernism, particularly surrealism, to articulate powerful emotions. The post-1989 rearrangement of the political landscape has swept him into nationalist territory, but his work stands independent of such political locations.

The youngest of these writers is Attila Bartis, who is also a photographer. His story appears more savagely anecdotal than Láng's, but it too demands a layered reading.

Gábor Görgey's work first appeared when he was 27, at the time of the 1956 revolution. He has worked in almost all branches of literature, as a poet, novelist, playwright and essayist, and there is the playwright's skill with spoken language in his poetry too. The recipient of many major prizes, he was formerly Hungary's Minister of Culture.

The legacy of the Second World War is dealt with by the poet, novelist and scholar Ágnes Gergely, who published her first book in 1963. One of the poems included here concerns her journalist father, who was taken away in 1944 and murdered. Being of the wrong background Gergely was shut out of higher education, took a job in a steelworks, then eventually qualified as a teacher, publishing translations first. Since then she has become established as one of Hungary's senior poets.

With Dezső Tandori, whose book, *Egy talált tárgy megtisztítása* (*The Cleaning of a Found Object*), was a milestone in modernist writing when it appeared in 1973, we are back with the prolific producers. Like Határ, Tandori is extremely productive, and it is impossible to represent his vast oeuvre of poems, essays, fictions and books about birds, racing and football in any adequate way. He is a one-man avant-garde. Tandori has something in common with the Scottish poet Edwin Morgan, but he brings us back to metropolitan Hungary too, to Budapest.

Ottó Orbán and György Petri are of particular significance in this anthology. In some ways they provide the programme for it, in that both of them are marvellously sharp, imaginative and often satirical mirrors of their times. Both died recently, and both are doubly represented by very late poems in the postscript. Orbán, the older, was the *enfant terrible* of Hungarian poetry in the '60s. He first came to prominence when he won a competition for institutionalised children after the war, a war he came back to time and again in his verse. After a breakdown in his youth, he became the translator of the Beat poets and their introducer into Hungary. A virtuoso, he was also the translator of Dylan Thomas and Robert Lowell. He learned something from all of them, from Lowell particularly the unrhymed sonnet, the vehicle he used most frequently for his political poems. Another highly prolific writer, his work includes prose poems, various technical tours de force, books for children, essays and travelogues. "The Father of the People" clearly refers to Stalin, but "A Roman Considers the Christians" is about 1989, as is "The Spirit of the Age". "A Nice Little War" captures the same spirit all too recognisably.

György Petri's work is probably better known abroad. Petri was a remarkable anti-heroic lyrical poet who, at the height of his career, decided to go samizdat, at which point his roughly bound books began to sell out almost as soon as they became available. The nature of censorship in Hungary has been eloquently discussed by Miklós Haraszti in his book *A cenzúra esztetikája* (translated as *The Velvet Prison*). What Haraszti describes is a kind of gentlemen's agreement: certain subjects being implicitly taboo, the writer does what he likes the rest of the time. The taboo subjects included 1956 and anyone involved on the revolutionary side, the presence of Russian troops, the basic tenets of Marxism-Leninism and the poverty that did not officially exist. With Petri, though, it is not a case of a few revolutionary gestures masquerading as poetry, but the poetry itself, which is of one substance with the politics. The sour-sweet lyrical stench of his work is evident in all the poems here, but "On the 24th Anniversary of the Little October Revolution" hits the points of shame simply and dramatically on the head. 1956 and 1968: the first the Hungarian Uprising, the second the invasion of Czechoslovakia in which relatively liberal Hungary took part. Uncle Imre is the executed Prime Minister of the revolution, Imre Nagy. Uncle Mátyás and Uncle Ernő refer to Mátyás Rákosi, the Stalinist dictator of Hungary, and his second-in-command, Ernő Gerő. Petri eventually returned to the fold of conventional publishing. His poetry had done its work.

With Szabolcs Várady, István Csukás and Zsuzsa Takács it is more often the individual persona that is confronted by the outside world in which political conditions set the climate of action. Várady works primarily through a refined, urbane irony, Csukás through semi-comic anecdote and Takács through a sense of emotional rawness. They reached maturity as writers in the late '60s and '70s as post-Prague Spring poets, in the world of half-comfortable disillusion and loss of faith. They serve in some ways as triangulation points for the period, as texture. Várady, the youngest of them, in fact precisely of an age with the late Petri, was already part of the ticking pre-1989 world, on the tip of the Comecon Islands.

The work of Péter Esterházy, like that of Péter Nádas, already has a wide international reputation. The son of famous aristocratic parents persecuted by the state, he became the leading novelist of his generation (his brother meanwhile became an international-level professional footballer, which shows where blue blood can take you). I have already said something about him. His major early work is a series of books under the general ironic title *Bevezetés a szépirodalomba* (*Introduction to Literature* or *Belles-Lettres*), from which the section title *Fuharosok* (a non-word sounding like *fuvarosok*, meaning "freighters", so translated here as "Fraighaoters") is included. The books are in fact a fireworks display of wit, post-modern devices, history, philosophy and Budapest life, spiced with intellectual jokes but underpinned by straightforward humanism.

The passage from *Jadviga párnája* (*Jadviga's Pillow*), the highly praised first novel by the sociologist Pál Závada, picks up the link with history. Závada was born in the south of Hungary, in one of the towns settled by Slovaks at the end of the Ottoman occupation. The history in the book is rendered polyphonic in that it is in the form of a diary voiced for two people and employs footnotes by a third.

In the "Crossing" subsection of the anthology, we move ever closer to a sensibility that may be termed vintage 1989. It could, of course, be argued that some of the writers in the previous subsection might fit in just as well, for it isn't merely a matter of dates or styles, and some of the writers at the head of this subsection would be equally at home with others included earlier. It is also true that tidying up literature nearly always involves terrible simplifications. It is no way to read an individual author. But as an exercise in introductions it may be excusable, and there is perhaps something in the writers of this section that hints at the decay and end of an old order and begins to sniff at, or directly to experience, a new one.

Ádám Nádasdy is a clear case in point. A very fine, elegant poet of wry love poems (and translator of various plays by Shakespeare), he is an early representative of gay literature in Hungary. Not that there wasn't such literature before, nor that his first volumes would have declared themselves as such, although his later work does. Its self-confidence is part of a new era, however.

István Baka was an important social and lyrical poet. His early death left a serious gap in Hungarian poetry. The poem included here is of the end of Kádárism and in some ways a scene familiar to us in the West: a railway station and poverty, with a full cast of passers-through.

At first sight Zsuzsa Rakovszky seems to occupy a comparable place, and her poems in this anthology bear that impression out, except that the collapsing social fabric she presents is seen in more intensely personal terms. The cinemas, cigarettes and matchboxes she mentions in "Decline and Fall" are part of a disappearing world furnished everywhere by passion. Thought by many to be the outstanding poet of her generation, she is now also regarded as one of its finest novelists. It is a pity that her work in this field is not yet available in translation, but judging by critical response it is bound to be soon.

Péter Kántor, a year older than Rakovszky, is represented by poems that already have 1989 in mind, that are in some ways reflections on it, for 1989 was not without its ambiguities, fears, political manoeuvrings and rhetorical overkill. (These were already referred to by Ottó Orbán in "A Roman Considers the Christians".) Kántor's work is followed by the last major batch of fiction. György Spiró has been a highly versatile writer since the mid-'70s, a novelist, a dramatist, a theatre director and a short-story writer. His major novel, *Az ikszek* (*The X's*) is set in nineteenth-century Poland, while his best-known play, *Csirkefej* (*Chickenhead*), is about vandalism and brutality on a Budapest estate.

Lajos Grendel belongs to the group of writers who are Hungarian but who work outside the country, in what used to be Hungary. Slovakian by citizenship, he is an important writer in his mother tongue. His story is included in this section because it is set in the post-communist era in Slovakia. It is part of the new world, which in many ways is not so different from the old one.

With László Krasznahorkai we enter the realm of apocalyptic writing. His mood is very black but oddly comic too. His enormously long sentences advance over the page like an endless dark shadow. W. G. Sebald and Susan Sontag have written glowingly of him, and a number of his works have been filmed, or rather transformed into the alternative medium of film, by the equally visionary film-maker Béla Tarr, most recently in *The Werckmeister Harmonies*, an adaptation of a part of his novel *Az ellenállás melankóliája* (*The Melancholy of Resistance*). The present excerpt is from a later novel, *Háború és háború* (*War and War*).

László Darvasi is a younger writer, poet and journalist whose reputation rose like a comet in the early '90s, particularly through his short stories, which present an acute balance between metaphor and reality. Szilárd Podmanicky came to notice at much the same time. His story is of the surreal aftermath of a drunken binge when the speaker finds himself saddled with the case of the old man next to him. There is a metaphor there to be picked out.

One of the most versatile of Hungarian writers, Pál Békés has authored children's books, film scripts, plays, novels and miniature short stories in the Örkény mode (a mode followed also by the younger Péter Zilahy). Much lighter in texture than Krasznahorkai and definitely less dark even than Örkény, who did after all live in darker times, Békés is essentially witty and humane. The little related pair of stories included here are about the importance of Elsewhere, an Elsewhere that is no longer quite as far away as it was.

The work of Károly Bari could fit anywhere in this anthology. Perhaps, as he is the leading Roma poet of the country and a historian of his people, he is best represented in this section, for the role and condition of the Roma people is a question the new Hungary will have to face in its own way. New regime: new roles. In terms of subject Bari is essentially rural and magical, and that links him with the Transylvanian group of writers.

Once we move past the poet, scholar and anthologist Győző Ferencz and the poet and short-story writer Ferenc Szijj, we are among writers whose maturity straddles the crossing point of 1989. Ferencz has served as a kind of ghost mentor to a number of younger poets. Formally inventive and playful, his work employs allusion, irony and, unusually for a Hungarian writer, a degree of diffidence. His tone can be difficult to pin down. It marks the establishment of a newer, more distanced, more intellectual and hermetic sensibility. Szijj has written minimalist verse. He too is wary of the lyrical "I" and treats it with caution. The time when the persona of the poet fulfilled an overtly political function, as with Petri for instance, seems to have faded into the distance.

It is too early to generalise about the new generation. There are certainly more prominent women writers, and I have tried to represent some of them. They are as likely to take their lead from Zsuzsa Rakovszky as from Ferencz. One of the younger poets, Mónika Mesterházi, has said that her generation favours "denser texts, music, form – not the looser language of conversational poetry (Petri diluted). And, yes, less philosophical, less articulating thoughts". And there is a harsher irony there too, particularly as articulated by Virág Erdős: a savage post-commercial, post-cybernetic anger. All choices from among a younger developing, thriving group of writers are bound to be somewhat arbitrary. Some, like Krisztina Tóth, have a strong lyrical presence. The poet and novelist Péter Zilahy is something of a globe-trotting part performer, part literary entrepreneur, part new media explorer. András Gerevich, the youngest of all, is also a short-story and screenplay writer. His poems may be related to Nádasdy's in their wry, erotic tone and subject. Flóra Imre, Mesterházi herself and Anna T. Szabó are very fine poets working from what seems a near- or post-'89 set of perceptions and values.

Many of the translations in this volume are from *The Hungarian Quarterly*, a remarkable and long-standing English-language magazine edited and published in Budapest. The anthology would have been impossible to compile in the time allotted to it had it not been for the material made available in this way. The current editor of the magazine (previously its literary editor), Miklós Vajda, is, in effect, a co-editor, or rather pre-editor.

The Hungarian Quarterly is an extraordinary survivor. Founded in 1936 by Count István Bethlen, Prime Minister between 1921 and 1931, its financing came from the government and leading industrialists and aristocrats. The magazine's primary aim was to find support in influential circles in Great Britain and the United States for the government's drive to achieve a peaceful revision on ethnic grounds of the frontiers drawn by the Treaty of Trianon. Another aim was a discreet indication that, despite the country's growing affiliation with Hitler's Germany – also motivated by revisionist purposes – the cream of Hungarian society and the government itself were still looking towards the Allies. Influential Western politicians were asked to contribute while conservative statesmen, as well as some of the best Hungarian writers, scholars, artists and journalists, regularly appeared in the magazine's pages. The elegantly produced, carefully edited, illustrated journal achieved some moderate success and continued to appear up until 1944, by which time the country had long been at war with the Allies.

In 1960, not long after the Soviets had suppressed the revolution of 1956, when the "Hungarian question" was still on the agenda at the United Nations and executions of revolutionaries occured regularly, the idea was mooted of an English-language journal to improve the image of the Kádár régime in the West. The concept, the format and even the title were taken from the pre-war journal, and thus *The New Hungarian Quarterly* was born. Half of its contents was straight political propaganda, but that gave the editor some leeway in the second half, where the best in literature and the arts could be published. This strong cultural section brought the magazine some respect and readers over the years, and, with the dictatorship also mellowing, the journal established itself as the prime source of information in English concerning matters of Hungarian culture and scholarship. An important novelty was the regular publication of poems by leading contemporary Hungarian poets in faithful translations prepared, with Hungarian help, exclusively by well-known British and American poets.

Since the great changes of 1989, the journal, which has reverted to its original title, has been an editorially independent publication and serves no political aims whatever. It does, however, continue to publish articles on political and social issues as well as the arts. *Encounters*, a selection of pieces from the magazine edited by Zsófia Zachár, appeared recently through a Hungarian publisher. That publication lay the foundations for this one. Miklós Vajda is in this respect the father of modern English translation of Hungarian literature. Any shortcomings in this book must be laid at my door. The credit for commissioning many of the translations goes to him.

GEORGE SZIRTES

PRELUDE

LANDLOCKED

SÁNDOR MÁRAI

from *Land Land* *(Memoir of Hungary, 1944–1948)*

I

Name days in Hungary have always been considered convivial, hospitable tribal holidays. And so, as the Gregorian calendar ordained, this year, too – 1944, on Sándor day, March 18 – we invited several relatives to dinner to celebrate the occasion.

As wartime shortages dictated, the dinner was modest. But this year, too, friends living on the shores of Lake Balaton sent us several bottles of full-bodied wine produced by the fiery volcanic soil. The early spring night was crisp, cold, and it was pleasant to have not only the meagrely stoked tile stoves heating the rooms but also the serious spirits of the wine warming our guests. We were sitting in the old house in Buda, in the flat which had been my home for nearly two decades.

There are days when persons live with an intuitive certainty, as if they have heard some news or word that will directly intervene in individual lives. One cannot tell what it is, but a moment has arrived, there is a smell to it. The name-day gathering had this kind of smell in mid-March 1944. We did not "know" anything for certain, but everyone scented that a fundamental, decisive change was brewing, indeed was close at hand.

At this time, in the blacked-out city, at the time of Voronezh and other war tragedies, its inhabitants, who had till then been relatively spared, were not leading the social life they formerly had. Still, on this particular evening my wife arranged the name-day dinner just as she had in times when we saw to our guests in peacetime. Our household had dug out of the bottoms of cupboards the family's Meissen china with the onion pattern, set the table with the old silver and lavishly lighted the table with candles in French candelabra in place of electricity. Eleven of us sat around the oval table. After that evening, these eleven beings never again sat down together at the same table. Now it is no longer possible for them to do so again, for several of them have died.

The intimate, ominous flickering of candlelight illuminated the faces, the bourgeois interior, the old furniture. I never bought any furniture; everything we owned was inherited from the estates of our two families, from two households in Upper Hungary. We didn't have any art treasures, but we didn't have a single piece of store-bought furniture either. The tastes and habits of our ancestors had selected everything arranged in our rooms.

The doors stood open between the rooms. Now, as I think back on this scene ominously lighted by the flickering candle flames, it all strikes me as if we, the bourgeois progeny of Upper Hungary and Buda, had reprised for ourselves the life of our fathers for one last time. On this night, everything that formed the props and scenery of those bygone days came to life again.

Conversation began perfunctorily, but the wine and the family chatter of old acquaintances helped us through the initial stiffness. After dinner we remained at the table, of course, and, following Hungarian custom, we began chatting over wine and demitasse.

Inevitably the moment arrived when the guests and hosts began to discuss politics with a passion. This evening was special and it remained memorable both in the light of the events that occurred afterwards – the sequel was nothing less than the total destruction and extinction of an entire way of life – and in another way as well: the moment had once again come when human beings sensed their fate with their instincts at least as much as with their intellects and with information. Our guests, all relatives, with a single exception, were unequivocally anti-Nazis. But they all feared the end of the war, and their wary conjectures were delivered in worried tones about what the immediate future would be like, what the chilly spring would bring, how the military situation would work out and how Hungary would fare in the cataclysm.

The majority of the disputants shared the concern that we could expect nothing good. But before long the relative who was a friend of the Nazis brought up the myth of "miracle weapons". At the time, the country was full of such tales; people were talking about a weapon that would "freeze" the enemy and about airplanes that flew with the speed of lightning so that pilots had to be plastered into their cockpits to keep them from falling out. We quickly dismissed such nonsense with a wave of the hand.

What could not be disposed of so readily was fear, fear of the reality that the final outcome of the war was near. When I stated that we must accept responsibility for the consequences and break with the Germans, most of the guests agreed, though rather diffidently – but not the relative who had befriended the Nazis. He now flared up. Tipsy, he pounded the table and repeated the preachments of "holding out" and "loyalty to the alliance" appearing in editorials.

When I took issue with him, he gave a surprising reply.

"I am a National Socialist," he shouted. "You" – he pointed at me – "can't understand this because you are talented. But I'm not, and that is why I need National Socialism."

The passionate words died away; the hot-blooded relative had declared the truth of his life, and, breathing a sigh of relief, he now stared straight ahead. Several began to laugh; but the laughter was bitter, somehow nobody was really in the mood to laugh. When we suddenly caught the drift of what he said, I answered that I don't put much trust in my "talent" – it is the kind of talent that must be proven newly every day – but I would not be a follower of the ideals of National Socialism even if I had no talent, which is not beyond question. The relative shook his head gravely.

"You can't possible understand," he repeated mechanically and struck his chest. "Now it's about us, the untalented," he said, with strange self-confession, like the hero in a Russian novel. "Our time has come!" . . .

Now we began laughing with relief and talked about other matters.

Towards midnight our guests said goodbye, for in the darkened city the streetcars ran only during certain hours of the night. When I accompanied the last of them to the vestibule, the telephone rang. I recognised the voice of a friend, a civil servant in the prime minister's office. He never phoned at night. For this reason I asked warily:

"What's up?"

"The Germans occupied Hungary tonight."

He said this in a very calm, natural voice, as if he were passing on a bit of social news. He was an outstanding, disciplined official. We were silent for a time. I asked:

"Where are they?"

"The Germans? Here, on Castle Hill. They are advancing in tanks. I'm watching them from a window."

"Where are you now?"

"At the ministry."

"Can you make it down to my place?"

"That's impossible now," he calmly said. "They won't let me pass between the tanks. But tomorrow, if they haven't arrested me yet, maybe I'll come down."

"Good night," I said, feeling what I was saying was stupid.

"Good night," he answered gravely.

He put down the phone. He wasn't arrested on the next day but on the third, and he was immediately taken away to a German internment camp.

. . . The maid came in and began clearing the table, wearing white gloves, as she did when serving, because this was also one of the rules of the house. I went to my room and sat down at the old desk. Before the windows, the city was silent in the spring night. Only occasionally did a tank rumble on its way to Castle Hill, carrying members of the Gestapo to occupy the offices. I listened to the clattering tanks and smoked cigarettes. The room was pleasantly lukewarm. I looked absent-mindedly at the books lining the walls, the six thousand volumes I had gathered together in various places in the world. Here was that Marcus Aurelius I bought from a second-hand dealer on the banks of the Seine, Eckermann's *Conversations* and an old Hungarian edition of the Bible. And six thousand more books. From a wall my father, grandfather and deceased relatives looked down at me.

2

I encountered my first Russian soldier several months later, on the second day of Christmas 1944. He was a young man, a White Russian, I believe; he had a typically Slavic face, with wide cheekbones, and blond hair, with a lock sticking out from under a fur cap pointed like a helmet and marked by the Soviet star. He galloped into the courtyard of the village's parish hall, a sub-machine gun in his hand; in his wake rode two older, bearded, sombre-faced privates. He levelled his weapon at me and asked:

"Who are you?"

A writer, I told him. We stood in the snow, the horses exhaling their fatigue from their lungs in steamy puffs. Like Russian soldiers generally, this one rode magnificently but did not spare his horse; when galloping, the Russian horseman does not raise his body in the saddle, the entire weight of his upper body bears down on the horse, cleaving almost immovably to his mount. After galloping, the horses came to a dead stop, neighed and snorted. The young soldier didn't understand my reply and repeated the question. Now – more distinctly, breaking the word into syllables – I said: "*Pisatiel.*" I didn't know any Russian, but I had learned this word because the rumour was that the Russians do not harm writers. And, in fact, the youth did break into a smile. The smile brightened up his young, proud, boyishly angry, ruddy-cheeked face.

"*Kharasho,*" he said. "*Idi domoi.*"

He jumped off his horse and rushed towards the parish hall. I understood he had dismissed me and I could go home. His comrades paid no attention to me. I hurried across the snow-covered yard and started out on the highway for the village house on the edge of a forest where I had been living for eight months. The house stood in a sort of no man's land, in a large garden, on the border of a settlement made up of half-village and half-summer places. I lived with escapees and refugees throughout these eight months. The lodgings on the forest's edge proved to be a proper choice. At this time, the Germans no more stuck their noses here than did the Hungarian Nazis and members of the new Arrow Cross squads trained to conduct man-hunts.

I hurried along the Danube's bank back to the abandoned house. The Danube was full of drifting ice floes. Two days earlier the Germans had withdrawn from the village and the entire area, unseen and unheard. On this day, the Russians had not yet completely encircled Budapest, and modern weapons of every type battled at the Danube's upper bend around Esztergom and then directly across on the other side of the river's bank. Russian artillery dubbed "Stalin pipe organs" and extraordinary and very effective mortars poured out a torrent of fire night and day. But it was relatively quiet on the right side of the river. Occasionally we caught a grenade, and sometimes a bomb, dropped absent-mindedly or mistakenly from some lost air-plane, would demolish a house in the village.

The Russians had occupied the island in the middle of the river days before. We observed them from the bank as they crawled around in the snow, building military positions, but on the second day of Christmas not a single Soviet patrol had blundered into our village. On the morning of this day, rumour had it that a Russian outpost had – at a major's command – moved several kilometres further on and occupied a former diplomat's house in the vicinity of a little town nearby. The villagers thought it would be a good idea for a delegation to go to the regular Russian army – with poppy seed and nut brioche and brandy – and ask the major to station a professional military patrol in our village, too; perhaps this way we could avoid abuses at the hands of loitering, looting bands of soldiers. The major promised to dispatch a patrol by nightfall, and he ordered the delegation to gather up all the weapons in the village. I was in the act of taking a hunting rifle to the parish hall when I encountered my first Russian soldier.

I trudged along the Danube's bank. It was growing dark. On the other bank of the river, in the dusk, blue, red, yellow and green flares crackled up high, like skyrockets on a special national holiday – the signals of the Russian infantry slowly advancing towards Pest with which they requested shellfire to cover their forward positions. The shellfire sounded close, and occasionally a rifle bullet whizzed past my ear. This whizzing sound was strange and unmistakable, but I had heard so many of them by this time that I paid no attention to it.

Village acquaintances passed by me in the dark; they recognised and greeted me in perturbed tones. In this locality were strangely mingled the most impoverished peasantry who barely survived doing cotter's work and the summer residences of well-to-do big city dwellers. On the hillside huts stood in rows; along the Danube, summer houses built after the First World War by the thriving middle class according to their diffuse tastes and in an odd hotch-potch of styles made a resplendent display, like some eccentric amusement park. Here were found Tyrolean houses, mansion-like summer villas constructed in gentry-empire style, imitations of Normandy castles and even Spanish garden homes reminiscent of South American haciendas. Few persons lived in the houses of the gentry; most of the owners had gone to the big city for the siege, because conventional wisdom held that Budapest "will fall in a few days" and in the city "the inhabitants will face field marshals", while in the village corporals will govern, and that will be more dangerous. In reality, one situation was just as dangerous as the other, but those who crowded into Budapest at the time of the siege shrivelled and baked in the cellars of the beleaguered city and experienced every horror of a large city's destruction. Many residents of the manorial houses in the village escaped to the West, and their homes were the first to be ransacked by the Russians, just as they had been by the locals.

Each and every person greeting me confusedly in the dark belonged to the village's proletariat. Their confusion suggested that the great change, the "historical moment", did not evoke the experience of "liberation" in their souls. A people that had already lived in servitude for so long seemed to know that their lot was not going to change: the old masters had left, and the new masters had arrived, and they would remain slaves as before.

The local shoemaker, who even for some time past had the reputation of being a Communist, hurried after me breathing heavily and began an emotional, confused discourse. The fat man stood without an overcoat in the biting cold and explained agitatedly to me that when the Russians marched in and caught sight of him at the end of the village, they shouted, "Bourgeois, bourgeois!" – and pulled off his leather coat, which he just happened to be wearing, shoved two hundred pengős in paper money into his hands, patted the terror-stricken man on the back and galloped on. "They thought I was a bourgeois," he explained in a whimpering voice, "because I am fat and have a leather coat. And I was waiting for them . . ." This was the first time I heard the voice of disappointment.

3

The house was dark. We had been without electricity for two days, and soon it wouldn't be available for months on end. We still had some firewood; we had flour, fifteen kilos. I had buried lard in bottles in the vineyard, twelve of them, and we still had soap and also some coffee. Extra clothing still turned up; I had hidden our remaining money, four thousand pengős, in the attic under a main beam, in a flat Lucky Strike tin box so mice would not nibble at them; at the time, this money was enough for two months. On that day I even had some cigarettes.

The household went to bed. I brewed some coffee and sat alone in the dark room before the slowly dying fire in the stove. I remember this night sharply, more vividly and powerfully than many things that happened later. Something had ended, an impossible situation had dissolved into a new, equally dangerous but entirely different state of affairs. The Russian soldier who entered my life today was, naturally, someone other than a ruddy-cheeked Slav youth from somewhere on the Volga. This Russian soldier – I had to think of this – entered not just my life this afternoon with every consequence, but that of all Europe as well. We didn't know about Yalta yet. What we did know was that the Russians were here, the Germans had withdrawn, and the war would soon be over. I understood this much about what had happened.

And I also understood that we must now answer a question. I couldn't put the question into words, but on this particular night, when a warrior from the East entered a dark Hungarian village – we "understand" only what we see and touch – I felt in my bones that this young Soviet soldier had brought a question to Europe with him.

At the time, the world for nearly thirty years had pondered, loudly and silently, what Communism was, what its meaning was. Those who replied gave very different answers, depending on interest, conviction, political creed, great power positions. Many lied, exaggerated. But then I spoke with those who didn't lie and read books which – the author's person furnishing the proof – did not exaggerate. In any case, I lived in an atmosphere in which Communism was considered one of the Seven Deadly Sins. This was why I thought the moment had arrived for me to forget everything I had ever heard about the Russians and the Communists. At the moment when – in the snowy, dark courtyard of the parish house – I first encountered a Soviet soldier, there also began in my life personally the great examination, the process of question and answer, the assessment of the Communist and non-Communist worlds; but this examination commenced simultaneously in the Western world as well. A power had appeared in Europe, and the Red Army was only the military expression of this power. What was this power? What was Communism? The Slavs? The East? . . .

In the night, muttering men walked around the house, came and left. The night loiterers spoke a foreign language. I sat in the dark room and decided that, to the extent humanly possible, I would purge my judgment of every bias and try to look at the Communists without any residual memories of my readings and conversations, without any of the preconceptions of official anti-Bolshevist propaganda.

That afternoon I had personally undergone an event which the so-called "intellectual" had lived through as a similar "experience" in Europe only twice up to then: in the ninth century, when the Arabs suddenly broke through to Autun and Poitiers, and in the sixteenth century, when the Turks transmigrated to Győr and Erlau. The Easterners were not allowed to advance further into Europe then either. The maraudings and conquests of the Genghis Khans, the Timur Lenks and the Attilas in the European plains were tragic but fleeting interludes, and one day, without so much as stopping to think, these hordes scurried home from Europe at some magical sign of some Asiatic tribal calamity. The Arabs, on the other hand, launched an attack with an ideological, racial and spiritual consciousness against another ideological, racial and spiritual consciousness, against Christianity, and when Charles Martel, the bastard, defeated them at Autun for good, they left in Europe not just the memory of their looting but also the great questions of Arab civilisation that demanded answers. They brought with them not only astronomy, navigation, medical science, new kinds of ornamentation and the Eastern view of nature but also a numerical system that made technical thought possible when it banished the complex and cumbersome numbers of the Greek and Roman numerical systems. They brought with them the self-consciousness of Hellenism, which by then was barely flickering in the dim cells and encapsulated souls of the Medieval scholastics, when, finally, Gerhard of Cremona translated several dozen Greek learned and literary works into Latin, including nearly all of Aristotle. To this "barbarian", to this first Eastern question, the Christian world would give a good answer at Autun; it answered not only with cannon but with the Renaissance and Humanism, which would, perhaps, not have emitted sparks in the soul of Medieval man for centuries without the impetus of Arab civilisation's Hellenistic, Aristotelian self-consciousness.

The Renaissance was, in any event, a response to the first massive Eastern ideological invasion. On the occasion of the second Eastern assault, at the powerful onslaught of the Osman world concept and Eastern imperialism, the Christian world would again reply not only with weapons but with a great attempt at renewal, the Reformation. How will my world, the Western world, respond to this young Russian soldier who today arrived from the East and asked me, an unknown European writer: "Who are you?"

I sat in the darkness, in this very strange darkness, listening to the cannon-fire rumbling in the night with the monotony of factory gear and destroying everything that, a few kilometres away, was for me not long ago still a home and a world concept; and I tried to figure out the tone of the question that the healthy blond Slavic soldier wearing a quilted Chinese coat would address to my world. I did not think about the "answer", because I knew that such "answers" cannot be determined. The humanists didn't "determine" the Renaissance either, nor did Luther "determine" the Reformation; such "answers" just happen somehow. Nonetheless, I tried to figure out what the Russian soldier really wanted of me.

He will, of course, carry off the pigs, the wheat, the oil, the coal and the machines; there was no doubt about that. (At the time I didn't suspect he would take people away, too.) But what does he want besides the pigs, wheat and oil? Does he want my "soul" and thus my personality, too? Not much time passed before this question resounded very powerfully not just within me in the night and in the secluded village house. We came to know that he wanted to take away all these things and, on top of it all, he wanted our "souls", our personalities. When we became aware of this, the encounter took on a different meaning, one that extended beyond the fate of a nation to that of the whole world.

Vast empires wither away more quickly than tropical forests; history is replete with the skeletons of such mammoth hulks as the Seleucian, Nubian and Libyan Empires – they bloomed for a few historical moments, then dust buried them all without a trace. Only a lunatic could believe that the fate of thousand-year-old Hungary has any significance for the large masses of peoples. If Hungary stands in the way, they will trample it underfoot, without anger, indifferently. If they can make use of Hungary for a moment, they will sign it on in some sort of subordinate role, just as the Germans "signed it on" yesterday, as the Russians will "sign it on" tomorrow. This is destiny, and a small nation can do very little against it. But to the question that the young Russian Bolshevist brought into my life – into the lives of everyone raised in the life forms of Western civilisation – one must answer without prejudgment and bias. I imagined I saw the strange, impassive young face in the darkness. It wasn't repugnant, but it was frightfully strange.

At this moment, in the phase of the war, I wasn't the only one to reflect anxiously on the Russians: a "bourgeois" Hungarian writer in a house in a Hungarian village. The English, French and Americans were also eyeing them with dubious expectations. At the cost of terrible sacrifices at Stalingrad, a great people turned around the wagon shaft of world history, and I had this very day encountered an embodiment of this great power. To many, to those persecuted by the Nazis, this young Russian brought along a kind of liberation, an escape from the Nazi terror. But he couldn't bring freedom with him because he didn't have any. At the time, this was not yet widely known.

4

For two weeks they came randomly and sporadically, singly or in pairs. They generally asked for something: wine, food, sometimes just a glass of water. After the initial anxiety, these encounters sometimes took place in a human voice, true, in a somewhat theatrical and studied voice. Once the rudiments of greetings and communications were clarified, only scant conversational possibilities remained to us. Staying in the house was a young woman who completed her university degree in Prague and spoke the Czech idiom fluently. She was our interpreter, and the Russians understood her for the most part.

They entered the house night and day without ringing or knocking. During the first days and nights, we were sometimes taken aback when, at the most unexpected moment, a Russian with a sub-machine gun stood before our bed or beside our table. But we became used to that quickly, too. Most of them stayed for only a short time.

Once three of them arrived, two officer types, or *kapitanos*, and a private. As we later learned, the officer rank started with majors in the Russian army; they had already completed the military academy and had orderlies, and most of them knew a little German. But below the rank of major, the officer types with several stars were not real officers. Also present were other ranks and relations between superiors and subordinates that a foreigner could understand only with difficulty. There was the "political officer" who monitored the regular soldiers on assignment from the Party, but it could also be presumed that the "political officer" himself had a monitor within the army. Some years before, at the beginning of the war, I read a book published in Switzerland whose author, a Russian named Basseneff, tried to draw a picture of the Soviet "People's Army". I now recollected this book, but I found the reality much more complicated than the one this Russian military writer delineated.

For instance, these three visitors held ranks hard to define in Western military terms. They were young – the private was a doltish sleigh driver, the officer types were mildly tipsy. They arrived about noon, and I tried to receive them politely, sociably, because I had already sensed that this way of treatment pacified my Russian guests the most effectively. I extended my hand, offered them a seat, treated them to my remaining cigarettes and brandy, and then waited to see what would happen. Sometimes the politeness, the external forms of hospitality, affected the Russians favourably. Generally, they arrived with great hubbub to search for "guns" and "Hermanns", that is Germans, but after the first polite words and hospital gestures, they grew tame. That's what happened now. When I raised the brandy glass and toasted their health, all three stood up and courteously returned the greeting with glasses in their hands. Then we sat around the crested tile stove and began conversing – exactly like billeted soldiers and locals during military exercises. Members of my family – my wife and a little boy, who was staying in the house at the time, and the young woman who spoke a Slavic language – sat with the guests. The situation was strange and different from what we expected on the basis of fugitives' alarming tales. I began to hope.

This hopefulness, at first, was not without cause. We got along without extraordinary damage and tragic mishaps with the officers and orderlies of the regular army, especially if they weren't drunkards, and there was also a high military command nearby. In the first days, some looters turned up, but they were more like pilfering sneak thieves in the night who arrived armed and demanded watches, liquor and cologne, and promptly took to their heels with the booty. Clearly, the thieves had an uneasy conscience because they feared punishment by the local high command. But in the early days, regular soldiers, especially the officers, sometimes behaved considerately here in the little village but differently in the big city nearby where open robbery and violent acts were authorised undertakings.

The three young men sat sociably around the large earthenware stove. The driver was hopelessly stupid, but he, too, made an effort to be well-mannered, visibly imitating the *kapitanos*' behaviour. They related what occupations they followed as civilians – one was a draughtsman – and they asked me what my profession was. This was my first lengthy conversation with Soviet men, and I again saw that the "writer" is a magical notion among Russians. At the moment when I said I am a writer, they looked at me with great respect and attentiveness, as if I were some extraordinary being. They looked around my room, whose modest furniture – some kind of bungalow furnishing – didn't really make a grand impression (the house wasn't mine, I had moved in eight months ago at the request of friends), and they were visibly affected by everything they saw. The younger *kapitano*, the draughtsman, said he was very pleased to have the opportunity to meet me because he "likes persons" like me. Then they wanted to know if the house belonged to me. When I said it didn't, they began asserting enthusiastically what a splendid lot Soviet writers enjoyed; they kept saying that in the Soviet Union I would have a house, a garden and a car by now. The older *kapitano* waxed unduly enthusiastic and asked if I wanted to move into one of the more splendid upper-class houses in the locality, because he would be glad to present it to me as a gift. Laughing, I turned down the offer . . .

This was different from what we expected, so completely different and surprising that I became cautious, like someone who has lost his way in the dark and is unable to find the road sign. What kind of people are they? For, a short time later, a maid from the neighbouring villa ran over and reported that these very same Russian officers who had dined at their place just a little while ago kissed the hand of the lady of the house, said goodbye graciously, came over to our house to look at a writer, and, when they departed, they sent back the chauffeur armed with a sub-machine gun from the highway to the villa, to their hosts, to demand that the master of the house hand over his gold wristwatch. The aggrieved man, who naively wore it and looked at it frequently during lunch in his guests' presence, later confirmed the news. "But then why did they kiss my wife's hand?" he asked, bewildered. We began to suspect that there was something astounding in the Russians.

Several Jewish refugees who lay hidden in the village through the months the Germans and the Hungarian Arrow Cross persecuted the Jews now ventured forth. An old man and his family lived close by; he was a pharmacist, a well-to-do bourgeois who had escaped pursuit by the Arrow Cross. But the women in his family were afraid of the Russians. At the time the first Russian visitor arrived, the old man – he had a white beard and was a venerable patriarchal figure – stopped solemnly in front of him and disclosed he was a Jew. The scene that followed was astonishing. On hearing the disclosure, the Russian soldier broke into a smile, removed the sub-machine gun from his neck, walked up to the old man and, according to Russian custom, kissed him gently – from right to left – on the cheeks. He said he was a Jew, too. For a time he silently and heartily squeezed the old man's hand.

Then he hung the sub-machine gun around his neck again and ordered the old gentleman to stand in the corner of the room with his entire family and to turn with raised hands towards the wall. When the old man didn't understand the order immediately, the soldier shouted at them to comply right away or he would shoot them dead. The women and the old man stood in the corner of the room, their faces turned to the wall. After this, the Russian robbed them slowly, at his leisure. He was an expert. With the skill of a wall-demolishing burglar he tapped the tile stove and walls from one end to the other and pulled out every drawer. He found the family's hidden jewels and all their cash, about forty thousand pengős. He put everything into his pockets and left.

5

The Russian soldiers sniffed out wine like hounds pursuing wild game. They pounded the length of the basement flooring with their rifle butts – in many places vintners had buried their wine barrels, but the Russians quickly got the hang of searching for them – and they dug carefully where the flooring gave a dull thud until they found the wine. The momentum of the Russian attack also stalled on two battlefronts: when the Soviet forces reached a wine district, their officers could only drive them on at the cost of bringing in new troops. This was what occurred in the Mátra and Balaton wine regions. All their behaviour showed this unpredictable quality.

It occurred that the Russian who dropped by in the morning, conversed amiably with a family, showed pictures of his own family back home sentimentally, patted the heads of the children present in the room and gave them candy and apples, departed and then returned in the afternoon or late at night and robbed the very same family he had made friends with in the morning. Since the power of the human imaginative faculty was keyed up during these days and later, I naturally didn't believe all the stories circulating about the Russians' behaviour, and I am now recording only what I personally experienced or what I am convinced actually took place.

It is certain that the "writer" was a magical idea for most Russians – just as the actor, the doctor, sometimes the priest, too! – but it was equally certain that this magical word did not always carry magical power for them. A Russian officer who turned up one morning demanded flour from me – naturally locals, neighbours, sent him who knew we had a little flour stashed away – and the argument that he had stumbled upon a writer's house carried no weight at all. He found the flour and carried it off, muttering furiously. Not a single morsel of bread was to be found in the house around New Year's. It was then I learned that need is more powerful than gold. At daybreak I headed with a ferryman and a dilapidated punt across the Danube full of drift ice to a place on the island just opposite, on the basis of a rumour that the miller there sold flour for gold. I found the village Shylock – a Swabian with a bloated, purple-blue face – in the mill and placed before him without a word a small gold-plated woman's Swiss wristwatch, one of our last remaining earthly treasures. The miller understood not only flour but gold as well; he sprang open the cover of the watch case with the technical deftness of a jeweller and looked at the assay mark of the gold worriedly. It was fine gold, eighteen karats. He sighed and handed it back with a scornful gesture. "I have no flour," he said, spreading his arms helplessly. "The Russians carried it off during the night."

And we veritably stood there helplessly – the gold-hungry miller and I, the flour-hungry writer – in the middle of a world situation. I went home empty-handed, and as the punt swam through the drift ice towards the other side – that morning heavy cannon-fire was sweeping along both banks of the river, the Russians were heading towards Pest with a large force – I reflected on the strange life situation I found myself in. In this moment I came to understand something about the gravity of the life lived by ancient bourgeois pioneers.

A good many exceptions cropped up, but in the first two weeks – thanks to the presence of the Russian high command that established itself in the village – I very generally got along with the Russians who called on us. More often than not, a nice manner, an affable intonation, won them over. The trust presented in advance, then the refusal, the adult intonation – that of an elder speaking to a young person – mixing these with the resigned voice of a defeated person – all this sometimes affected them. Not the meaning of the words – I could barely speak to them even with the help of an interpreter – it was rather the tone only, the manner, the look that made an impression on them . . .

6

They were childlike, sometimes wild, sometimes edgy and melancholy, always unpredictable. Since I could not do anything else anyway, I decided to keep at my profession, and so, after the first surprises, I began observing them, and wrote down briefly what I experienced. Not long ago I read over these notes, and even after reading them, I can only repeat what I set down on several occasions at the time: there is "something different" about the Russians that someone raised in the West cannot understand. I won't pass judgment on this "something different", I won't even assess or disparage it. I shall simply establish what it is.

When I come face to face with someone from the West – a Frenchman, Englishman, American or German, say – I can by and large figure out the primary reflexes ensuing from the situation and the moment within the situation itself independent of his personality.

But I could never decipher the Russians' primary reflexes and even less so those of the second or third degree. I wasn't the only one who looked at them with such ignorance, everyone in the Western world who encountered them during this period did so, and they, too, the Russians, watched us closely. The Russians walked with piercing looks among us; a primitive people with powerful impulses watched us warily.

The magic word "writer" wasn't always effectual, and I couldn't entertain the hope that the soldiers of the Red Army hanging around during the siege of Budapest would spend time attending literary seminars in my room in an abandoned country house. But a Russian always turned up who looked at me with respectful, reverential regard when I introduced myself. And because I needed protection on the occasions of these visits that were not wholly without danger, and because the Russians were extremely suspicious and didn't believe I really was a writer, and I, secretly, in the depth of my soul, shared their doubt then and even more so since, I was compelled to look for some kind of certificate that would confirm my audacious claim to my sceptical visitors. And because a trustworthy "*bumashka*" verifying that someone is a "writer" is issued nowhere in the world, I was glad to find a French edition of one of my books in the small reference library of the owners of the house. My name was on the title page, and on the back of the book, the publisher fortuitously included among the advertisements, in a list of its publications, a noted Soviet writer named Ilya Ehrenburg and the title of one of his novels.

During our literary conversations at this time, I had already noticed that the Russians generally were not telling the truth when they boasted of being widely read, but I also found that among Soviet writers it was the name of this Ilya Ehrenburg that they were most likely to know. I later learned that at this time he often wrote for the army in officially distributed camp newspapers and also in other Russian publications, so that even those who hadn't read any of his books knew his name.

One night towards dawn, a dishevelled, bearded, ill-tempered Russian arrived, a Kirghiz or some other Eastern type; he asked for something, wine or bacon, and when I didn't give him what he asked for, he began grumbling irritably. He gripped his sub-machine gun and shouted unintelligible words in a threatening voice. The situation was turning hostile. I decided to resort to the last recourse of defence: I introduced myself. But the Russian was suspicious. "Writer?" he asked distrustfully and grumpily. "What kind of writer?" I took the

French book off the shelf, showed him my name, then pointed to myself and said with the help of the interpreter: "Leave, because, as you see, you have got into a writer's house by mistake. See, I wrote this book. Here is my name. But that's not all," – I turned the book over – "I'm not just an ordinary writer but one whose books were published at the same time as those of a famous Russian writer. See, you can read Ilya Ehrenburg's name here." The short, bearded Russian was still suspicious. He bent over the book with the weapon in his hand, spelled out the name on the back and asked with a black look and sceptical voice:

"Ilya Ehrenburg?"

"Yes," I said. "How about that?"

He looked me over from head to foot. Then he flung out his arms, threw his head back and shrugged his shoulders.

"Propagandist!" he said contemptuously.

He turned and left the room. I stared after him with my mouth open. This man, it seemed, understood literature and had heard something about the difference between a writer and a propagandist.

But this and other kinds of encounters could not enlighten me about that "difference" I sensed in the Russians: what it was that set them apart from the people of the West. For they were different, not like a Hindu or a Chinese, but I am certain that a German peasant, an English repairman, a French veterinary or an Italian housepainter would reply differently from them to the prime questions about life in the *attitudinal* sense. We watched one another closely, for the Russians also kept an eye on us. They watched us not only in the "manor houses". They didn't take a look at just the accessories of bourgeois life; they were interested in those, but they also looked around and observed the poor in their abodes, and it was apparent that what they found there was not only unfamiliar but also astonishing and amazing to them. What was this "difference"? Was it the "Soviet man", actually, and thus a new, engendered and conditioned human breed who discerned and surveyed the world and humanity from a different perspective? Or was the Russian simply someone who, not for the first time in history, but now, it seemed, emerged with all its consequences from his Eurasian home and headed for the world to prowl about a bit, wary but curious? I couldn't come up with an answer.

Of course, they had the piglets and the flour carted away, but there was nothing remarkable about this, not even typical. At this time they also had the bicycles on the highway carried off; they pedalled them for a while and then threw them away or gave them to someone as a gift. Their obvious penchant for collecting watches couldn't be explained easily either. They actually demanded watches with a collector's passion; there were Russians who rolled up their coat sleeves and proudly put on their most recently stolen trophies next to the four or five wristwatches already on their arms. In the First World War, I was acquainted with some Russian prisoners of war – officers, peasants and workers – but not one of them was so passionately interested in watches. What was going on here, why did the time machine engage the Russians' interest so fervidly? I recollected Spengler's observation in his great pessimistic work that the people of a harmonious and lively culture have no awareness of "recording", thus of time measured in moments; the Chinese and the Greeks feel and think in large time perspectives, the *Olympian* being proof of this indifference to time as a unit of measurement, but when a culture comes to a period of crisis, that civilisation, in short the principle of utility, occasions the same feelings of panic in the souls of human beings, and it is then that the anxious measuring of time commences. It is possible that Soviet industrial experimentation elicited this feeling for time. I couldn't say. It was more likely that there weren't enough watch factories in the Soviet Union, and the muzhik developed a fancy for this special toy. Or, more simply, the watch was the one valuable that could be bartered most easily. Since I am speaking about the Russians, I can't give a definite answer.

Their coming and going, visits, vanishings – everything about them – was baffling and unpredictable. Days passed without our seeing a single Russian; then, unexpectedly, they would arrive en masse. They would pass through the village in motor vehicles, but in other ways as well, in wagons, dishevelled, like Gypsies. It wasn't only the service corps that advanced like this; the infantry also had itself transported in countless wagons. Privates, officers, woman soldiers and boy soldiers, twelve and thirteen years old, in regular uniforms with insignia of rank lay stretched out on the straw. I didn't see any chaplains among the troops, but it's possible I just didn't recognise them.

The Germans always advanced with mechanised detachments, as if the Krupp factory had sallied forth; even the stacks of their field-kitchens spewed smoke as if cannon barrels had been converted to this purpose. The Russians had everything required to wage war; but what they had was "different" – not as mechanised and systematically regulated. It was as if a monstrous, dreadful, enigmatic Eastern travelling circus had set out from the distance, from the dim remoteness, from the East, from Russia. This travelling circus was, in reality, one of the largest military machines on earth. And those who led it did so incomprehensibly but magnificently in the eyes of foreigners: everything was in its place, everything functioned in the apparent confusion; mysterious supervisors and monitors gave timely signals about everything to one another within the great machine.

Their intelligence network, information service, transmission of commands and internal procedures could not be detected. But seemingly, everything in the Russian army happened in accord with some very ancient system; the warfare experiences of the Genghis Khans, Tatars and the Golden Horde manifested themselves in the systematic way they marched, moved on, ate, threw bridges across rivers, pitched tents and then suddenly disappeared at some mysterious signal. The warfare of the ancient Magyars and Huns may have been like this; Scythian patrols galloped like this, not sparing the horse, and every forty kilometres – so scholars say – a garrison and fresh mounts awaited the horsemen, who tore open their tethered horse's arteries, drank its blood for a brief time measured by an hourglass and then quickly sewed up the horse's wound and galloped on . . . These Russians were closer to nature than the soldiers in the Western armies: even as the chiefs of the ancient Mongolian armies arrayed their forces galloping on white and different-coloured horses by the course of the moon in a certain eastern or northern line of attack – heaven knows what sort of streamlining war technique this was millennia ago! – so these later descendants of the Mongols were still able to perceive a measure of nature's power to support or obstruct.

It is difficult for me to speak about this because I can't substantiate it, but during the months when I lived in the closest intimacy night and day with the Russians, I distinctly felt, perceived, something of this kind. All this constituted the "difference". Moreover, they were cunning, crafty and scornfully and maliciously guileful; they were happy if they could fool us, the "Westerners". They were filled with childish joy if they saw us taken in. I had many dealings with the Russians then and sometimes later as well, but not once did a Russian who asked me for something and promised earnestly to return what he borrowed – a tool, book, any worthless article – ever keep his word. And if I called on them to fulfil the promise, they laughed happily and openly in my face because, well, being smarter, they had outwitted me.

I remember some strange characters: a young soldier who, on patrol, is riding a horse on the Danube's bank in the foggy January dawn, and the trotting and the face of the Mongolian horseman – all this is coming from so a great distance that I stop along the road and follow the apparition with my eyes for a long time. This horseman clearly isn't "different" from the others, he isn't an individual. He is the Mongolian horseman, and he has for millennia trotted like this in his quilted Chinese coat on the banks of the Volga or some other river, and he will ride his horse with the same impassivity if one day he should be sent out on patrol in the Pyrenees. He does not so much as glance at his surroundings; an absolute indifference is reflected in the Mongolian face. On another occasion, two straggling horsemen are plodding along, a sort of Zoro and Huru – one gangling, the other paunchy and stubby, like Sancho Panza. They are singing and making gloomy, ridiculous faces. Struggling and mimicking themselves, they amble along the highway, and when they reach me, they howl whoops into my face that suggest the braying of a jackass; then, shrugging their shoulders, they move on, two country buffoons.

They liked to play, to act a lot. But their idea of acting was also "different". It lacked any awareness of *homo ludens* or the civilised reflex of *commedia dell'arte*; in every one of their impromptu amusements there was a bit of sorcery, something tribal, ritualistic – and for this reason, they were somewhat frightening when they started to play.

Sometimes officers showed up with whom we could converse at length and seriously, in German, too. Naturally, I didn't enquire about their life and lot at home, because they would have misunderstood my purpose. Rather, it seemed most sensible for me to nibble at the only topic of conversation that I could check out – literature. They answered my questions vaguely, sometimes stupidly, mostly with misinformation, but then sometimes with amazing intelligence. Since many of them tended to tell lies, I accepted as true only answers containing factual proof that the person I asked knew what he was talking about.

[AT]

JÁNOS PILINSZKY

Harbach 1944

(to Gábor Thurzó)

At all times I see them.
The moon brilliant. A black shaft looms up.
Beneath it, harnessed men
haul a huge cart.

Dragging that giant wagon
which grows bigger as the night grows
their bodies are divided among
the dust, their hunger and their trembling.

They are carrying the road, they are carrying the land,
the bleak potato fields,
and all they know is the weight of everything,
the burden of the skylines

and the falling bodies of their companions
which almost grew into their own
as they lurch, living layers,
treading each other's footsteps.

The villages stay clear of them,
the gateways withdraw.
The distance, that has come to meet them,
reels away back.

Staggering, they wade knee-deep
in the low, darkly muffled clatter
of their wooden clogs
as through invisible leaf litter.

Already their bodies belong to silence.
And they thrust their faces towards the height
as if they strained for a scent
of the far-off celestial troughs

because, prepared for their coming
like an opened stockyard,
its gates flung savagely back,
death gapes to its hinges.

[TH/JC]

On the Wall of a KZ-Lager

Where you have fallen, you stay.
In the whole universe, this is your place.
Just this single spot.
But you have made this yours utterly.

The countryside evades you.
House, mill, poplar,
each thing strives to be free of you
as if it were mutating in nothingness.

But now it is you who stay.
Did we blind you? You continue to watch us.
Did we rob you? You enriched yourself.
Speechless, speechless, you testify against us.

[TH/JC]

ISTVÁN VAS

Pest Elegy

Remarkable city: mud slopping filth. February strives
To cover the purple of mourning with slush, and a hard rain drives
The rubbish before it, the rubbish which thickens and thrives.

Soot settles, blackening turrets of snow: skeletal, bloody,
The city is shivering in puddles, both of us muddy,
Emerging together: the city is one with my own frozen body.

Fog swathes the Ring Road; a thin ersatz gauze serves for a binding,
Above the hulks of the Royal and Emke the smoke has stopped winding,
Through teetering gaps new lights in the New York are pulsing and blinding.

A tortured frivolity flickers, struggles once more to its feet,
And clings to the city a murderous climate failed to defeat,
Refusing to flounder in mortar or drown in the swill of the street.

Ten o'clock. Life's neons are blinking. Soon they will stop.
Despair is a drunkard who lurches and heaves in the slop.
A thin throbbing of motors at night: Pest hunched for the drop.

What voices have rung down these streets, or flew to address
Impossible hopes but whistled out nevertheless
The youthful and brilliant logic of ultimate cleanliness!

The light in our eyes, in our mutual glances, remembers the glow –
We remember it all, the lot, my poor friends, is it not so?
The irregular beat in the stone heart of town gives our hearts the go.

Though the stone heart of town keeps on missing, its beats never die.
But even if fate should leave not a stone standing, time would raise high
The stack of her walls once again, with its right of reply.

For it's neither the stone, nor the beam, nor the wall, nor any such quiddity;
Demolish the fabric a hundred times over, there still stands a city:
She has purchased from Death itself her share of eternity.

The city has purchased herself and redeemed me as well:
My guilt floats in gutters and ditches, in winter's apparel.
The great absolution is here, in the present, and I can feel hell

Slip from my heart with the sorrow that's stamped and suffered alone:
Redeeming herself, the city redeems me as one of her own.
Forgiveness, unhoped for, glows from her body, from bruised flesh and bone.

The lights are all out now but faith dawns through faint foggy weather.
The record remains, entered by somebody, somehow, wherever:
I lived here, nor wanted any place else. Not then and not ever.

[GS]

Dialogue between Strangers

– And again the roses.
– And summer again.
– Do you notice still?
– More than ever.
– The year runs on.
– And grows shorter and shorter.
– Slowly you run out of time.
– I do.
– And what will happen?
– What could? What they say is natural.
– In a word, you bear it?
– No, just endure the unbearable.
– And how do you prepare for it?
– I don't.
– What does your hand hold now?
– The usual. Cigarette, wine glass, a pen.

– Of course. The sorry trash you are attached to.
Personal stuff, keepsakes, faces, your own things.
How long will you hold them? Better throw them away
And start empty-handed and walk away from the roads,
To the hill's crown.
                    – What for?
                                        – By then it will be autumn again.
And at the top of the hill, among neither tree nor bush,
A cold rain beats down the needlegrass,
And atop the bare hill the rain beats you to the bare skin too,
And leaches out of you what you believe important,
And facts and faces seep out of you,
And what is bare to the core you may transcend, you know where.
                                                            I don't want
To transcend anywhere, if not as I am.
And I won't climb the bare hill.
                                        – Don't be headstrong.

– But I am headstrong and still collect what fills me up,
And obstinately don't want to be naked to the core.
I know, my time runs out. But I don't want to run out of
What may sometime flare up even in cold rain.

– And what do you think? By the light of that flare
You will gain what awaits you? Or would you perhaps impose
Its conditions?
                    – No, I just cannot accept its conditions
And I do not need what has no need of me.
Because I am what I am, and I do not give myself up.

– In any case you will be compelled to.
                                                – If there is such a power, so
                                                  be it.

– Time is running out. Be ready, for what awaits you is ready to
  meet you.
– And till then?
                    – Roses again, and again, summer.

[DHo]

SÁNDOR WEÖRES

Monkeyland

Oh for far-off monkeyland,
ripe monkeybread on baobabs,
and the wind strums out monkeytunes
from monkeywindow monkeybars.

Monkeyheroes rise and fight
in monkeyfield and monkeysquare,
and monkeysanatoriums
have monkeypatients crying there.

Monkeygirl monkeytaught
masters monkeyalphabet,
evil monkey pounds his thrawn
feet in monkeyprison yet.

Monkeymill is nearly made,
miles of monkeymayonnaise,
winningly unwinnable
winning monkeymind wins praise.

Monkeyking on monkeypole
harangues the crowd in monkeytongue,
monkeyheaven comes to some,
monkeyhell for those undone.

Macaque, gorilla, chimpanzee,
baboon, orangutan, each beast
reads his monkeynewssheet at
the end of each twilight repast.

With monkeysupper memories
the monkeyouthouse rumbles, hums,
monkeyswaddies start to march,
right turn, left turn, shoulder arms –

monkeymilitary fright
reflected in each monkeyface,
with monkeygun in monkeyfist
the monkeys' world the world we face.

[EMor]

Antithin

At last it has leaked out – thin men are the cause of everything.
They wait in ambush on street corners and if an old woman comes
by
they don't even greet her. They are more concerned with
exchanging their
straw hats for lottery tickets, and with naturalising crocodiles in
the waters of Europe, so that even there there should be no safety.
They always begin their fishy deals in their beds at dawn, and
afterwards go to the street. Some work in offices, others ostensibly
are waiters or locksmiths – they all disguise themselves. But their
true trade is thinness. At last it has leaked out – thin men are, etc.

[RL]

Queen Tatavane

O my winged ancestors!
Green branch and dry twig you gave me
for my two empires, to plant one and to lash one.
I am small as a weasel, pure as the eastern Moon,
light-ankled as a gazelle, but not poised for flight –
my heart lies open to you, to every silent suggestion.

The Elephantstar took my fifteenth year,
the Dragonstar brought this, the sixteenth.
I am allowed three husbands by ancestral decree
and seven lovers beneath the holy jasmine-leaves.

Not for me to escape with girlfriends to the fields,
for happy laughter, goats to milk, fresh milk to drink,

instead I sit on the throne in your light year after year,
an ebony idol with the world's weight on my neck.

Negro caravans, Arab ships are my traffic and merchandise,
I pay well, though I see most as polecats and monkeys,
but even the sky rains on unchosen ground, seeds burst unchosen.
I survey the naked hosts lost in their prison,
all of them I love as if they were my children,
punishing them with the rod and if need be by the sword,
and though my heart should bleed my looks are frozen.

Wake up, my fathers and mothers! Leave the ash-filled urn,
help me while the mists crawl;
your dark little daughter pleads with you as the last queen,
waiting among the garlands of the cedar-hall.

My seat among stone lions, the man's throne empty at my side,
my brow is glowing ruby-wreathed like the dawn-clouds,
my purple-tinted fingers, my drowsy almond eyes
shine like a god's as they strike down and raise;
what you found sweet and bitter I come to, I taste.

Orange veils on my shoulders, fireflower wreaths on my dark hair,
the reedpipe cries, the eunuchs drone, the altar's set.
Come Bulak-Amba my starry bull-browed ancestor!
Come Aure-Ange my lovely holy milk-rich ancestress!

Mango, areca, piled on the altar,
the year's brimming rice, brown coconut, white copra,
all round, red flower thrown on red flower,
sweet sandalwood fumes float up into the air.

Great man-spirit with no name: eat!
Great woman-spirit with no name: eat!
Huge emptiness in the silence behind the drumbeat: eat!

I call you, my father over the foam,
my old begetter, Batan-Kenam,
you are coming in your sun-chariot, four-elephant-drawn,
through the head-waving rattlesnakes of five cosmic storms,
my soldier, ageless, coral-garlanded,

blue-shirted arms,
lance of sky's shark-bone, turtle shield,
cut-off locks of the seven dancer-stars shimmer at your belt,
your elephants lumber and stamp, tiger-herds are felled,
and you rest on your elbow at the world's end in the lee of the loud
  blue mountain –
I salute you my glittering visitor, my far-off father!

I am wrapped in my veil, I am hidden,
the welcoming hostess is timid,
I hand out half-peeled oranges on a gold dish:
look at me here, I am your own flesh,
you know I am supple and clawed like a forest cat,
you pause if you see my dark green shining eyes,
my white-hot teeth-embers,
behind, my skeleton is lace-fine, a dragon-fly:
see your one-day-old woman! one smile is all she would wish!

I summon you Aruvatene, my mother!
I call you. I am your daughter. Do you love her?
Your little one, will you be her protector?
Look, Nightqueen, at your tiny drop of dew:
the sparkling skin, the swelling breast!
You thick-starred heavenly palm-tree, I dance for you.

Blow the pipe, roll the drum,
my dance-wind skims about you, let it come!
my silver ankle-jangle chatters – from you it came!
my orange shawl flies out – you gave it my name!

But if your beautiful face goes ashy as mist
I give you my blood to drink from your ancient chalice,
turn back, I leave you in peace,
eat, drink in silence.

Come too, Andede, good grandmother,
you are as old as the wind
that snuffles in the oven-cinders.
I shall never be so old,
fugitive with blowing flowers.

Andede, good grandmother,
you are as wrinkled as the stone
that snaps off from the mountain.
I shall never be so wrinkled,
I am the rock-escaping fountain.

Andede, good grandmother,
you smile like a yellow desert place
grinding its bones, toothless sand-cascades
skirting the cosmic border.
That is not my smile,
I am the lady of two empires,
sword and bread on my lap together
under the trickle of my tears,
Andede, good grandmother,
you champ and smack like the green dragon
that swallows up the wildest moor.
But I can never be satisfied,
two nations fight to eat from my hand
and bread forever lusts after sword.

Andede, good grandmother,
perpetually decaying, never destroyed,
you are puny but sinewy like a root in the earth,
I am the mother of everybody,
I would take them all on my lap,
I would let them all eat and sup,
but when I even raise my hand, I die.

Great man-spirit, with no name: eat!
Great woman-spirit with no name: eat!
Huge emptiness in the silence behind the drumbeat: eat!

Come forward, now, great, ancient, unforgotten,
every sky-dome-breasted queen,
every lightning-dashing king!
I know that your good
is our only food,
but if misery surges again,
here I am – my blame alone,
I your shadow, your orphan,

prostrate under your cane,
beg for that bastinadoing!

For heaven's sake help me then!
Oh I am the virgin peahen
who instead of living eggs
found red-hot stones between her legs
and with anxious wings spread wide
broods to hatch a void.
Pain of two nations is fire under me,
who will ever hatch the happiness of the world?

[EMor]

IVÁN MÁNDY

On the Balcony

He was watering the plants. Sprinkling them. Rather half-heartedly. Without conviction. The plants sensed it, the plants on the balcony. They were coated with dust in the faded-green box. The climbing plant crept up the worn, crumbling mortar wall, and yet . . . It was barely possible to stir on the tiny balcony. He cautiously turned around. He looked down at the street, at the square. Trucks below the window. People walking dogs on the pathways of the square. A girl in jeans with two dogs. One a gloomy-looking bulldog. An over-aged detective. The other distinguished, long-haired. They never speak to each other. A black-haired boy with a black dog heaved into sight behind the girl. Thank God!

And he must be on this rickety balcony.

Yes, on the balcony with the shattered, blackened stone facing. A piece of its ledge is missing. As if a bite had been taken out of it. The whole thing is falling into decay, just like the building itself.

He splashed a little water on the deck. Then he just stood there holding the empty can.

This balcony could give way at any time. A girl actually said: "Listen, I wouldn't go out there if I was you."

Some day he will fly away with the balcony. Stones, stone fragments plopping around him. He'll fly over the trees. Across the square.

The night is a sweat-soaked shirt.

This appeared before him. This was on the slip on the writing desk inside. One single perplexing line.

The night is a sweat-soaked shirt.

What is he getting at? What kind of story is he getting entangled in? Come now! He isn't getting entangled in anything. There is no story. Moreover, his stories! Just that night from the years of the Fifties. From the depth of the Fifties.

I couldn't sleep. It would have been very important to get some sleep. At least for a couple of hours. But it was hopeless! I tossed and turned in the tangled covers. I adjusted the pillow time and time again. Maybe I had a fever. I didn't dare take my temperature. My throat was scratchy, it twinged and burned. I went to the window, stared out into the darkness. The yellowish light of a window across the way. The only light. They are sitting up with a sick person. He will never die and never get up. Those keeping vigil take turns. The light is always on. The house of sickness.

I watched this for a time.

Back to bed.

I lay motionless. My eyes closed, my hands clasped on my chest. I sleep. Actually, I am already asleep. I sat up. I hurled the little pillow into the darkness.

The morning's uncertain greyness. The hurled pillow in the corner.

Getting up. Setting out for the railway station. Then the journey to Pereszlény. A lecture on a book at the student hostel. Popov's *Steel and Slag*. We salute the comrade author!

The comrade author had not authored anything for a long time. He had lost out everywhere. Actually, no place was left for him to be lost out of. The periodicals in which formerly some of his stories had appeared also ceased publication.

How many of us could have been in the smoke-filled compartment? It's odd, but again I saw only the pillow tossed into the corner. The absurdly crumpled bedsheets.

Railway workers were playing cards. One took off his heavy railway coat, another just unbuttoned it. A woman was drinking. She sat in her shabby fur coat. She leaned her head back and drank. Or rather, she was plied with drinks. A man was bending over her with the bottle. She laughed barely audibly. She put her hand on her mouth, only to pull it away immediately.

"Why are you doing that?"

He heard the quiet voice very clearly. As if someone had just now spoken up from the square. Or simply from the air.

An old man in the compartment:

"Tell me, why are you doing that? Don't you see she is . . . ?"

Then immediately an old woman:

"Stop! Stay out of it!"

They sat huddled together in the corner.

I took out the Popov. I tried dipping into it. Balázs is travelling on Mikszáth somewhere to Kecskemét. And I on Popov.

The muddy floor. The doddering seats. Aren't they heating the train at all?

The two old people huddled together. The rail workers played cards. The woman wearing the fur coat slept.

I couldn't imagine we would ever arrive anywhere.

The train ran through the fog. Ran! Crawled. Jolted. Stopped, winded.

Several passengers got off.

A postman went through the compartment with an enormous black bag hanging from his shoulder. He was heading towards me. What's this, a letter? Is he bringing me a letter? Maybe from Adrienne Fiam?

The permit! The entry permit!

I didn't attack my pockets right off. I didn't turn them inside out right off. Instead, cautiously with the tips of my fingers. This is my Army Reserve Status card. Temporarily unfit. What is this "temporarily" bit? What do they mean? My fingers stopped for an instant, then moved on . . . The Writers' Association membership card. They haven't ejected me yet. They just called me in. They chatted with me. A woman with pale blue eyes sat on the other side of the table. We haven't seen anything from you for a long time, Comrade Zsámboky. She fastened her eyes on me. Are you working on something? I am working on . . . yes. A novel . . . a kind of novel. What is it about? About a soccer team. A flabbergasted face. A soccer team? And how are you coming with it? Good Lord! How am I coming with it? Anyway, I said something. She just looked at me. Rather drearily. We haven't given up on you yet, Comrade Zsámboky.

They hadn't given up on me yet.

Meanwhile, the searching went on. A card. It could be an invitation. Who is inviting me? And where? The Army Reserve Status thing again. But the permit! To enter the border zone! I will have to get it stamped. And again on departure. Arrival and departure. Except I won't get there because . . . But why don't I have a wallet. A miserable wallet in which . . .

"Lose something?"

"No, nothing."

The old gentleman leaned towards me for a little while. His wife pulled him back.

And I in front of them with the police permit. Completely exhausted!

I got up. I gazed out.

Fog-choked houses. Ghostly houses.

I went into the corridor.

A forsaken, frozen field. Mounds of dirty snow.

Back to the compartment.

They stared at me. The two old people. Who is this character? He gets up, sits down, gets up again. He gropes through all his pockets. He rummages through his briefcase. He leafs through a book. He shuts it immediately.

The others like in a dream.

That character in a brownish-purple coat gets off the train. She totters around the station with her ridiculously little bag. She asks someone something.

The police?

The police station on the side of the hill. A family house. In years past it welcomed guests warmly. The host came out to the gate.

A fat policeman stamped the document in some kind of hall.

"It must be stamped on the way back!"

"Yes, on the way back."

When will this "on the way back" take place? In any case, I will have to get up at dawn again. Until then a bed or a chair.

Now to the hostel. But how do I get there?

I should have asked at the police station. Well, there I didn't ask about anything.

Now, however: "How do I get to the hostel? The vocational students? Please, which way is it?"

Please, which way . . . ?

Please, which way . . . ?

A narrow bridge above a narrow creek. A girl in a blue wrap on the railing, her knees drawn up. A schoolbag under her arm.

No bridge of any kind! No girl of any kind! That must have been some other place. Some other trip, some other town.

Down on the square a white-maned man embraced a tree with one arm. As if taking it to dance. He eased himself slowly to the ground with a serene intimacy. He reposed beside the tree. He gazed up with a rosy smile. He beckoned towards Zsámboky. Zsámboky drew further back.

There wasn't a creek. There wasn't a bridge. And there wasn't a girl.

Gardens. Desolate gardens giving way to each other. Fallen leaves. Yellow, yellowish green, pale green, rust-red leaves in listless piles. When did they fall? This autumn? Last year? Or longer ago? The gardens overflow with them. They overflow with hatred. The hatred of the dead leaves.

"Have you ever thought of joining the party?"

Where did that voice come from?

From a room again. From the other side of the table again. I could barely make out the woman's face. She pulled back from the range of the lamplight. Maybe only when her chin moved.

Actually, I had long expected this question. For it to be delivered in a room during a conversation. Still, I could just barely utter: "I haven't reached that point yet."

"You haven't yet?"

I looked at that chin, at the mouth's faintly visible outline. Then it tumbled out of me: "God . . . (the woman gave a start) I believe in Him."

She stiffened.

I repeated it: "I believe in Him."

Then we just sat sunk in silence.

A hand rose from the other side. It reached across. It brushed mine barely perceptibly.

"I do too."

Rotting benches in the garden. Seats broken. Or already gone. Only those arms rising into the air. Unexpectedly a willowy yellow bench. Almost elegant. Yes indeed, elegance itself. Listen, sir! You are really holding your own well. But be careful because one of these days . . . In short, I'd better be careful.

The gardens were left behind.

The houses receded. Just like the Danube in its own sulkiness. Suddenly I found myself on the bank. So unexpectedly that I nearly walked into it.

A prison-grey building. Solitary, ominous. The hostel. A sign on the gate. I didn't read it. If I am asked sometime where I'd been, in which hostel, I don't know, I don't remember.

Dogs escorted me across the courtyard. Shaggy, sleepy-looking dogs. And a lanky young man with a stooped back. Is he the one who checked my identification at the gate? Or did he just now appear? Join me now? With a scarf, without a coat. The scarf carefully wrapped around his throat. His throat is sensitive.

"Well, yes . . . I also have a lot of trouble with my throat."

He didn't hear me. He just walked beside me bundled up in his scarf. Go and choke!

"We are going to the office."

The dogs followed us silently. They didn't even let out an occasional yelp. At times they stopped for a moment. They turned towards me. Did they want to ask me something?

Boys dressed in blue overcoats crossed the courtyard. Faces of iron filings. Of fallen wood shavings.

The dogs bowed their heads low. As if scrubbing the pavement. These were humiliated at some time. Badly humiliated.

The light was on in the office.

Portraits on the wall. The very same portraits always and everywhere. In offices, schools, rooms, corridors. And now here.

I didn't look up. I didn't want to see those faces.

An older woman in a pink sweater in the range of the lamplight. The sore throat behind me as he delivered me.

"The comrade lecturer."

The woman glanced up as she took me over.

"Comrade Jávor?"

"János Zsámboky."

Her glance died away.

"I don't know why Mrs Morvai does this to me! I can never get Dezső Jávor."

The escort was silent.

I was silent also. Well, naturally. After all, Dezső Jávor is something else. A model lecturer. You just can't get him from the Society.

She examined my papers. The escort had not moved yet. Who knows, he may have to take me back.

The woman with a sigh:

"All right!"

She pointed for me to take a seat. She became absorbed in some sort of ledger.

The escort disappeared.

I sank into my coat. My briefcase beside me.

She made notes. She twisted her hair with a finger. Her pencil glided across a sheet.

"You still have to wait."

I nodded.

Maybe I should take off my coat. At least unbutton it. But I only loosened my scarf.

Whispering behind my back. Someone entered, someone left.

The door opened again. Papers were put on the table.

The woman, as she looked at them:

"I say, enough of this matter!"

She went out. I was left to myself with the lamp and the faces on the wall.

Matter? What matter? Did they get a new principal? Did somebody escape? They caught and brought him back?

My fingers began moving on my coat buttons. They moved and drew back.

A man in the lamplight. An indifferent back bending forward. He was scribbling in a notebook. He leaned back. He stared into the air. Behaving as if absolutely alone.

Maybe there really isn't anyone else in the room. Just a coat thrown on a chair. A briefcase beside a chair.

"May I have a cup of tea?"

He looked at me a trifle offended. Offended and suspicious. He sat there motionless for a while. He stood up and went out. He returned with a tin mug and a little porcelain plate.

"Thank you."

He nodded and left. Somehow this business about the tea had irritated him.

The tea was tepid, watery. Stale, broken crackers on the plate. Crushed pieces of a sugar wafer. Where did he scrape them up? In any case, he vanished. Just like the woman. They won't ever come back again. Maybe they are talking about me in a room.

I slipped out of my coat. I sipped the tea.

Steps resounding in the corridor. A marching column. The marching of a brigade.

Someone will enter in a moment.

I stood up. They must not catch me off guard.

Nobody came in. The steps died away.

For a few minutes I remained standing facing the door.

Darkness outdoors. Only light from lamps in the courtyard. The dogs are circling each other. Occasional sharp barks. Deep, throaty sounds.

Some singing in a distant room? No, nothing.

"We can go!"

A man in the doorway? His face invisible in the darkness.

I took Popov out of my briefcase. I tried to smile.

"Well then . . ."

A cold stone corridor. Greenish-grey doors. Schoolrooms? Workshops?

My guide descended on metal stairs.

"If you will permit me, I will go ahead."

"This way, comrade!"

What is this? A prison corridor? A cellar?

He suddenly turned towards me.

"I will give just a few words of introduction. What is the comrade's name?"

"János Zsámboky."

Suddenly I stood before them. As if abruptly pushed into the large room. Into that large room under ground.

The boys in a semicircle. In blue coats, overalls. Such tired faces! If they could sit down, they would fall asleep. But they can't sit down.

After a few short steps I stopped in front of them.

The introductory words were delivered. Silence. But not the silence of expectation.

I heard my voice:

"*Steel and Slag* . . ."

This voice came from a distance. Ill at ease, dusty. At times it rasped unexpectedly.

"In this novel . . . in this great novel about building . . ."

Again the voice lapsed into nothingness.

I tried to capture a glance. Hopeless. But somebody is watching closely. Somebody in the rows. Then he will write the report.

". . . faces rise before us. We recognise them . . . these resolute . . ." Don't let me say exemplary, at least not that!

The shoes! The shoes lined up before me! I should say, hobnailed boots. Heavy, cumbersome boots. When do they clean them? At night, before going to bed? How often do they get a new pair? Annually? Once every year?

"Because this novel has its power . . . its significance in . . ."

A rat scurried across the room. With the furious haste of latecomers. It stopped in front of me. It looked at me sideways. Well, what's this? What can you say to me? Immeasurable mockery in its look. And it seems a bit tipsy. The author of polemical essays. Polemical essays dripping with mockery. It shook itself irritably. Don't get mad, but you aren't a partner in the controversy. Then it disappeared.

And we remained in numb immobility.

I heard my voice again. Then nothing . . . I stood and waited. For what? Questions? What sort of questions?

I bowed.

"Thank you for your kind attention."

Someone stepped up to me, shook my hands.

The rows moved. The brigades marched out. They left the room.

That guffawing outside! The faces they must have made! That character, old chap! Did you watch him? Standing there, just grinding away. He didn't have an inkling of what he was talking about. He never opened the book. He never had it in his hands. They doubled up with guffaws.

No, they didn't guffaw. They didn't make faces either. They simply marched off.

Zsámboky leaned over the stone parapet.

He raised the sprinkling can. He shook it. He shook nothing out of it.

And then? Did I have supper? Surely they gave me some supper! Or did they take me right to that upstairs room?

I came upon my coat several times. Somebody always brought it after me. They took it by the collar like some slippery character. Like someone wanting to make a getaway. Or to look around a bit. Not so fast! No, not that! Let's keep moving along, buddy!

The room upstairs. In a deserted corner of the upstairs. Alone with my coat and my briefcase.

Someone spoke from the outside.

"When do you head back, comrade?"

"In the morning. On the 6.10."

"Do you have a watch?"

"A watch? No, I don't."

"Then I will call you."

With that he left.

I went to the bed. I tested it a few times. It didn't take umbrage. It had no umbrage in it at all. An iron bed. An army cot. A discharged army cot. A veteran. The covers not the most reassuring. Probably thin. Well, then the coat.

Thrown over a chair for the time being. But it knows what to expect.

Maybe I won't lie down. They won't wake me up anyway. No one will knock. Why wouldn't they? They really don't want to get saddled with me. They've had enough of me. On the other hand, it's not such a bad idea . . . If I strolled into that office. To that woman who expected Dezső Jávor.

In the morning I will cross the garden again. The desolate garden.

But first the night. They don't heat the room very much. Really, what kind of room is this? A guest room? They certainly won't stick an important guest in here. A tiny washbasin next to the wardrobe. I take the toothbrush out of my briefcase. Toothbrush, toothpaste, soap.

A hurried ablution, an extremely hurried ablution.

Throaty barking from the courtyard.

The guards, the hostel's guards. It seems there is nobody around but them. Just them. And me in this room. They know about me, about my every movement. My turning off the light. My undressing. I spread my coat over the bed. I get under the covers. Under the prickly covers.

I don't hear them any more.

Have they slipped into the building? Are they roaming the corridor? In front of the door?

The chair. The solitary chair beside the table. For an instant it vanished. Then it rose again out of the darkness. And now they also could be seen.

Those two old people. The ones on the train that I . . . And now here in this room. Beside each other on this chair. Huddled together. They sit holding hands. The man seeming to smile, the woman more frightened somehow. But madam, you have nothing to fear. You can sit here as long as you like.

The door opened soundlessly. A woman spoke from outside:

"Sanyika knows 'Childe John' by heart."

She stopped. She waited for me to say something. She stood outside and waited.

"Should I send him in?"

I wanted to raise my head. To shout at her. Shut her door and go away!

"Don't you want to hear him?"

"No! No!"

With great agony I raised my head.

"He will recite it all by heart."

"No! No!"

I sank back. I lay motionless. They are here . . . beside me. The mother and Sanyika. They huddle together on the edge of the bed. But the mother immediately gives the sign. She gives Sanyika's arm a yank. And he promptly begins "Childe John".

What do I care! Let him recite "Childe John". Let him recite whatever he wants to.

I was standing on a street in the sunlight. In the sharp sunlight of early spring. For a time I just gazed at the rooftops. Then I began to stroll. Without a coat.

A tall, dark woman from the other side:

"Listen! You are getting careless."

"Oh, come on, Adrienne. I never wear an overcoat in March."

"You will catch cold. You know how much trouble you have with your throat."

I broke into a laugh.

"Adrienne, don't worry about my throat."

I looked up at the sky. At the cold blue sky. I shivered a little. Then a waiter emerged from a café. An old flat-footed waiter.

"We'll put the tables out on the terrace immediately."

I nodded. I called over to the other side:

"Adrienne, did you hear? They are putting the tables out on the terrace right away."

"But that's not so sure yet."

"Not so sure? What do you mean?"

But she had already vanished. Just like the waiter. I shivered, but gloomily this time. Better to sit down inside.

Where is it?

A dark hole between two lowered shutters. A dark hole in the hollow of the wall. Still, someone is moving around inside.

I called in: "When will you open?"

No answer.

They banged the shutters ever more furiously.

Then only that banging.

I sat stiffly in bed. Darkness around me. The banging from the outside.

"Five fifteen!"

"Yes . . . thank you!"

The knocking stopped. Receding steps in the corridor.

The covers half slid down. The coat at the end of the bed.

I raised the covers. I lay back for an instant. As if wanting to really sleep right now.

I stood in my pyjamas at the table. I leaned over it.

"Adrienne Fiam!"

How long had I been standing like this? Suddenly terror tore through me. Icy terror. Have I lost my mind? What am I waiting for? It must be at least five thirty already. And the police! The railway station! How do I get out of here? Surely someone will come.

Nobody came.

Dressed in the room. Hand on the briefcase. For some reason I felt very sticky. Something stuck on me that already . . .

Keep brooding, you beast. Meanwhile, you will miss the train.

I held the briefcase. I looked back from the door. Maybe I wanted to say goodbye to the room.

Lost in the darkness of the corridor.

The stairs! I must find the stairs!

A small point of light somewhere in the depth. The dorm rooms must be that way. The washrooms. In a moment the place will be stirring. The boys must be up by now. They are sleepily tottering to the washrooms. They are opening the taps. The sneezing of the taps. Giggling, swearing. As they jostle each other in the showers.

Nothing could be heard. But I found the stairs. I grabbed that brown banister very gratefully.

The point of light like a lamp choked by fog.

I stopped on a landing. My hand on the banister. One more step and I'll sit down on the floor. And then just sleep, sleep!

I looked down into the depth. One or two more floors and then . . .

Sharp, cold air.

The courtyard.

Ghosts came towards me. The ghosts dispersed.

Muffled growling. Short, angry yapping. Somewhat longer. Long drawn-out howling.

The dogs.

They surrounded me. They circled around me. They stopped barking. They kept stalking me. They sniffed nervously. Nervously and intensely. They gave a growl at each of my movements. Others came out of the darkness trotting feverishly. Their fervour abated slightly when they came close. Still, they didn't leave.

Flickering yellow eyes. Their breath lashed at my face. Their reeking breath.

I didn't move. I couldn't.

Pressed against the wall beside the climbing plant.

Rooftops before him. Closed and open windows. Trees on the square. Pathways.

Broken-off twigs and branches on the pathways. Entangled like antlers.

It was growing dark.

He didn't move. As if there wasn't a room behind him. Nothing at all!

All of a sudden he picked up the sprinkling can. He went into the room. He circled the table. He walked the circles maniacally. He kept striking the can against his knee.

He stopped.

He bent over the table. Before him the slip with the lone single line.

The night is a sweat-soaked shirt.

[AT]

At the Movies with Father

He didn't turn towards him as they sat in seats eight and nine on the left. He simply observed the boy out of the corner of his eye in the drizzling incandescence. He touched the shoulder for an instant and asked:

"Can you see all right, old fellow?"

[AT]

ISTVÁN ÖRKÉNY

1949
(*show trial*)

Foreign Minister László Rajk, the respected Party man, was sentenced to death today. His execution, carried out at his own request, will take place before a select audience of invited dignitaries.*

[JS]

We're a Small Nation

Executioner's Wife: This cheese soufflé is delicious.
Executioner: Light as a feather.
Condemned Man's Wife: You must try the cupcake too.
Executioner's Wife: I've never tasted cupcake quite so mouthwatering before.
Condemned Man: We should get together more often.
Executioner's Wife: It's the only way to learn about each other.
Executioner: Every meeting brings new understanding.
Condemned Man's Wife: We're a small nation. We should stick together.
Condemned Man: Sticking together is what we do best.
Executioner: Shouldn't we be on a first-name basis, friends?
Condemned Man: Don't you remember? We already are.

* László Rajk was Minister of Foreign Affairs in 1949 when Hungary's Communist Party Secretary Rákosi put him on trial for spying for the Western Imperialists. Since such trials had no basis in fact, they quickly became known as show trials. One curious aspect of these trials was the way the authorities managed to convince the accused that they must play along for the good of the Communist cause. Hence the reference here to Rajk being executed "at his own request".

Executioner: I'd like to get to know you better.
Condemned Man: I'll drink to that!
Executioner: To your very good health!
Condemned Man: And to yours, Comrade!

[JS]

Rondo

She pulls a slip of paper from the
carriage of her typewriter.
She takes two new slips of paper.
She slides a sheet of carbon paper
between them. She types.

She pulls a slip of paper from the
carriage of her typewriter.
She takes two new slips of paper.
She slides a sheet of carbon paper
between them. She types.

She pulls a slip of paper from the
carriage of her typewriter.
She takes two new slips of paper.
She slides a sheet of carbon paper
between them. She types.

She pulls a slip of paper from the
carriage of her typewriter.
She has been working for the same firm
for twenty-five years.
She eats a cold sandwich for lunch.
She lives alone.

Her name is Mrs Wolf.
Remember the name.
Mrs Wolf. Mrs Wolf. Mrs Wolf.

[JS]

*Ahasuerus**

Two Jews are walking down the street.
The first Jew asks the second a question.
The second Jew answers him.
The two Jews continue walking.
The first Jew who in the meantime has thought of another question asks it.
The second Jew answers him.
Sometimes this amuses them.
Sometimes it does not.
And so the two Jews continue walking.
They also continue talking.
Life, as you can see, is not always a bowl of cherries.

[JS]

Life should be so simple

1. remove fire extinguisher from bracket
2. open valve
3. approach source of fire
4. extinguish fire
5. close valve
6. replace extinguisher on bracket

[JS]

November

The morning fog was heavy, the traffic slow. The tram had pulled out right in front of Kordova Kordován's nose. The forty-year-old salad chef of the Restaurant Royale stood waiting at the stop. After a while

* Ahasuerus was the Old Testament king who, having given his deputy Haman permission for the massacre of the Jews, was persuaded by Queen Esther to save them.

he got fed up with standing around and so, with his right hand, he took a firm grip of his left thumb and with a quick jerk, pulled it off. Taking it between two fingers he studied it, wrapped it up in a clean handkerchief and, reaching inside his coat, slipped it securely in the rear pocket of his trouser. He looked around. The next tram still hadn't come. But Kordova Kordován just shrugged. He wasn't about to get worked up over every little trifle.

[JS]

GYULA ILLYÉS

A Sentence about Tyranny

Where tyranny exists
that tyranny exists
not only in the barrel of the gun
not only in the cells of a prison

not just in the interrogation block
or the small hours of the clock
the guard's bark and his fists
the tyranny exists

not just in the billowing black fetor
of the closing speech of the prosecutor,
in "the justified use of force"
the prisoners' dull morse

not merely in the cool postscript
of the expected verdict
there's tyranny
not just in the crisp military

order to "Stand" and the numb
instruction "Fire!", the roll of the drum,
in the last twitch
of the corpse in the ditch

not just in the door half open
and the fearful omen,
the whispered tremor
of the secret rumour

the hand that grips,
the finger before the lips,
tyranny is in place
in the iron mask of the face

in the clench of the jaw
the wordless O
of pain and its echo
and the tears

of silence-breeding fears,
in the surprise
of starting eyes

tyranny supplies
the standing ovation, the loud
hurrahs and chanting of the crowd
at the conference, the songs

of tyranny, the breasts
that tyranny infests,
the loud unflagging
noise of rhythmic clapping,

at opera, in trumpet cry,
in the uproarious lie
of grandiose statues, of colours
in galleries,

in the frame and the wash,
in the very brush,
not just in the neat snarl
of the midnight car

as it waits
outside the gates

tyranny permeates
all manners and all states,
its omnipresent eyes more steady
than those of old Nobodaddy,

there's tyranny
in the nursery
in father's advice, in his guile,
in your mother's smile

in the child's answer
to the perfect stranger;

not just in wires with barbs and hooks
not just in rows of books,
but, worse than a barbed-wire fence
the slogans devoid of sense

whose tyranny supplies
the long goodbyes;
the words of parting,
the will-you-be-home-soon, darling?

in the street manners, the meetings
and half-hearted greetings,
the handshakes and the alarm
of the weak hand in your palm,

he's there when your loved one's face
turns suddenly to ice
he accompanies you
to tryst or rendezvous

not just to the grilling
but to the cooing and the billing,
in your words of love he'll appear
like a dead fly in your beer

because even in dreams you're not free
of his eternal company,
in the nuptial bed, in your lust
he covers you like dust

because nothing may be caressed
but that which he first blessed,
it is him you cuddle up to
and raise your loving cup to

in your plate, in your glass he flows
in your mouth and through your nose
in frost, fog, out or in
he creeps under your skin

like an open vent through which
you breathe the foul air of the ditch
and he lingers like drains
or a gas leak at the mains

it's tyranny that dogs
your inner monologues,
nothing is your own
once your dreams are known

all is changed or lost,
each star a border post
light-strafed and mined; the stars
are spies at window bars,

the vast tent's every lamp
lights a labour camp,
come fever, come the bell
it's tyranny sounds the knell,

confessor is confession,
he preaches, reads the lesson
he's Church, House and Theatre
the Inquisition;

you blink your eyes, you stare
you see him everywhere;
like sickness or memory
he keeps you company;

trains rattling down the rail
the clatter of the jail;
in the mountains, by the coast
you are his breathing host;

lightning: the sudden noise
of thunder, it's his voice
in the bright electric dart,
the skipping of the heart

in moments of calm,
in chains of tedium,
in rain that falls an age,
the star-high prison-cage

in snow that rises and waits
like a cell, and isolates;
your own dog's faithful eyes
wear his look for disguise,

his is the truth, the way
so each succeeding day
is his, each move you make
you do it for his sake;

like water, you both follow
the course set and the hollow
ring is closed; that phiz
you see in the mirror is his

escape is doomed to failure,
you're both prisoner and gaoler;
he has soaked, corroded in,
he's deep beneath your skin

in your kidney, in your fag,
he's in your every rag,
you think: his agile patter
rules both mind and matter

you look, but what you see
is his, illusory,
one match is all it takes
and fire consumes the brake

you having failed to snuff
the head as it broke off;
his "vigilance" extends
to factories, fields and friends

and you no longer know or feel
what it is to live, eat meat or bread
to desire or love or spread
your arms wide in appeal;

it is the chain slaves wear
that they themselves prepare;
you eat but it's tyranny
grows fat, his are your progeny

in tyranny's domain
you are the link in the chain,
you stink of him through and through,
the tyranny IS you;

like moles in sunlight we crawl
in pitch darkness, sprawl
and fidget in the closet
as if it were a desert,

because where tyranny obtains
everything is vain,
the song itself though fine
is false in every line,

for he stands over you
at your grave, and tells you who
you were, your every molecule
his to dispose and rule.

[GS]

ÁGNES NEMES NAGY

Trees

It's time to learn. The winter trees.
How head to toe they're clad in frost.
Stiff monumental tapestries.

It's time to learn that region where
the crystal turns to steam and air,
and where the trees swim through the mist
like something remembered but long lost.

The trees, and then the stream behind,
the wild duck's silent sway of wing,
the deep blue night, white and blind,
where stands the hooded tribe of things,
here one must learn the unsung deeds
of heroism of the trees.

[GS]

from *Journal*

Mind
I know I have no reasonable grounds
for thinking, but watch the thoughts as they go round.
And since contempt's appropriate to the act
mindlessly I trust to intellect.

Nightmare
From a world of rotting rags and clout
The marsh-light of cold reason flashes out,
Plays on the corpse, the softening skull beneath,
And illuminates its naked row of teeth.

Revenge

He who cannot take revenge,
Nor yet forgive, must find redress
In burning forever the low flame
Of his unquenchable bitterness.

Sic Itur ad Astra

Compared with these I am a saint
   no judge would dare try me;
if the world wags on like this
   they will deify me.

July

Light and light and sunspots, fragrant colours,
In place of my heart, de rigeur – bouquets.
Just this once, dear world, I will forgive you,
But from now on you'll have to mend your ways!

You sit and read

You sit and you read. How alone you are, even you don't know.
But sometimes you guess and then with a leisurely movement
And a hint of mild animal sadness your simple features
Dip into the light.

Before the mirror

You take your face and slowly remove the paint,
But would remove the face that fate assigned you,
You wait for the armchair to rise and with a faint
Gesture of boredom to appear behind you.

Contemplative

The old pose lost its charm. Let's take
A new one out. Yes, this will do.
In matters of dress it's all the same
What you fit your body to.

The dress, the body and the soul,
The same applies to everything.
When Thespis prinks does she at all
Suspect what change the colours bring?

Sincerity
Inspecting myself makes me bilious.
It's easier for the spontaneous.
I would if I could be the driver of the dray
Who washes great blonde horses all the day
And has nothing to say.

[GS]

LÁSZLÓ NAGY

Squared by Walls

Couldn't you have died,
or at least bled,
instead of pacing the floor
stunned with despair?
You kept clear of the trouble –
bullets, armoured tracks, emblazoned
girls' screams. Not for you broken
wheels, scattering rooftiles,
grim gangs of working lads,
and soot-brindled petals.
You did not spill one drop
of blood, and when it stopped,
you had only gone grey and mad.

In usual winter weather
you stand here; no other
but yourself, and wide awake,
squared by walls that echo
a cough like raking
gunfire. It's not merely
your flesh that's cold;
mind and heart are frozen – crowned
by knives of ice.
You are ashamed of your melting phrases;
as if it were a sin
to think of spring
or lilacs – the lung-like trees blossoming.
What agony for a Lord of Life!
Yet, deep in the secret places
of your being, furtive with guilt,
you are breathing on the frosted pane,
that you may look out at the world again.

[TC/GG]

FERENC JUHÁSZ

The Boy Changed into a Stag Cries out at the Gate of Secrets

The mother called after her son
from the far distance
The mother called after her son
from the far distance,
she went out in front of the house, calling
and she loosened her hair's thick knot
which the dusk wove to a dense, stirring veil,
a valuable robe sweeping the earth,
wove to a stiff and heavily flaring mantle,
a banner for the wind with ten black tassels,
a shroud, the fire-slashed blood-heavy twilight.
She twisted her fingers among the fine tendrils
of the stars, the moon's suds bleached her features,
and she called after her son shrilly
as she called him long ago, a small child,
she went out from the house talking to the wind,
and spoke to the songbirds, her words overtaking
the wild geese going in couples,
to the shivering bulrushes,
to the potato flower in its pallor,
to the clench-balled bulls rooted so deeply,
to the fragrant shadowy mulch,
she spoke to the fish where they leaped playfully,
to the momentary oil-rings, mauve and fleeting.
   You birds and branches, hear me,
listen as I cry,
   listen, you fishes and you flowers,
listen, I cry to be heard,
   listen, you glands of the pumping soils,
   you vibrant fins, you astral-seeding parachutes,
decelerate, you humming motors of the saps,
screw down the whining taps in the depth of the atom,

all iron-pelvised virgins,
sheep alive under cotton,
listen as I cry,
I am crying out to my son.

The mother called out to her son
and her cry climbed in a spiral
within the gyre of the cosmos it ascended,
her limbs glancing in the light-rays
like the skid-scaled flanks of a fish,
or a roadside boil of salt or crystal.
The mother called out to her son,
Come back, my own son, come back,
I am calling, your calm harbour,
Come back, my own son, come back,
I am calling, your pure fountain,
Come back, my own son, come back,
I am calling, the breast where your memory sucked,
Come back, my own son, come back,
I am calling, your almost sightless lamp.
Come back, my own son, for this world of spiky objects has put out my eyes,
my eyes are sealed under yellow-green bruises, my jaw contracts,
my thighs and my shins are skinned,
from every side things batter in on me like crazed rams,
the gate, the post, the chair try their horns on me,
doors slam against me like drunken brawlers,
the vicious electricity snaps at me,
my scaling skin leaks blood a bird's beak crushed with a rock,
scissors slither off like spider-crabs of nickel,
the matches are sparrowfeet, the pail hacks back at me with its handle.

Come back, my own son, come back,
my legs no longer lift me like the young hind
festering blooms open on my feet,
gnarled tubers screw into my purpling thighs,
the skin over my toes glaze to bone,
my fingers harden, already the flaking flesh
shells off like slate from weathered geologic formations,
every limb has served its time and sickens.

Come back, my own son, come back
  for I am no longer as I was,
  I am a used-up shadow from the inner visions
  that flare through the thickening organs
  like an old cock's crowing, on winter dawns,
from a fence of shirts hanging board-frozen.
I am calling, your own mother,
come back, my own son, come back,
force new order on to the anarchic things,
discipline the savage objects, tame the knife and domesticate the
  comb,
because now I am only two gritty green eyes
glassy and weightless, like the dragonfly,
whose winged nape and mouth, that you know so well, so delicately
  clasp
two crystal apples in the green-illumined skull,
I am two staring eyes without a face,
seeing all, and one with the unearthly beings.
Come back, my own son, come back into place,
  with your fresh breath bring everything again into place.

  In the remote forest the boy heard.
  He jerked up his head in an instant,
  his spread nostrils testing the air,
  his soft dewlap throbbing, the veined ears pointing
  tautly to that lamenting music
  as to the still tread of the hunter,
  as to hot wisps fronding from the cradle
  of a forest fire, when the skyline trees
  smoke and begin to whimper bluely.
  He turned his head to the old voice,
  and now an agony fastens on him,
  and he sees the shag hair over his buttocks,
  and he sees, on his bony legs,
  the cleft hooves that deal his track,
  sees, where lilies look up in pools,
  low-slung hair-pursed buck-balls.
  He forces his way towards the lake,
  crashing the brittle willow thickets,
  haunches plastered with foam that spatters
  on the earth at his every bound,

his four black hooves rip him a path
through a slaughter of wild flowers,
sock a lizard into the mud,
throat ballooned and tail sheared,
till he reaches the lake at last,
and looks in at its lit window
that holds the moon, moving beech boughs
and a stag staring at him.
For the first time he sees the bristling pelt
covering all his lean body,
hair over knees and thighs, the transverse
tasselled lips of his male purse,
his long skull treed with antlers,
bone boughs bursting to bone leaves,
his face closely furred to the chin,
his nostrils slit and slanted in.
The great antlers knock against trees,
roped veins lump on his neck,
he strains fiercely, stamping he tries
to put out an answering cry, but in vain,
it is only a stag's voice belling
in the throat of this mother's son,
and he scatters a son's tears, trampling the shallows
to drive out that lake-horror, scare it
down into the whirpool gullet
of the water-dark, where glittering
little fishes flicker their laces,
miniature bubble-eyed jewellery.
The ripples smooth off into the gloom,
but still a stag stands in the foam of the moon.

Now in his turn the boy cries back,
  stretching up his bellowing neck,
Now in his turn the boy cries back
  crying through fog from a stag's throat,
    Mother, my mother,
    I cannot come back
    mother, my mother,
    you must not lure me,
    mother, my mother,
    my maker, my nurse,

mother, my mother,
fresh foaming fountain,
safe arms that held me,
big breasts that fed me,
my tent in the frost,
mother, my mother,
my frail silky stem,
mother, my mother,
my gold-mouthed bird
mother, my mother,
you must not lure me.
If I should return
my horns would split you,
from point on to point
tossing your body,
if I should return
you would fall under me,
your loose veiny breasts
shredded by hooves,
I'd stab with bare tines,
I'd rip with my teeth,
and stamp in your womb, even,
if I should return
I'd hook your lungs from you,
blue flies would be clouding,
stars would gaze
on your spilled flower-vitals,
which once housed me,
they were summer suns over me,
a glistening peace
their warm clasp unbroken
as once the warm cattle
breathed gently to Jesus.
Mother, my mother,
do not summon me,
your death would be home
as my shape entered,
as this son approached you.
Every prong of my antlers
is a golden thread,
every branch of my antlers

a winged candelabra,
each spine of my antlers
a catafalque candle,
each leaf of my antlers
a gold-laced altar.
It would be your death
to see my grey antlers
lifting in the sky
like an All Souls
candlelit cemetery,
my head a stone tree
and the leaves flames lengthening.
Mother, my mother,
if I came near you,
I would burn you like tinder grass,
scorch you to charred clay,
you'd explode like resin,
and I would roast you
to black rags of flesh.
Mother, my mother,
do not summon me,
I would devour you
at my coming,
your bed would be havoc,
your flower garden
ploughed by the thousand
blades of my antlers.
I'd chew through the trees
in the stag-torn coppice,
empty the one well
with one swallowing,
at my coming
your cottage would be blazing,
then I would run
to the ancient graveyard,
with my narrow soft nose
with my four hooves
I'd dig up my father,
my teeth would be wrenching
the cracked coffin lid
to scatter the bones.

Mother, O mother,
do not lure me,
I cannot come back,
if I come back
I bring your death.

In a stag's voice the boy cried,
And in these words his mother answered:
Come back, my son, come back.
I call you, your own mother,
come back, my own son, come back,
I'll cook brown broth and into it you'll slice onion rings.
They'll crunch in your bite like quartz splintering in the champ of a giant,
I'll bring you warm milk in a jug
and trickle wine from my last keg into bottles necked like the heron,
and I know how to knead bread under my stony knuckles, I know how you like it,
bread to bake to soft-bellied buns, the sweet bread for feasts,
come back, my own son, come back.
From the live breasts of screeching geese I have pulled the down for your eiderdown,
weeping I plucked my weeping geese, and the bald patches
whitened angrily on their breasts, like the mouths of the dying,
I have shaken out your mattress in the sun, freshened it for your sleeping
the yard is swept for your coming, the table is laid.

Mother, my mother,
for me there'll be no homecoming,
do not lay the plaited white bread out for me,
or the goat's sweet milk foaming in my flowered mug,
do not prepare my soft bed for me,
or ravage the breasts of the geese for their feathers,
pour away your wine, let it soak into my father's grave,
braid the lovely onions in a garland,
fry up for the little ones the big-bellied frothy-topped dough.

The milk would be vinegar at a touch of my tongue
and the white bread would be struck to a stone turtle
your wine spilling like warm blood into my tumbler

the eiderdown dissolving in a silence of blue flame
and the brittle-beaked mug splintered to swordgrass.

O mother, O mother, my own good mother,
my step will never ring out in my father's house,
I have to live in the thick of the forest,
your shadowed house has no room for my meshed antlers.
Your yard has no room for my cemetery antlers
because my reaching-out horns are a loud world tree,
their foliage arches to constellations, their green moss is the Milky
Way.

Into my mouth comes only sweet-breathed herbs,
only the first-growth grasses that melt my saliva
and I can never drink again from the flowered mug you bring me,
only from a clear brook, only from a clear brook.

I do not understand, I do not understand your strange and
tormented words, my son,
you speak like a stag, a stag's spirit has possessed you my
unhappy one.
When the turtledove cries, when the turtledove cries, when
the little bird sings, when the little bird sings, my son,
why in the whole Universe am I the last soul left, the
solitary one?
Do you remember, do you remember, your small once-young
mother, my son?
I do not understand, I do not understand your sad and
tortured words, O my long-lost son.
Do you remember how you came running; running home to me, so
happy with your school report,
you dissected a bullfrog, splayed his freckled paddle feet
on the fence,
how you pored over books about aircraft and followed me in to
help with the washing,
you loved Irene B, your friends were VJ and HS, the wild and
orchid-bearded painter,
and do you remember the Saturday nights, when your father
came back sober how happy you were?

O mother, my mother, do not speak of my sweetheart of those
days, or of my friends,
they flit by like fish in the cold depths, that painter with
his chin of vermilion
who knows down what road he has gone shouting, who knows,
mother, where my boyhood has gone?
Mother, my mother, do not remember my father, for sorrow has
bloomed from his flesh,
sorrow flowers out of the dark earth, do not remember my
father, my father,
he'll heave from the earth, gathering about him his
yellowing bones,
and stagger from the grave with his nails and his hair new
grown.
Oh, Oh, Uncle Wilhelm came, the coffin maker with his puppet
mask, he told us to hold your feet and drop you
neatly into the coffin,
and I retched because I was frightened. I had come that day
from Pest,
you too, my father, went back and forth to Pest, an office
messenger, till the rails writhed up,
such rending knives in my belly then, your tight cheeks
gashed by the candle's shadows.
Your new son-in-law, Lacy the barber, shaved you with care,
while the candle dribbled like a silent baby,
regurgitating its glistening entrails, its long luminous
nerves like vines,
the choral society surrounded you under their purple hats,
mourning you at the tops of their voices,
with one fingertip I traced the rim of your forehead,
your hair was so alive,
I heard it growing, I saw the bristles thicken and your chin
blackened by morning, and the next day your throat sunken in
under spines of new hair like the snake-grass,
curved like a soft-haired cantaloupe, cabbage skin blue under
the yellow hair of the caterpillar,
Oh and I thought your hair, your beard, would bush the whole
room full, and would overgrow the yard
and the entire world, that the stars would nestle like cells
in the living strands.
Ah the ponderous green rain began to fall then, and the team

of red horses on the hearse whinnied in terror,
one lashing out over your head with a thunderbolt hoof, the
other relentlessly pissing,
so that his purple parts passed out with it like a hanged
man's tongue, while the coachman cursed.
The downpour sluiced around the huddled brassbandsmen, and
then all those old friends blew with a will
blew as they wept, by the chapel wall studded with
globethistles,
the old friends blew till their lips swelled purple and the
music spiralled out and up,
the old friends blew till their lips cracked, till their lips
bled, their eyeballs staring,
blew for the cards and the booze, and the trumped women, the
bloated and the withered,
blew for the beer-money of their red-letter days, the tips
tossed whirling into space after you,
blew as they sobbed, blew sadly down into sedimentary layers
of silted sadness,
music poured from the burnished mouths, from rings of brass
into putrefying nothingness,
out of it streamed the petrified sweethearts, rotten women
and mouldered grandfathers, out of the music,
with little cottages, cradles and a whole generation of
silver-bellied watches thick with enamel, rolling like
onions,
Easter bells and multitudinous Saviours flew out on the wide
spread wings of the sound,
with railway wheels and infantrymen brass-buttoned at the
salute, and satchels,
the old friends played on, teeth crimsoning under lips that
peeled back swelling like blackened liver,
and yourself conducting the choir: well done boys, that's
grand, don't stop now, keep it up,
all the time your hands folded hard, and those gold spiders
with their huge wheel-spoke-jointed legs sitting on
your heart,
and in the cupboard your collapsed boots wait for their
relatives, the white socks on your curling bread–
crust feet,
the old friends blew for you that day out under the crashing

rain, valves snapping like Adam's apples of steel,
fangs of antediluvian birds, teeth of the Carcharodon,
cruising for carrion out of the brazen mouths of
the trumpets,
O mother, my mother, do not recall my father,
let my father lie, lest his eyes erupt from suddenly opening
earth.

The mother called after her son
from the far distance,
come back, my own son, come back,
turn from that stone world,
you stag of the stone forest, the chemical air, the
electric grids,
industrial lightning, riveted bridges, streetcars, lap
at your blood,
hourly they attack you a hundred times afresh, yet you
never hit back,
I am calling, your own mother,
come back, my own son, come back.

He stood on the perpetually renewing crags of time,
he stood over the Universe, on the ringed summit,
there the boy stood at the gate of secrets,
his stag's antlers were toying with the stars,
and his stag's voice down the lost paths of the world
answered to his mother his maker.

Mother, my mother, I cannot come back,
new gold boils in my hundred wounds,
every day a hundred bullets blast me off my feet,
every day I get up a hundred times more whole
every day I die three billion times,
every day I am born three billion times,
every branch of my antlers is a double-based pylon,
every tine of my antlers is a high-tension cable,
my eyes are ports for sea-going tankers, my veins are
tarry hawsers, my teeth
are iron bridges, in my heart surge the monster-infested
seas,
each vertebra is a seething capital, and a barge belching

black smoke is my spleen,
my every cell is a factory, my every atom a solar system,
and sun and moon swing in my testicles,
and the Milky Way is in my bone marrow,
space's every point is a part of my body,
and my brain's rhythms come in from far out in the
circling galaxies.

O my lost son, no matter for that,
your mother's eyes are sleepless, they watch for
you still.

Only to die shall I come back, only to die shall I come back,
yes, I shall come back to die
and when I have come, but only to die, O my mother,
then you can stretch me out in my father's house,
then with your marble hands you can wash my body,
then you can close my glandulous eyelids with a kiss,
and then when my flesh falls to pieces
and lies in its stench, yet deep among flowers,
then I shall feed on your blood and be fruit of your body
then I shall be your own small son once more,
and this shall give pain to you alone, O mother,
to you alone, O my mother.

[TH]

COMECON ISLANDS I

THE ISLE OF MEMORY

GÉZA OTTLIK

from *Buda*

EVERY ROAD

You have returned to Buda, then, where you were born. This was a miracle. The city was there: you had borne the unbearable, interminable years that had after all come to an end. What happened was that the four, no, the forty – no: the four hundred years came to an end, ran out. The prophet Nehemiah rained curses on his people's heads, for they had forgotten the miracles the Lord had accomplished for them.

Well, I, Benedek Both, have not forgotten them. It happened in 1926, and it was a miracle, almost beyond belief. Like three or four decades later, when, after a fresh span of years without hope, you could suddenly travel abroad again and Europe was there, and you found your way back into your childhood one morning at the railway station in Lille. That was a miracle too, and beyond belief.

"I've had so many miracles happen to me in my lifetime, three, four – no, more, five – that I should not be allowed to write a novel," I said to Márta one evening, on July 21, 1979.

After a few moments of thoughtful silence – she was perhaps counting – she nodded.

"True."

Life is not like this. I would be misleading the readers. "Well then don't write a novel, BB," said Márta. "Leave writing to your friend. Or perhaps to Lexi. Or there's Gábor Medve's manuscript. You just go on painting, BB."

"Is it all right to paint miracles?"

"Yes. Painting them is all right."

We laughed. It was Saturday. Painting is not truth. It is cheating, a bit of hocus-pocus, like poetry. (Of course it's just a bit of hocus-pocus, said Medve, but it's sacred.) Reality is what is, and untruth is what is not, that is what I say. Never mind, it was a splendid summer evening, a Saturday. The colours of the city were mellow and ripe like once – not so long ago – in my dream, on the Oktogon. Márta knew that I never forgot my miracles – I am a cowardly, God-fearing man. To sum up, I said to myself:

I have always failed in everything. I thought that at thirty, forty, fifty I would have a proper studio, a large one. I did not. That at forty, I would have an exhibition of my work. I did not. That at fifty, Márta and I would have our own house, with an overgrown garden surrounded by a stone wall with a couple of devoted old servants – on the coast, in the bay of, say, Beaulieu and Cap Ferrat. We did not. Forty years ago, Márta and I thought we would soon be divorced, that we would find wonderful new loves, real ones, for our own love, though it had been real, had faded and come to an end and was not of the kind that could be replaced by sibling affection.

So we thought. We were mistaken. It could and was. We did not get divorced. In this, too, I failed.

True, I thought, but to this I must add:

I've always succeeded in everything. Everything that I most desired subconsciously, desired so much that I did not dare hope for it, even in secret. I made the great school team: Hilbert-Both-Rodriguez-Medve. I became a free man in 1930. When there was no-one left who wanted what I was painting, the "New Eights", the greatest and most exacting, received me in their midst. For forty hard, hard years I succeeded in keeping Márta. And in the end the world, too, recognised me as a painter, and the miracle in this was that there was no price to pay for this recognition, which again does not happen often, is a fortunate accident of fate. I would never have dared to dream of setting myself these aims. And they did not become, as it often happens with our fulfilled desires, caricatures, travesties, the mockery of fate.

"I've always failed in everything," I said to Márta, grinning, because Márta knew that it was true, and that it is just as true that I've always succeeded in everything. She was the only one who knew, no-one else could understand even if I explained, but there was no need for anyone else to know. Márta had to know, though. She knew, and laughed. I told her about my dream – which I have never done until now.

Not so long ago I dreamed I was walking along the boulevard, crossing the Oktogon, it was late afternoon, balmy and mild, and I noticed that the city was beautiful, full of colour. I noticed this despite the sadness in me, knowing that I must die tomorrow, and there was nothing we could do about it. Sad, but what can one do? The houses, the trees, the pedestrians, Andrássy út: the late afternoon had never been so mellow. It was mild. Ripe. It did not hurt. Strange. It should have hurt, but it did not. The air, the Oktogon, everything was balmy, soft. Mild? Mellow? No, there is no other word for it – it was ripe.

"Like that time in 1926?" asked Márta. No. Not at all. On the contrary, almost. I shook my head.

"Well then, why don't you paint your dream, BB?"

Yes, it's true. I could perhaps paint that, paint the dream, but the other, that bygone summer when we broke free of humanity and Buda, Júlia, my mother and even the Szeredys were there, we had survived the insufferable – that summer I could never paint. So many things that cannot be omitted must be included, so dreadfully many, says Medve, that the scant sixty or eighty years of a human life are insufficient even for a perfunctory survey.

WHAT IS UNQUESTIONABLY THERE

So you got started on it after all, BB. You're sorry you did, aren't you? began the dining-room window of No. 15b Fehérvári út. The bare walls opposite, blind archways shedding plaster in a new, unaccustomed light as the early morning sunlight falls upon them, you had just begun school, it was miserable, getting out of bed, washing, getting dressed, Júlia, your mother, you try to paint it and get nowhere. It is too much for you.

Márta doesn't think so. She thinks I can start anywhere, in 1926, or on the Oktogon of more recent times, all roads lead to Buda. The feeling that contains Buda and my whole life so far is one thing, a single thing: something like the concept of plain cobalt blue or lead grey, or a single C sharp sounded on one of the strings of a cello. If you cannot make a great painting or a symphony out of these, your dream obligingly dissolves it into a spectacle, reduces it to its components, to empirical facts, motifs that can be painted in sections. Sadness and desire, one must die, time running out, not enough left for the beauties of the city because of the countless things that make it up and cannot be left out, and – as was deftly pointed out by the dream – it is not Buda, not even sections of Pest that would be beautiful for you, where you would feel more at home (like Kecskeméti utca, for example), though they are of course familiar, but unfamiliar too, memory and desire, a map, openness, expectancy and patience, the ripeness of the late afternoon hour.

Could all of this go into it? Into that single feeling of what it was like crossing the Oktogon? All of it fits in there, and many other things besides, so many that you could shovel in the words uncounted. It is not worth it though. They do not exist. What is unquestionably there, Medve says, is the feeling. Nothing else exists with the same certainty. The existence of the world, of other people is hypothetical, conjecture, a presumption that you can render probable after a sufficient amount of experimenting. You accept them as existing because you have no other choice, but you'd better not forget that the only thing that is not hypothetical, that is unquestionably there, is the feeling.

THE LACK OF PRECISION

I received a blow-up of a photograph of the cadet school in Pécs where we stopped for a couple of days in June 1926 after our boat trip to Mohács. A friend of mine enlarged one of Medve's so-so snapshots for me as a favour. Well, this enlargement, when I took a good look at it, gave me a perfectly precise idea of that imprecise feeling of what that summer was like.

The feeling is imprecise. Writes Medve. Words are useless in any case – the first duty of times to come will be to abolish language, every national language. But the feeling is imprecise even before we try to find words to fit it. It is imprecise from the outset, in itself. Let us begin the story at the beginning, at the beginnings of the beginning, with existence before birth. "Something exists." – A thought? Yourself? No, not yet. Let us begin with "Exists". – If it exists, then it is something. – From this something we need that which is unquestionably there: the feeling. The more certain its existence, the more imprecise it is. The more we try to define it, the less certainly we can say that it exists.

The north-north-east view from the dining-room window of Flat 19 on the second floor of No. 15b Fehérvári út, illuminated by the rising sun, exists. If I add the countless things that add up to it and cannot be left out, I will smudge its certain existence. Yet I shall have to paint Júlia (who would wake me with her soft tinkling on the piano, *alla turcas* played with much pedal and film music – she was staying with us at the time, like Auntie Terka), my mother (who used to cut me slices of smoked bacon at breakfast, because she knew I preferred it, and ate the more easily sliceable boiled kind out of laziness – I didn't know about my preference, believed it was all the same to me), and Petár Halász, and certainly the Billroth cambric compress.

It's true that the façade of the cadet school at Pécs leads to Buda, as we shall see, I shall take a closer look at it myself. And in fact it does "lead" there – as did the intersection in London where I lost my bearings at the age of fifty-one. I did not lose my way, the map was there in my head, just like when I was five (in Mátyás tér), as one always draws it, it was just that there, on the corner of Tottenham Court Road, as in Mátyás tér, I had, for a moment, lost my sense of orientation. Does this great street lead north to south or south to north? Which is the way home? Should we turn right or left? You'll soon find out, BB. An exquisite, feverish feeling of excitement, expectancy, the same imprecise feeling (I don't know, happiness?) overcomes one at fifty-one, just as it does at the age of five. (Well, if this gives me a feeling of happy expectancy, then this is Buda again. Buda is still there. It was still there in London.)

NEW SEPTEMBER

Buda, the place to which we have so miraculously found our way back, is that part of the Hungarian capital that lies on the right bank of the river Danube. It is an ancient settlement, large enough to rate as a town as early as the Bronze Age. It survived a succession of residents, Celts, Romans, Huns, Goths, Lombards, Avars – it shall probably survive us Hungarians as well – and stayed forever young because it was always being destroyed and rebuilt again. The 1st district: the Castle, Krisztinaváros, Tabán. The 2nd district: Víziváros, Highroad. The military academy of Hűvösvölgy stood in the area known as the Törökvész dűlő, in the fields beside the Ördögárok that ran between the hills of the 2nd district. You had to change at the Retek utca loop to a No. 83. "Cadet school!" the conductor would cry, calling it by the old name still in use. Here the city tram clattered along on sleepers on the embankment, smothering the distant sound of the bugle as it passed. We assembled at the foot of a statue in the centre of the garden. It was the beginning of September. That year, after the ratification of the treaty of Locarno and before the general strike in England, R. A. Locke in Nebraska ran the 200 in 20.5, which was three-tenths better than Paddock's world record. Everyone was trying out Szeredy's new guitar.

A senior shepherded us over to the belfry beside the wide flight of stairs leading to the main building. Here too we stayed apart, keeping a distance from the unfamiliar faces of those who came from the other junior cadet school and were to be our classmates. We eyed them. With caution. Trying to pick out the ringleaders. Of us all, Medve was the most vehement in insisting: "Let's not go over!" So when he caught sight of Kornél Hilbert and rushed over without a word, I found myself shouting after him in vain. I was so angry that I just turned round and dashed off in the opposite direction. I thought I heard someone shout after me:

"About turn!"

I turned.

"BB, you fathead. Didn't you hear me say you weren't to trample all over the bloody track?"

It was a senior who had shouted at me but was already turning back to his friends. I circled back from the edge of the track. They were fussy about it because it was they who had laid it three years earlier. The cinder track was in quite good condition at present. Perhaps I should also explain that this senior was a tall boy with an agreeable habit of blinking at you, that is, he would keep closing his eyes and slowly opening them again while he spoke, and the "fathead", stated in a calm, almost conversational tone of voice, his recognising me so matter-of-factly and remembering my impossible name after three years, all made for a more than cordial welcome. It was a cosy, fraternal kick in the pants. And was directed not only at me but at all of us rookies.

For here we fourth years had gone back to being new boys again. And there were four more years, four years, who knows how long, four years of relentless service. This blinking senior and the loafing round the track without restriction after being told to dismiss, the whole "garden party" atmosphere that replaced the expected roll-call – it all seemed too good to be true. Somehow suspect, like the behaviour, the very being of Tibor Takátsy, the black-haired senior in June before the trip to Mohács. We had been given the morning off, and before briefing he had made me put on his spare pair of white gloves because the favourite pastime of the duty officer (a captain who had been wounded in the head several times) was to tear up the pass of anyone whose gloves were not clean enough to pass muster. As I said, it seemed just too good to be true, our getting this battalion duty officer in June. How many Tibor Takátsys will we get? And how many Captain Joneszkós?

All that happened – that we had borne the unbearable four hundred years – was not sufficient explanation for why returning to Buda was a miracle, why I felt at the bottom of my heart that everything was perfect as it was during that river trip to Mohács – but the experience, the content of the ten calendar years of childhood preceding it (worth about forty thousand years of adulthood) must be added to it, and the knowledge of the years that would come after.

I knew, with sudden, profound tranquillity acquired one morning before reveille on the second-floor corridor, that some day I would be a painter, that at forty I would be painting with real oil paints on real canvas on a lake shore in the mountains with a cigar in my mouth, that some day I would be free.

Medve calls this "some day" a necessary condition. "Some day, his mother too will understand what a simple and true person he is."

"Some day, she'll see that he – he does not know exactly what as yet – but he will be doing something genuine and worthwhile with his life, something he likes and is content to do. Like sunlight falling in stripes across a carpet sometimes, for example. Or like facing one's destiny in the main square of Bilbao with night falling around you and your collar turned up against the rain. Or perhaps even like the scent of elderflowers to someone who happens to like it."

(Kornél Hilbert asked me once whether I was going to be a gunner too. "Of course not." – "What will you be then?" – "A painter." – "A painter!? What kind of painter?" – "A Spanish painter," I said. He turned to Medve. "What about you?" – "Who, me? A poet and a general, of course." (If I can't be an elder, thought Medve.)

Before our time, the senior cadet school had legendary runners. The school record for 100 was held by Elemér Veress with 11.1. Consequently, one's greatest ambition, that is, to be the hundred-metre champion, was so far beyond one's reach that it was best forgotten. Miklós Zrínyi? That was quite another matter. It may not have been a more humble or reasonable ambition than 11.1, but Medve could not afford to consider his boundless ambition as presumptuous self-conceit or idle fantasy because he used it as a working theory, a hypothesis which can be held only so far as it can be held. If it is illusion and comes to nothing, it involves a grave risk that makes it legitimate. But legitimate or not, it serves as a basis for discussion for him at least, a platform, there is no other way of doing it. Understand it who will – he wrote.)

Well, for once, I understand what he means. (Platform? Basis for discussion?)

Márta and I had a similar unspoken agreement. From the beginning. That some day we would make a simple and true something out of our lives, that would please both of us without lies. Unspoken? No.

It was not only never put into words, but was never even thought out properly. We felt, felt it with unquestionable certainty, therefore imprecisely. I could not put it in words even today, and "some day" was lost somewhere along the way. What is left is: For once, I understood what he meant. I want to be a painter. Which is grandiose self-conceit.

JUNE 21, 1926. FREE MOVIE

And then, on the boat to Mohács, in the summer night, Medve suddenly says: "My mother's arranged for me to move to the Cistercian *gimnázium* in the autumn."

Szeredy looked up. He was playing "La Cumparsita" very softly on his strange instrument. "And Warrant-Officer Schulze shall wear a cassock." "And Zsoldos will be the Prince Primate," I said. This was all just part of our usual horsing around. Though it wasn't quite the same as usual. In an even more suspicious-sounding voice, Medve said:

"There's only one supplementary exam to take, in Latin."

Szeredy stopped strumming "La Cumparsita". I stopped kidding Medve back. We were all silent. Only the ship's engine kept on huffing and puffing and wheezing. In the morning we had been given leave to go into town, were allowed a half-day at home. Szeredy went up to the Svábhegy and brought down his brother-in-law's saxo-viola. Júlia, too, had thought – or so I gathered from something she said – that perhaps this time I would be going home for good. She must have known that it couldn't be true. But the way she looked at me, with a hopeless little look full of hope, that hurt.

At one point Medve writes: "Are we to be prisoners or are we to be free? First of all, there is no question about it. We are all prisoners. You come into the world, to an unfamiliar place that has nothing to do with you. And the reel begins to turn, a free movie just for you, and you are a spectator. But a small part of the cinema is your own body, and as it is the only, special little part with which you are in contact, you call this yourself too. But this number-two 'self' is an actor in the free movie, in the strange world where everything is accidental, and independent of your state of spectator. We are actors here, prisoners, we are not free to choose. But spectators are free. They cannot be made prisoners.

"Secondly, if you can choose whether you are to be a prisoner or at liberty, then you are already free. A single alternative, a single other option in place of nothing, of naught, is unlimited liberty." (For me, having reached the departures side of the Keleti railway station – I used to go to Monostor on my leaves from school, and always tried to catch the express, it was there in thirty-five minutes – the possibility that I could, at my pleasure, enter the building either by the big central doorway, or by the doorway in the corner that was nearer, and so along the passage, gave me not only a feeling of being free but also a sense of terrific, exciting adventurousness.)

That autumn after his escape, when he came back as a Spectator-Actor amalgam into the hypothetically existing world erected upon a morass, Medve said we should go on with the free movie. (Your life is a trial-life, experimental. To the end. The world, space, time, matter, power, other people, are all concepts. Ideas to be tested in your head. With repeated experimenting you can render your concept of the arrangement of the world probable, but you cannot prove it. Not even if you continue experimenting until the Day of Judgement, and all your hypotheses prove true: because of the nature of the procedure. You are not in the same place. You unquestionably exist, the existence of the world is not such an unquestionable certainty. So carry on, BB, but don't forget that you are just a visitor here, a spectator. But to be able to do anything, build, create something here, to be able to live, you must forget this. And if you forget it, if you do not preserve your beginning, your state of impartial observer, disasters will befall you. An hour may come, a year may come, several years may come when you will not be able to think, offhand, of anything else to put in the album, except let the world perish and the peoples of the earth die out, every race, to the last man.)

SHALL WE BE PRISONERS?

Marcell let some of us go before nine, those of us who had relatives living in town. Medve rang the bell and Veronika was struck dumb when she saw him. She just stared at him, could not speak. Medve hugs her, they go inside. "I'm not really home, Veron. That'll be on the fourth. I can stay until half past twelve, today." "Oh, Lord! I'll just run down and get you some fresh rolls for your breakfast . . ." His mother, too, is happy to see him.

They go in together, "I'm glad you came, son. I've something important to tell you . . ."

They do not pay attention to each other. Medve is rummaging in his cupboard.

"Gábor . . . what are you looking for?"

"That paperback. *Serpolette* . . . that was the title."

"Gábor! I've arranged for you to go to the Cistercians in the autumn!"

But Medve had squatted down to reach the lower shelves and spoke to her without turning around: "Really? Blast. I can't find it."

No wonder he can't find it. It wasn't there at Easter, either. But he had hoped then that he had returned it to Formes. But no.

"Gábor!" The woman takes hold of her son's hand. "Didn't you hear what I said? You've been accepted at the Cistercian school!"

"Really? I'm sorry, Mummy, but I see you've been rearranging the furniture in my room – I don't suppose you came upon it by any chance, did you? It was just one of those cheap little paperbacks, a novel in the Contemporary Library series. *Serpolette*, I don't remember who wrote it." He looks up diffidently at his mother. "You chucked it out, didn't you?"

"Of course I didn't!" his mother shakes her head angrily. For he had given voice to this suspicion at Easter – it must be said, not without foundation.

"Are you listening to me? You can change schools in the autumn. I've already spoken to the inspector of schools!"

At last Medve understands. He claps his hands together and burst into uncontrollable laughter.

"There's only one supplementary exam to take, in Latin."

Medve laughs, giggles, shakes his head, his mother is crestfallen.

"Didn't you want me to take you away from that school?" – "No."

She doesn't understand. "Why, Gábor, do you want to be a soldier after all?" Of course he doesn't. (I already am one, he thinks, cursing to himself.)

"You hated it. Have you come to like the military school?" (Like hell. Well then, why not? Why?)

Why? Because one can't walk out of reality with a supplementary exam in Latin, thinks Medve. Because we've begun something and I can't start shouting "Quits!" For that's not the way to choose liberty. To choose liberty you first have to choose to be a prisoner. Why did I go back from no man's land? Who can say? No-one knows better than I what it means to be free. And to be free to choose captivity. (The hypothetical world erected upon a morass. Continuing the Free Movie. Your trial-life, experiences, render probable, but never prove, your concept concerning the existence of the physical world and other people presumed similar to yourself . . .)

His mother would have taken him home after he ran away, as soon as that first October. Then came that great gift of fortune, the minor operation in hospital, his first protracted stretch of liberty. And a great many things belong there that cannot be left out. Now they are at liberty again, but this escape must be completed. Four more years.

[EMol]

IMRE KERTÉSZ

The Union Jack

fog before us, fog behind us, and beneath us
a sunken country

—MIHÁLY BABITS

If I may perchance wish now, after all, to tell the story of the Union Jack, as I was urged to do at a friendly gathering a few days – or months – ago, then I would have to mention the piece of reading matter which first inculcated in me – let's call it a grudging admiration for the Union Jack; I would have to tell about the books I was reading at the time, about my passion for reading, what nourished it, the vagaries of chance on which it hinged, as indeed does everything else in which, with the passage of time, we discern what, whether it be the consequentiality of fate or the absurdity of fate, is in any event our fate; I would have to tell about when that passion started and whither it propelled me in the end; in short, I would have to tell almost my entire life story. And since that is impossible, in the lack not just of the requisite time but also of the requisite facts, for who indeed, being in possession of the few misleading facts one deems to know about one's life, could say of himself that he even recognises right away as his life that process, course and outcome (exit or *exitus*) which is so totally obscure to himself – and himself above all; so probably it would be best if I were to begin the story of the Union Jack with Richard Wagner. And though Richard Wagner, like a persistent leitmotif, would lead us with uncanny sureness by a direct path, to the Union Jack, I would have to broach Richard Wagner himself at the editorial office. That editorial office exists no more, just as the very building in which that one-time editorial office then (three years after the war, to be precise) was for me, for a while, still very much in existence exists no more – that one-time editorial office full of dark corridors, dusty crannies, tiny, tobacco-smoked rooms lit by bare bulbs, ringing telephones, yells, the quick-fire staccato of typewriters, full of fleeting excitements, abiding qualms, vacillating moods and, later, the fear, unvacillating and ever less vacillating, which seeped out from every cranny, as it were, to squat over everything, the one-time editorial office that had long since *not* conjured up long-bygone editorial officers, where in those days I was obliged to turn up at some execrably early hour, something like 7.00 every morning, say. With what sort of hopes, I wonder? – I mused aloud and publicly in the friendly gathering that had been urging me to tell the story of the Union Jack. The young man (he would have been about twenty) whom, through a sensory delusion to which we are all prey, I then considered was, and prized as, the most personal part of myself I see today as in a film; and one thing that very likely disposes me to this is that he himself – or I myself – also saw himself (myself) as in a film. This, moreover, is undoubtedly what renders tellable a story that otherwise, like every story, is untellable, or rather not a story at all, and which, were I to tell it in that manner anyway, would probably drive me to tell precisely the opposite of what I ought to tell. That life, that 20-year-old young man's life, was sustained solely by its *formulability*; that life lumbered along, with its every nerve-fibre, every fitful effort, solely at the level of *formulability*. That life strove with all its might *to live*, and in that respect stood in contrast, for example, to my present striving, hence also my present formulations, these incessantly miscarried formulations, colliding incessantly against the unformulable, grappling – naturally, to no avail – with the unformulable: no, the striving for formulation, then and there, was actually aimed at keeping the unformulable – namely, the essence, which is to say this life, grinding and stumbling along in the dark, lugging along the burden of darkness – in the shadows, because that young man (I) could only live this life in that way. I made contact with the world through reading, that epidermis around the layers of my existence, as though some form of protective clothing. Tempered by reading, distanced by reading, obliterated by reading, that world was my fallacious but sole liveable, indeed, now and again, almost tolerable world. In the end, the predictable moment arrived when I became a lost cause for that editorial office, and thereby a lost cause for . . . I all but said for society too, had there been a society, or rather if what there was had been a society, then I became a lost cause for what passed for society, for that horde which now whimpered like a whipped dog, now howled like a ravening hyena, always greedy for any provender that it could tear to shreds; I had long been a lost cause for myself, and I almost became a lost cause for life as well. But even at that rock bottom – at least what, at the time, I supposed to be rock bottom, until I got to know depths that were deeper still, ever deeper, depths that were bottomless – even at that rock bottom the formulability was retained, the camera setting, one might say: the camera lens of a pulp thriller, for example. Where I acquired it, what its title was, what it was about, I have no idea. I don't read thrillers any longer, ever since, in the midst of reading one thriller, I suddenly caught myself being utterly uninterested in who the murderer might be; that in this world – a murderous world – it was not only misleading and actually outrageous but also quite unnecessary for me to fret about who the murderer was: everybody was. That way of formulating it, however, did not occur to me at the time, some 40 years ago, perhaps; it was not a formulation that would have seemed of any use to my strivings at that time, some 40 years ago, perhaps, as it was merely a fact, one of those simple – albeit obviously not entirely insignificant – facts among which I lived, among which I had to live (because I wanted to live): it was much more important to me that the main protagonist, a man with an exciting job – a private eye, maybe – had the habit, before embarking on one of his deadly dangerous enterprises, of always "treating himself" to something, a glass of whisky, or occasionally a woman, but sometimes he would make do with an aimless, headlong spin along the highway in his car. That detective novel taught me that a person needs pleasure in those rare intervals in one's torture sessions: until then I would not have dared to formulate that, or if so, then at best as a sin. In those times, deadly dangers were already menacing in the editorial office, deadly boring dangers, to be quite precise, but no less deadly for all that, ever fresher ones every day, albeit the same ones every day. In those times, after a short and utterly inexplicable temporary hiatus, food coupons were again in use, most notably for meat, though quite unnecessarily as it happened – most especially for meat – since there were insufficient meat stocks to justify the reciprocatory gravity of issuing coupons for meat. Around that time, next door to the editorial office, they opened, or re-opened, the so-called Corvin Restaurant, which is to say the so-called Corvin Restaurant in the so-called Corvin Department Store, where (the store being under foreign ownership or, to be more punctilious, in the hands of the occupying power) they even served meat, and without meat coupons at that, although the meat was on offer at double price (in other words, they asked double the price that would have been asked for elsewhere, had meat been on offer anywhere else); and around that time, if the prospect of a fresher, deadly boring deadly danger lay in wait for me at the editorial office, usually in the form of one of those otherwise so splendidly styled "staff conferences", on such occasions I would "treat myself" beforehand to a breaded cutlet in this restaurant (very often out of an advance on my salary for the following month, since the institution of the advance, obviously as the result of some oversight, still remained operative for a while, everything else having long ceased to be operative); and however many and whatever sort of deadly boring dangers to life I might have to confront, the awareness that I had "treated myself" beforehand, the awareness of my foresightedness, my secret, even my *freedom*, that inhered in the couponless breaded cutlet and in the advance on my salary that I had procured to pay for it, about which nobody besides myself could have known, except perhaps the waiter (but then he knew only about the breaded cutlet), and perhaps also the cashier (but then he knew only about the advance) – that helped me through every horror, every ignominy, and every infamy visited on me that day. For around that time the everydays, the everydays that stretched from dawn to dusk, were transformed into systematic ignominies that stretched from dawn to dusk, but how they were transformed into that, the formulation – or series of formulations – of that otherwise most certainly noteworthy process no longer figures among the formulations I recall now and so, most likely, did not figure among my formulations at the time either. The reason for that, obviously, may be that my formulations, as I have already noted, served solely for the rehearsal of my life, for the bare sustenance of my life that stretched from dawn till dusk, while they looked on life itself as a given, like the air which I am obliged to breathe, the water in which I am obliged to swim. Quality of life as an object of formulation was simply left outside the scope of my formulations, as those formulations did not serve to gain an understanding of life but, on the contrary, as I have said, to make life liveable, or in other words, to avoid any formulation of life. Around that time, for example, certain trials were grinding ahead in the country, and to the questions of the friendly gathering that had been urging me to tell the story of the Union Jack, the pressing, badgering questions of this gathering, mustered mainly from among my former students, and so from people mostly 20 to 30 years younger than I, though by that token no longer quite so young themselves, heedless to the fact that with their very questions they were interrupting and distracting me from telling the story of the Union Jack – so, to those questions as to whether I had, as it were, "believed" in the accounts of the indictments laid out at these trials, whether I had "believed" in the guilt of the accused and so on, I replied that those questions, and most particularly the question of the credibility or incredibility of the trials, did not even cross my mind at the time. In the world that surrounded me then – the world of lies, terror and murder, as I might well classify that world *sub specie æternitas*, though that does not even begin to touch on the *reality*, the *singularity*, of that world – in that world, then, it never so much as crossed my mind that every single one of those trials might *not* be lies, that the judges, prosecutors, defending counsels, witnesses, indeed the accused themselves, would not all be lying, and that the sole truth that was functioning there, and tirelessly at that, was not the hangman's, and that any other truth would or *could* function here except the truth of arrest, imprisonment, execution, the shot in the head and the noose. Only now did I formulate it all so trenchantly, in such decidedly categorical terms – as if then (or even now, for that matter) there had existed (or exists) any solid basis for any sort of categorisation – now that they were urging me to tell the story of the Union Jack, and so I was obliged to tell it all from the viewpoint of a story, to attribute significance to something which has only subsequently acquired significance in the public mind – that bogus awareness raised to the status of generality – but which in the reality of those days, at least as far as I am concerned, had only very slight, or an entirely different, significance. For that reason I cannot assert, for example, that I would have felt morally outraged, say, in connection with the trials that were grinding ahead around that time: I don't recall that I felt that, and I don't even consider it very likely, if only because I did not have a sense of any morality whatsoever – either within me or around me – in the name of which I might have been outraged. But all this, as I say, is to massively overrate and overexplain what those trials meant for me – for a self whom I now see only from a great distance, as on some faded, shaky and brittle film – because in reality they barely grazed my consciousness; they signified, let us say, a gelling of the constant danger, and with that, of course, of my constant disgust, a heightening of a danger that might not yet have been threatening me directly, perhaps, or to express myself poetically, a further darkening of the horizon, in spite of which, however, it was still possible to read, if there happened to be something to read (*Arch of Triumph*, for example). What affected me was not so much the morality of the trials that were grinding ahead then, but rather the influences that ground along at the level of sensibility; hence, the reflexes evoked from me were not moral, but rather those acting at the level of sensory organs and neurological paths – mood reflexes, one might call them, like the aforementioned disgust, then alarm, indignation, fleeting scepticism, general disconcertment and the rest. I recall it being summer at the time, for instance, and that summer had announced itself from the very onset with an almost unbearable heat. I recall that during that unbearably hot summer it had occurred to somebody in the editorial office that the "young colleagues", as it was phrased, ought to partake of some higher, theoretical indoctrination, as it was phrased. I recall that on one especially hot evening of that very hot summer, a bigwig in the editorial office – a party first-something, a party bigwig, a bigwig held in general terror, a bigger and more senior bigwig than the senior editor-in-chief himself, though, as far as his authority went, one who was held in a fair degree of hiddenness, if I may be allowed the Heideggerian paraphrase – imparted to us "young colleagues", as it was phrased, this theoretical indoctrination, as it was phrased. I even recall the room in which the lecture was held, the now no longer existing room, the vanished site of which is itself now built over, the so-called "typing pool", by which is to be understood the typewriters, the female typists who operated those typewriters with a furious clatter, the writing desks and ordinary tables, chairs, commotion, countless telephones, countless colleagues, countless sources of sound, all of which, that evening, had already been silenced, removed, tidied away, and transformed into a pious audience, duly seated on the chairs, and the lecturer who was indoctrinating them. I recall that the double-panelled balcony door was wide open, and how much I envied the lecturer for the frequency – by the end, virtually every minute – with which, as if by way of punctuation marks to the lecture, he was able to step outside to cool off on the vast balcony, not stopping until he reached the balustrade, where, leaning out over the parapet, he would look down each time into the steaming chasm of the Grand Boulevard, and each time, in the stifling room, I too thought longingly of the dust-choked, leafy boughs of the roadside trees, perhaps just stirring in the twilight air, the passers-by sauntering beneath them, the dilapidated terrace of the Simplon (later Simpla) Cafe opposite, the clandestine streetgirls clacking by afresh, far from clandestinely, on their high-heeled shoes towards their beats in Népszínház or Bérkocsis Street. It was all the more conspicuous, though only later did I attribute any significance to it, that at the end of the lecture this bigwig, face burnt red as a lobster, sweat pouring from his brow and literally trembling – from the effort, I supposed at the time (if I supposed anyting at all at the time) – was in no great hurry to get down to the street; quite the contrary, he was hardly able to tear himself away from us, addressing several of us individually, until at long last we were rid of him, and I too was able to step out onto the balcony and, with a sigh of relief, look down at the street where, at that very moment, the bigwig stepped out of the building and, at that very moment, out of a black car that was idling by the pavement jumped two ominously helpful men to assist the bigwig most assiduously, but perhaps a touch insistently, into the black car, while in that unexpected hush which sometimes falls for a brief moment, like a climax or an orchestral pause, to interrupt the din of the city in the settling twilight at the end of each unbearable day, the nightmarish lights of the street lamps suddenly lit up. It will come as no surprise to you, mature, cultured people that you are, I said to the friendly gathering, mustered mainly from my former students, which had been continually urging me to tell the story of the Union Jack, to learn where that black car took its victim, or that the bigwig had been continually spying down from the balcony on the black car waiting down below, hoping, for a while, that the black car was not waiting for him, then as time passed – during the lecture – slowly ascertaining beyond any doubt that it was indeed for him that the black car was waiting, and after that ascertainment all he could do was spin out the time, that is, as far as he was able, delay the moment of departure, the stepping out from the entrance gate of the building; as for me, however, I hardly know what surprised me more, and of course more disagreeably: the encoutner four, five or six years later, on what was then still a tree-lined Andrássy (and later Stalin, Hungarian Youth, People's Republic, etc.) Avenue, with a battered, half-blinded, broken old man in whom, to my great horror, I recognised the erstwhile bigwig, or the "ad-hoc meeting", as it was called, that was convened in great haste at the editorial office the day following the balcony scene, in the course of which I was obliged to listen to certain things, each more absurd than the last, about this bigwig who, just the day before had been a figure of general terror, general homage, general creeping and crawling. These absurdities were brought to our attention now by the hysterically twitching ravings of a pampered youth, now by the incomprehensible outpourings of rage from the senior editor-in-chief himself, a being who, in his mortal terror, had been reduced to some human primeval condition, a pulsating amoeba, a mere existential jelly, and had stayed utterly transfixed in that reduced state, yet who only the previous day had been scared rigid, kowtowing and smarmily creeping and crawling in the presence of the selfsame bigwig. It would be utterly impossible, and utterly beside the point, for me to recall this man's choice of words, more absurd even than his absurd assertions: they consisted of a farrago of allegations and abuses, protestations, excuses, insults, pledges, threats and such-like, expressed in the most extreme manner, not eschewing the use of animal names, with the names of canine beasts of prey prominent among the abuses, for instance, and dragging in the language of the most bigoted religious sects among the pledges. Now I would be very curious as to whether the friendly gathering that had been urging me to tell the story of the Union Jack was able, even dimly, to imagine that scene, as I asked them to do at the time, since I myself, sadly, do not possess the requisite powers of evocation or means of expression; however much they may have nodded, strained and tried, I am sure that, in the end, they were incapable of it, simply because it is quite impossible to imagine such a scene. It is impossible to imagine how a grown-up man, well into his forties, who eats with knife and fork, wears a necktie, speaks the language of the educated middle class and, as an editor-in-chief, can lay claim to unreserved trust in his faculty of judgment; impossible to imagine how such a man, unless he were drunk or had suddenly gone off his head, could all at once wallow in the mire of his own fear and, amid spasms of twitching, squawk streams of such patent nonsense; impossible to imagine such a situation occurring, or rather, since it did occur, impossible to imagine how such a situation could have occurred; and in the end, it is impossible to imagine the situation itself, the scene and all of its details: the group squashed together facing the ranting buffoon, our group of adult men and women, reporters, stenographers, typists, technicians of every sort, in their thirties, forties, fifties and even sixties and seventies, who listened in consternation, with earnest-looking faces and without a single objection, to these near-meaningless ravings, that belied all common sense, reason and moderation by their self-negating anger, their veritable paroxysm of self-negation. Let me reiterate: the question of the credibility or incredibility of the words and accusations – words more fitting to a pulp thriller and accusations reminiscent of medieval chronicles of heresy, which went far beyond the orbit of critical judgment – did not so much as cross my mind at the time for who could have made any judgment there, apart from those who did the judging? What sort of truth would I have been able to perceive here aside from the truth of that ludicrous and, in essence, childish scene;

oh yes, and aside from the truth that anybody might be carried off, at any time, in a black car, aside from that, in essence, again plain childish bogeyman-truth? Let me reiterate: the only thing perceived by that stupefied, irresolute, 20-year-old young man (I), torn between unremitting horror and an unremitting itch to laugh, was that the person who only yesterday had still been a bigwig here was today fit only to be abused with the names of canine predators and to be taken off anywhere, at any time, in a black car – in other words, all he (I) perceived was a lack of permanence. And now, before that friendly gathering which had been urging me to tell the story of the Union Jack, I was unexpectedly moved to declare that maybe morality (in a certain sense) is nothing more than permanence, and maybe people create situations that can be designated as lacking in permanence for no other reason than to prevent a condition of morality being established. If this declaration, uttered at the dining table, may seem exceptionally slipshod and probably, indeed in all certainty, untenable under the rather more considered circumstances of writing, I still maintain that there does at least exist a close connection between *seriousness* and permanence. For death, if we constantly prepare for it in the course of life as the true, indeed – as a matter of fact – sole task that awaits us; if, in the course of life, we rehearse it, so to speak; if we learn to see it as a solution, an ultimately reassuring, if not satisfying, solution, is a serious matter. But the brick that happens, by chance, to drop right on our head is not serious. The hangman is not serious. And yet oddly even someone who has no fear of death fears the hangman. All I intend by the foregoing is to describe, inadequately as it may be, my state, my state as it was then. The fact that, on the one hand, I was afraid while, on the other, I was laughing, but above all, in some sense, I was confused, or I might even say that I had reached a crisis point, lost the refuge of my formulations; my life, maybe due to a quickening of tempo or *dynamics*, had become ever more unformulable, hence the sustainability of my way of life had become ever more questionable. Here I must remind you that professionally I was – or ought to have been – pursuing a formulation of life as a journalist. Granted, that a journalist should demand a formulation of life is a falsehood in its very essence: but then anyone who lies is *ipso facto* thinking about the truth, and I would only have been able to lie about life if I had been acquainted, at least in part, with its truth, yet I was not acquainted, either in whole or in part, with the truth, even the truth of the life I was living. Little by little, I was therefore recaterogised in the editorial office from *talented* journalist to *untalented* journalist. From the moment that I slipped, for a while at least, out of the world of formulability, and thus the sustainability of my way of life, the events going on around me – and hence I myself as an event – disintegrated into fragmentary images and impressions. But the camera lens that captured the jumbled images, sounds and even thoughts was still, agonisingly and irreducibly, *me*, only a me that was growing ever more distanced from myself. The diabolical wooden spoon had once again scraped the very bottom of the human soup in the cauldron of so-called *world history* in which we all stew. I see myself there, in depressed listlessness, at meetings that stretch out to dawn, where the hounds of hell yap, the whip of *criticism* and *self-criticism* cracks on my back, and increasingly I just wait, wait for when and where the door will open through which I shall be ejected who knows where. Before too long I was to be stumbling around in rust-tinted dust beneath the interminable labyrinth of pipes of a murderous factory barrack-complex; bleak dawns smelling or iron castings would await, hazed daytimes when the dull cognitions of the mind would swell and burst like heavy bubbles on the tin-grey surface of a steaming, swirling mass of molten metal. I became a factory worker, but at least it was possible, bit by bit, to formulate this afresh, if only with the vocabulary of adventure, absurdity, mockery and fear; that is, with a vocabulary consistent with the world around me, and in that way I more or less regained my life once more. That I might regain life *fully*, indeed that a *full life might be possible at all* – but now that I have already lived this life, now that what still remains of this life (my life) may also be considered as already lived, I must formulate it more precisely, indeed absolutely precisely: that a full life *might have been possible* – that is something I only began to suspect when all at once, after the formulations of adventure, I unexpectedly found myself, dumbfounded and fascinated, face to face with the *adventure of formulation*. This adventure to surpass all my adventures however, I have to broach, as I remarked in my preamble, with Richard Wagner, but before broaching Richard Wagner, I have to start at the editorial office, as I have likewise already signalled. At first, when they "took me on" at the editorial office, when I started going to work, day after day, at that office, when, day after day, I telephoned in to the office from the city hall (having been given that column, the "City Hall" column, as my assignment) the latest city-hall news, indeed reports, I always formulated this aggregation of facts, and not yet entirely without reason, as "I am a journalist", since the appearance, and the activity that engendered this appearance, truly did permit me, by and large, so to formulate it. That was my period of naive formulations, of unbiased formulations, when my way of life and its formulation did not yet stand irreducibly opposed to one another, or in an opposition that was reducible solely by radical means. What had carried me into that career, and therefore into that editorial office, was a formulation, a book I had read, that – above and beyond the necessity of making, so to say, a "career choice" and, yes, above and beyond my irrepressible longing – I might cast off the shackles of parental harassments and a childhood prolonged by education. After stints as a commercial traveller in wines and in building materials had been brought to a close by risible results, indeed quite simply by having become a laughing stock, then attempts at the printing trade or, to be precise, as a type-setter, had merely introduced me to the experience of futile torment and monotony, quite by chance – if indeed such a thing (that is to say, chance) exists, though I personally do not believe it – a book came into my hands. This book was a formulation of the life of a journalist, a Budapest journalist who moves about in Budapest coffee-houses, in Budapest editorial offices, in Budapest social circles, pursuing relationship with Budapest women – more particularly, two women, one an aristocratic lady, referred to only by the French brand name of her perfume, the other girl, a simple, poor honest creature, palpably finer than the lady with the branded perfume because she was endowed with virtue but born to be oppressed, thereby evoking perpetual twinges of social and metaphysical conscience, so to say – a totally false and falsified formulation, but one that, if memory serves me right, was presented with genuine longing, and thus with genuine plausibility. The book told about a life, a world, that could never have existed in reality, or at best only in formulations, the sort of formulations for which I too was later to strive, for purposes of the sustainability of my way of life, formulations which draw a veil over a life that is unformulable, that lumbers in the dark, stumbles about in the dark, lugs the burden of darkness – in other words, over life itself. This book about that journalist, and thus also, to some extent, about journalism itself, gave no inkling about journalism in the disaster era, or about disasters at all; the book was *light-hearted* and *wise*, in other words, a nescient book, but a book that, with the allure of nescience, exercised a fateful influence on me. The book may well have lied, but, as I remember it today, the lying was certainly honest, and it is highly likely that I was in need of just such a lie at the time. A person always lights upon the lie he is in need of just as unerringly and just as unhesitatingly as he unerringly and unhesitatingly lights upon the truth he is in need of, should he feel any need at all of the truth, that is, in winding up his life. The book presented journalism itself as a sort of happy-go-lucky pursuit, *a matter of talent*, and that accorded fully with the totally absurd and totally nescient fantasies I spun at that time about leading a happy-go-lucky but nevertheless somewhat intellectual life. In some respects I soon forgot about the book, but in others, never; I never re-read it, it never again came into my hands, and in the end the book itself went missing somewhere, somehow, and I never looked for it again. Later on, however, as a result of discreetly thorough asking around, I came to realise that the book could have been none other than one of the works of Ernő Szép, more than likely – though this is just an assumption, since I have not corroborated it for myself – his novel *Adam's Apple*. And now that I had mentioned the book that influenced my life so profoundly, with the peculiar determinacy of dreams of a revelatory nature, after some hesitation I also said to the friendly gathering where they had been urging me to tell the story of the Union Jack that the author of that book, Ernő Szép, without my being aware that he was the author of the book (by no means one of the most significant of his life's works, perhaps, if indeed truly significant at all), around the time when the disaster had not only been undeniably visible, present and obvious, but nothing other than the disaster was visible, present and obvious, and, apart from the disaster, nothing else functioned, Ernő Szép was pointed out to me, a so-called "cub reporter", on one or two occasions in the erstwhile so-called "literary" coffee-houses and cafés which still existed at that time, albeit by then only as disaster coffee-houses and cafés, of course, into which strayed only shadowy figures seeking some warmth, temporary shelter, temporary formulations. And on one or two occasions – perhaps even two or three – I, the "cub reporter", was even introduced to Ernő Szép (who naturally never recalled my earlier introductions), purely for the sake of being able to hear him introduce himself with the phrase that has since attained legendary, nay mythical status: "I *was* Ernő Szép." At this juncture, I proposed a minute's silence to the friendly gathering of my former students who had been urging me to tell the story of the Union Jack. Because, I told them, as the years and decades pass not only have I not forgotten that form of introduction, it actually comes to mind increasingly often. Of course, I said, you would have had to see Ernő Szép, you would have had to see the old chap who, before you would have been able to see him, *was* Ernő Szép: a tiny old chap who seemed to be relieved of his own very weight, swept along the icy streets like a speck of dust by the wind of disaster, drifting from one coffee-house to the next. You would have had to see, I said, his hat, for example, a so-called "Eden" hat of a shade that had evidently once been what was called "dove grey", which now teetered on his tiny bird's head like a battle-cruiser pummelled by numerous direct hits. You would have had to see his neat, hopeless-grey suit, the trouser legs bagging on to his shoes. Even then I suspected, but now I know for certain, that this introduction "I *was* Ernő Szép" was not one of those habitual disaster jokes or disaster witticisms of this disaster city which, in the disaster era that had by then undisguisedly set in, were generally believed and accepted because people could not believe, because they did not know or want to believe or give credence to anything else. No, that introductory form was a formulation, and a radical formulation at that – a heroic feat of formulation, I would say. Through this formulation Ernő Szép remained, indeed became the essence of, Ernő Szép, and at the very time when he already only *was* Ernő Szép; when they had already wound up, finished off and taken into state ownership every possibility by which Ernő Szép had once still been permitted to be Ernő Szép. Simply a lapidary formulation of the actual truth condition (the disaster), couched in four words, which no longer had anything to do with wisdom or light-heartedness. A formulation which lures nobody towards anything but with which nobody can ever be reconciled, and by that token a formulation with a far-reaching resonance – indeed, in its own way, a creation which, I will hazard a guess, may survive all of Ernő Szép's literary creations. At this, my friends and former students started to mutter, some of them sceptically objecting that anyway the oeuvre, as they called it, is "irreplaceable", as they phrased it, and moreover Ernő Szép is at this very time gaining a new lease of life, at this very time people are starting to re-read and re-evaluate his works. I knew nothing, and in this instance once again did not even want to know anything, about this, since I am not a literary man; indeed, for a long time now I have not liked and don't even read any literature. If I search for formulations, then I usually search for them outside literature; if I were to strive for formulations, I would probably refrain from formulations that are literary formulations, because – and maybe it suffices to leave it at this; indeed, there is truly nothing more that I can say – literature has fallen under suspicion. It is to be feared that formulations that have been steeped in the solvent of literature never again win back their density and lifelikeness. One should strive for formulations that totally encapsulate the experience of life (that is to say, the disaster); formulations that assist one to die and yet still bequeath something to posterity. I don't mind if literature, too, is capable of such formulations, but what I see increasingly is that only *bearing witness* is able to do this, possibly a life passed in muteness, without its being formulated, *as a formulation*. "I came amongst you to bear witness to the truth" – is that literature? "I *was* Ernő Szép" – is that literature? Therefore – and only now do I notice it – the story of my encounter with the adventure of formulation (and at the same time with the Union Jack) does not start, as I originally supposed, with Richard Wagner after all, but with Ernő Szép; but in either case, one way or the other, I have to and had to start with the editorial office. In the editorial office to which my fantasy, under the influence of Ernő Szép, had borne me – with external circumstances ready, as ever, to comply with steadfast fantasy – in that editorial office, then, on a briefer and more condensed trajectory, so to say, though of course without leaving behind an intellectual trail of any kind, I trod the very same path that Ernő Szép had taken, from the ignorance of wisdom and light-heartedness up to the "I *was* Ernő Szép" – type of formulation; all that I found on the site of the alleged erstwhile Budapest was a city that had tumbled into ruins, lives that had tumbled into ruins, souls that had been tipped into ruins, and hopes trampled underfoot amid those ruins. The young man whom I'm speaking about here – I – was also one those souls, stumbling around on the way to nothingness amid those ruins, although he (I) at the time still construed the ruins merely as some kind of film set and himself as an actor in a film – in any event, some splenetic, some acerbically modern film that was fraudulent in an acerbic and modern manner – a role that, being based entirely on an illusion seen from the auditorium, and oblivious to all disturbing circumstances (that is to say, reality, or the disaster), he (I) formulated as "I'm a journalist". I can see the young man on drizzly autumn mornings, the fog of which he inhaled just as he did the rapidly evaporating freedom; around him I can see the set, the blackly glistening wet asphalt, the accustomed bends in familiar streets, their expansions into the void over which the swirls of thinning fog gave hints of the river; the sopping-wet smell of the people who waited with him for the bus, the wet umbrellas, the hoarding plastered with garish advertisements which concealed the wartime rubble of a ruined building, on a site where today, 40 years later, another ruin stands, a peacetime ruin, the wartime ruined building having been replaced by a peacetime ruined building, a decrepit, eight-storey monument to total peace, corroded by premature death, patinated by air pollution, vandalised by every sort of squalor, theft, neglect, infinite provisionality and futureless indifference. I can see the stairway up whose stairs he will hurry before too long, with the same sense of security that delusion-driven people have which had impelled him (me) to declare "I'm a journalist" – with a certain sense of self-importance, in other words, which even the stairway in itself nurtured, that already long-non-existing stairway which hinted at a then unambiguous reality, the reality of *real* editorial offices, *late* journalists, *one-time* journalism and the mood and reality that embraced all this; I can see the lame porter, the so-called "errand-boy" or, more accurately, office messenger, that singularly essential person who in those days was still so singularly essential merely through the singularly essential services he rendered, limping nimbly between the rooms of the editorial office as he fetched and carried manuscripts and galley-proofs and performed trivial but indispensable errands as zealously as he was ready to act as a lender of last resort for cash loans (at low interest), if the worst came to the worst; a person who only later on turned into an all-powerful, implacable, unapproachable Office Assistant, wrapped in his cloak of arrogance, of the sort familiar to us solely from Kafka's novels and, to be sure, so-called *socialist reality*. On one such autumn morning, no, it was more likely forenoon already, most probably around the time of the gradual decrescendo from the clamorous chords of going to press, the "deadline", in those languid moments of slackness deriving from a certain sense of what could be called satisfaction, it happened that one of the stenographers in the editorial office raised with me the question of which theatre I wanted free tickers for. This stenographer – I still remember him today: his name was Pásztor, and although he was at least 50 years older than me, I, like everyone else, called him Wee Pásztor, since he was a diminutive, exquisitely dapper little chap, with his neat suits, fastidious neckties, French-style footwear, one of those cast-off *parliamentary stenographers* consigned to oblivion here in an era when Parliament had long ceased to be a *p*arliament, and stenography was no longer stenography in an era of ready-made texts, off-the-peg texts, prefabricated, pre-digested and meticulously censored disaster texts – this stenographer, then, with his rounded little eunuch's paunch, his bald egg-head, his face reminiscent of carefully ripened soft-cheeses, his little eyes shifting anxiously in their narrow slits, therefore required especially tactful handling, all the more so as he was hard of hearing, something of a paradox, to put it mildly, for a stenographer, and as such – when in prisons and diverse penal institutions in the selfsame city, indeed just a few blocks away, the numbers of people standing in corridors, hands behind their backs, faces turned to the wall, were already starting to multiply rapidly, when summary courts were churning out their sentences at full blast, when everybody outside prison walls, everybody indiscriminately, could be regarded as only a prisoner released on indefinite parole – he continually fretted that his deafness, which everyone knew about, might accidentally be exposed and he might be sent into retirement: this stenographer, then, was the one who used to keep the records of claims and entitlements to free tickets of so-called colleagues in the editorial office. I can still recall the ambivalent surprise that caught the young man, whom, as I say, I sustained and felt myself to be at the time, in the wake of the stenographer's accosting me at all, for on the one hand, he (I) had no heart for going to the theatre, simply on account of the disheartening plays that were performed in the theatres, while on the other hand, he was entitled to regard the mere fact of being accosted as marketing the end of his apprenticeship, his coming-of-age as a journalist, so to speak, since free tickets were earmarked exclusively for fully qualified and paid-up so-called colleagues. I remember that we pondered the miserable options for a while with honest, one might say fellow-suffering, scepticism – he, an old man simplified to his trivial practical fears, and I, a young man with more complex and more general anxieties – during which our gazes, so foreign and yet so intimate, communed for a few seconds. There was one other choice: the Opera House. "*Die Walküre* is on", he said. At that time I did not know the opera. I knew nothing at all about Richard Wagner. All in all, I knew nothing about any operas, had no liking for opera in general, though as to why not, that would be worth reflecting on, but not here, not now, when I really ought to be telling the story of the Union Jack. Suffice it to say that my family liked opera, which may make it somewhat easier to understand why I didn't like opera. What my family liked, though, was not the operas of Richard Wagner but Italian opera, the pinnacle of my family's taste, I almost said tolerance, being the opera *Aida*. I grew up in a musical milieu – insofar as I can call my childhood milieu a musical milieu at all, which I cannot, because I would call my childhood milieu any other milieu but a musical milieu – where the remarks that were passed about Richard Wagner, for example, were of the kind "Wagner is *loud*, Wagner is *difficult*" or, to mention a remark made in connection with another composer, "If it has to be a Strauss, then only Johann", and so forth. In short, I grew up in a milieu that was just as stultified in respect of music as it was in every other respect, which did not leave my taste completely unscathed. I would not venture to state categorically that it was exclusively the influence of my family, but it is an indisputable fact that, up until the moment when I got my ticket to Richard Wagner's opera *Die Walküre* from the stenographer Pásztor in the editorial office, I liked instrumental music exclusively and disliked any music in which there is singing (excepting the Ninth Symphony, and by that I mean Beethoven's, not the Mahler Ninth Symphony that I got to know later on, much later on, at just the right time, at a time when thoughts about death were manifesting, when I was making acquaintance with thoughts about death, indeed, what I would have to call a process of familiarising myself with, if not exactly befriending, thoughts about death), as if in the human voice alone, or to be more precise, the singing voice, I saw some kind of polluting matter which casts a poor light on the music. All the musical precursors of which I partook prior to hearing the Wagner opera had been purely instrumental precursors, chiefly orchestral, which I got to at best sporadically, primarily through the agency of that exceedingly testy old man at the Music Academy, known to every student or student type who, due to some eye defect, wore a perennial look of distrust but, for a forint or two pressed into his palm, would let any student or student type into the auditorium, ordering them brusquely to stand by the wall and then, as soon as the conductor appeared at the stage door leading to the podium, would direct them in a harsh voice to any unoccupied seats. I now wonder idly why, how and on what impulse I came to like music; it is a fact, however, that around that time, when I was still not yet able to call myself a journalist, when my perpetually problematic life was perhaps at its most problematic because my life was prey to my family, a family that was already on the point of breaking up around that time and subsequently, during the disaster era, broke up completely to be dispersed into prisons, foreign countries, death, poverty or even, in rarer cases, prosperity, a life from which already then, as ever since, I was constantly obliged to flee; it is a fact, therefore, that even then, as little more than a child, I would have been unable to tolerate that life, my life, without music. I think it was that life which prepared me, or in truth I should say rather that life which *rehearsed* me, for the disaster-era life which ensued not long afterwards, palliated as it was by reading and music, a life comprising several separate lives that played into one another's hands, each one able to annihilate the others at will, yet each holding the others in balance and constantly offering formulations. In this sole respect, purely in respect of this balancing, the balancing of small weights, my seeing and hearing *Die Walküre*, being receptive to *Die Walküre*, being overwhelmed by *Die Walküre*, undoubtedly represented a threat in a certain sense: it cast too big a weight on to the scales. What is more, that event – Richard Wagner's opera *Die Walküre* – had an impact like a street mugging, a sudden attack for which I was unprepared in every sense. Naturally, I was not so uninformed as to be unaware that Richard Wagner himself had written the librettos of his operas, making it advisable to read through the texts before listening his operas. But I was no more able to obtain the libretto for *Die Walküre* than Wagner's other librettos, a state of affairs to which pessimism induced by my milieu and lassitude induced by that pessimism – a lassitude that was always instantly ready for renunciation of any kind – no doubt contributed, though to be completely fair I should add that in the disaster era, which happened to be the era in which Richard Wagner began to interest me, Richard Wagner was classified as an undesirable composer, and thus his opera librettos were not available for sale, his operas were generally not performed, so to this day I don't understand and don't know why *Die Walküre*, of all his operas, was being performed, and with a fair degree of regularity at that. I do remember that one of those so-called programme booklets was on sale, the sort of disaster-era programme booklet, which, alongside (disastrous) synopses of other operas, ballets, plays, marionette shows and films, also provided a five- or six-line synopsis of the "content", so to speak, of *Die Walküre*, out of which I understood nothing at all and which presumably – though this did not occur to me at the time – had been deliberately contrived in such a way that nobody should understand it; in truth, to hold nothing back, I was even unaware that *Die Walküre* was the second piece in an interlinked tetralogy. That was how I took my seat in the auditorium at the Opera House, which even in the disaster era was still an exceedingly agreeable, indeed splendid place. What happened to me is what came next:

. . . the auditorium was plunged into darkness, and the overture commenced with a wild cadence down below. Storm, storm . . . Storm, a raging tempest, tumult in the forest. The bluff command of the God rang out and was reiterated, distorted by anger, with a compliant crack of thunder on its heels. The curtains whisked open as if blown asunder by the storm. There was the pagan hall, dark save for the glow of its hearth; in the centre, the towering outlines of the ash tree's trunk. Siegmund, a rosy-cheeked man with a straw-coloured beard, appeared in the timber-framed doorway and leaned, harassed and exhausted, on the door-post. His sturdy legs, swathed in hides and thongs, carried him forward with tragically dragging steps. The blue eyes beneath the blond brows and the blond forelock of his wig fixed the conductor with a broken, almost imploring gaze; then at long last the music receded, paused, to allow the tenor's voice to be heard, which rang clear and true, though dampened by his panting for breath . . . A minute passed, filled by the eloquent, singing, portentous steam of the music, a flow which surged onwards to the head of the events . . . Then Sieglinde entered from stage-left . . . which resounded low down as a profound, winding song. Again their glances met and mingled, again the deep melody unwound yearningly down below in the orchestra . . .

Yes, that is how it was. Try as I might to follow it, straining my ears and eyes to the utmost, I understood not a single word of the text. I had no idea who Siegmund and Sieglinde were, who Wotan and the Valkyrie were, or what motivated them. "The end was approaching. A huge vista, a sublime purpose opened up. Everything was pervaded by an epic solemnity. Brünhilde slept; the God mounted the rocks." Yes, whereas I stepped out of the Opera House on to Stalin Avenue, as it happened to be called at that time. I shall not attempt – naturally, it would be pointless to do so – to analyse right here and now the so-called *artistic impact* or *artistic experience*; in essence – to resort, against my better judgment, to a literary simile – I walked in much the same way as the main protagonists in *Tristan and* Isolde – another opera by the same composer, Richard Wagner, which at that time I knew about only by hearsay – go around after they imbibe the magic potion: the poison penetrated deep within me, permeated me through and through. From then onwards, whenever *Die Walküre* was performed, as far as possible I would always be seated there, in the auditorium, the only other refuge I found, where I might occasionally shelter myself, if only with an all too fragile fugacity, during that period apart from the auditorium of the Opera House and the, sadly, all too sporadic performances of *Die Walküre*, being the Lukács Baths. In those two places, immersed in the pure sensuality of the then still green, hot-spring water of the Lukács Baths and in the both sensually and intellectually very different ambience of the ruddy gloom at the Opera, every now and then, in lucky moments, I would become aware of a presentiment, unattainably remote of course, of the notion of a private life. Even if such a presentiment, as I have already mentioned, was fraught with a certain implicit danger, I could not help sensing its *irrevocability*, and I was able to place my trust in that solid sentiment as a kind of *metaphysical consolation*: put simply, in the lowest depths of disaster, and in the lowest depths of consciousness of that disaster, I was never again able to carry on living as if I had not seen and heard Richard Wagner's opera *Die Walküre*, as if Richard Wagner had not written his opera *Die Walküre*, as if that opera and the world of that opera did not subsist as a world in the disaster world. That was the world I loved; the other I had to endure. Wotan interested me; my editor-in-chief did not. The enigma of Siegmund and Sieglinde interested me; that of the world which was really around me – the real disaster world – did not. It goes without saying that I was unable to formulate all this for myself so simply at the time, since it was not, nor could it be, so simple. I suppose that I conceded too much to the terror of so-called reality, which thereafter appeared to be the inexorably reality of the disaster, the one and only, unappealably, real world; and although for my own part I was now – after *Die Walküre*, through *Die Walküre* – *unappealably* aware of the reality of the other world as well, it was like being aware of it only in secret, in a certain sense with an illicit, and thus incontrovertible but nevertheless guilty, knowledge. I suppose I did not yet know that this secret and guilty knowledge was in fact a *knowledge of myself*. I did not know that existence always sends word of itself in the form of secret and guilty knowledge, and that the world of the disaster was in fact a world of this secret and guilty knowledge raised to the point of self-denial, a world that rewards only the virtue of self-denial, that finds salvation solely in self-denial and that is therefore – however we look at it – in some sense religious. Thus I saw no *connection* of any kind between the disaster world of *Die Walküre* and the real disaster world, even though, on the other hand, I had unappealable cognisances of the reality of both worlds. I simply did not know how to bridge the chasm or rather, to be more accurate, schizophrenia which separated these two worlds, just as I did not even know why I should feel it was my task – and a somewhat obscure, somewhat painful, yet also somewhat hopeful task at that – to bridge that chasm or rather, to be more accurate, schizophrenia.

. . . He looked down into the orchestra pit. The sunken space, standing out bright against the auditorium, was a hive of industry: hands busy fingering, arms bowing, swollen cheeks puffing, humble mortals labouring assiduously in the service of the work of a great passionate force, a work enacted up above in childishly sublime visions . . . Creation! How did one create? A pain gnawed in his breast, a fervour or yearning, something like a cloying anguish – for where? for what? It was so vague, so shamefully unclear. He sensed two words: Creativity . . . Passion. And while his temple throbbed fiercely, a craved-for insight: creativity is born of passion and in turn assumes the form of passion. He saw the pale, exhausted woman clinging to the breast of the fugitive, he saw their love and distress, and he felt: this was how life must be to be creative – I read these words like somebody who was reading for the first time in his life, like somebody who was encountering words for the first time in his life, secret words that spoke to him alone, interpretable by him alone, the same thing as had happened to me when I saw *Die Walküre* for the first time in my life. The book – Thomas Mann's *The Blood of the Wälsung* – was about *Die Walküre*, as its very title divulged; I began reading it in the hope that I might learn something about *Die Walküre* from it, and I put the book down in a shock of amazement, as if I had learnt something about myself, as if I had read a prophecy. It all fitted: *Die Walküre*, the fugitive existence, the distraughtness – everything. I ought to note here that between first receiving *Die Walküre*, my first engulfment by *Die Walküre*, and my first engulfment by this little book, years – suffice it to say, years full of vicissitudes – had passed; so, in order to clarify my assertion that "it all fitted", I shall be obliged at this point to digress slightly, to give at least an outline of the circumstances in which I was living at the time, all the more so that I too can find a steady bearing in the weft of time and events and not find I have lost the thread of this story, the story of the Union Jack. This book – *The Blood of the Wälsung* – came into my hands after I and my wife-to-be, with the assistance of a good friend of ours, one fine summer morning traversed half the city, from the former Lónyay, then Szamuely and today once again Lónyay, Street, with a four-wheeled tow cart on which were piled, to put it simply, the appurtenances of our rudimentary household. This happened in the nick of time since the lodgings in Lónyay (or Szamuely) Street that my wife-to-be and I had been inhabiting had by then started to become unbearable and uninhabitable. I had become acquainted with my wife-to-be in the late summer the year before, just after she had got out of the internment camp where she had been imprisoned for a year for the usual reasons – in other words, for no reason at all. At that time, my wife-to-be was living in the kitchen of a woman friend from earlier days, where the woman friend had taken her in – for the time being – because somebody else happened to be living in my wife-to-be's apartment. That somebody else, a woman

(Mrs Solymosi), had taken over the apartment under extremely suspicious – or if you prefer, extremely usual – circumstances immediately after my wife-to-be's arrest, through the intervention of exactly the same authorities who – essentially without any verifiable reason, indeed on no pretext at all – had arrested my wife-to-be. Practically the moment she learned of my wife-to-be's release, that somebody else (Mrs Solymosi) immediately requested my wife-to-be (by registered letter) to instantly have the furniture my wife-to-be had unlawfully stored in the apartment that rightfully belonged to *her* (Mrs Solymosi) removed to the place where they were currently lodged (which is to say, the kitchen of the woman friend from earlier days who was taking her in, for the time being). When later, thanks to a protracted legal action, but above all to unpredictable circumstances – let's call it a stroke of luck – my wife-to-be got her own apartment back, we discovered, among some abandoned odds and ends, books and other junk, pegged together with a paper clip, a bundle of paper slips covered with the pearly letters of a woman's handwriting, from which I don't mind quoting a few details here – under the title of, let's say, "Notes for a denunciation" or "Fragments of a denunciation" – purely as a contribution to a legal case-study or even to an aesthetics of the disaster, as follows:

"She has lodged various complaints against me at the Council and the police, that I illegally moved into the apartment and stole hers . . . She imagined she could scare me with her slanders and I would give up the apartment to her . . . The apartment has been allocated definitively, there's no space for her furniture in my apartment . . . *Furniture*: 3 large wardrobes, 1 corner couch, 4 chairs . . . She should put them into storage, I am under no obligation to keep them after what is already 1½ years . . ."

There follow a few items of data that would appear to be reminders:

"17/10/1952 application, 29/10 allocation, 23/11 apartment opened up, inventory taken, 15/11 move in, 18/11 AVH [State Security], Council = AVH, AVH 2x – no response, Rákosi's secretariat . . . In September of 1953 Mrs. V. [i.e. my wife-to-be] Mrs V. morning . . . Asked her by reg. letter to remove furn . . . Have to keep my own furniture in cellar because I'm looking after her stuff . . . Her wardrobes are crammed full of √[dirty] clothes, under AVH seal, can't be aired . . . She says she doesn't have an apartment and is staying as a guest with somebody. Does that mean she doesn't need the things in the wardrobe? The woman puts on a good act and is quite capable of sobbing if required, but I've had enough of that and I won't tolerate her furniture in my apartment any longer –".

So we had had to spend the disaster winter that lay before us, which was ushered in at the very start by temperatures of 20 to 25 degrees below zero, in various temporary shelters, including the aforementioned kitchen of the woman friend from earlier days, a spare room of distant relatives surrendered on a very explicitly temporary basis, an exceptionally charmless rented room, made especially memorable by its ice-cold latrine on the outside balcony, and so on, until a miracle – admittedly, all too temporary as it turned out – in the shape of Bessie, a former snake charmer and her Lónyay (or Szamuely) Street rented apartment, dropped into our lap. It doesn't matter in the slightest now how and why this miracle occurred, although it would be wrong to leave out of this story – the story of the Union Jack – the earthly mediator of this heavenly miracle: a grey-templed gentleman, known as Uncle Bandi Faragó in the cafés and night-clubs around Nagymező Street, who, somewhat flashily for those times – the disaster times – and the occasion – the disaster – used to dress in an aristocratic, green hunting hat, short sheepskin coat and English-style tweeds, whose face glowed with a permanent suntan even in the deathly pale winter, and besides that allegedly pursued the exclusive occupation of a professional conman and adulterer, as was indeed confirmed decades later when, from a newspaper bought out of sheer absent-mindedness (since the so-called news was of no real interest), I was silently and genuinely shocked to learn about his death in a well-known common prison, where, allegedly, a cell, slippers and bathrobe used to be aside for him even during the days that he spent on release; and who one afternoon, in one of those cafés around Nagymező Street, one of these cheap, noisy, draughty, gloomy and dirty cafés with music which, since the state, though holding them to be iniquitous, at least heated well and kept open until late at night, had become an illicit day-and-night shelter for outcasts and which, while it was temporarily taking the place of our temporary residences, could be said to have been the main living quarters for my wife-to-be and me, suddenly came up to our table, and, really without any prior or more direct introduction, declared: "I hear you're looking for lodgings, my lad." Then, to my apathetic admission, which ruled out all hope in advance: "But, dear boy, why didn't you come to me?" he asked, in a tone of such self-explanatory, such deep and uncomprehending reproach, that, in my shame, I was lost for words. Later, after we had gone to the imparted address in Szamuely Street, where the door was opened by a lady, getting on in years and of – as Gyula Krudy might have put it – statuesque figure, with yellow forecurls peaking from under her green turban, the face slightly stiffened by heavy make-up, and wearing a curious silk pantaloon besprinkled with magical stars and geometrical designs, who, not content with a verbal reference, did not allow so much as a toe into the hallway until she had glimpsed the message written in Uncle Bandi Faragó's own hand on Uncle Bandi Faragó's own calling card; so when this lady led us, my wife-to-be and me, to the room that was to let, a spacious corner room with a bay window, the dominant furnishings of which were a decidedly oversized divan, big enough for at least four persons, a mirror placed in front of it, and a standard lamp with a shade plastered with all sort of obsolete bank notes (including the million- and billion-*pengő* denominations that had been in currency not so long before) that gave a mystic lighting effect, my wife-to-be and I did not doubt for one second the original purpose to which the room had been put, and it seemed most probable (and at once a clue to the miracle) that around that time, in that era of denunciations, the room's intended purposes all of a sudden – who knows, perhaps due to a denunciation that just happened to be pending – did not, to be concise, seem expedient. Things might have changed by the spring, but during that winter we had the chance to peek into our landlady's past: we could see her as a young woman, wearing an ostrich-plumed silk turban, a giant speckled snake coiled around there naked back, in some night-club in Oran, Algiers or Tangiers, which there, in that Lónyay (i.e. Szamuely) Street disaster-sublease, struck one as indeed quite extraordinarily implausible, and we could handle and ritually marvel at a profusion of relics which were every bit as implausible; later on, however, the snake charmer became despondent, and it was apparent from her increasingly consistent demeanour that, above and beyond the hostile feelings towards people that naturally arise in one as time goes by, she was not guided not so much by the random targets of such transcendental antipathy as by palpably down-to-earth goals: she wanted to regain her room because she had other, presumably more lucrative, plans for it. I shall try to skip the details as rapidly as possible, for I can only relate those details in this spirit, the spirit of formulabiltiy, which is by no means the same thing, of course, as the real spirit of those details, which is to say the way in which I lived and survived that reality; and this nicely illustrates the iron curtain that rises between formulation and being, the iron curtain that rises between the storyteller and his audience, the iron curtain that rises between one person and another, and, in the end, the impenetrable iron curtain that rises between a person and himself, between a person and his own life. I woke up to all this when I read these words: ". . . he saw their love and distress, and he felt: this was how life must be to be creative". These words, all at once, awakened me to my life, in the light of these words, all at once, I glimpsed my life; these words, or so I felt, changed my life. The book which, from one second to the next, swept away the haze of my formulations from the surface of my life, so I might see that life, all at once, face to face, in the fresh, startling and bold colours of seriousness, I discovered in the new (that is, repossessed) apartment – absolutely out of place, absolutely improbably, in the manner, as I remain convinced to this day, of a miracle that spoke to me alone – among the forgotten odds and ends, the above-mentioned denunciation slips and, thumbed to tatters, some volumes of pulp, shock-worker, partisan and romantic novels, the latter of defunct imprints. That book, so I felt, marked the start of the radicalisation of my life, when my way of life and its formulation would no longer be able to stand in any sort of contradiction with one another. By then, the time when I had been a journalist, or even a factory worker, had already long gone; by then I had committed myself to my seemingly unlimited, but also supposedly unlimited and intentionally unlimited studies, being able, thanks to a congenital ailment, to absent myself from my occasional jobs for months on end without running any immediate risk in the meantime that my mode of existence would, in all likelihood, qualify as the crime of so-called "publicly dangerous work-shyness". At that time all this completely preoccupied me, producing in me a sense of exaltation, of *mission*. I suppose it was then that I became aquatinted with the experience of *reading*, *reading* for nothing in particular, an experience in no way comparable with the experience of reading as it is generally understood and designated, the sort of reading bouts, or mania for reading, that might overcome a person at best just once or twice in a lifetime. Around this time there also appeared a book by the author of *The Blood of the Wälsung*, a volume of essays, in which there was an essay on Goethe and Tolstoy, whose chapter titles alone – "Questions of Rank", "Illness", "Freedom and Eminence", "Noblesse Oblige" and the rest – were enough in themselves almost to dumbfound me. I recall that I read this book all the time and everywhere I went; the essay on Goethe and Tolstoy was tucked under my arm all the time and everywhere I went: it was with me when I boarded the trams, went into shops, wandered about the streets – and so also, one especially fine early afternoon in late autumn, when I set off for the Instituto italiano di cultura per l'Ungheria, the Italian Institute of Culture, where at the time, in my unlimited thirst for knowledge, I was learning Italian, and during my passage across the city I registered, indeed, here and there, even participated, at least as an astounded spectator, in the intoxicating events of a day that was later to become memorable, a day that I or anybody else could hardly have guessed would turn into that particular memorable day. I was, I recollect, somewhat surprised when I turned off Múzeum Boulevard into the otherwise normally deserted Bródy Sándor Street, hurrying towards the nearby palace of the Italian Institute, which had originally been built as the one-time Hungarian Parliament. The lesson, however, started at the normal time. After a while, the street noise penetrated into the room even through the closed window. Signore Perselli, the finicky, jet-black-moustached *direttore*, for whom, on his rare visits to lessons, it took no more than a blatantly clumsy pronunciation of the word *molto* to be excited into demonstrating how it should be done with Italian fluidity, with the initial "o" closed and the final "o" short, the intervening consonants being articulated with the tongue drawn back, almost like saying "malto", on this occasion burst into the room in genuinely frantic haste to exchange a few no doubt diplomatically apprehensive words with our teacher before scurrying on to the other classrooms. A minute later, everybody was at one of the windows. In the slowly gathering dusk I could clearly see that on the left, towards the front, green rockets were being launched from the Hungarian Radio building above the heads of the darkly milling crowd of protesters there. At that very moment, from the opposite direction, three open-topped trucks turned into the street out of Múzeum Boulevard; from above, I had a good view of the militiamen with the green markings of border guards who were seated on the benches, rifles squeezed between their knees. On the back of the first truck, leaning against the driver's cabin, stood a lieutenant, evidently the commander. The crowd fell quiet, opened ranks, then roared. It is quite unnecessary here for me to evoke the manifestly pathetically affecting words that they started to shout to the soldiers down below, words which only at that given moment, that elevated moment of pathos, were able to exert an effect of genuine pathos. The trucks slowed down in the dense crowd, then came to a halt. The lieutenant turned about, raised his arm aloft. The last of the trucks now started to back out of the street, to be followed by the other two, amidst jubilation from the crowd. At this moment, we who, from an Italian diplomatic viewpoint that held itself to be above and beyond all this, had no doubt suddenly become unwelcome guests, capable of who knew what sort of emotional or other manifestations, were ordered to gather downstairs, beneath the long, neo-Renaissance vaulting of the entrance. The heavy, two-leafed gate was bolted from the inside with iron bands. We squashed together, between the sounds assailing us from outside and the security guards standing by behind us, until the Institute's burly porter, evidently on some signal, swung the iron bands back and swiftly threw open the gate through which each and every one of the 60 to 80 of us, on a vigorous shove being applied from the rear, found ourselves, in a trice, deposited outside on the by now twilit street, in a vortex of buffeting sound, swirling movement, ungovernable passion and inscrutable events that teemed between the buildings. In the ensuing days my attention was divided between the essay on Goethe and Tolstoy and the events that raged outside; or, to be more precise, the cryptic and unformulable promise that inhered in the essay on Goethe and Tolstoy, in the gradual comprehension and eventual acceptance of it, was linked in my mind, in a strange but quite self-explanatory manner, with the equally unformulable, similarly uncertain but, at the same time, wider-ranging promise inherent in the external events. I cannot say that the events that were stirring externally diminished my interest in the essay on Goethe and Tolstoy: to the contrary, they heightened it; on the other hand, I also cannot say that while I was totally immersed in the world of the essay on Goethe and Tolstoy and the spiritual and intellectual jolts of that experience, I *also* absent-mindedly paid occasional attention to the events that were stirring in the street: no, that is not what happened at all, I would have to say instead, however strange it may sound, that the events stirring in the street *vindicated* the heightened attention paid to the essay on Goethe and Tolstoy; the events stirring in the street during those days thereby *bestowed a real and incontrovertible sense on the heightened attention I was paying to the essay on Goethe and Tolstoy*. The weather turned autumnal; several quieter days ensued; down below on the street, of course, but especially on looking out from the window, I could see how much the street had changed: detached overhead tramway cables snaking between the rails, dangling bullet-riddled signboards, smashed windows here and there, fresh holes in the peeling stucco of the houses, dense throngs of people on the pavements of the long, long street, all the way up to the distant corner, and very occasionally a vehicle, a passenger car or lorry, tearing by at great speed, with some highly conspicuous distinguishing marks, the more garish the better. A hurtling jeep-like motor, suddenly appeared with the British red-white-and-blue colours, a Union Jack, draped over the entire radiator. It was scudding at breakneck speed between the crowds thronging the pavement on either side when, sporadically at first but then ever more continuously, evidently as a mark of their affection, people began to applaud. I was able to see the vehicle, once it had sped past me, only from the rear, and at the very moment when the applause seemed to coalesce, almost solidify, an arm stretched out hesitantly, almost reluctantly at first, from the left-side window of the car. The hand was tucked into a light-coloured glove, and though I did not see it from close up, I presume it was a kid glove; probably in response to the clapping, it cautiously dipped several times parallel to the direction in which the vehicle was travelling. It was a wave, a friendly, welcoming, perhaps slightly consolatory gesture which, at the very least, adumbrated an unreserved endorsement and, by the by, also the solid consciousness that before long that same gloved hand would be touching the rail of the steps leading down from an aircraft on to the runway on arrival home in that distant island country. After that, vehicle, hand and Union Jack – all disappeared in the bend of the road, and the applause gradually died away.

So much, then, for the story of the Union Jack. "Johnny rejoiced wholeheartedly at the prospect of the fight; I think neither he nor Brattström shared any of my apprehensions," I read during the severe winter that soon set in, during which my aforementioned ailment flared up again, so to speak, in the form of a fever of reading, or perhaps it was my feverish reading which flaring up again not long afterwards in the form of the aforementioned ailment. "Johnny repeatedly assured me, with that charming rolling of his r's, that the two boys really meant serious business, as befitted men; then, with a complacent and somewhat sarcastic objectivity, he weighed the chances of victory . . . He gave me my first impression of that peculiar sense of superiority, so typical of the English national character, which I later came to admire so much," I read.

What naturally also belongs to the story, perhaps needless to say, is that several days later, on that same bend in the road, but coming from exactly the opposite direction to that in which the Union Jack had disappeared, tanks suddenly veered into sight. All but wavering in their haste, their uneasiness, their fear, they always paused for a moment at the bend, and though the road, the pavement, the district, the city, everything was by now wholly deserted, with not a person, not a sound, not a soul to be found anywhere, the tanks as if anticipating even a stray embryonic thought, each and every time let off a single cannon round, strictly one, before clattering onwards. Since the gun position, direction and trajectory were always the same, for days on end they always pounded the same first-floor windows, outside and eventually interior walls of the same decrepit, Secessionist-style apartment block, so that finally the yawning void looked for all the world like a corpse's mouth, gaping in terminal wonderment, all of whose tooth were about to be knocked out one by one.

But here we really do reach the end of the story of the Union Jack, this sad but maybe not all that significant story. It would never have entered my head to tell it had that friendly gathering of former students, mustered to celebrate, there's no denying it, my all too round-numbered birthday, not appealed to my better nature, while my wife was busy in the kitchen preparing a cold snack and drinks for them. For them, they said, for "younger people", there are no longer any, as they put it, "primal experiences" . . . they only ever know and hear about tales of heroism and horror stories, or perhaps horrific tales of heroism and heroic horror stories . . . that birthdays are a fine thing, but with due consideration to my fluctuating blood pressure, my "revolutionary" pulse of at best 48 beats per minute, the pacemaker that I will anyway, sooner or later, find is unavoidable . . . not to put too fine a point on it, lest I too should take my stories and experiences, my whole knowledge of life, with me to the grave, when there are hardly any more authentic witnesses and tellable tales, and that they – a "generation", as they put it – are left here with their wealth of objective but totally lifeless and routine knowledge and facts . . . and so forth. I tried to reassure them that there was nothing wrong about this; that, anecdotes apart, every story and everybody's story is one and the same story when it gets down to the essentials, and that these essentially selfsame stories are really essentially all horror stories; that essentially every event is really a horror event, and even history too had long, long ago become, essentially, at best just horror history. But then how come, they asked at this point, that in the course of my own particular horror history I was able to recount spiritual and intellectual experiences of the kind that I had recounted; what had become of the continuation of what, in the course of my account, I had called "my mission"; or had I, perhaps, given up on the "mission"; moreover, what had stood out for them from my entire story was something, they said, that they had actually always suspected and assumed about me, namely, that by retreating inconspicuously into my own narrow area of expertise, I had lived a diminished life though I might also have pursued an intellectual existence and, if merely in my area of expertise, I could have been creative – in other words, as they said, where and how had the "break" in my, so to say, "career" occurred. I was staggered to hear this for it meant I had told them the story of the Union Jack to absolutely no purpose; it seems that they, children of destruction, no longer understand, are *unable* to understand, that the devastation of total war was turned by total peace into complete and, so to say, perfect destruction. Just one comment about an intellectual existence: even if I had happened to pursue an intellectual existence, I could only have done this at the price of self-denial, that is, I could only have pursued at best the *appearance* of an intellectual existence; thus, whether I chose an intellectual existence or I chose to foresake an intellectual existence, in any event self-denial had been the one and only choice open to me. And so, reckoning that naturally they would anyway not understand, were *unable* to understand, I tried to explain to them that it was not at all a matter of my, as it were, "relinquishing" what I had characterised as my mission, which is to say that there should no longer be a contradiction between my way of life and its formulation, or at least not a radical contradiction. I cited that great philosopher of history, Wilhelm Dilthey, with whom I had endeavoured – so far as I could, so far as I was free to do so – to familiarise them, my former students, when they were still in their student years: "Understanding presupposes existence, and an event only becomes a life experience if understanding guides existence out of its narrow and subjective being into the sphere of the whole and the general." I, so I feel, had done that. I had understood that I could only be creative here in the act of self-denial; that the sole creation possible in the world, as it is here, is *self-denial as creation*. I may have expressed myself extremely, but that doesn't matter since they didn't understand anyway: to that extent, and in consistent cognisance of that, I told them, I had lived, understood and fulfilled, if I may put it this way, the morally obligatory experience of life – life *as it is here*, and to that extent my life is a life of paying witness – so I am content. I reminded them of the formulations cited in the story, the story of the Union Jack: "I came amongst you to bear witness to the truth", and "I *was* Ernő Szép". There is no more ultimate lesson, no more complete experience than those. As to what it is all for, what *precisely* this is for, what experience is for, after all – that's another question, I reflected later. Who sees through us? Living, I reflected, is done as a favour to God. And while attention turned to the arrival of the dishes, the glasses raised and clinked in celebration of my birthday, I reflected, if not exactly with impatience but with a certain sense of expectant relief, that the more promising future which is nowadays threatened from all sides is something that I myself neither have to live through nor understand.

[TW]

PÉTER NÁDAS

Blown Away

In early January, when the shop reopened, only a few items were on the shelves. But there was more stuff in the large cartons that stood behind the counter. These were being unpacked now. Everything seemed new, clean, bright, fragrant. It had been snowing steadily for days. In the mirrors, on the ceiling, the yellow glow of the store's recessed lights seemed to clash with all that white. A young woman stood on a ladder, while an older one, the sleeve of her white smock rolled up to her elbow, was handing her bottles of liquor. Only my eyes took note of the fact that this older woman was one of those who had been branded. Just inside the curve of her elbow, on her forearm, was her number, tattooed in blue ink. Actually, it began with a letter, which was followed by a short line, sort of a dash, then the number itself, perhaps six digits in all. Normally, you saw such tattoos only when men wore short-sleeved shirts and women were in sleeveless summer dresses. A stranger's bare arm would reach for the leather strap in a streetcar, grab hold, and then you'd see it. Some people had them removed surgically, but then the skin graft itself, the wrinkled or discoloured scar tissue, became the distinguishing mark. The streetcar would rumble along, generating a pleasant breeze, and whoever noticed such an arm, *if* they noticed it, would rather stare out the open window, at streets baking in the summer heat. I know I did. Years later, the crippled and maimed war veterans also began to disappear from the city, they must have died out. At one point, I don't know just when, they even stopped marking special seats for them on the streetcars. But back then there were still quite a lot of them around. Some had an arm missing, others a leg. They would use safety pins to fasten their trouser legs or shirtsleeves, and thus cover the place where limbs should have been; or they'd let the sleeves dangle freely over the stumps. Jacket sleeves were pinned inside jacket pockets. There were peg legs properly shod; crutches strapped to the stump of an arm or to the hip. And scars, marks, holes, disfigurement; traces of burns and frostbite on horrifying faces. None of this required any explanation, though I never could decide what was more considerate: to look as if there was nothing to see, or to quickly turn away. I'd rather do the latter. Either way, the shame lingered, for I could never look, or turn away, without them noticing. They knew well why I had turned, or why I'd made believe there was nothing to look at. In our neighbourhood you performed this pathetic little ritual rather frequently. Cold indifference offends. But my sympathy wasn't much good either, because my revulsion, my disgust, was even stronger. The most I could bring myself to do was turn away slowly.

Almost every morning I saw a man who had been reduced to a mere torso. He propelled himself between people's feet on a wheeled wooden platform. My own father would not have been any older if – even in such a state – he had survived. The man rolled out of Szófia utca and braked his vehicle with his two hands, which were swathed in heavy leather gloves. In front of the large pharmacy the pavement slanted quite a bit. I had no idea where he was coming from. Most people were in a hurry, of course. He'd repeat the same two phrases each time. And always address a man. He would wait for his chance. He could get that contraption to come thumping down from the pavement, but on the other side of the street he needed help with it. First he'd swing forward, raise himself on his two fists and stay that way, almost allowing that dolly of his to slip out from under him and tip over the pavement. But then with another push he would yank his truncated limbs back on the board, and with his gloved hands quickly slow it down, to keep it from rolling out into the street. What had remained of his body was clean, sinewy, nice. It probably wasn't just due to the physical exertion, but sweat poured from his forehead and neck. A handsome face looked up at passers-by – on his moist forehead his long, smooth, dark-brown hair had got all matted – and asked that he be helped back on the pavement. His voice remained clear, steady: "I will only need assistance on the other side, if you wouldn't mind. An unfortunate war veteran appreciates your kindness." The person to whom these words were addressed would become flustered, not knowing just what he was supposed to do. But the miserable creature wouldn't say another word. He swung forward, rose, bounced back, slowed down in such quick succession that whoever saw him do it for the first time could hardly follow the precisely timed sequence.

Seeing him drive himself across the street, the helper would follow him rather helplessly. I saw him many times myself, and followed him. I wanted to know where he was going.

The men who were able to walk on their own two feet were overcome with shame. And a kind of childish eagerness. The same inexplicable shame marked their faces, their whole demeanour. If only they didn't have to follow an athlete's torso with their healthy feet. Maybe then their backs wouldn't sag quite as much. The rolling board made an infernal racket as it bumped and bounced and clattered on the uneven cobblestones. Cars had to stop. When the torso reached the other side, it bent forward, the two gloved hands propped up against the pavement, the shoulder muscles tense, and then, as though completing an exercise on the parallel bars, he swung himself quite gracefully up on the pavement, keeping his body suspended. The man helping him just had to slide the board under the two stumps. All this was clear enough, no words, no special instructions were needed. But the men walking on their own two feet wanted to do something more, something that required strength and skill. They looked as if they were really trying to help. However, the torso wanted nothing else from them. And as he rolled away between scurrying feet, they were left there, ungratified, frustrated. I never did find out where he was going.

And then there was this walking, talking third-degree burn. Judging from her fine clothes, graceful movements and refined vocabulary, she was a youngish lady. Under the huge hats she wore there was not a single lock or strand of hair. The turned-down rim of her hat covered her forehead and threw a shadow where her face should have been. On her forehead there was this altogether unlikely dent, as if the spot where the frontal and cranial bones fused had been smashed, flattened, even though the skin itself showed no trace of injury. In fact, her sunken forehead was the only place where the skin was more or less unscathed. Her face was full of scars, cuts, odd creases, suture marks. She had no nose, and no lips either. A lipless slit was all she had, and above it two dark holes. She wore dresses with high, closed collars, and her silk scarves were wrapped tight around her neck. But if her scarf came a little loose, you could see that her neck had suffered burns too. Her whole body must have been covered with burns. She wore suede gloves and dark, thick stockings. Her breathing had an odd wheeze to it, the sounds came from her throat, from the hollow of her mouth, as if she were unable to put her words into final form. They never did become real words, only her intonation suggested their meaning. If I ended up standing next to her in a queue, I had to pretend I had important business elsewhere. At close range I couldn't stand listening to those throaty, muzzy sounds, they hurt my ear, though it was my heart that was ready to burst. But that I couldn't admit to her. Then again, how could somebody else's heartache have helped her? Others were rather more indifferent, or more considerate, and she probably got used to this unemotional kind of solicitude. But you could be sure of this only if she had had a face with which to express her feelings. Otherwise she spoke like a self-assured lady who knew how to handle tradespeople.

"Any roquefort left? If not, then let me have some bologna, but do slice it thin. No, not from that, from the one over there, yes how very kind of you. And you will make sure it won't be more."

The last time I saw her was the day our store had run out of bread. They didn't let you inside, they sold whatever they still had from a table they'd set up to block the open door. The overnight curfew lasted until eight in the morning, and if you didn't queue up at dawn, you were out of luck. The queue on the pavement stretched quite far. There were reports on the radio almost every hour that the fighting had ended and a ceasefire was in effect. But even if the shooting did stop in one section of the city, it flared up in another, and before long it picked up everywhere. What's more, this had been going on for three days, and few people had anything by way of reserves. I still can't understand the general attitude, though. It's no doubt important that people have bread, but they have to be alive to eat it. Yet that's not how we thought then. There was always something we needed a fresh supply of, everybody was out searching, as if that was the most important thing, to find that one item.

The store manager called out in the early-morning darkness that all the bread was gone, he would not get another delivery that day, the bakery on Király utca was ordered by the authorities to resupply the hospitals. A few people yelled back: He could have told them earlier. Only those waiting for sugar, flour, oil or farina should stay, the man said. He had nothing else in stock. No, madam, there was no salt, it was no use asking. No yeast, no matches either. But over at Glázner's they'll be baking all day, there should be enough for everybody. As soon as he said this, the queue began to dwindle.

She was there that morning, too, wearing a short Persian lamb coat, long trousers and boots, and explaining something to the person next to her. So we all had to adjourn to Glázner's on St Stephen Boulevard. This sort of thing happened a lot during those days, but nobody seemed to mind moving on. In fact, it wasn't thought to be a good idea to stay in one place too long. And sometimes you didn't need an official announcement – word simply got around that at another location there were still things to be had. And then small bands of anxious shoppers would begin their trek towards yet another destination. Nobody complained. True, nobody knew what to expect. Was the next place going to be less safe? Was any location really safe? You simply succumbed to need, that's what caused your anxiety. So you moved on. But sometimes you couldn't get to the next place, not even by taking long detours, because of the fighting. Or you did get there, only to find out that the store was closed, or it had never opened, or had been reduced to rubble in the meantime. But something would always turn up. And in the hope of this something, everyone worked out his private strategy. They knew which roads to take and which ones to avoid. It wasn't wise to go off on your own, though. That way you didn't get to hear the latest news. But sticking too close to crowds also had its dangers. Things changed constantly. So you navigated between crowds that were either dispersing or becoming more dense. Daylight was not much better than these foggy, early-morning hours. It looked as if everyone was following their own instinct, but in reality they were all very much aware of what the others were doing. Maybe they did know better. And this odd feeling, which in more peaceful times may have alienated them from one another, made them stick together more. Yet this togetherness didn't feel right either. It made everybody think that only *they* knew what was best for them, all the others did was run off at the mouth, it might just make more sense too, that others viewed the same uncertainties very differently. But when it came to deciding, for instance, whether to cross an open square or choose a different route, you just couldn't make up your mind alone.

And the real danger spots weren't even where the skirmishes raged on without a let-up. If shots were fired at more or less the same height, or if we could tell where they were coming from, where they were aimed, then we could dodge them at least, or cling to a piece of railing or an overturned streetcar, and wait for a pause between two bursts and bend down and make a dash for it. That is what the others were doing, too. Of course, you had to count on stray bullets. When just about everyone made it across, somebody would get hit. And the victim would stay on the roadway, unless somebody was willing to creep back and pull him out from under a hail of bullets. And then there he was, somebody nobody knew, either injured or already dead. By then there was no more milk anywhere. One woman's milk can was hit by a flying bullet. This happened during the day. Feeble sunlight cut through a light autumn fog. The woman was running towards us from the other side of the street, while a few of us were still waiting for the right moment to dash across. At such moments, faces got all twisted, mouths stayed wide open, eyes narrowed to slits. As if at once two sentences were on everybody's lips: "All right, *now*" and "Good, I made it." When the woman's can was hit, she stopped, her face frozen in disbelief. The milk poured out of the can in two gushing streams. Which meant that somewhere around there, milk *was* being sold. Or had been. And the spilled milk seemed more important than anything else. She didn't even duck, but in her fury slammed the can against the ground. Three times, four times, without letting go of the handle. The others, too, hollered for a while, but it didn't change anything.

What remains even more memorable is the quiet. An inert square, a silent intersection, where everything is ominously still. Locked doors, closed shutters. Lightness or dark, it doesn't seem to matter; not even footsteps can disturb such silence. Yet deep inside it something stirs and fills the air. That was just the kind of unnerving dawn that greeted us around the Western Station. No light anywhere, not behind the windows, not on the street – no sound, no movement of any kind. It was chilly and foggy, you felt it on your skin, in your nostrils. But there was nothing to see or hear, not there, not yet. Perhaps cats or rats have such presentiment. The square was still far away, you could just about make out the heavily damaged railway-station towers against a still dark sky. Up to this point we'd been like a bunch of spirited and noisy tourists. But there was no question that now we'd have to be quiet and keep away from the square. Afterwards all we could hear was the shuffle of our receding footsteps. It rebounded from the walls of apartment buildings. We knew what we were doing, like cats and rats. It looked from here as if the upper end of Podmaniczky utca was open. We'd seen others turn in, so it seemed like a safe enough crossing point. But we didn't walk together, each of us was on his own. You told yourself: You'll get to Bajcsy-Zsilinszky út somehow. And didn't even ask: And then what? All you saw before you was Kálmán utca, where the trolleys used to run – that's the street you had to reach first. If you were calculating probabilities, weighing possibilities, your only concern was the next step. Just how you were going to get there didn't interest you, only the very next step. Not before or since then have I felt the city to be so much a part of me. One pressing need highlighted a single spot for me, and with that my situation was placed under microscopic scrutiny. It was as if I saw right away where everything was, and what sort of landmarks and hiding places and natural defences – what dangers – I could count on or anticipate. I was like an animal that knows every trail and track. Right now it was Kálmán utca, and after that it would be another street, though I knew I mustn't get too close to the Ministry of Defence building or the Parliament. Alkotmány utca would pose a problem because it was so wide; and crossing the Boulevard might be an even bigger problem. But right now only Kálmán utca was under a magnifying lens; I didn't ask myself what I would do once I'd made it there. Something was bound to happen, and then again, something else might, or maybe nothing at all. Somewhere in the distance you heard the rattle of machine guns. But you heard that rattle everywhere – nearby, a little further away, in the remote distance. It became dangerous only when you heard it echo right in your own street. Then it was like being inside a sack, with you having to find a way to climb out. But you never could figure out such a thing beforehand.

While I kept walking, somebody stopped me to ask what's up. There's bread at Glázner's, I said. Just then the whole street had a respite. People appeared in several doorways. Rebels, too, bringing stuff out, carrying things back in. Lights went on in the apartments upstairs. The autumnal leaves had changed colour, but the boughs were still full. This and all those lights made it seem as if this whole thing had just about run its course. Streets heaving a sigh of relief always looked this way, though now this one kept taking quick, sharp breaths, for nobody really knew how long the respite would last. It was probably a caretaker's helper who'd stopped me before. From a well-lighted window just overhead, a woman called out to him: "Will you be a dear, Stevie, and turn on the water for us?" He was carrying a box of ammunition on his shoulder. "Fuck you, man, you'll never get through here. Don't you see what's happening?" Sure I did; if he said so. I didn't think his contempt was entirely unjustified. Perhaps it wasn't even contempt. Maybe all he meant to say was that I was a stupid civilian. Mind you, it wasn't that hard to get hold of a gun. I had seen people on trucks handing them out to all comers.

It wasn't fear that stopped me from grabbing one. I couldn't even say that I objected to all the shooting. On the contrary, I approved. I couldn't imagine it happening any other way. Justice was done. And where there was shooting, there were bound to be deaths. But my job now was to find bread. And other stuff, too. "We already turned it on, miss. You just go ahead and try it." It was at the next intersection where I learned, from somebody else, that the Russians had pulled as far back as the Basilica. And had brought out their heavy guns. But the Western Station was still in rebel hands. Which meant it was a good place to cut across. What you didn't know was when it would start up again. On the corner there was a large photography studio. And in front of its shattered window, a bunch of familiar faces. Broken glass crunched under our feet. Somebody had better start moving, we all thought, but no-one could say this out loud. Everyone was privy to some piece of new information, and therefore committed to this or that course of action. An interminable discussion ensued, everybody had his say, though it was not all that interesting. The only nice thing about it was that in this unfamiliar neighbourhood, you got to see familiar faces. People looked at one another in the dark, they spoke their mind, they kept gesturing with their hands. Still, there were those who didn't say a word, who only listened, and it was mostly these people who later would lose their patience. Which was bad. You had to decide, after all, whom to side with, which faction to join. Either way, it was bad. In the end, everyone was waiting for his turn, only no-one wanted to go first.

Strung over the deserted street, a single crippled arc light still burned. The trolley bus's overhead lines fell on the cable, the weight shifted the lamp's dish, the glass cover broke, but the light itself worked. In between piles of ripped-up paving stones there were dead bodies. On the corner of Kálmán utca smoke rose from a burned-out tank on the pavement. From a distance it looked like steam. Perhaps the tank caught fire as it tried to avoid the pile of stones. Skidding out of control, it ran up the pavement, hit a tree, its limbs came crashing down, and then both tree and tank went up in flames. The charred branches stuck out of the wreck like horns. A single collapsed wall was all that remained of a newspaper kiosk. The foggy, early-morning air cradled a few sheets of newsprint. Nothing else stirred. Now and then the sheets of newspaper rose in the air, were wafted along, then deposited.

Even at this point I could see her. But only her eyes. Her face was shielded by her scarf. On this particular morning she wore a turban instead of a hat, and the colour and pattern of her turban matched the cashmere scarf perfectly. It was not unusual to see such fineries, or even a fur coat, during those few days. People pulled out many things which earlier they would not have dreamed of putting on. As if it were a holiday of some kind, though in truth, these articles of clothing hardly suited the occasion. She held her shopping basket on her arm the way she always did – as though she'd just run down to do some last-minute shopping. And while the others were still busy conferring and weighing alternatives, she apparently whispered something from behind her scarf to the man standing next to her, who didn't seem to understand. This man was wearing riding boots, which, too, were things one hadn't seen much of in recent years. Then she started walking, and it looked as if the man was going to go after her. Broken glass and other debris crunched under their feet in the continuing stillness. But then the man thought better of it; he wasn't going to follow her, which didn't seem to bother the woman. She stepped off the kerb and continued walking, shopping basket in hand. She wasn't running or hurrying, she didn't even lean forward very much as she walked. She was simply someone going shopping. The man stayed in the middle of the pavement, which wasn't too smart of him. In those days the pavement at this spot jutted out in a salient. He stood there, as though on a spit of land, facing a sea of danger. He should have either turned around or walked on. We also watched the woman, anxious to see what would happen to her. She got to the arc light all right. It would be harder after that, on account of the corpses and the ripped-up paving stones. The streetcar tracks protruded from the exposed roadbed like two lifeless spines. The city then was full of objects that had lost their function, their reason for being. But nothing happened. She walked between the two tracks where there were gaping holes now, regular trenches. She could easily fall into one. But the dark depths were still, we heard nothing suspicious. At least twenty of us were waiting at the corner for the final outcome. At such moments you didn't hear the person breathing next to you, or if you did, you were oblivious to it. When she got past the tracks, she stepped out of the patch of light, though we could still see her running. If she got that far, let her not be cut down. These were times when it was so easy to understand what people did, and why. When she reappeared, she stood in front of a house, on the other side.

I saw her even at Glázner's, later on. It was light by then. She had to have been there for some time, because she'd already joined the queue. I took one look at this queue and felt like giving up. But then what would I do for bread? Whenever you saw a long queue, you tried to figure out what your chances were. But this time all figuring seemed futile. And I even dawdled, by walking ahead, as far as Katona József utca, to see if the situation was really that bad. In the meantime, of course, new people had joined the queue. But others wavered, too. Not believing their eyes, they also went ahead to check or tried to size things up from a distance. But the more you thought about it, the worse your chances got, because other people took the place that technically, on the basis of time of arrival, belonged to you. The queue spilled out of Fürst Sándor utca, its fringes coming to an end on the Boulevard. That was to be my place in a queue that wound massively around an entire city block, all along Sallai Imre utca, and then curved back on to the Boulevard and the baker's main entrance. And this queue did not move an iota, for the simple reason that there was no fresh bread, and no way of knowing when the next batch would come out of the ovens. There were people who'd brought chairs or stools with them; others just stood and shuffled their cold feet or leaned their backs against the masonry. Either I gave up or I didn't. No more hesitation. But as I dragged myself back to the end of the queue, it occurred to me to walk all the way to Petneházy utca, where the central bakery was. Not that I had any sort of premonition then.

On the whole, things looked calm here, which may have been the main reason why I didn't go off on my own. I took my place at the end of the queue. There was no more room on the pavement. Those who came after me had to stand in the intersection. We could always creep up just a little. Which didn't mean that they'd finally begun serving people inside the shop – it was quiet impatience that closed up the ranks. A half-hour or so passed, after which things began moving inside; and pretty soon there was a stir outside as well. First, just restlessness, some quiet grumbling, a little shoving. Everybody would have loved to press forward, but there was no room. "Just where would you want me to move, madam?" In such a situation everyone has to say something. "Just a minute, my good man, just one minute." Then the helpless shuffle of feet, the rumble of irritability, the first solitary shouts. People given to such outbursts are held in contempt by the crowd, and rightly so. In order to squeeze your way into the shop, you must make room for the happy few who are on their way out with their fresh loaves.

Whoever doesn't understand the psychology of waiting might think that nothing's more natural than letting these people pass – it's in your best interest to do so, after all. If people aren't allowed out, no-one'll be able to go in. But the fact is that people in such circumstances have to contend with several different pressures at once. And no matter how reasonable or good-natured a person may be, in a crowd he will not be able to yield to all of these pressures. His common sense and his sense of justice will inevitably clash with his sense of urgency, and past a certain point he will not be in control of his conflicting impulses. His common sense will become especially vulnerable. Let's just imagine that someone at the back of the queue has an urge to move forward, even though he has no idea what's going on ahead of him. He may move up just a little, no more than an inch or two, yet already tensions flare. Instinctively, or on purpose, he's slouched forward. But if he didn't, someone else would, or he'd be irritably nudged along by the others. And if that happened, his sense of justice would surely suffer. But however much this person may cherish his common sense or his sense of justice, he couldn't possibly resist the will of so many people bearing down on him – right now he'd buckle under his own body weight. Nevertheless, for a brief moment everyone is anxious for him to stand fast and push back, for people *are* for the most part well-meaning and reasonable, yet no-one can ignore the insidious machinations of their own animal selfishness. It's not their fault, they will say, that this person is simply too weak to get that pushy creep off his back. In any case, if people are not equal in strength, not equally capable of resisting the pressure on them, then the tiny space I gain by virtue of my own strength will surely be filled by the weak ones, or invaded by the petty schemers, who'll then manage to shove me aside.

There are those who wait for just such a moment. For needless to say, physical strength is not the only thing that varies in people – mental fortitude and understanding are also apportioned unevenly. So there are those who will valiantly put up with the massive weight on their backs and will even have the stamina to withstand the pressure, but all they really want is to keep others from obtaining what they would like for themselves. And this desire for a slight advantage can be so easily justified. This one's been standing here for ten hours. It's cold. He simply must go to the toilet. And that one's child hasn't had a bite to eat in two days. If she doesn't make it into the shop, or if the next batch of bread is gone before her turn, it means another one-hour wait, and that's more than she can take. Perhaps she is right, it *is* more than they can take. They have high blood pressure, cancer, heart trouble. And what if they run out of flour in there? Or if the bakery gets hit? Or if these crazy people trample them to death? Common sense hasn't got a chance, everyone can see that. There is always someone who still clings to his sense of justice. Although the only thing he really wants by now is to be treated justly by others. Everyone roars; everyone screams. He can't help himself and screams along with them. Even those who do not open their mouths scream. There are those who knew the bitter truth all along and now let it all out. And those who are shocked to learn that people can act this way and who now likewise proclaim their discovery. And those who do not yet know that the neighbour with whom they've just had a friendly chat is in fact a maniac. And there are also those who are pressed against the plate-glass window; who are pushed out of the queue; who are kicked and stepped on. There are children and there are old people. Those who desperately try to leave the shop, and those who accidentally get pushed inside. The experienced hysterics and the ones who really are gasping for air. And there are many who still don't believe that something like this can actually happen to them. It's something inside them, their soul, that screams. And though no sound may come out of their mouths, they are shaken by a strange fever, stirred by other people's screams. A fine membrane ruptures inside.

I must have been screaming, too, just about everybody was. When this happens, nothing can help except a moment of grace, a stroke of luck, an accident. Nobody feels responsible any more for what they do. Should they come out of this unharmed, they wouldn't know whom to be more grateful to. But how odd that even a violent commotion in a crowd can quickly quieten down. I still don't know what happened; but at least the shop windows weren't smashed in. Lifting their loaves over their heads, the first people managed to fight their way through the crowd. The human mass clogged the entrance, it wouldn't budge, yet they squeezed through. All you saw were lurching shoulders, colliding backs. At such moments people are faceless; memory has little to preserve. I saw it all. I stood no more than thirty feet away, yet I don't know what really happened. Backs, shoulders, the white blur of faces. My hearing remembers, though. Above the throng ringing the entrance, frantic screams cleaved the air. We, however, who stood at the very end of that twisting, block-long queue (and thus were only about thirty feet from the spot where at any moment irremediable disaster could have struck), responded by merely shouting. Hoping that these shouts would remind the screamers that a modicum of common sense remained, all was not lost. They could still stop. Or do this some other way. The shouts were meant simply to force back the screams, yet there was anger in the shouts, the anger of frustrated self-interest. After all, if something irrevocable happened up there, then I'd end up with no bread back here. All along the line, as far as the eye could see, there was commotion, unrest. People stopped resting their backs against the sides of buildings, they got up from their chairs and stools. Still not knowing for sure what was going on, they jostled and clamoured and were ready to press forward. Whatever happened, happened then, in that confused hubbub, amid angry shouts and hysterical screams, in the air, where polar opposites – helplessness and wilfulness – collided head-on.

Just when the first group of lucky breadwinners managed finally to squeeze through the door and stood there dazed, happy, some choosing to take off in a hurry, afraid that someone might actually snatch the prize out of their hands – just then, the jolting, nerve-racking uproar reached its climax. This was it. Nothing could be louder. They all saw these people come out, and they all wanted to take their place. Going as far as stopping others from leaving the shop. Molten lava might feel this way when it has to crack the earth's crust. Or the crust itself, when it tries to hold out around the cracks but then caves in. The pressure inside became simply intolerable, without significantly weakening the pressure outside. The loaves exhaled a hot, heady fragrance. And naturally, those still inside, thinking that the gods must love them to be bestowing these loaves, were most eager to break out. While those trying to fight their way in saw their whole life now as a tremulous uncertainty. The ones elbowing their way in were sure they were doing it for the bread – while those on their way out were defending their lives along with their still hot loaves. Nothing got resolved, of course, but the screams and shouts abated somewhat. The line began to move, though this didn't lessen the confusion, it just turned it into an indignant bustle. No-one screamed any more, but everyone argued and pleaded and cursed. We crept forward slowly. And in the soles of our feet felt nascent hope.

I could see her even then – her turban, the uncertain outline of her charred face. The sun came out and we moved forward rather briskly. The sunlight warmed us, we could breathe in the smell of the nearby river – it mixed agreeably with the scent of fresh-baked bread. Nobody talked about what had just happened, or what could have happened. But then, it really was nothing. And if we kept up this pace, we'd have our bread in no time. In a matter of minutes we were at the corner of Fürst Sándor utca. Happy shoppers were coming out of the bakery again. We moved steadily along and kept a sharp eye on each other's shuffling feet. At this point you realised that your situation had changed significantly. You were no longer stuck at the end of the queue, you were on your way. And you watched, lest somebody pulled a fast one on you – and made sure others wouldn't get the same impression about you. The queue is moving, your antennae are up and finely tuned, you are ready to pounce. Everyone is pushing for some advantage, a half-inch lead if nothing else, just as long as the other guy is left behind. It's as though, in the name of common decency, you are always reining in the other guy, except that the reins are held by him. People hold back in their own greed. If you can't have the upper hand, you should at least make sure you don't lose out. When the queue starts moving, there is no time to argue, and when it comes to a stop again, it's too late to turn things to your own advantage. It has to be done now. That half-inch lead must be grabbed right now. And it has to appear as though the other guy's slowness or clumsiness – and not your despicable selfishness – is responsible for that lead. By the time we reached the corner of Katona József utca, the queue had stopped moving. The narrow street was still dark and cool. A bit of sunlight seeped through between the rooftops, but it penetrated only the tiny side street that connects Fürst Sándor utca and Pozsonyi út.

The moment the queue stops moving can be amazing. Everybody has to admit that for all their watchfulness they did not end up with the same people who were there when the procession began – the line-up is different. You made every attempt to ensure that things wouldn't change, yet they did. Familiar coats and familiar faces have turned into enemies simply because they somehow ended up ahead of you. Any moment now you'll have to team up with strangers. It will be a bitter moment. Quarrels can break out at such moments. Which may degenerate into fist fights. Or it may suddenly turn quiet, if only because the hopeful scuffing and shuffling has ceased. In this silence a chair or a stool hits the ground, a sigh is heard. Somebody says something, somebody else answers. For a while you have to make this spot your own. Trouble starts when somebody objects. This is not where I ought to be standing, he may say to himself, and in an unguarded moment may voice his dissatisfaction openly. Everyone's afraid of such a challenge. Their common fear may stifle even ongoing arguments. What's at work, however, is not the voice of reason – people are simply afraid.

It did turn quiet, and felt like the quiet of an ordinary autumn morning. No shots could be heard anywhere. I was lucky to be able to rest my back against the side of a building. True, I had to manoeuvre a bit to end up in the right position. On the walls of this particular building you could still see the scars of the last war. Over the years the bullet holes filled up with soot and almost blended in with the mouldering plaster. I grew up in this city and couldn't imagine buildings not looking this way. But the quiet I sensed was not real quiet after all – it was overtaken by a distant, even rumble. I knew by then that inside the large shop the baking was done in three different ovens, and a new batch of bread came out every thirty-five minutes or so. We figured that with each baking cycle we'd advance about thirty yards. If the ovens could handle the load, that is. And if there was enough firewood. And they didn't run out of flour. Or could get a new delivery if they did. And if they could prepare the dough fast enough to feed the ovens. Which was not very likely. At this rate, one of us calculated, they'd have to go through twenty-seven cycles before our turn would come, probably sometime in the late afternoon. The question wasn't whether we could wait that long but whether we would make it inside the bakery before dark. And if we didn't, would the curfew be lifted by then? It was more dangerous to violate the curfew at night than early in the morning. And almost impossible not to get caught, because at night there were patrols all over the city. By morning the fighting usually died down.

But now that rumbling noise kept getting louder. Past a certain threshold, there could be no doubt – a column of tanks was approaching. Now these convoys weren't all that frightening. With a rumble and a roar they would move from one location to another. As long as they didn't stop, there was nothing to worry about. Besides, it was highly unlikely that they would turn into such a narrow street. They preferred wider thoroughfares and kept to the middle even there, to make it harder for people to hurl petrol-filled bottles at them from their windows. The rumble came from the direction of the Angels Field district, and you could tell from the sound that they were going to pass through either Pozsonyi út or Pannónia utca. When you distinguished the clatter of the caterpillar treads in that maddening racket, you could be sure they chose Pozsonyi út. For in those days Pozsonyi út was still surfaced with yellow road bricks, which made the noise much screechier. First the clatter and the screech reverberated amid the tall buildings, and then, at the other end of the sunlit side street, you saw the tanks themselves. They passed, one after another, equidistant from each other. Just as one left your field of vision, another entered it. The exhaust fumes dimmed even further the listless sunlight.

Nobody in our queue moved. Those of us who could see into that tiny side street kept looking. The fumes got so bad, and the roar so evasive, that everybody fell silent. Not that they would have heard even if people had kept on talking. And there was no end to the convoy. The vibration was picked up by the surrounding buildings, I felt it come together in my hands and feet, as though I wasn't the one shaking. And the rumbling and shaking grew even stronger, because the tanks, with the shrillest of shrieks, turned on to the ramp of Margit Bridge, and as they did the entire substructure began to shake. You felt the bridge in the soles of your feet. I had a city which was split in half by a river, but the familiar bridge was now reduced to a sensation. The vibration was picked up by the span itself, it spread to the block of houses around the bridge, I even felt it on my back. It made you oblivious to everything around you, for you kept concentrating on your own shaking body. It didn't occur to me that we might be in danger, though it didn't sound as though this procession was going to end anytime soon. Yet such manoeuvres were not rare, the Russians kept regrouping their forces, people on the street didn't pay much attention to these comings and goings. For a few days back then it even seemed possible that they'd leave for good. At least leave the city; maybe the whole country.

From where I was standing I had a fairly good view of that small side street. The tanks passed a café called Samovar, and I could even see that. Behind the café's sun-streaked window there was a large photograph showing Hedda Hiller, the lovely chanteuse, who only a few nights ago had performed here. The café was open and crowded with people, all of them looking through the window, watching the tanks go by. There were also people on the pavement outside the café, and they, too, were watching. Then something happened which to this day I have difficulty assimilating. Sluggishly, though still as if it had a sudden change of heart, one of the tanks turned into this side street, its treads grazed the pavement, the friction caused sparks to fly. The people standing around scattered in every direction. Some sought refuge in the café, others ran into the nearest apartment house. In a matter of seconds the street was empty. What remained was the heavy smell of petrol and bright shafts of sunlight creeping down from the rooftops. Those of us standing in the queue did not move. With its gun-barrel raised high, the tank was coming towards us.

For a moment it occurred to me that all it was doing was securing the column's safe passage, in which case all this was strictly routine. It got to the middle of the tiny street, stopped, but didn't cut its engine. Nothing was happening. At this point I even thought that perhaps it was having engine trouble, and that's why it left the column. But I also sensed trouble. At that very moment the tank's gun began to move. It came down, quite gently, as though it were aiming at the apartment house in front of it, or at the wide awning over the entrance of the Duna cinema. But there was nothing there. We stood under the awning – a motionless crowd waiting in a queue. It all happened so fast, my mind couldn't react, only my eyes. Even so I couldn't believe that the burst of flame darting out of the turret, the tank's twitch and shudder, meant that a shot was fired. And then another. Two frozen images. But in between the two, a terrifying explosion. Then a third shot, though all that could do was hit the blast, the mayhem, the clouds of dust, and follow up with yet another explosion. Everything was blown away.

[IS]

GYÖRGY KONRÁD

from *The Case Worker*

It is not duty that keeps me here. If I really wanted to I could go home this minute; by this time of day most of my colleagues are watching television. I live with my family in a pleasant part of town, in an apartment commensurate with my professional status, with neighbours of like social standing. I came here only on a visit, to familiarise myself with the environment, and no amount of cheap metaphysics, born of fatigue, will convince me of the contrary. I know all about what goes on in these apartments – things heard and seen make for a kind of bond between them and me – but it is not a bond that holds me fast. These prehistoric beds have never carried me from baroque nights to naturalistic mornings. This hedge of decrepit objects never surrounded my awakenings. Though I am well acquainted with it, neither my hair, nor my skin, nor my clothes, are impregnated with the smell of poverty, that yellow star. I participate in the squabbles of the natives as a neutral but armed observer, a soldier, as it were, of the United Nations. Very little of what I see happens to me. I have never been paralysed, crippled, deaf-mute or blind, mine shafts have never collapsed on top of me, I have never fallen from scaffolding, no chemicals have exploded in my hands, no press has ever crushed me, no transmission belt carried off half my arm, no streetcar wheel amputated my foot, I have never had heart trouble or suspicious symptoms calling for histological analysis, no shock electrodes have been applied to my temples, thus far no peace-time death has started out in my direction. My family life is orderly, my mother is not confined to the chronic diseases ward or my father to a padded cell, my wife is not in jail. My loved ones do not sleep with axes under their pillows, nobody pushes me from behind when I lean out the window, nobody throws knives at me or puts dynamite in my cigarette, nobody pours lye in my wine, nobody denounces me to the police, I have not been shut up in a mental hospital or been thrown out of my home; I am generally well liked. I know that most of the people in this house spend their days as peacefully as I do, though perhaps in their case the backdrop is somewhat barer. There is a minority, however, who live in a state of perpetual siege; of course they've got used to it, but they complain and I listen to them day in and day out – this minority is composed of my clients. I know it's absurd, but it is becoming more and more difficult for me to close the door of my complaint-filled filing cabinet when I leave the office for the day. Sometimes I think that spending my days amid lost causes when I myself stand to lose nothing, living amid endless debt when I myself have no creditors, allotting twenty minutes or at the most half an hour to each appointment because others are waiting, putting off complainant and complainee on formal pretexts, trusting that they will shortly exchange roles, disposing of hopeless cases with a semblance of action, making hasty decisions on the basis of unconfirmed reports and prejudiced testimony, sacrificing lesser interests to greater interests with a minimum of hesitation, using preposterous legal phraseology to drown the unique individual case in an ocean of remotely similar cases, neglecting the usual for the unusual, taking the handy legal shortcut rather than the roundabout path of sympathy and indignation, dealing superficially with thousands of clients instead of giving three or four, or even one, the attention they deserve – all this, I sometimes think, is plain fraud.

Actually, what I do amounts to nothing. I regulate the traffic of suffering, sending it this way and that, passing on the loads that pile up on me to institutions or private citizens. But for the most part I wait, and try to stop others from doing anything. The raw material I work with fools me time and again, and since time will in any case modify my decisions, I try to get it to work with me. There's no hurry, no situation is irreversible, today's mortal danger will be nothing tomorrow and vice versa, today's nothing will be death. If I don't help my client, someone else will; if nobody helps him, he'll help himself; and if he can't, he will learn to bear his lot. But try as I may to encourage myself with such phrases, this child has undeniably become my lot.

This morning I was glued to the telephone, waiting for a line. I slammed down the receiver, dismissed my clients, told the doorman I wasn't in, pleaded, raged, shouted. My colleagues and my superiors, the other departments and the head office, would all have been glad to help me; they saw my point, they agreed with me, but unfortunately it was out of the question. Regular homes won't take him, neither would the psychiatric institute because he's unteachable; but there's no room in the mental hospital, and even if they let him share another patient's bed, he'd have to wait six weeks, because they've been quarantined for scarlet fever. The machinery has broken down, pull is ineffectual, even the back doors have closed. I hunt for relatives, acquaintances, anyone who will take him – I've got to do something quickly. I've never heard of any Bandula relatives, and they seem to have had no friends; no-one could stand them. And besides, who would be crazy enough to saddle himself with Feri? So here I am, busily doing what needs to be done. I get up from the bed, sit down on the chair, pick things up and pack them away, feed the child, wipe him with a wet cloth, endeavour to comb his helmet-like tangle of hair and rake the flakes of tobacco and dried moths out of it.

I can't take him home; our two rooms are barely enough for the four of us. There would be no-one to take care of him, because my wife works and my children go to school. And besides, Feri, what with the way he stamps, bounces, snarls and stinks, would hardly fit into my family. My wife would be sorry for him; in her spare time she would take better care of him than I could, but she wouldn't give up her job for his sake. My son and daughter wash their hands before meals without being told to; if they see a drunk in the street they turn their heads away, and when visiting Grandmother in the hospital they stand stiffly by the bed like soldiers being passed in review. They are good children, though perhaps a little too serious: they put on their school uniforms on holidays, think the history in their schoolbooks is more reliable than my stories, respect their teachers, disapprove of premature kissing and take me to task, employing the stock phrases learned at the day nursery, kindergarten and school; I don't think they would exactly welcome the idea of taking in my grimy protégé – who would be capable of biting them – for an indefinite period. If there's no other way, I'll have to take my holiday now and move in for a few weeks. That would settle it; perhaps I'll just stay here and fall asleep on Bandula's bed.

I look at the crowd scattering over the marketplace; I implore them to help me. I feel like the ageing clerk who, after smiling at his companions and greeting his superiors in the front ranks, is just about to slip away from the May Day parade, when someone thrusts a heavy banner into his hands. Now he can't leave, this cumbersome banner holds him fast; it's tiring, it's ridiculous, but he has to carry it; he can't palm it off on one of the women, or even on one of the younger men unless somebody volunteers. He looks around for someone to take it, but nobody does; and so, grimly bidding goodbye to the hoped-for day of rest, he trudges onward on swollen ankles, the heroic banner waving over his thinning hair.

[PA]

SÁNDOR TAR

Special Treat

The child waited in the dark, narrow frisking room beside the porter's cubicle with Miss Anna, her supervisor. Unbutton your coat, said Miss Anna, it's warm in here; did you hear what I said, she said later in a whisper, people came and went through the doorway, the barrier rose slowly before a blue lorry. Forty-two twenty-seven, shouted the porter standing outside. State Fuel and Building Material Company! Excuse me please, called Miss Anna through the partly open doors of the frisking room. There was a man sitting in the porter's cubicle writing something, you couldn't see the table. Hello, cried Miss Anna with her hands pressed against her breast, hello? The porter looked up, looking first in another direction before he spoke, Yes? Couldn't you call them again, asked Miss Anna, they may have forgotten we were coming today. Which workshop did you say, asked the porter and put on his glasses. The whetters, said Miss Anna, her voice faltering with excitement, then cleared her throat, the whetters, she repeated. I told you to unbutton your coat, didn't I? The little girl stared out through the crack in the door, counting the beads of perspiration trickling down her back and tickling her skin with her mouth open. Cosmos Workers Brigade, cried Miss Anna in the direction of the porter's cubicle, that was the name, Cosmos Brigade! There's no such thing as brigades here now, Miss, said the porter, who were you wanting to speak to, from the whetters? Miss Anna took out a handkerchief and wiped her face with it. I don't rightly know, she said, the people who were the child's patrons until now. Or is there no such thing as patrons either, any more? We used to come once a month, they give the child a special lunch and show her the factory. The porter hummed and hawed, shaking his head, then began to dial. Miss Anna pushed up the sleeve of her fur coat, looked at her watch, you stay here, she said, and stepped out into the foyer. Unbutton your coat, dear, she called back loudly, it's very hot in there! Through the crack in the door that cut a long strip out of her, she appeared to have only one leg, twenty, sighed Supa, the little girl, happily, darkness enclosed her, thick as mud, and she knew she couldn't move, ever again. She closed her eyes. They said you're to wait, said the porter, someone will be along soon, it's just that they're rather busy at the moment. Fine, said Miss Anna, thank you. The gate barrier rose again, something came in. Did you see that, dear? The nice man in there pushes a button, and the barrier rises. She pointed at the porter sitting in his cubicle. Supa stared at him with loathing. I told you to unbutton that damned coat, hissed Miss Anna, but I'm just wasting my breath, aren't I? With quick, strong fingers she began tugging at the buttons of the little girl's coat, have you got a handkerchief, she asked later, wipe your nose! Out in the street a car sounded its horn, Miss Anna looked at her watch again, then went to the porter's cubicle and knocked on the door. Hello? Look, she said, I'm in a rush, I've got to go, I'm very sorry I can't wait to meet the factory representative but I've really got to go! What? said the porter. Would you please just keep an eye on the child until these whetters or whatever you call them get here? The porter looked up in surprise, yawned, waited a moment, what, he asked finally, what do you want me to do? I'd like to leave the child here if I may, I've got to go. All right, said the porter, it's all right with me, and went on writing in a notebook. Miss Anna looked around. Don't you dare come out of there, you hear me? she told Supa, just do everything like I said. I've got to run. The little girl did not reply, goodbye, said Miss Anna, they'll bring you home when you're done. Then she knocked on the glass front of the porter's cubicle, goodbye, she said, goodbye, she said again to the other porter outside who, glancing after her, saw the large red-haired woman squeezing herself in beside a man into the waiting car.

Would you all please stop fucking around now, said Gémes, the foreman, the porter's called me up for the third time, saying there's some kid down there and to do something about it. Do what? Who's the kid, anyway? Whose kid is it? It isn't mine, said Bread, and put a handful of workpieces into his lap, I'm divorced and the wife got custody. He pulled the mask back over his mouth and pressed the first piece against the whetstone. The machines were aligned along the walls of the narrow, corridor-like workshop, slim, snaking pipes sucked and carried the dust away, rattling bronchitically, the walls, the floor, the windows were black, there was a smell of burning tallow in the air and bits of fluff floating, crates and boxes stood on the floor and whetstones stacked up in piles. Rozika, the foreman persisted, do you know anything about this? The thin dark woman stopped what she was doing, shrugged her shoulders and said, no more than the rest. They're just putting it on. She must be the brigade child, Andrea something, the kid the brigade used to be patrons of, it's all written up in the brigade diary. Mrs Nyári organised it all. Organised what? asked the foreman. The child, of course. What was there to organise about the child? Well, we helped her with her lessons, and every month one of the brigade members took her out to lunch as a special treat. Lunch? Yes, lunch, asserted Rozika, the foreman stared at her blankly. Me too? he asked. That's right, you too, said Kelemen, the burly, bald whetter, joining in the discussion, and what's more, me too! And me a bachelor! You can imagine the trouble it took me to make her a cup of tea! There was a burst of laughter. But I never even saw the child, said the foreman indignantly, once they were quiet again. Neither did we, said Német, glancing at him from above the rim of his glasses, but we got really fond of her. Didn't we, Bagos. Loved her like she was our own. There, in the diary. You mean it was written up in the brigade diary, helping her with her lessons and the lunches and all, and the child never . . . Exactly, said Rozika, Mrs Nyári put in something about her every week, you should know, you were the one who authorised it. We took them presents from Santa, which the children reciprocated with a lovely programme. The children did what? Reciprocated our kindness, that's how it was written in the diary. Anyone seen that diary about somewhere, asked the foreman, no, said several all at once, Mrs Nyári took it with her to her next place, she thought she could flash it around but we all know the rest, Rozika added. And how come they brought the kid here today, if they've never done it before? For a while no-one answered, there was just the drone of the machine furthest away and the steady, shrill whine, Bread did not take part in the discussion, he went on working. And there was the money we collected, Német said later, but I've spent it. What money? For the points. You authorised it, and patronising meant a lot of points, we came first, sometimes second. And they gave us money for the points. You leave me out of all this, said the foreman irritably, who the hell bothered to check what one signed, when it came to brigade affairs. Well, then . . . is someone going to take her then, or what are we going to do? Bread, lay off a minute, I can't hear a thing! Bread looked up, I can lay off all right, he said, if I get paid for it.

There was no mad scramble, Bread said his budget did not allow for unexpected expenditures of the kind. Kelemen's a bachelor, I'm not much of a hand at housekeeping, he said, there may be a little brandy or beer at home, if not I'll lay in a supply, depends on how many miles the kid does per gallon. Német asked whether the child was a boy or a girl, he hadn't quite caught the name. A girl? Nothing doing, then. And if it were a boy? Nothing doing then either, the wife's been feeling out of sorts ever since she fell against the philodendron, she won't even cook for him, let alone for a strange kid. Bagos said it was the last thing he needed, he was already paying maintenance for one kid, why should he take on another? And Rozika commutes. The foreman's eyes flicked nervously from one to the other, I can't take her home, he said constrainedly in the end, and everyone knew why, he was divorced and living with a young woman. Let's just carry on as if we didn't know about her, said Bread, just walk right past her when we go past the porter's cubicle, she doesn't know us. How can you say such a thing, Rozika snapped indignantly, you should be ashamed of yourself! And besides, the porter knows us, said Német, and he'd hand over the little orphan to one of us for certain. Someone suddenly came up with a bright idea, let them take her back then, that would be the best thing, let them take her home! That's right, cried the others, relieved, we've got to tell them brigades and patronising have been scrapped. Rozika shook her head in disapproval, well I hope you don't mind my saying so but I for one feel ashamed of myself. To do this to a kid! But the foreman had already rushed off to telephone, the others had set the machines going, put on their masks, the drone and the whine grew louder, the specks flying off the whetstones sparkled like fireworks.

The foreman put down the telephone, feeling like he'd been beaten up. The woman who brought the child had left, telling the porter that they would be taking the child home, once they had taken her out to lunch. On top of it all, we don't even know where the child comes from, because she doesn't know herself, he told Rozika discouragedly. A fine state of things, said the woman, poor child. Well, there's only one thing we can do, said the foreman later, I'll just have to call up and find out the addresses of all the institutions and which of them's missing a little girl called Andrea something. What does she look like, asked Rozika, I didn't see her over the phone, snapped the foreman irritably, all I know is what the porter told me, she's about ten years old and won't take off her coat, she's pouring with sweat and when you ask her what her name is all she'll say is Supa. Otherwise she's a sweet little thing, he added wryly. I'll take her home, said Rozika, but I can only bring her back in the morning, and I'll bring her here. After all, we can't just . . . out of all these people, there's not one who'll . . .

All right, said the foreman gruffly, I'll take her home! But where shall I take her afterwards? Would you tell me that? We'll leave a message with the porter, said Rozika, if anyone should come looking for her . . . Gémes sighed and said, go and take a look at the child, I'll be along in a minute.

Elvira! Virácska! Gémes was calling her name before he had shut the door behind him, pushing the little girl ahead of him. A thick-lipped woman with too much make-up on appeared from somewhere within the depths of the flat, wearing a lacy nightgown of sorts, coming up with lazy steps, then stopped, who's that, she asked. Gémes began to explain, took off his coat, kissed the woman, laughed confusedly, we'll bear it somehow, just this once, he said, someone will be coming to fetch her soon, darling, don't pull that nice sulky face at me, come on, what shall we do. The woman did not say anything, she stared at the child as though she were a plant or something, stared at this pale, skinny, sweating, unkempt little figure whose eyes were burning with hatred. What's your name, dear, she asked later, but the child did not reply. Her name is Andrea, Gémes finally said instead of her, and the little girl glanced at him contemptuously. Supa, she cried in a harsh, bitter voice. All right, all right, said Elvira, there's no need to jump down my throat. If it's Supa you prefer, Supa it will be. Were you planning on having her eat with us, she asked, turning to the man, or what? There's room enough, said Gémes, or would you rather not? It's all the same to me, said the woman, just get her unwrapped somehow, or she'll be roasted alive before our eyes, I don't know, I don't want to touch her. We're having soy-bean stew for lunch, and a mixed salad. Marvellous, enthused Gémes, marvellous!

Nuisance, thought Supa, then something else came into her head, nonsense. Nonsense nuisance. They told her to take off her coat and wash her hands. She stood in a room. It was a pity she had lost count, another drop of perspiration was running down her back, melting away a little lower down this time, somewhere around her waist, if she moves there won't be another. She pushed her right foot slowly forward, it's nice and warm in here, she felt the tiny beads forming on her forehead and under her lip, it's nice here. She did not hear what they were saying, she felt several drops trickling down her back all at once, Gémes wanted to take off her coat from behind, he spoiled everything! And the woman, with finger and thumb, from the front, AND HER FACE WITH A RAG! She bit her hand.

All right, get the little beast out of here, said Elvira, pressing a paper handkerchief to her hand. I can't stand the sight of her! She's not a child, she's an animal! Darling, did she bite you very hard? Show me! Gémes put his arm around the woman's shoulder but she shrugged it off, and repeated, syllable by syllable, get-her-out-of-here! Go on, get going! Then she went into one of the rooms, the man followed her, look, there's nowhere to take her, what do you want me to do with her? Where do you want me to put her? Out in the street or down the drain, came from somewhere within the room, it's all the same to me, I just don't want to lay my eyes on her again. Colonial-style furniture in the spacious living-room, a fireplace with green tiles around it, armchairs, fur rugs, an enormous mirror, soft carpets, a bunch of flowers, peace and quiet, and now in the middle of it all there stands this little monster with her dark stare and grubby face in her filthy soiled coat, not saying anything, not moving. For a moment Gémes could not believe his own eyes, he hoped he was only dreaming. See what you've done, he asked the child, but she just stared at him with wild anger in her eyes. All right, said Gémes, we're going to get in the car and we're going to drive until we find this institution of yours. Come on, get going, out! The child did not move, just stared at him, Gémes made to touch her, and at last she spoke, you creep. And smiled faintly, as though she were glad she had thought of something. Then she moved towards the door of her own accord.

Gémes stopped the car when, on a sudden impulse, Supa leaned forward and snapped off the sunshield. Until then she had squirmed restlessly, struck the window once or twice with her fist, stood up. Damn and blast you, he said, turning round to face her, what the hell have you done now? What the bloody hell's the matter with you? Hey? The child's face was still perspiring, though the window was down in front. Have you gone out of your tiny mind? Just you wait, I'll chuck you out of here by the scruff of your neck, like a cat, or else hand you over to a policeman! Silly little nit. The child banged the sunshield down on the floor of the car, I'm peeing, she retorted at last. You doing what . . . ? It took a while to register but Gémes finally realised that he had to jump out of the car, drag the kid out, make for the nearest pub and shove her in the loo. Dear God, he grumbled to himself, wiped his brow, took a look around. It was an ordinary pub, a couple of tables, noisy, smoke-filled, ill-smelling. At one of the back tables sat Kelemen and Németh, yes, no mistake! He waved at them but they did not notice him, he moved aside so they'd have a better view of him, at last! Kelemen raised his bottle of beer in greeting, Gémes grinned and waved at him. We're not having anything, he said when they came over, we're well away, aren't we, pal? You said it, said Német, you said it. Listen, said Gémes, you've got to help me out somehow. You know I took that little girl home . . . That was real kind of you, said Német, and we were saying, among ourselves you know, that the foreman, well, it just goes to show you . . . That's not the problem, complained Gémes, the problem is that the child bit my wife, I'd take her back but I just can't cope with her alone. She bit her, did she, asked Kelemen, showing interest and leaning against Német, and which part of your dearest did she . . . Silly bugger, said Német, and where are you going to go now? He hiccuped. I'm trying to find out where she belongs, I'd have taken her back already but I can't because . . . And where are they now, I mean the kid, asked Kelemen, I expect they're taking a walk while you take a nip . . . She's in the toilet, replied Gémes nervously, and taking her time, he thought. Which one? Oh, I don't know . . . this one, I think. That's the men's, said Német, and someone's got to go in and fetch them? Yes, agreed Gémes, and I need someone to keep an eye on her while I go find that orphanage or home or whatever . . . You know, you're a good man, said Kelemen, just don't spread it around, I live nearby, if I remember right, which way was it, Német? Out this way and then how was it, anyway, they can stop over at my place while you go . . . wherever . . . They argued for a little while longer until Kelemen finally understood that Elvirácska hadn't come, only the little orphan was here, and she had gone for a pee, had been gone for a good half-hour, her kidneys must be something special, shouldn't have given her so much beer to drink, at that age they don't need assistance to drop off to sleep, well, fetch the girl then, Német, she'll be all right with me, we'll rub along somehow, she'll hand me the beer and do the wash and the whitewash and the washing up. I've got a shopping bag on me, you know, he said later, when Német had dragged Supa out of the toilet, and Gémes got the message and ordered five bottles of beer to put in it. The child might fancy a drop, said Kelemen, while her daddy's away. He isn't her daddy? Well then, who is this girl? Oh! Yes, of course! Come along then, girl, or d'you want a snifter before we go to make up for all the fluid you just lost, where did all that pee come from, how d'you do it? Just when and if you fancy, and . . . Német joined them up, you take hold of your daddy here, here's his hand, just don't let go of it or else he'll fall and all the bottles will be broken, there now . . . The child looked up at Kelemen with stern eyes and gripped his hand firmly. Gémes watched them from the car, he knew where Kelemen lived, he was the one who had been with him when he'd been taken home in an ambulance. He watched them stagger along and saw that the child kept such a tight hold on the old man's hand that his shoulder was bowed. I don't envy him, thought Gémes, and started the car.

Kelemen lived in the building that housed the pub but in the back of it, in a lean-to, one room, a kitchen and a tiny entrance hall and that was it, there was a shed of sorts rotting to pieces a little way off, a couple of trees, it was dark, the light of the street lamps did not reach this far. Kelemen fumbled with the door for a long time before they were finally able to get in and did not stop speaking all the while. He sometimes called Supa Miss, and sometimes Madam, here we are, then, he said, when he succeeded in opening the door, I'll have the light on in a minute, this way. An unmade bed with a rumpled quilt, a pillow, no sheets, two tables, a single chair. A piece of coloured material hung from the top of the window, in front of it stood an old-fashioned bench and under it an array of empty bottles. It was warm in the flat, so warm that even Kelemen noticed it, it's warm in here, he said, suddenly breaking off the story he was telling, but there's nothing we can do about it, he patted the radiator, the heat comes from the pub, he explained, and it can only be turned off from there, what does it matter. Well, it would be better if it was beer coming through this thick pipe, but it's no use telling them that. Sit down, your daddy will be coming to fetch you soon, he's a good man, I remember . . . Kelemen suddenly stopped, no, he said after a while, I don't remember any more. He opened a bottle of beer with the cap of another and drank.

Supa stood where she had let go of the burly man's hand, it was nice and warm in here, just like in the other place, clothes strewn about everywhere, Miss Anna will give her a beating, the smell, the old man took off his shirt and, and, he was sweating all over! She too could feel the warm wetness on her back, waited for the moment when the first one would start trickling down, but HE had oceans of them! On his back, on his chest, on his brow, and he drank, and told stories, and now, now, it had started! Supa breathed a sigh of relief, then unbuttoned her coat without taking her eyes off the old man for a minute, watched this beautiful, great body bathed in beads of perspiration, all pearls, then slowly lowered the coat to the floor, come on, she heard, have a drop of beer! Back in the old days, in the foreign legion, this was the way your uncle Németh and I tore the snakes into ribbons, like an expander, and the Arabs went out of their minds 'cos it was a sacred snake or something . . . Supa went up close to him, put her hand on Kelemen and laughed, the old man went on talking, gesticulating, later he showed her some kind of dance, at times the child was gasping for breath she was laughing so hard, then suddenly found herself telling stories in turn, about her father, who was a giant and came and went among them with a whip, and her mother, who tried on her father's tie and hung like that and laughed until they took her down, and she was still laughing when they were trying to find her shoe because it had fallen off her foot, and someone found it on the window sill, and about Miss Anna too, who always takes someone out to lunch to some factory and leaves them there, and they all know she's on the job meanwhile, but it's better if she isn't there, all the same. Supa talked and talked, the words rushing out, sometimes swallowing hard, the old man, blinking stupidly, laughed at everything she said, and the girl too laughed at it all, sipped beer, lit matches, then suddenly fell silent. What's up, asked the old man. I peed in my pants, said the child happily, upon which Kelemen burst out laughing again, why, that's nothing, never you mind, he said in a while, gasping for breath, so did I! So did I! There . . . stop laughing now, it's a serious matter, this . . . He tried to get up from the puddle but never quite made it, he kept falling back, waved his hand sadly, and went on laughing, Supa too, they couldn't stop.

When Gémes opened the door on them around midnight, Kelemen was snoring on the bed, and the little girl was sitting on the bench in a long green dressing gown and smoking, beside her on the floor lay an empty beer bottle and a comb. She stood up slowly. She knew by then she would never leave here.

[EMol]

MIHÁLY KORNIS

from *Lifebook: The Hero of Our Story*

I

TO DIE

A hot, muggy day. The minute he opens his eyes he feels his bad temper, the lead settle on him. Lying hairy and naked on the sheet he blinks his eyes, surprised as always at the suddenness. Surprised that the pleasant taste of some inconsequential dream is still in my mouth, he's already thinking that every moment of the day will be pure hell. That once again defeat lies waiting for him at the starting line. All is lost, the world's gone mad, Hungary is lost, I'm forty-three, and not writing . . . Try as I might, it just won't come. It won't. What should I do? What can I do? My writer's cramp. I loathe it. I've made a thorough mess of my life, writing plays out of impotence, while the knowledge, the knowledge, it's stuck inside, fossilised in some dark recess of the heart.

He climbs out of bed.

My wife sees his face and tactfully retreats to the kitchen.

She gives him fruit. She pretends she's reading the papers. We say nothing.

The aggressive sun shines through the kitchen window. Yellowish-red shafts of light. Back perspiring, last night comes to him, when after hours of fitful desperation worse, even, than usual, he stands up pale as a ghost from his desk and gropes his way to the bathroom. I hang my head.

He's terrified of sympathy.

Still, later on they quietly sat down side by side anyway and something he did not usually do, he spoke to his wife of his literary wasteland, how awkward! He said to her, listen, if I can't write, I don't want to live. But the thought of suicide is obnoxious to him, you know, it's the coward's way out . . . He's been at a loss lately, honest! Altogether too bitter to play the fool, the addict, the alcoholic. Or to weep . . . It's just that I have no idea what I'm doing here! His parents, his relatives, they're all dead. My friends have deserted me, and I have deserted them in turn. He won't chase after women, I wouldn't want to break your heart, nor mine neither, for that matter; besides, as he gets on in years, the diminishing casual bouts of cheating – need he spell it out? – lie heavy on his conscience. In short, it's just not worth the bother.

Not to mention Aids.

It was a bitch, but he even gave up smoking. He needed his strength to work, should it ever come to that. For the same reason, he wouldn't allow himself to smoke grass either – goodness, I've got to watch the purity of my infertile thoughts, if you know what I mean; besides (it's no use hiding it from you) literature bores me to tears, politics ditto, while the atmosphere's turning more fascist by the hour, there's no stopping it; which, considered together – his writer's dementia especially – leads to himself catching himself flirting with the notion of sudden death as if it were the grand prize in the state lottery, an unlooked-for stroke of good fortune, a legal escape hatch, and that this morning, when he went to the cemetery to see his parents, because he hadn't been out there in years, I caught myself counting how many headstones I could find of people who had died younger than me, and he was relieved to note that on this earth it did not count as bad manners to die at the age of forty-three . . .

Naturally, I will not give in, he kept repeating as he paced up and down in front of the terrified woman, no sirree, not me, it's the sheer improbability of it that makes me want to believe in my rebirth. Besides, running scared is against his principles; having come this far I want to see it through, and he wants his wife to understand, the fact that at times he is capable of writing something promising while at other times he is blocked for years on end, not to mention the fact that he's got to vacillate between these two extremes all his life, having to put up with the curious – and at times malicious – prying of others, well, this is pure torture, my daily bread!

And our lives, too, Manyika, gone bad, in the past year or two everything's gone bad. Or have we simply grown old?

Jumping to my feet, I get into my clothes – in the sweltering heat he's heading for the pool, he, the writer who does not write . . .

Should I turn back now that I am here? Why did I come?

So I can go home, he thought.

Swimming bores me to death. It always has.

I want to die, he thought.

He'll go home and lie down on his bed, never to get up again. Manyi's going to beg me in vain, no, I'll say, no, no, stop pestering, and if you won't support me, have the kindness to lock me up in an asylum. But she won't. She's going to feel sorry for me. And support me until I croak.

Of course it's just a thought, the foolish Tábor thought.

And then the Jewish cemetery came to mind on that muggy, stifling morning yesterday, all that dark green around him, and a light intermittent drizzle, the foliage oozing, death perspiring, death the good, death the inconsequential, sluggish non-existence on the periphery of town, et cetera, et cetera; food for thought when I write my novel, he thought at the far end of the cemetery as he was looking for his aunt's grave, stroking the blackened gravestones under the heavy foliage moist under his palms despite the sweltering heat, except just then something terrifying – though considering the unrelenting failures of the past fifteen years, the terrifying certainty was only natural – crept into his heart, to wit, *you will never write about it because you cannot write novels, it's all you can do noting down what you remember, the fact that you had a family, you know, they're all dead now to the last man, your father, your mother; keeping a record, tallying! the Book, Writing . . . badly, but the main thing is that it be done, you're the last of the lot, you scum, it's not the novel but their favourite food and their laughter, that's what you should be noting down!*

Sure, sure, but what's the use of remembering for its own sake, the foolish Tábor asked himself. Who cares about my family's history? These people don't, the fascists don't, while Gyuri Perl, all he does is drink, and as for the rest, I don't give a damn. We have no children, we have no-one, tomorrow or the day after it's the end of the world, I'll never write anything ever again, I am bereft of hope because I have no hope, though who knows, possibly this afternoon, a miracle . . . that's how I launched into **a handful is not enough: in praise of over-developed honkers** back in '75, and though he'd been walking along the narrow corridor for some time unawares, heading for the exit, the foolish Tábor changed his mind once again and, gaping into space, turned around and trampled into the locker room, an obese mouse, after which for forty straight minutes, desperately gasping for air, he agonised in the water over how he would start this thing in the afternoon.

To be perfectly honest, he hadn't the foggiest.

2

NIHT FORDEM KIND

The cemetery, all that green, dark green, poison green, death green!

When they first took me I was just a child, though not to a dead relative, but so we could probe, sound and fathom the wall of the martyrs, the Wall of the Martyrs – or however it's got to be written! – the newly finished wall of the martyrs (Wall of the Martyrs), or at least my father did, to be precise. Anxious Sunday morning preparations; before starting out they brushed me several times, my hair, my clothes, Grandad put on spats, Mother checked my teeth in a small compact mirror, and her own, too. Dad she just warned to do likewise. I was made to grin into a small hand-held compact and she grinned, too, then took me to the bathroom. Healthy we were, that's for sure, but by the time we got on the tram we were at loggerheads, Dad whacked my bottom, his bass baritone booming on the back platform so his head turned purple, with Grandad hissing at him, which just made Dad bend into it all the more, "I want to get off, my family hates me, my lot is misery!" he ranted, the sweat trickling from under his hat as we got off on the outskirts of town.

That's when I saw how far out they had put the cemetery of the Jews.

In '55 – or was it '57? – a couple of days after the unveiling of the Wall of the Martyrs, driven by curiosity, Dad took the family to the Jewish cemetery.

Where I had never been before.

Or who knows. You never know. Kozma utca number 6.

They were stumped. What were they going to say to me? I could see that right away. We're going to the cemetery, they said, but don't you worry, it'll be very nice. While I felt sorry for them thinking I don't know about death, I decided to be tactful and not ask any questions. Instead I turned my back to them and played hopscotch on the parquet floor.

They said, too – it was Dad who said, I guess – we are going to visit Grandmother, what I mean is, you're going now to visit both your grandmothers, while I added to myself, "who are in the ground", though I couldn't see it too concretely in the mind's eye, or anything, see what it's like. "Like the dead are." Or who knows. As I've just said, it was going to be my first time. I didn't bother my head much about it. Not that there wasn't plenty of furtive jabbering about the Wall of the Martyrs for days beforehand, during dinner, for instance – **niht fordem kind**, not in front of the child! – but for some reason I figured this Wall of the Martyrs was like a statue, except it wasn't a statue but a wall, because the government had at long last bowed to an old and legitimate demand of the Working Masses, a bunch of grown-up nonsense, nothing to fret about.

At the time I had no very clear notion of the Jews, who they are. I still don't. And yet I racked my brains a lot more over this problem than anyone would expect, or (especially) expected at the time! Poor Mum and Dad. Because for one thing, it was around this time that Albert Russell's book on the history of the liquidation (a quaint contemporary expression) of European Jews, *The Scourge of the Swastika*, was published, and it being profusely illustrated with a bunch of riveting pictures, Grandad spent months poring over it without losing interest, ever, but having to make frequent visits to the loo, he'd often forget it on the couch, alas!, which is how I got my first glimpse of mountains of corpses, death marches, sterilised twins and charred skeletons.

Or whatever.

I had this thing about photographs, you see, and generally pictures of all kinds, and I'd sneak a look at such stuff with trepidation, as if I'd seen it before but wanted to see it again, whereas this book (among others) was strictly off limits to me. Yes indeed. Naturally, I got all worked up and queasy, knowing right away I shouldn't have looked, what's more, that it was really very thoughtful of my parents forbidding me in no uncertain terms, because it really was not for my innocent soul, I might get scared witless thinking I was a Jew myself.

Because it just so happens I wasn't. Just my folks. Like in those Jewish jokes.

For one thing, I was not circumcised, ha-ha!, and no rabbi ever saw me, and I wasn't given a Jewish name or entered in the congregation records, which means I'm non-denominational, my parents explained, only to repeat it over and over again later, around '56, should anybody ask, you are non-denominational, and don't you forget it!

But this is just an aside to this other incidental cemetery episode when . . . but where was I? . . . when at the gate I had to take their hands, and I was excited and a little awed because right by the fence I saw all those mausoleums with the sooty walls, a bunch of shitty old death houses, the graves – which of course I didn't know at the time

– of barons and bankers' families, and so I said, could we please leave and go to the two grandmothers instead?

In short, where are we headed? And why are we headed that way?

Because we were keeping to the side wall, you see, stubbornly to the side wall, as if Mum and Dad had no intention at all of visiting the graves. But they wouldn't answer this question of mine either, which scared me. They had changed beyond recognition, the skin taut around their faces; they had grown old, their shoulders stooping in such a strange way, my father taking his father's arm, whereas usually he wouldn't even talk to him! I turned to Mum, but she didn't hear me either, or pretended not to, her pretty lips becoming repugnantly thin, as if she had meant to close them once and for all.

She yanked me along by the wrist. I felt the heat.

A hot autumn day, not too hot but hot enough, a broody, misty day, leaf-cluttered, stifling. And no-one heard me squall! They dragged me along the ground, no reproaches, no whacking my behind, they just stared ahead, into thin air. They had also turned sooty, or so it seemed to me . . . Also, I would have liked to ask something I had pointedly and conveniently forgotten till then, namely, what was I expected to do when we got there? On the playground it's playing on the swing, at kindergarten it's being a good boy, on the bus it's looking politely out the window. But now? What are we children expected to do in a case like this? But by then I was breathless from the excitement – no, it was fear! – the picture before me shattered into a thousand fragments, as it always did in moments of panic, the air like oatmeal, and brown; I might have even shrieked, I'm not sure, but no, because Dad's turning to face me after all, I can see it in the mind's eye, his lips ashen, he stamps his foot, he's promised himself to turn a deaf ear to my histrionics at least here, within these walls, but too much is too much and I'd better come to my senses or else, but it's him who is not in his senses, I see, his eyes flashing as if the roots of his hair hurt, a blue flame darting in his eye! and he's trembling like an aspen leaf, trembling, and on the verge of tears . . .

Then suddenly we're there, in a clearing, abruptly, a colossal emptiness as if somebody had first bombed it, then carefully raked it. **Somebody. The Hungarian fascists, the Arrow Cross. A janitor, to ease his conscience.**

"The death wall," I hear.

Which makes me prick up my ears. And wouldn't you know. There, to the right, something that looks to me like gigantic walls of stone. **Death walls.**

At their base hunch-backed couples, married couples, Sunday people. Hardly any children. But plenty of bow-legged old women, though, with glass jars and flowers, and men like my father, in hats. But the way they move about, it's really peculiar, first sneaking up to the wall real close, as if trying to sniff it, then backing off hurriedly, as if they didn't really want to see, just make sure . . . Sure of what?

Hands clasped behind their backs, necks craned, puny bird-folk, Jewish cranes, glancing at the wall one minute, blinking cagily at us the next, what do we make of it? **You people are Jews, too, are you not? Well, the boy's bound to grow out of it. Besides, you are lucky. It hardly shows by the size of your family! We should have it so good. However, let us not look at each other any more, you mind? It's too obvious!** Some of them kneel by the wall, murmuring . . . I feel sick to my stomach.

"The death wall," Grandad repeats matter-of-factly.

Mum and Dad swallow hard. Their cheeks ashen, they assume the cagey bird posture, then gingerly ease up to the wall, all the way up . . . For some reason I decide it would be best after all if I ran off to play at a distance, a familiar, comforting game, nothing to worry about. Make myself scarce. It's just another one of those excursions, really, when grown-ups get themselves muddled up in those ridiculous self-consciously grown-up things; but they're bound to stop after a while, no need sticking to them, "death wall", what a way of putting it! Well, let them have their fill of looking, a monstrosity, but they'll stop sooner or later, and then we can go visit the two grandmothers in the ground.

But I can't resist the temptation and go up the wall myself.

Why?

Because even at the gate I was probably squalling because it struck me – never mind that I didn't want to know – **that I know, though it is strictly forbidden, yes, we were liquidated in the war. But fine, I don't know, I pretend I don't know. Except I'm mature, grown old before my time, and when they first told me I already knew how it's these camp Jews that were jammed into the wall, slapped into the back, poor souls, first carefully slapped into the brick by the sadistic fascists then fired in a kiln, but it doesn't hurt because once you're dead nothing hurts any more, so it was no use them wanting to hurt, except now they can't be let out again, it can't be done, these ashes-and-dust Jews, Auschwitz**

Jews dragged home against their will, but why, I wonder?, so the survivors can see and touch the wall, at least? they've piled their relatives up to make a wall for Sunday-morning strollers, monstrous, they come here then haven't got the nerve to go up close, they're secretly afraid of it, for all they know it might bite, the anger, the anger of the innocent stuck inside the wall; of course, if I were to ask them – you can bet your sweet life they'd flatly deny it, and when I grow up I'm going to flatly deny it in front of my children too, let the dead do their thinking in the ground, what did they go die for, why, when I have hardly lived!, that's the sort of miserable Jews we are, except the proletarian state has graciously allowed us to join the ranks of the workers and if we don't act up, we might even survive, not to mention a cemetery, way out in shitsville but our very own, but the main thing is not to make an issue of it, going round bragging from pillar to post, poor Mother, too, where is her other husband? and Dad's fat sister, what a disgusting, pitiful lot we are, if only I knew what there was in that wall worth gaping at, what a laugh, first they bring them here, then they goggle at them like a shop window, phew!, contemplating their own deaths with other people's eyes . . .

In short, I tiptoed over, you might say, and – now comes the interesting part – I saw . . . I see the death wall is scribbled full of names, hundreds of thousands of names, **names and names and names** like ants marching in thick columns up and down and sideways, the names of all those burnt Jews, I realise with a shudder, and as if that weren't bad enough, **these names got incised into them, into the wall, as if dying wasn't bad enough, their bodies written on, some religious dictate, perhaps? one of those batamt Jewish things?** I wonder; however, as I draw closer, hopping on one foot to get a better look at the Sunday-morning survivors, curious to see what Jewish custom prescribes must be done in front of one of these whatchamacallit martyr walls or whatever, because I happen to know from Grandad's goings-on that they have some real queer customs, **or had**, the Israelites, **who are they?**, a good thing it's been discontinued, legally banned, otherwise the family would be kept busy all day, like Grandad in the closet, when nobody's looking –

so then: I look and see the poor things standing by the wall, feeling more and more familiar, not looking at each other quite so intensely, most of them not even concerned with the dead names, the newcomers, it's they who are trying to make them out with a faint blush, with guarded interest, lest some unauthorised stranger should think they're also Yids, God forbid, **oh, no, they're just studying this thing or whatever out of idle curiosity, isn't it fascinating, those Hitler victims, the ovens, all those names, is that a fact . . . ?** while their heads covered with handkerchiefs Dad and Grandad, for instance, are murmuring something on their knees, Grandad's flung his greatcoat on the ground, he's kneeling right up against the wall, gesticulating vehemently and talking –

talking?!

yes, bowing and muttering

and doing stuff with his arms

and Dad too!

But by then I hear the droning. Like a circling band of insects, louder and louder, I'm all ashiver, yes, it's coming from the wall, and those that come here secretly come for this.

They're all chit-chatting with the wall!

Especially the elderly, shouting soberly, but impatiently, WHAT'S WITH LICI, TELL ME ABOUT LICI, MRS ÁRMIN RÓNA, BORN LICI MINK, LISTEN, ÁRPÁD'S GONE OUT OF HIS MIND, HEADING FOR AUSTRALIA WITHOUT A PENNY TO HIS NAME, LEAVING A SECURE LIVELIHOOD BEHIND, AND THE PARTY, TOO, WHAT SHOULD I TELL YOUR DAUGHTER, FREIDMANN, HOW DID YOU DIE, DAD, HELP ME, PLEASE, THAT CHILD'S A NERVOUS WRECK NOW THAT YOU'RE NOT AT HIS BECK AND CALL, THEY WON'T TAKE HIM AT UNIVERSITY BECAUSE OF HIS PAST, AND THAT MANCI BÍRÓ, COMPLAINING ABOUT EVERYTHING, IT'S ENOUGH TO DRIVE ME NUTS, THE HOUSING MANAGEMENT NATIONALISED THE ENTIRE STOCK, UNDERSTAND? EVERYTHING WE EVER HAD! THEY'LL MAKE NO EXCEPTIONS, BUT YOUR STROMAN, HE'S A DECENT SORT, GIVING US BACK WHAT HE COULD, TELL ME, YOU DO EAT FROM TIME TO TIME ANYWAY, DON'T YOU? I AM LOOKING FOR ATTORNEY-AT-LAW SAMU HAJÓS, BÉRKOCSIS UTCA. 17/B, SECOND FLOOR, APARTMENT THREE, BLUE EYES, BROWN HAIR, ALL GOODNESS AND PURITY PURPOSE and the like

but the chatter, the feverish answers coming from the wall I couldn't make out very well partly because the excited cackle of the living, husky with emotion, drowned out the hundred-thousand-million voices of the dead, and partly because, to be perfectly honest, you couldn't make it out even if there were a deadly silence around the wall, there being too many of them talking all at once, **inside the wall too squirming and writhing baked together in a raving frenzy**

probably all hoping someone would come specifically to them begging giving name and address pleading for news of lost relatives just in case but never oh it's out of the question in this infernal din it's always somebody else the relatives are looking for and the dead too are looking for somebody else, their numbers so great they have to outshout each other till their lungs burst, all those Jews screaming themselves hoarse and beyond **ah! at last I understand** but of course I don't, repulsed, I sneak a furtive look at Grandad Miksa, his palm pressed hard against the wall, his head, mad-relentless, lowered towards the ground, shouting on his knees **who to I wonder, did others in our family also die in the war? did everybody? and not just Magduska and Uncle Poldi? except they didn't have the nerve to tell me to my face before, poor Grandad, he's probably trying to introduce me to the family right now, but it's no use screaming and shouting among these millions, and it's no use pretending that he can**, a handkerchief tied into knots at its four corners trembling awkwardly on his bald pate, I'd like to run over to him, he's not far, but just then Dad bars the way, picks me up and kisses me feverishly on the cheek, he's pulled off his coat too now and sits me on his arm, covering my eyes with kisses dripping with saliva and emotion, "let him be, it's what he's been pleading for, let him bark himself hoarse, well, how do you like it, what have you got to say," peevishly I stretch myself in his arm, "nothing, and how much longer is this going to last, and where is Mum," I feel a profound depth of shame, I cling to his arm, "put me down," wonder of wonders, he does as he is told, he puts me down, what's more, he runs to the other side of the wall, his shirt ridiculously bobbing over his belly, he must have heard something, his name, most likely, yes, **they're calling out to him, it's his turn now, but who?** I sneak after him but at the corner of the wall I bump into my mum, she's out of sorts, her eyes cold and empty, looking in her handbag for a cigarette, "leave your father be, why don't you run on back to play, and don't mind about us," she's pacing up and down the symmetrically raked gravel, leaning slightly forward, her light coat flapping in the resurgent lukewarm wind, I'm thinking **she won't even look at me** and **her lipstick, it turns her lips the colour of raw meat** and it also strikes me how **her other husband is here, too, the one she loved more** and I forget to go search for my father, I stare back at that horrible wall, it's so brazen which is something else I mustn't talk to anybody about either, I bet.

– – – And it was no use me wailing on the way out either, let's go to the two grandmothers in the ground – – –

. . . On the other hand, Dad made a special point of taking me to the glassed-in iron cage across the entrance-exit, it's still there today, a stone's throw from the mortuary

and unhappily it transpired that in that ear-splitting din and cloud storm of frayed nerves whirling around the memorial candle I thought I heard that the red tongue of flame Dad said would never die away, that this feeble, greyish nothing of a flame burning in the iron cage, that it is truly **eternal, eternal fire**.

In short I believed that it was never lit and would never be extinguished, and that it was burning for us. What's more, that possibly it's us Jews burning in there, in our very own cemetery, as a warning, what I mean is, a warning to others how **never again, Europe, take care**, and the like. Because at the time that's the sort of spiel that was in vogue.

Yes, this is us – there I stood, a bundle of confusion and none too happy either – puny enough as the flames go, but eternal.

A Jewish flame.

3

GREEN GRAVEYARD FIELDS

In the morning, headed for the cemetery.

I set off, perky as can be, yes indeed. In the passage leading to József Boulevard he even catches himself heading for his father's and mother's grave with such lithe steps, holding his tears together like an orator his say or a future bridegroom his bouquet of posies. But between Stáhly utca and Népszínház utca the metropolis, gone bad, launches its relentless assault on him, it's like trying to keep from bumping into some old beggar woman grown oblivious to the world around her who'd like to pick his pockets too, but it is late, death in the offing, my native town a filthy bag lady dropping greyish clumps of cotton from her panties on to the sidewalk, or what is this, this morning's head-on collision. The thing is not to look. Autumn in midsummer, the July sky the colour of whey. The atmosphere oppressive.

The muted melancholy, the newspaper stands on Blaha Lujza

Square with their frightfully bad atmosphere. He just stands there, asking for nothing, looking the hoodlums that call themselves newspaper vendors resolutely in the eye. But cowardice wins the day and in the end, he buys a *Kurír*. He's profoundly disappointed. He'd hardly set out, and already he's forgotten to grieve. As I approach Kőbánya I stash the paper away, under my bum, and I look out, at nothing, then preoccupied I take it out again, nothing there either, I put it away again . . . He's there before he knows it. Beyond the Christian plots the semolina-dumpling sky is yellower, perhaps, than here. Leaning more to yellowish-grey, though legally the same. We do not discriminate here: this is one jailhouse Globe, with Hungary on it, and the so-called cemetery block, the size of an ant's supper, if that. A pinprick. It won't hurt. He trips over the streetcar rail overgrown with grass, springs hurriedly to his feet and is soon inside. The trap is sprung.

Past the gate, the small office building, in the rain. Around it steaming paving-brick and the cement path leading to the inner gate, where it is not raining. Which is only natural. The office, it's wicked. Always has been. It's legendary. I'd never seen it when it wasn't raining. Even the sky's got to put up defences. It's always pouring on top of the office. Just ask anybody. It's a bad place, an evil place, pernicious and pestilential, mean, corrupt and vulgar. A while back, seven years ago, Mr Havasi's hypocritical, grovelling Gypsies, at my mother's funeral, some rotten deal, lousy, the whole thing, and that shamus too in the opaque heat of the mortuary, who for the furtively presented tip from me furtively uncovered the "recently deceased" laid out in the furtively presented coffin, and that lady clerk with the nasal voice sitting behind the glass contemplating her two hands atop the catalogue as she worked, not to mention the long lines . . .

For them. It's raining for them.

I wasn't in the habit of visiting the place before because we weren't in the habit of dying before. For decades I didn't even know where it was, much less that there were disguised jail offices such as this, various forms of payment, plus windbag-rationalist priests. So-called rabbis.

I storm in.

Past the gate, though, he hesitates, stopping in his tracks.

A middle-aged woman in a white smock hurries past him. She's heading for the office. She looks at him, her eyes the colour of fading forget-me-nots.

Can I help you?

She has pulled a hood over her head. A transparent raincoat is stretched over the office whites.

Jahrzeit?

It's not a question but a statement, sad, understanding.

No! Of course not! I'm here to visit my relatives

the hero of our story mumbles in his embarrassment, then quickly looks away, looks at nothing

"it's not that embarrassing"

but it's embarrassing all the same

"it's just silly"

it's not that silly.

". . . I wish I knew, *year-week*, what could it mean, *year-week*?"

he wonders

Excuse me, you seem familiar with the place, could you tell me how frequently the grave-sites need to be renewed. Or will I be notified by mail?

he asks with a tentative, fleeting smile

"why is this woman so familiar, this beauty past her prime, who on her cheeks uses crrrr-reams, a middle-class widow who came here in hopes of finding employment, a volunteer, possibly, the victim of her state of mind, it wouldn't be the first time, **the widow and the soldier**, Mother appeared in it at the National in forty-six or whenever"

"yes, it was this woman who provided the proper ritual nightgown for Mother's corpse back then! it was this woman who amid profuse apologies sold me those whatchamacallits for a couple of forints, I have no idea what the Hebrew name is for them, for anything, and I had to decide about Mother's hair, could it be? her hair? yes, that's when this widow told me how **after a bereavement in her own family, in her profound grief she offered her services to the congregation for the remainder of her days, and ever since, day and night, without a word of complaint, there is nothing for her but this, and"**

"she recognised me, yes, it's her, letting me know, even back then, that I am famous, oy oy"

the hero of our story continues in his reflections

Never, my dear sir, what are you thinking! For the Jews there is no renewal! Our final resting places come with a guarantee. As long as this country goes by the name of Hungary, at any rate, and is a sovereign state!

but even the kind-hearted volunteer realises that this may have been a little too much

In short, put your mind at rest, honoured sir, we will never lay so much as a finger on them, it's been our way ever since we're Jews

and now she places her hand on the foolish man's arm

"she's on this side of sixty, and pale forget-me-nots swimming in her eyes"

"her lips, too, light and soft, the upper and the lower, too, while her body, it's one of those eternally youthful types; but why is she resting her hand on my muscular lower arm, where will this lead, oh, tell me, what's the use"

You know, I don't like coming out here because, for one thing, I keep running into the mafia . . .

"yes, yes, yes!"

Pushy types, moonlighting

"that's what I am"

It's bad enough them cheating me out of the money for the grave tending, but I can't get rid of them, I haven't got a moment's peace alone with . . .

the woman waves me off, it's coming out of her ears, this shoddy excuse

Put your mind at rest! We have a new director, new men, they're different, or so I'm told. Just ignore them is my advice! And if they talk to you anyway, talk back in some foreign language . . .

her light hand is only just now stirring from . . .

"then she rests it on my arm again, how about that!"

then she withdraws it again with a sad little laugh

"groping relentlessly for my hand, why, I wonder? **hers like a big, obese butterfly, mine like a hypersensitive languid worm**, it makes me smile, albeit fatigued from the dirt of the morning and from all that's waiting for me in this cemetery; it's not unpleasant, I wouldn't call it unpleasant, but all the same I'm glad none of the dead are passing by just now"

. . . If they stop at hiring new help, tell me, what has changed? It's just a matter of time before they band into a new mafia, don't you agree?

the hero of our story goes on with the embarrassed conversation

the lady grips foolish Tábor's wrists with both hands like a vice

her head bent to the side, looking to meet his eyes

"as naively melodramatic as a rebellious-libertine orphan girl of the Belle Epoque who wishes to penetrate to the heart of her corpulent uncle's reliability, oh, right into the very centre of his pupils, as if this weren't the dismal entrance area to the Israelite city of the dead at

Rákoskeresztúr but the farther end of the garden of a Swiss girls' school on a sunless summer's morn when the suffragette, having grown tired of her involuntary incognito, has made a decision past recall to give vent to her wild passions behind the handy pile of bricks, the degree of freedom of which – not to mention its mere existence! – this foolish man can have no inkling of!"

Well . . .

and good! Well and good, my dear sir, still, you mustn't be surprised, it's inherent in the nature of the thing, is it not?

"yes, yes"

the lady drawing ever closer, well and good,

her glance in tow and her impish, rueful smile

sidling up to the man's lips, he'd left them parted

from below, eagerly, with a song in her heart, wet

behind the pile of bricks, where they'd dumped the rubble from some truck

next to the eternal light, what breach of etiquette! still, he feels a pointed

and jabbing excitement in the pit of his stomach which he can never quite

suppress in short, the most potent, the most pernicious kind

"who will disappear, who should I be ignoring?"

he stammers, but by then there's pawing

hurried and intimate, as always

"what I mean is, not always!"

that's what's so nice about her, she's so "Jewish, so graveyardish!"

greying wisps of hair above the soft upper lip

must be around fifty, NO, MORE – MORE!

"just seven years more than me"

the foolish man reassures himself, and reaches under feeling the warmth, everywhere the warmth, a lukewarm breeze wandering among the ornate gravestones, the sky made of lead, the soil damp, the soil greasy-black, graveyard soil

"she's in heat" he thinks idiotically, and "lost", meaning him, **he's lost, and I can't find my way back, I've lost my way, nothing but grey vaginas for me now and neglected cemetery paths, I'm not even Jewish, my parents wanted me to be Hungarian, like the patriotic poets Petőfi or Attila József, I-prostrate-myself-before-thee-my-sweet-sweet-homeland-take-me-to-your-bosom** and the like, then alarmed, he concentrates under himself, "in the mud" **I am lost if you are lost**, the Jewish soil of Pest trembles, sad-eyed mirage, soft-lipped lady, oh, how she nabbed me, right by the gate, the body coated with dew, the skin parched and covered with forest litter though the thighs are smooth, a homeland without lustre, I'm not used to this, he wails, I'm not accustomed, I crave young women who squeal with delight while this woman of Rákoskeresztúr screeches, belying her age, the effort paling her face, a network of wrinkles, hot little veins in the furrows of her thighs, it is early in the day and humid, and let's assume I've got myself entangled with this petal-eyed woman of the graveyard crying with no end in sight behind the pile of bricks ———

. . . though her outpouring of generosity was not unwelcome, to be sure, its hidden significance upset and outraged me all the same, that the mere fact of my "origins" should make somebody, anybody, more intimate, helpful and excited, somebody who as far as I'm concerned is a total stranger and who from this moment on I should respect for at least two reasons, firstly because she respects me, too (though she knows nothing about me), and secondly because I ought to be joining her in the self-glorifying ritual of a shared fate which she has initiated with certain melancholy and cryptic exchanges of the eye and other trifling . . .

. . . nauseating and in bad taste, I thought even as a child, and if in my presence someone hit a tone like this with my parents – because luckily they did not do this themselves, but clearly thought it natural coming from others – well, at such times I'd run away from them without a second thought, out of the room and to the next corner where, taking several deep breaths, I'd wave with annoyance when they called me, the way Jewish children who are taken too seriously by their parent, so-called spoiled Jewish children, have a way of doing . . . ———

——— In the end I was almost sorry we hadn't become better acquainted, two birds of differently frenzied feathers . . .

I studied the layout of the cemetery carefully to make sure beforehand I wouldn't lose my way.

I'd lost my way more than once in the past and was determined not to do it again. I didn't feel like it. Staring at the signs painted on sheet iron he repeated over and over again: I must head for the Wall of the Martyrs, head left, because we're all lying that way, to the left, Father's and Gran's graves are both to the left, and Mother's and Granny's and Erzsi's, my favourite relative who was my aunt, what I mean is, she still is, she's also lying to the left of the main path with her parents, my great-grandfather, the shoemaker David Klein and his wife, Franciska Pilisi (who according to family lore kept a kosher kitchen), they live off to the left, yes, at the end of the cemetery, plot 38, sheer coincidence, we had our share of family problems to be sure, but our participation in left-wing politics was negligible, whereas my going ga-ga and not being able to write THE BOOK in thirteen long years, let's face it, now there's a problem of far greater proportions; he just stands in front of the cemetery layout, anxiously memorising our grave sites, "I am going to lose my way, I am going to lose my way";

his face ashen, he shrugs off the woman who is still clinging to him and sets off; when he reaches the vast desolate area in front of the mortuary he practically breaks into a run, it's so awkward passing the Corpse Showroom, it invariably brings back his mother's burial and his former self, unburiable, indigestible, unbearable, as he's looking at his mother in the metal coffin, for instance; as he passed the dromedary-grey ballroom with its bestial function he thinks, again and again, **I told her to show me, and she did, the pig**, but by then he's running past the Wall of the Martyrs, not stopping, though, why should he, "he's otherwise engaged," but he glares at the ocean of names, like he's done at the Directory set up by the entrance, the marble is dirty, he notes, and not from the sacred, convoluted, angular pencil marks of the elderly either, the likes of "and also Izidor Tauber and Irén, Mór, Lili, Gyurka, Gyula, Réga, Heliane, Carrys", or, "we're back from Montreal, Pál Spitz and his wife," and so on and so forth, but because "nobody bothers to clean it any more," *how shall I put it*, "these people have been written off," not in the cemetery, or not just in the cemetery, but more of that – – –

– – – It was easy finding Dad's and Gran's grave. No. 11/A fourth from the left. Even if at first I generally don't remember, still, my feet will take me there every time.

It's one of your so-called preferred spots:
aisle row along the pedestrian path,
so you don't even have to walk into the plot.
Right away I embarrassedly smoothed the earth from the stone slab
"some sort of storm"
my soul suffocating, I also forced a branch of ivy to the side
so I could see the slab, the slabs.
Two marble slabs, a smaller one,
ISTVÁN TÁBOR (1909–1970)

on top and under it
a yellowed larger one
which he had had made for his mother when he finally got the money together
in the mid-sixties,
because until then Gran had nothing but a sort of slip,
a sort of sheet iron slip,
and Dad was awfully ashamed on account of it
and so he had the stone inscribed with:
My beloved mother MRS MIKSA TÁBOR
I remember how he agonised over what should go on the stone,
once he shoved a crumpled piece of paper in front of me
where under the name that was on her ID
it also said among other things
née Regina Weisz
"is that how it's done?"
he asked gravely, stabbing a finger at the slip,
and when I crossed out *née*,
"are you quite sure? won't it lead to complications? is that the proper way?"
and when with no small effort I put his mind at rest
he ran to the phone to call the gravestone man,
"it's too impersonal, understand? you mustn't, I will not allow it, you just leave
Regina Weisz 1880–1970
and under it
these nine Hebrew letters"

וחלנחשלמה

which he then insisted on
though he couldn't read or pronounce them himself,
but he knew what they meant,
his mother's Jewish name, I think.
Sitting in an armchair, wheezing, his head tilted to the side, through glasses
slipped partway down his nose he stared at the badly crumpled tombstone plans,
at his mother's Jewish name,
if that's what it was,
and these characters shaped themselves into a woman's name.
I should ask a Jewish rabbi from Pest

but don't feel like bothering.
"I will not let anyone talk me out of this!"
he warned, whereas I had no intention of talking him out of anything,
"this has got to go on there!"
he said repeatedly before he shoved the tattered cemetery slip
into his wallet, I thought as I forced the green leaves of the ivy to the side
to make the writing visible.
Suddenly I found it all so domestic,
this cleaning up around the grave,
like an old mammy who finds peace only in the cemetery,
I laid my *Kurír* on the ground, kneeled down on it,
pulled the small black cemetery pamphlet from under my arm
and slapped a piece of ragged silk on top of my head which I got here in the office, once, in lieu of a capelle.
I looked ridiculous, I knew,
as I kneeled with that piece of capelle lining on my head, turning the pages
looking for a Jewish prayer I could read, printed in an adulterated form, but now it didn't bother me somehow,
this time around, my looking ridiculous,
it felt almost good,
a rare thing for a man as vain
as the hero of our story, "and **the Lord's Prayer** too
I will not go home without it, so even if I don't find anything suitable in this thing here, it's okay . . ."
but I did, for **he who seeketh shall find**, and **he who asketh shall receive**, and **he**
who bangs loud enough shall have the gates thrown open on to him,
as a likeable martyr rabbi once said.
And so I found the ***maskir***.
Which is what I ended up reciting
first over the graves of Gran and Dad, though later, as I discovered at home,
in a wholly sacrilegious manner,
because according to the exegesis of the Law
maskir is to be said
"during devotional prayers in the synagogue",
"but why can't this dark-green stroll through the cemetery,"
I later reflected stubbornly,

"be regarded as a devotional prayer in the synagogue,"
why not, why on earth not; besides,
"maskir",
I'd heard this atmospheric-ugly word first as a child,
I don't know from whom,
nor on what occasion,
but hear it I did many times, with a sense of shame due to the aura
of the word? or was I ashamed of myself?
it could well be, nothing could be more typical,
but that's another story.
Anyway, this time around it felt good rolling the guttural sounds
around my tongue
as if I were shovelling pear compote into my mouth by the
spoonful, careful
so the mealy, sugary syrup shouldn't drip down the corner of my lips.
I said *maskir* three times for Gran and three times for Dad, too,
and then the **Lord's Prayer**, once,
not because it's any less important in my heart than that other,
or anyplace else, it might even be the other way around,
anyhow, I don't know how it happened, but as I ground it out,
bowing repeatedly,
I could feel that due to some extraordinary circumstance wholly
independent of me
this time the prayer hit home,
ripping open that certain generally unreachable caul,
and my plea fell where I had intended.
Not so at other times.
But this time, definitely. Who can explain?
And then, taking heart, I even asked them in my own words
for help. Help in my present state of distress!

——— After what happened, it was easy as pie finding his mother's grave. All he had to do, he knew, was retrace his steps on the path that led to the grave of his father and paternal grandmother, then turn right the first chance he got, counting out twenty-six rows, then stride headlong through the mounds run riot with weed, careful not to trip as he stares eagerly ahead in anticipation of spotting the sandstone obelisk with the cone top that in 1950, after the funeral service, his mother had put up for her mother, a memorial carved out of some pitiful, perishable material for which later, when the builder herself was placed under it, the Gypsies, shaking their heads, said they would take no responsibility, "it's going to crack, if we so much as touch it, it's going to crack in two," we were told with something that verged on real feeling, though with blank, bright, gleaming eyes. "Think it over, Mr Tábor, an injection of concrete is what you need if you want to avoid catastrophe," "why don't you go fuck off," the hero of our story said facing the line of gravediggers, his suit drenched in sweat, careful to avoid their eyes — — —

Dried-up rabbit shit. Chirping crickets. A foggy summer. The sky like the greyish, tattered rubber flesh of a hot-air balloon burst asunder. "We writhe, we squirm. But soon it's over . . ." He stumbles over to his mother's grave. For the time being he feels nothing. Panting, he glances up at the sky, then timidly puts his fingers to the obelisk. He has to pee. But he doesn't — — —

My dearly beloved Mother
Mrs Zoltán Kelen
born Ilona Klein
1880–1950
Katalin Kelen
1915–1985

According to family lore, they had a horrendous fight over the memorial, too.

By 1950 rampant nationalisation and the secret police divested his father of whatever little he might still have had. You want to spend the money on a dead woman when we're starving? He has no trouble imagining it, he'd seen it a thousand times, it's the only thing he ever saw: the merchant, hurt to the quick, screaming at the top of his lungs at the actress who had been kicked off the stage because of her bourgeois origins, not to mention her "bourgeois beauty", *between '45 and '48, she was a real star beauty in Pest!*, the delicate blue vein he could never take his eyes from bulging at her temple, he's standing with belly distended like a schoolmaster, stabbed to the quick in his pride, slamming his fist on the coffee table, roaring, knowing he's in the wrong, his head crimson, even if he's right he shouldn't, he reflected, *it's no way for a dignified man to behave*, he could easily become an object of ridicule, he feels it himself, *like some sort of fool*. Across from him, in her armchair, his mother bows her head, shielding her eyes with her arm, sobbing bitterly, a cigarette trembling between her fingers, but she's holding it extended sadly over the table somehow so the ashes should fall into the alpaca ashtray, "Oh, Mother! my darling! the light of my life!" he blubbers like a babe, it doesn't suit him, but the pain is real, he's not pretending, at times like this he is calling his mother in earnest ———

I prayed, just like before.

. . . and already on the way here, traipsing along the path to the grave, a sense of great joy welled up in him, yes, an enormous fount of joy; it is what he felt in kindergarten when he was waiting to be reunited with his mother. When I hadn't seen her for half a day anywhere at all and wasn't even absolutely sure, perhaps, if he'd ever see her again, and whether it wouldn't always be like this from then on, with him stuck in this much more credible darkness, this bleak waiting outside the apartment door or in kindergarten, stuck with the usual hypocritical neglect on the playground or in the hospital, the dark neglect at home. And then, when someone would finally call, "your mother's here," I didn't even hear her voice yet, but the mere thought – "Mother's coming!" – it was like, oh, it was like being freed from a subterranean dungeon every time, and me working my way blindly through a mist of ecstasy from which now, now! she's coming! coming! and she folds me in her arms at long last, this whiter, brighter, more precious life, for whose sake it is worth going through it all, for this more noble, more comforting fairy-tale ending, this joy and hope, this refinement of soul. **A better world**. What's there to be surprised about?

——— . . . Once I was among the graves, it was like slowly, familiarly, penetrating a fragrant cloud, sweet and heady, my heart jumping for joy, for nothing, for no reason at all. Just because I was at my mother's grave! Near her disintegrating body . . . Still, though his heart was beating merrily, he felt his anger just the same, he's angry with my mother, even in her grave! How distressing, really, there's no finding her, grabbing her and telling her in no uncertain terms . . . but what? And what for?

Good Lord.

Moving aside, I relieved myself in the misty sunshine.

I have no will-power. Besides, I couldn't hold it back.

. . . I'll just step aside a bit, I thought, and pee, it can't harm anybody around here any more.

But I prayed, too.

. . . so back I traipsed to the gravel path after I'd peed my fill near my mother's grave, like an animal, and goggled with my bulgy eyes until I found a couple of suitable memorial pebbles for her grave, and her mother's grave, too . . .

— — — . . . But as I reached the heap of stones, my feet passing noisily over them, I saw a graceful wisp of ivy. It had crept up over Mother's name. I urgently pulled it away, down to the ground. But I was immediately sorry.

"Maybe it was her."

"Inspired by her sense for beauty."

"Her love of life . . . She was peeking out of the ground."

And so on.

4

GRANDAD

It was not easy finding Grandad's grave.

I never can find it. I catch myself running up and down the cemetery paths, alarmed I won't find it. This feeling, however, indistinctly, has me in its grip every time: "Grandad. He's lost." *Kidnapped. Gone. Never was here to begin with. Your life the product of a fevered imagination. You are not even alive. And you never had a grandfather to begin with. You are not who you think you are. It is high time you woke up! Cock-a-doodle-do!* You have grown old. *Want proof*? Just look at yourself, wandering through a cemetery, for kicks, searching for relatives under the heaped-up mounds, a battered briefcase under your arm, and constantly losing your way . . . You should start wearing a notebook where your head is. Comes from eating too much meat. Consuming his own brain. He'll croak faster than his ancestors . . . His belly, too, bulging like a barrel, a man pregnant with Death. That's where he hides all his sadness, stuffing it all in, hey?

. . . I'm traipsing frightened, and very lonely, too, in this section of the cemetery to the left, my soul howling at the sight of the rusty sector signs, *he's surrounded by the dead, they've been watching him, he knows, for some time now, testing him*, uncanny, how the cemetery is testing him! Then, when pale as a ghost, muttering and panic-stricken he counts yet again the sectors of the row in question of the lot in question, something comes unexpectedly to mind, and he stops in his tracks. He's found it. He's standing on it. I couldn't find it before either only because even the possibility that there is NO TOMBSTONE here I had erased from my mind. No tomb. Not for him. He hasn't got one. What he's got is a heap, a tentative little mound, an ocean of weeds. Plus what's left of the former lilac bush, planted out of love, long since gone wild. Also what the caretaker mafia perpetrated against it under the guise of "ivy planting" . . . This is what I constantly forget, that there's no sign of any sort here to stand as a reminder that below lie hidden the ashes of a human being. Even the provisional sign with his name is gone. What remains is a thinnish marble slab behind the irregular heap or mound, sunk into the ground, and even that not fixed in place . . .

I did not attend Grandad's funeral in '59.

He did not attend. They asked him if he wouldn't like to attend, his father no doubt asked him, and he must have felt the need to come up with some sort of serious-sounding excuse, like oh, my goodness, I should go, really, seeing how Grandad always loved me. But . . .

But what? What did I say?

Something like, "You know how upset I get in a cemetery"? If that's what I said, I was aping my father, who had a bad heart. "So just this once, don't make me think of how sensitive I am, think of my soul." Yes, I was quite capable of saying even that. And still am. Or: "Look here, Dad, don't make me go, just this once, please. Leave me out of it. A person mourns with his heart anyhow, not his actions, his whatchamacallit, his . . ." Yes, I said plenty of things like that even when I was ten, I am sorry to say. But maybe I just sighed and said, "I don't know how to put it . . . The thing is . . . no fooling . . . I'm not inclined."

I must have made a special point of saying that, I just know it.

This whining in imitation of the grown-ups, this searching for the right words.

But that's not what he remembered, but what it felt like saying no when my father had brought it up, nervous and in passing, a day or two prior to the funeral, barely just touching upon it one winter's morning; he was in the dumps and was in the devil of a hurry to be off someplace; he was in his topcoat and hat and he barely just stopped behind me for a second, and after I'd started hemming and hawing by way of an answer in a sing-song manner, having been startled from my reading, because I had jerked my head up from some book or other, which means I had to turn around, and – but he wouldn't even let me finish – "I don't want you to either, I just thought I should ask, it's better if you don't," he cut in brusquely, irritably, then averting my eyes he hastily fixed his scarf, and was off

and then, but afterwards, too

yes, even as I was making my excuses

I felt a burning sense of shame! Burning, raging . . .

Inextinguishable!

I felt my cheeks burning, then to my surprise I started whining inside, God forbid Father should notice how "his cheeks are on fire, he's blushing, lying, he's lazy and selfish and thumbs his nose at us, he's spoiled rotten", that's what he's thinking, so while I was making my excuses I never took my eyes off his, "will he buy it," but he didn't look like he wouldn't, still, with every word things went from bad to worse, it sounded worse, and maybe it was, and that's why the hero of our story found this so utterly shameful, among other things, because . . .

because . . . ?

because for days I'd been expecting the question; I even suspected that it would be popped in an off-handed manner, and so, pretending I didn't even know what I was doing, feigning preoccupation, I rehearsed over and over what I hoped would be an artless and unstudied sort of answer which, when I actually got to say it, turned into a monstrous lie, and this surprised me all the more because when I had rehearsed it inside I was pleased as punch, what's more, I even thought how suitable it was, *what a sensitive child, he couldn't even say why, still, he just baulked at seeing his grandfather's coffin, poor thing, how he stammered, lost for words, grown old before his time, he knows too much, alas!, the Jewish cemetery, it gets him down*

and I couldn't see why this good little alibi

should sound so implausible, even in my own eyes

not to mention Dad's

but when he stormed out of the house and I began pacing in front of the window, shivers like lightning zigzagging up and down my back, and I found myself incapable of digesting what had just happened, chewed over the dialogue between my father and myself, replaying it as it were, over and over again, the shame, it ate into me something awful.

Or whatever. Not just the shame. But the shame, too.

I couldn't have said what. It was too indistinct. Besides — — —

Father hadn't even asked what he had asked. What he actually asked was, should I get rid of the corpse all by myself, or are you going to lend me a hand? And I said, I'm sorry, forget it, no way, do it yourself. Do you imagine just because you made me is no reason I should do your dirty work for you. Not now. Or ever.

Grandad lies on your conscience. You made your bed. Now lie in it.

I was heartless because I am heartless.

And unfair. (Really? It's not *my* problem.) Still, that my own father – that I should be ashamed of a Zeus, when I should have been ashamed of myself. Those old wives' tales about children and innocence! Must've been thought up by sentimental evil-doers to ease their consciences, the old shitheads. To lie about something, as if in a trance, when it is too late . . .

Whoever loves the light and prefers clarity knows that a child is a wolf. A child is the most heartless of all creatures.

I have not changed.

Possibly, what made this impertinent and cheeky laziness of mine so surprisingly laden with shame was the fact that my father did not bawl me out right away, that he didn't smack me, backhanded, on the spot . . . ? Because the one thing he never would tolerate, then or ever, was for me to say something I did not mean!

What a father. A foolish father. I lied, and he didn't smack me on the kisser. Out of a sense of fair play. Because he was lying too. Why did he have to ask if I felt like going with him?

By then, Grandad hadn't been living with us for years. He was wasting away in a Jewish old-age home in Óbuda, a victim of cerebral sclerosis. Dad had him taken there in the winter of '57, when he accidentally set fire to the bed linen.

Our visits to him were few and far between.

I didn't miss him either — — —

". . . and then, stumbling, I wedged my body behind the grave, no easy feat when you consider the effusive growth of the wild lilac busy – not that it was all that difficult either, though it was unpleasant – you try wrestling with the unyielding bushes behind a grave is all I say, go try it! – then with a groan I bent into it, grabbed the marble slab, but no, sorry, that's not how it was, because I pushed through the waist-high weeds, panicky-blind, to see if it's still there, if it's him, my grandfather, am I with my grandfather, lest I end up trampling over the grave of some so-called strange Jew, and so, first bending down, the blood rushing to my head, I pushed my livid countenance forward and down and studied the slab, brushing the sand off with my hand so I could see in the greenish half-light – it felt rotten, by the way, not knowing whether I'm desecrating a grave or bending over Grandad! – but there he was, I'd found him, in person!, I let escape a self-satisfied groan, my lower lip covered with sand, a wisp of hair in my eye, I'm old, I'm worn out, **I've arrived**, in a manner of speaking

[JS]

LÁSZLÓ PARTI NAGY

A Swell on the Balaton

They've had their lot for today, so they are still zilching up – flake out after just a word or two. Their soles slither on the concrete, they huddle together, their downy groins falling and rising in sync; the fat, the hormones, the marrow, the wee, dumb will carries on working within them. To look at, they're identical, but one will turn into a dead loss, another into an Olympian. Who knows, after all, how it is with ability? I give them a look-over then ponder on my own lad, but I've no way of telling. It comes from deep down. It could be the ability comes from deep down, and for a long time it grows faster than the body, bigger and bigger – a "gift", as they say.

I'm not saying the body don't grow, what's to stop it? The tissue stock perliferates, the skin expands continuously: it has no chance to wrinkle, at most it marbles. The ceaseless work shows; it automatically pays dividends. Nowadays I give a lot of thought to this, the skin and all. I have the time, can lay up as and when I want; I gaze out of the window, watching my mob shifting around. I do no more than goes down well and write it all down in my notebook; I don't show even that around too much – though true, there isn't really anyone who would be interested.

The Balaton, one way or another, has been a constant companion in my life. Even when I'm starkers, even in that wispy, wee strip, I sit down to my task, but usually I can't be bothered with the time. I just listen to the cane cracking under my teeth, its rustling surface, one after the other – like eternity, sort of. On sunny mornings, every now and then, I even shed tears at the thought of it. I'm getting on, that can't be ruled out. Maybe I ought to check it out, but a couple of years ago the Association promised a trailer at preferential rates, but nothing came of it. All the tracksuited monkeys said it was regulations, that sort of thing only goes with the European championships and higher. Stuff you, I thought to myself, you dopey huskies.

This is something that's been part of me ever since I was a little kid, though it was a very ordinary family, nothing in the background or the upbringing. Except Mam was a scullery-girl down the canteen, so I was able to put in practice from early on with plain pasta and bread. Oh, and the freebie grease as well, of course. I often called in on her so someone could keep an eye on me. No stopping me then. She didn't much like me, poor thing, thought I was hormonal. That was just coming into fashion then, being hormonal. Get down from there, you ninny, or you'll grow into such a fatso the cats will get you, she was always saying that, I remember. It was a big works canteen, so there were plenty of moggies around, if only because of the rats. She didn't like me, but she did once show me off to the cook. Well look here! So this'd be little Kálmán. He's only starting infant school in September and can already put away a kilo of fat.

The fellow just laughed: get away, not this snipped of pork scratching. Next thing he'll be pegging out on us, Piri. But he still doled it out, just for a laugh, and smeared it on a lid. So, go on then, show us, laddie! Did I want to try against the clock? Glad to, I'm sure. My mam shifted from one leg to the other, giggled, all embarrassed she was. I did one minute twenty-nine for that sticky, blown-out cooking fat. The cook looked from the stopwatch to the empty lid, slapped a gobsmacked expression on that big bulldog boatrace of his, and gasped. Still, he did give us a bottle of grape juice for free, and a two-forint ice lolly. That was a big deal, since I had only eaten fifty-fillér lollies up till then. He said I could come by other times as well, to practise on the leftovers, with his personal permission, and I should chew a lot of rubber – erasers, whatever – to build my jaws up. And, like, would I care to turn up for a spot of training.

The hell I wouldn't! So that's how I started going twice a week down the Slaughterhouse. You couldn't call it real training, just one long hall, the stuff in mixing bowls, everyone doing his own thing. I was only in my second year at school but was put into the junior team. A pipsqueak-nobody like me among the big teenage boys. Oh sure, I had the weight, but nothing else. Only the will, the aspiration. Back then they competed in pressed head-meat, black pudding, factory pork rind, whatever was to be had, though never explicitly in fat. With the more sinewy stuff like that, of course, the accent's on the chewing, so it's no wonder, what with my tiny jaws, that I got left behind in the snacking. Still, I got a few good placings on quantity.

I didn't work out with the sweet stuff in the early days: in our eyes that was training for girls, like, young rookie proles that we were. At school, all they could see was that I was putting on the flesh, getting stronger, but otherwise they showed no interest. I was an average learner, all C's and D's, except for A's in arithmetic. One autumn, we were off on some study trip or whatever at the Sweet Goods Factory. The bloke at the factory said we could eat as much as we could tuck away, but no filching anything away in our pockets or satchels. You mean that? Sure I mean it, he said. We happened to be hanging around the line for Inota chocolates – the melt, that is, before it's formed and stamped out. And still warm. I'll have a go, I thought to myself. There was a girl called Violet, and I wanted to impress her that I too could do something, there was more to the world than tonic sol-fa and climbing ropes.

Will you give us a spoon and some bicarb? You bet, he says. I didn't have a wristwatch, needless to say, I just counted to myself – guesswork, like. By the first ten-minute split I must have done something like two kilos twenty. At three-eighty I asked for a time-out, all by the rules, a bob, a small straddle, left arm up, right arm over the stomach. I zilched up behind the warm glazing rollers. Back then they didn't have all the drugs they do now, no sprays, nowt, so it had to be a finger or the corner of a handkerchief. "Keep it small," I thought to myself, which was enough for me to carry on till I got fed up. The factory bloke was white as a sheet, heaving up right beside me, when he said that would do, he wasn't going to have an ambulance called out. That was the first time the sheer rapture got to me.

It's wobbly feeling that your capacity is bigger than you are yourself; that you're expanding more and more inside, just growing more and more, and unknown chambers are opening up deep down inside, and you're pushing death off. Dumb-ass kid that I was, I still had that inkling! I wanted to have a challenge on doing two hundred cherry brandies. They were rarities then, all for export, and we didn't see them even at Christmas, but he said that was it, we had to move on. Lying motherfucker, I says to him. He didn't dare lay a hand on me, for all that I had cut him to the quick; he went off and called in the security chap.

Anyway, this chap smoothed the whole thing over with a word or two, then he took me to one side, offered me a walnut cream and asked if I was a regular anywhere. The Kinizsi Meat mob. Well, I should pack it in with those dead losses, they just put on weight, no technique. He'd sign me on: tram money for each training session, a bite to eat after competitions, salami baps, pop, they weren't a big club themselves. So that's when the Sweets Works signed me up. It was proper professional there, what with the theory, the training, the peristaltics – the lot. I began making serious strides too. In just a couple of years I won on Balaton slices at the Pioneer Olympics.

I was a second-year industrial trainee and already in the starting squad with the seniors – just fifth table, mind you, but in the A team all the same. It was only afterwards the reform came in and they started monkeying with age limits for seniors as well and ended the single-dish contests, saying that was all a thing of the past, amateurs could only enter for menus. That didn't go down at all well with me, I can tell you, a whole new ball game, right, having to keep several things going all the time, like in modern pentathlon – on the level, it calls for quite a different mindset. To say nothing of the fact that there wasn't much of a tradition for it here: the Bulgarians and Russkis used to sweep the board.

It was the soup, most of all, that was a problem – the very first course. The basic standard in the seniors was quite high, ten cubic decimetres, preferably ham stock or jellied aspic, warmed up. My kidneys were bound up something chronic, right, they couldn't take all that flushing, and that was a drawback, for sure. I'd never make it big, the doc said. But what eighteen-year-old believes that? Do my mob believe it when I tell them: only one out of ten? I couldn't have cared less, just gritted my teeth and went onto diuretics. It was prohibited, you bet, but I pushed on all the same, carried on anyway. Then it was my heart that couldn't take it.

I wasn't too bad on lipids, let's say – that's what they called the meat officially, the second course. I could do as much as four-seventy on lean bacon. On desserts I was the discipline leader, hands down – on Neapolitans, what they called filled wafer biscuits, or pissingers. That was the only thing we did in square metres, and my PB was two-ninety-eight. Just to give you an idea, three-twenty-one was enough for Igor Vokstogonov to become European champion at Sofia in '69.

When they reversed the reforms and speed-scoffing was again permitted – well, I had another go at that, hoping it would put up my earnings. I was conscripted anyway; the army signed me on. But more grief – that's all that came of that, and injuries. My jaw muscles were very dicey, then there was trouble with the gullet too. Of course, back then they weren't yet doing those transection operations here, only in Halle and Leningrad.

I almost bought it at Kecskemét, at the Friendly Armed Forces Spartaciad. At the request of the Soviets, they put horse Veronese on for the compulsories, and we were shit-scared of that, right, we knew only too well what that was. So wouldn't you just know it, a wadding got wedged in the gullet – one of those gauzes, or whatever. So that's me substituted pronto, a laryngotomy, and I had to lay off almost six months, Army Hospital and what have you, one long torture. I still believed in myself, though, whatever the doctors might have said. I got better and in the second week started practising with infusions, which was totally banned, but I was flat on my back, what was I supposed to do? It leaked out, and the major came by to bawl me out. You want to kill yourself? Not me, I shakes my head, but I have to keep in trim. So anyway, they allowed that after getting a special ministerial order, but even so it really put me out of commission, the nerves worst of all.

Not long after that, I had what was reckoned to be an asthmatic lockjaw attack in Katowice – that did me in. Really put the wind up me, that did, and somehow everything slipped internally. No-one definitely wrote me off, understand, but you sense what people are really thinking. Whether you have the bottle. They didn't even support me politically. I'll join the Party, I thought to myself, but they sniffed, so I didn't push it. I'd made the national B team a few times, had a drawer full of medals and certificates, but nothing else. That's it, I said, I'm jacking it in. I'm a qualified mechanic, I thought to myself, I'll survive. I turned in the equipment; they didn't shed any tears, neither did I. No bouquet, not so much as a wristwatch, did I get out of them.

A few months afterwards, I got married, one of those sports romances, you could say. The wife was First Division at Canned Goods, brought up from Nagyatád she was, a well-knit country girl. Not badly placed in the movement either, so she even got to the Worlds in Havana. So anyway, they put on a small demonstration there: they had a special military plane bring the material along after them, and she was first in Bean Soup with Sausage. Even the Party daily reported that Fidel Castro clapped so hard he almost fell off the platform.

The thing was, though, that Gizi was too short for her build; she had perpetual capacity problems, and later on I myself wasn't too happy about her being away so much, because élite sport is a big commitment, what with training camps for this, Eskimo therapy for that, and meanwhile the housework goes to pot, no cooking, no washing, no family life. The truth of it is, though, that she was already getting past it; she was afraid of operations, she couldn't stand the constant dilatation, her gullet was totally shot with the plaster pump.

As it was she called it a day after the first kid – the only one, that is to say. Little Louis was premature, just one-eighty at birth. Vitamin deficiency, so they said, and it may well have been, but she was only Second Division for Veg, so even the pregnant women weren't too happy about having her transferred to them, internal directive or not. Well, you can understand why; but they barely paid the calorie money, which mattered a fair bit for women in the family way. They chose to say it was a cyst for as long as they could. Or a myoma.

Suffice it to say, both of us slowly lost weight; then, through the wife, we were allocated a flat, did it up and lived like anyone else. I was a demonstrator with North Budapest Catering. I would occasionally drop in on Kinizsi Meat, but only the way us veterans get together, without umpire or jury panel, just between ourselves, doing marrowbone jelly, tripes, whatever could be had. The main thing was we were happy as Larry: we'd zilch up, muck around in the showers, and that was that. Afterwards we would go somewhere to tuck a meal away. Then there were the beer contests.

Gizi was still quite active; it was mostly her insisting we should put ourselves around, like. She'd go to the Women's Council and places like that, give talks to Pioneers, guest at gala dinners for workers' militias, and she hassled me into doing the same. Truth is, I was missing something, so me and the wife started making these challenges – Party Congress, November 7th, Liberation Day, that sort of thing.

There was one time when Comrade Biszku himself, the CC Secretary, had a look at us. It was even on TV, right. It was the thirtieth anniversary, and District headquarters had a word with the wife that it might not be a bad idea, after all, to come up with something. Something nice. So anyway, with help from firms, and with the Party Committee pushing as well, we got together a hundredweight of caviar. Not the black stuff, that wasn't possible, which was a relief for us anyway.

I remember it well: April 3rd it was, the eve of the day itself. A fine, sunny day, raincoat weather. The Szakasits centre was all dolled up with crêpe paper, the whole auditorium, Young Communists, workers' militia, you name it. The agreement was bread, nothing on it, and the wife was scared: Hey, we're not going to make this! Remember Elly Fibinger? We're going to be left with egg on our faces. Don't worry, lambchop, I tell her, four evacuations – it just has to work. Well, the District were pretty leery about it at first, but then they cleared it with the high-ups and went along with it: like, we could go backstage to zilch up, meantime there'd be speeches, then we carry on. Right, so three intervals, bicarb ad lib, but straight time to count. We haggled them down to splits, so there wouldn't be any misunderstandings.

Anyway, we come on. Big ovation. The MC announces that Kálmán so-and-so and his wife are here today, and they've taken on such-and-such a challenge. On one side of the stage are the honorary presidents, Comrade Biszku, a Russki general, veterans and what have you; on the right, the challenge. The two national anthems are played, the Pioneers hare on with the cellophane-wrapped carnations. We get some too, of course, and toss them into the audience, the way it had been arranged, and we race over to the ping-pong table.

We duck under the red cord and sit down. The table is nicely tilted so everyone can get a clear view, and in the middle is a big 30. We had that stuck up early in the morning, two decorators and a cook, and really good it looked too. Forty-five kilos of red caviar: we'd had to polish off fifty in practice, the rest went to the doc and the umpires. The wife had even dreamed up the idea of putting in these, like, horizontal bands every five kilos, a sort of scale out of bacon: quite a nice ornamental touch, but then again it also helped to hold the material, as well as letting us keep a running check on where we were. We started at 2.00 p.m. on the dot, after the general, with a horn blast. That way, with intervals and the programme, it fitted in well with the dinner.

What they said was that when we wanted a time-out the wife should wave her hankie, or give some sort of signal with it, then we could go off behind. Meanwhile they'd have the Red bigwigs on, the choir, the rest of the bill. We were at twenty-six kilos by the second interval. So there we were, sitting out back, doing a bit of diaphragm breathing, me dressed up as a factory worker, with Gizi as a peasant woman, in a pretty, embroidered Matyó folk costume. All of a sudden, the wife whispers across that she can't make it out, her stomach is giving her real stick. What else do you expect after throwing up, I tells her. We were just over the peristaltics. But she was sweating just like Elly Fibinger in the Parliament building. Don't be silly, I says, that was different; with her, she had the bad luck to be blockaded with goose liver. Well, that may be so, she says, but something isn't right. All right, lambchop, then you take it from the bottom of the zero; as far as I could make out, that's stickier and maybe a bit looser. If it comes to it, bicarb more often. That was allowed, you see, even out in the open – burping. We're standing OK on time, we'll make forty-five minutes, for sure.

But then in the last break all she did again was retch and weep; she was pale as my shirt. As soon as the doc went out, I gave her a cuddle: come on now, *you* of all people crying? From Canned Goods? Well, her eyes sparkled a bit at that, but the poor thing was drooping, I was getting nowhere pumping her up. Well, in that case, no ifs and buts about it, health has to come first; you know the rules, I'll go and tell the doctor. Oh, you can't do that: he'll tell the umpires, they'll call the whole thing off, and that's the trip to Sochi down the pan. That's what we'd been promised, provisionally like, with return flights. All right then, pull yourself together; we can finish off the last eight kilos at a squat.

I grabbed her round her waist and we go on that way, embracing, but she was finished. The rest was just dabbling; I don't suppose she put even two kilos away, poor soul, and all she could do with the bacon was thrust it down her blouse. Anyway, we made 49.34 in the end, though we really wanted to beat forty-five minutes, on account of the anniversary – that plus as a mark of respect for the heroes. Still, it wasn't a bad effort even so. We take our bow, hands on heart, and there's a big ovation, bravos. The agreement was that we would finish up with a jog right round the stage, but the way things were with the wife, we just plodded it.

We hadn't even got to the changing room when along comes the Deputy Director of the Culture Department, shakes us by the hand, pecks us both on the cheek twice over, she's all flushed, she's so moved. She invites us to stay on for the gala dinner: Comrade Svigadurin wants to congratulate us in person. I take one look at the wife; she's dropping but signals with her eyes, no, we can't get out of this. We zilch up, get our breathing sorted, and I tell the doctor to give her an injection. It didn't help. We have to take our seats right at the high table. Have a nip of cognac, Gizi, I whisper in her ear. She takes a sip, but that only makes it worse. They had just brought in the second course when she passed out – not just any old how, either, but face down on to the fried chops. I couldn't catch her in time. Never felt like this since I was a kid, she says, and flops over like a sack.

The ambulance came. By then we're outside at reception, so as not to create a stir. What did she eat, the doctor asks, a hearty, well-upholstered woman like her, no doubt she put away too much. Just the same amount as me, doctor. Fair enough, but what was it anyway? Caviar, I say. Oh, then it had probably gone off. I didn't argue. Nor did I tell him what our challenge had been. Suffice it to say, the wife all but died.

Two years after that we got divorced. She hitched up with a trainer friend in the baking industry and they defected to New York. Now they make appearances in, like, all manner of variety shows and, supposedly, nightclubs. I've heard tell that they have a fairly successful routine in which Gizi kneads pastry dough, shapes it into these little globs, then tosses them into the fellow's mouth, but from five yards, six even, and he eats them, just like that – raw. The Two Hungers, that's what they call themselves. I think it's rather tasteless, though, to make a joke that way out of bread of all things. She once wrote that I should forgive her; she herself wasn't angry with me, but she only has this one life, and she would like to spend it in love. Things were going well for them, they went swimming a lot in the sea, give little Louis a million kisses, she would like to bring him out of the country to give him an education. I didn't bother to send an answer.

So over time, bit by bit, it's all fallen by the wayside. No regrets about it either: I'm sufficient to myself, just holed up here, dismantling and building up. And I listen to the heartbeats of my mob, their little pitter-pattering. I even hear their tissue stock perliferating – the lot. My son says that he'll get the entrance done up properly, all it needs is to chop a bit off the kitchen area and a double-panelled door could be fitted. But then, what with being on the fourth floor and no lift, why bother?

The main thing is I have no yearnings. I live inwardly, the infinite billows inside me. Now I compete only with myself. Or how to put it: it's not even a competition – a display. I'm telling you, the way it is, I'm at peace in myself, unhurried anticipation. And my skin is still expanding – nothing wrong there. When it gets to the end, if I notice some day that it's coming to the end, I'll have a thorough wash, spruce myself up and shut the door on that Gizi.

The old security guy, that trainer from the Sweet Works, when he comes by with the material, he cooks for a week; he takes the equipment away to have it scrubbed and brings clean gear. It sometimes helps in doing the peristaltics, particularly since I've started doing it along with the wrapping. No-one believes me when I say the silver paper gets incorporated as well. I hit on the idea of this Balaton championship thing, the Miss Foam Cup. I go by various names, Gordon Siófoki, Joe Buffalo, Ratata the Eyetie, that sort of thing, and pit my skills against the field every Sunday afternoon.

It's neither here nor there, in the end, but I keep accurate record: I can do four hundred bars an hour with the stripping, and five-seventy not taking off the silver wrapping. The young kids line up in a row like dominos; I turn the standard light on them. The view from Badacsony must be something like this on a sunny day, or more likely from Tihany: it's the same to me, but old Jenő says Tihany. And, sort of, the light powders on the water like the spangles in vaudeville shows. All it takes is for me to shove the first one, and the whole lot ripples.

Oh, and I feed my cats. One of them, Gizella, she's a hundred and seven kilos, fifty-three centimetres tall, a tabby. She'll make something. She can put away ten kilos of margarine, the cheaper stuff. I have her do a special chewing exercise for two hours a day; there's a Czech rubber brick thing for that, mostly that. But she turns her nose up at Balaton slices, just claws at the air. I don't know what to think, sometimes I wonder if there will be anyone still around to take these little boobies on a study trip to the Sweet Goods Factory.

Little Louis, well he can't stand even the sight of them, and him already a qualified rifleman, a marksman with the army. He grits his teeth, doesn't say a word, lets one off. He brings game innards, rosehips. I don't much like him coming by. He puts the wind up us. But that's the way these things go: Gizella, she doesn't like me. There was nothing for it, I had to have bars put up between us. She bites. For my part, I don't want to rush the meat, there's no hurry: a few years will be soon enough, when she's in her prime. Take me: I started with the greasy stuff, back when. Don't push it, young Gizi, I tell her, first you have to work hard at getting there, you for this, me for that. But it's no use. The wee mite's a big muttonhead.

[TW]

LÁSZLÓ GARACZI

from *Lemur, Who Are You?*

Teacher Justice hates children. She'd like to see the world as a different kind of place: one without children. Teacher Justice isn't a very nice communist lady. Her favourite saying is, "I'll smack you so hard you'll slide home on your own snot." She isn't very tolerant with her own son, Danny, either. She likes to hit him with her pocketbook while they stand at the bus stop. Danny speaks very little. Actually, he hardly speaks at all. Since he never says anything, he never really seems to notice if he's being spoken to. Just now his mother asked him a question pertaining to the subject of his extra maths lessons, but his attention was completely absorbed by the yo-yo glistening in the window of the toy store. He'd never had a yo-yo before, but he would have liked to have one in the worst way. When he failed to answer his mother's question he was slapped with her terrible pocketbook.

"Listen when I talk to you!"

Freddy, Petey and I were hanging around the neighbourhood one Saturday afternoon. The streets were empty, policemen with German shepherds stood on every corner. We went over to Balassi Park, where Zombai and his gang played soccer every afternoon and then went to Szalay's to have an ice cream with whipped cream, but today no-one was there. The park was completely empty. The grey sky hung down all the way to the rooftops. After a long time we finally understood why everything was so deserted. This is a dangerous day when everyone stays at home. October 23, 1966. Petey tells us how last night his old man listened to some programme on Radio Free Europe where they talked about how the Russians killed a lot of Hungarians ten years ago. Probably it was mostly those Hungarians who were wicked, counter-revolutionary and bourgeois capitalists. They deserved it.

On the corner stands a Wartburg with its door only half closed. We can see a box of Swallow cigarettes in the open glove compartment. We could steal it, but the guards at the gate of the Parliament are watching. Plus a security guard could show up at any moment with a German shepherd.

We walk to a nearby park. There are hardly any people on the streets and the ones that *are* out are scurrying home. The city is ours! Should we take the tram over to Buda? I could play around with the controls at the opposite side of the tram in the other driver's seat. Yes, let's ride over to Buda. Look at the souls of all those wicked capitalist Hungarians fly above the Danube in big clumps.

The rain stopped. We played jacks in the middle of the abandoned park in the wet sand. Jacks are totally different in the wet sand: the ball doesn't pop properly.

I ask my dad the reason for this state of alarm.

"It's to catch the enemies of the people," he says.

"Is Teacher Vera at school an enemy of the people?"

"Teacher Vera probably isn't *exactly* what I mean by an enemy of the people," he says, "though she probably isn't a friend of the people either."

"I don't think so either, considering how she twisted my ear because of the girls' bathroom incident. But why are the people hiding if the power is in their hands?"

"They stay at home because they don't want to be provoked."

Provoked. A nice, scary word.

"What does 'provoked' mean, Dad?"

Teacher Vera is fat, has a moustache and despises all children. Still, she isn't a typical provoker, a ranting counter-revolutionary, a Doctor Mengele, that guy Dad talks about. She acts a little like she can't overthrow a nation, like she can't provoke, like she doesn't want to do that at all, so she settles for torturing children. She doesn't have any higher aspirations. But Dad won the battle with Teacher Vera so what are the people whining about? I don't understand the people. I don't want to be the people.

The other thing I've been meaning to ask (only I don't dare ask it) is about the policemen. How come they're the good guys, whatever the scenario, and still everyone is scared of them? I'm always told, "Love, adore the nice policemen." So why was Mister Master allowed to say the other day that the customs officer is a fishmonger? He's allowed to say things like that and I'm not? Is he an enemy? Or is he just a non-friend? Or is the fishmonger the enemy?

Maybe Teacher Justice slapped Danny because the two of them came out to the bus stop to provoke the people but the people stayed at home and Danny just stared at that blasted yo-yo in the window.

Now Teacher Justice and Danny are sitting at home in the kitchen, dipping boiled potatoes into fried grease. Teacher Justice is telling

Danny what it'll be like when his Daddy comes home from Canada. Meanwhile, in between Daddy and the grease Danny is imagining that one day he will have a yo-yo like no-one else, and he'll be the best yo-yoer in the school. Day and night, ceaselessly he will practise his yo-yo skills. He'll walk to school playing with his colourful striped yo-yo, and when he steps into school everyone will say, "Here comes Danny, the yo-yo king." He will study and brush his teeth and eat and dress and visit his Grandpap on the farm all the while playing with his yo-yo, and he'll break all the records. The kids at school say there is a kid in Australia who played with his yo-yo for ten straight hours. He's in the *Guinness Book of World Records*. But what would be ten hours for Danny? If he could only have that yo-yo in the window, he'd yo-yo constantly. Who cares about the rumour going around the school that a boy developed chronic tendon problems from yo-yoing. Danny doesn't care two sticks about his extra maths classes and the story someone told him about the yo-yo that escaped from its string and crashed into a movie projectionist's ear so hard that the ambulance had to carry him off to the traumatology ward. No, these things will never stop him, never deter him. He knows that soon he will get a letter from the White House asking him to come to the inauguration ceremony of Richard Nixon to perform his endless, amazing yo-yo presentation, but his daydreams were intercepted by the strict maternal bag swatting Danny's ecstatic face for the second time.

Frederick Try, our Russian teacher. I can't help liking him: so precise, so merciless, that reptile smile, those pursed, blade-like lips, the half-lowered eyes. True, he has a bit of a sour personality, as if he were always looking into the bottom of a greasy pan he will have to clean.

He asks about our homework. There's no way to make him forget, he always remembers, and he says that even if he *did* forget (which he never does), we would spend the next class covering the homework of two classes: even worse!

Frederick Try opens his mouth very slowly.

For thirty years Teacher Freddy here has been showing the inside of his mouth to students. A huge beam of saliva stretches between his bloodless lips. That great, grooved tongue in his mouth looks as if Gellért Hill wanted to slide into a reddish-grey, flooded Danube. The moment has finally arrived. I hear the booming death sentence shooting out of the black bat-cave of a mouth:

"Miklós Lemur, please step up to the blackboard."

Frederick Try, our Russian teacher, went to Moscow once. In the transit waiting room he gathered all his courage and struck up a conversation with a cute gal in a skirt-suit. When they got on the plane, however, the air pressure popped the cartridge of his fountain pen and the ink leaked all over his cream-coloured jacket. Right above the heart. This embarrassing incident obviously severed all further possibilities of conversation. Freddy sat in anguish all the way to Seremetyevo. True, when he got to Headquarters and changed into his cardigan, he was offered a Georgian *dyevushka* to have some fun with. Well, something bad had to happen for something good to happen. Unfortunately, the conference about the exchange programme was moved to Senyezs, a city on the outskirts of Moscow, and the educational centre of Senyezs didn't have enough rep. money to pay for the Georgian *dyevushka* any longer. What's more, the infamous Russian insects came up from the drains of Senyezs and settled comfortably into the ink-stained jacket of Frederick Try. They stared at him all night from "under cover" with their beady little eyes. It seemed that everything had to turn out well in order for it to turn out badly again. To worsen things, because he had consumed excessive amounts of vodka, Frederick got anginal cramps and spent the night rolling around on the carpet doubled over, kneading his chest where? Right in the same place above his heart where the ink stain was.

Only minutes remain of this Russian class.

He poses the question nice and slow. Students gasp, beg and moan. Falling out of their seats they stretch their arms towards him: please, call on me please, please, pleeeease. They all imagine receiving the reward Teacher Freddy tempted them with. The students who sit at the front try to block each other, while those sitting in the back of the room feel they have the right to slide forward. Teacher Freddy just stares at them with dreamy eyes. The gloating smile of victory stretches across his blade lips, while the students, caught up in this dramatic moment, love him more than anything else. There they are, crouched around him, genuflecting. They are like a huge, shaking cluster of grapes. They cling to his body almost, waiting for the movement of his lips. He's not a stinking pig, who said that? They are reaching towards him, stretching with two hands, and then the stinking pig, or rather not a stinking pig, points to Emma Say. What will Emma Say answer? The class releases a unified cry. No! That's not the answer, please choose me, I beg of you! They stomp on each other to get closer to Teacher Freddy. But if Teacher Freddy, the biggest jerk of a teacher you've ever seen (well, maybe that's overdoing it a little), will not call on someone in a few seconds, all the students will throw themselves on him and tear him to pieces.

Our school encourages the active participation of students.

Mezdunarodny zensky dyeny. This was the grammatical error Emma Say made. She crash-landed: Women's Day is masculine. She's a very proud girl. "Nice double milk bar bouncing on your chest, baby," the boys jeer. She tries to slap one of them. Laughing and running they call, "Emma, I love you, but not today."

By the end of class everyone is fantasising about lunch, but Teacher Freddy Try poses one last question.

"And the correct answer receives an A plus." (Pause.) "What was the name of the shuttle Lunyik 1?"

The name of Lunyik 1. Hmm. What *was* the name of the Lunyik 1? Good question.

"Any ideas, class?"

Margaret Mazányi raises her hand: "Lenin," she says. George Navratil raises his hand: "Stalin, the name of Lunyik 1 was Stalin."

"Sit down," he says, "you're more stupid than I thought. The person who knows the correct answer gets two A pluses, but if you give the wrong answer, you get an F. I will not allow guesswork."

The rusty cogs of Mickey Lemur's brain begin to creak loudly. He has to locate information inside his head that was never there in the first place. He even knows how to say the word *velocity* in Russian. But the name of Lunyik 1?

"Three A pluses! Nobody in this class wants three A pluses? All idiots here?"

Mickey Lemur sets his brain to super-speed overdrive. Three A pluses! That's six forints from Mum and then it's smooth sailing to my report card! The name of Lunyik 1, the name of Lunyik 1 . . . maybe Lunyik 1 didn't have a name? Is that the answer? It's a trick question. The name of Lunyik 1 was Lunyik 1? Six forints, that's three bags of crackling gum!

It's the last class before lunch and Mickey Lemur's stomach is gurgling with hunger. If it's not Lenin, not Stalin, what could it be? Moscow, Volga, Vostok? Maybe Communism? Or . . . or . . . Mickey Lemur's stomach roars. Or: wet cabbage. Boiled cabbage? The name of Lunyik 1 was Boiled Cabbage? It's impossible to concentrate like this.

Teacher, sir, I know the answer!

Yes? Let's hear it, I'm listening.

The name of Lunyik 1 was Boiled Cabbage. They wrote it on the side with big red letters, BOILED CABBAGE, and then whoosh! They sent it out into outer space!

Teacher Freddy slammed his grade book shut. The great dream of three bags of crackling gum disappeared as fast as Boiled Cabbage whizzed out from the stratosphere.

"The name of Lunyik I was *Mechta*, meaning Dream," he said condescendingly and left the room without a word.

For the past few months now, every week I have been giving lectures to the class for extra credit. My series is called "Famous Battles". I have a map on the board, drawings of uniforms and weapons, sketches of the actual battle, as well as the mandatory cholera epidemic and peace ceremonies following the battle. To top it off I've got historical consequences, important outcomes and so on. Each battle is an A from Teacher Sophie for me, which is two forints at home from Mum, which is a bag of crackling gum at the store.

I'm studying the battle plan of Waterloo lying on the green divan. I can almost taste the harsh raspberry taste of the crackling gum in my mouth. If you put too much in your mouth at once your nose and ears start to pop too. But I spend my battle money on other things as well: I paid some debts off to Herendi with the Battle of Austerlitz and added a detailed explanation of the Crimean War to the ceasefire of Világos to buy two new forwards for my soccer team. Before that, I bought a sorbet at Szalay's with the Gorlic Battle money, and the siege of Végvár got me a whole bunch of stamps for my collection, while the victory at Nándorfehévár established my place among the top gamblers. My mother didn't pay for the Battle of Rigómező because I broke the lampshade by accident. But my Doberdó money became gum (Bazooka Joe), and the blood and guts of Verdun turned into the cake I got from the German vending machines at Marx Square. The money from the Great Armada demolition I lost at cards. The siege of Mohács got stuck in between two panels of the floor and I had to pick it out with a match. I had a boat ride on the Danube to Margaret Island with the Battle of Trafalgar. The Battle of the People at Borodino was a small tool and a piece of menthol candy.

It was amazing: I had triggered an inexhaustible stream of A's and forints. But one day at recess Teacher Sophie pulled me aside. In a tired but kind voice she suggested that maybe I should take a break from my series for a while. She didn't even let me do World War II. And I had started to save up for a bike!

There I stood, lost, in the middle of the kitchen with the gas attack of Ypres, oh God, why did I ever grow up?

If the leader of a gang can't climb the rope during gym class, if he can't remember the words to songs in music class, if he can't paint a cloud and a dog with watercolours without having them blur into one another during art class, if he sews the buttons to the spool of thread during home economics, then the days of even a great gang leader are numbered.

His servants and foot soldiers stare at him from the ground as he struggles, panting, up the yellow rope. White stripes painted on the floor in complicated geometric shapes label the different kinds of ball games that can be played in the gymnasium. While they were painting these stripes we had gym class in our homeroom. We put all our things away, changed and did our gymnastics on the desks. Afterwards we had to open all the windows and the door because it smelled like a zoo. The gang leader twists spastically on the rope. He simply can't get any higher. He starts to feel, starts to realise, that he will never get any higher than this.

No, this is not possible. I can't fail so utterly, not this way, not in front of everyone, Jesus help me, please. Grinding his teeth, he attempts one more time to bunch the rope between his legs, but he's already sliding down, the rope grazes his legs, he arrives on his bottom, splat! Damn it, he thinks. He crawls away.

Teacher Tony doesn't even evaluate his attempts, he just ejaculates the words "Three times twenty flags on the bars!" Judy Tausz looks at him from the girls' line with gentle pity, staring shamelessly. She's scrawled an ugly heart with an arrow through it on the wall of the courthouse next to the school. Inside the heart are the names: Mickey L. and Judy T. How embarrassing!

Teacher Tony calls on Mickey Gyulay, the lowest of the gang leader's foot soldiers. He climbs up the rope in a matter of seconds. He goes up and down three times, and then stands back into the line in an orderly fashion.

Slowly the gang leader understands what he sees from his frog's perspective as he hangs from the wall bars in total humiliation. The End is near. Mickey Gyulay, my lowest foot soldier, why have you betrayed me?

He's so low already, I can't even demote him.

Doing "the flag" on the bars looks like this: hanging on the wall bars, you lift both legs in unison, as your shoulder blades get crushed and your muscles snap. Meanwhile, Teacher Tony is already showing a new and interesting exercise: jump up and down on one foot, clap behind your back, do circles with your head while making clicking noises with your tongue. And then another fun game: run around and freeze when you hear the whistle. If you move, you're out.

The gang leader hangs on the bars, his legs dangling somewhere between heaven and earth. But then suddenly the metal bars melt off the windows, the grey, winter sky floats in through the bombed-out hole. A woman in a black shawl stands below him, a stale piece of bread in her hand. Dust and ashes drift in the air, hay, excrement and ashes litter the gymnasium floor. The woman taps the hind legs of the horse and shakes her head, disappointed.

The horse, the woman and the gang leader.

Teacher Justice turns around. But no, she isn't looking at him. She stares at the floor. She's not a woman, she's still a girl. Girl Justice. He lowers his legs down from the flag pose. Soldiers lie in front of the wall bars. One of them tries to sit up. "*Hilfe*," he whispers. Bloody froth streams on to his uniform from his mouth.

"What happened in school today?" asks Mom before tucking me in. I can see down her nightgown. "Uh, what?" What *did* happen? Oh yes, in gym class I learned free-falling.

The members of the kayak clique move off together during recess to have a secret conference about yesterday's jerk-off contest in the boathouse and to gossip about which Olympic gold medallist they had Coke with in the club's cafeteria. They act condescendingly with the rest of the class and avoid Mickey Lemur like the plague. Nevertheless, Freddy Takács, eminent member of the kayak clique, still talks to Mickey and tells him how he found a corpse in the Danube.

"The police pulled her out with a grappling-iron. She was green and bloated: a woman."

A comatose hope awakens in the heart of Mickey Lemur: if he's telling me this story, maybe all is not lost yet!

"A naked woman. They covered her up. She was all green and bloated. They laid her on the rocks of the beach and her bare feet stuck out from under the sheet." Freddy's voice shakes as he stares madly into nothing beyond the eyes of Mickey Lemur. Mickey feels the good old, confidential intimacy. Ha! So when it really comes down to basic, instinctive questions, it turns out they can only count on one another! With a hopeful shudder, he asked Freddy to tell him once more, in detail, what it was like to find the body during kayak practice, those green ankles lying on the rocks but Freddy had nothing more to say.

The cold distance, the contempt, the indifference returned. When Mickey is ill, Freddy doesn't bring him the homework any more, or if he does, it's just because the teacher told him to. He stares at the floor and leaves quickly so he doesn't have to talk to Mickey. He doesn't tell Mickey his ideas, he goes his own way, speaks an unintelligible language. Mickey can't share his jokes, he doesn't know how to make contact with him, and can't understand why their relationship has become an embarrassment, how it became an undesirable association from one day to the next.

If he goes near the kayak clique they stop talking. What are *you* doing here? they seem to say. They tease and molest him. Little Gyulay bumps into him in the doorway and yells at him, "Are you blind as well as retarded, dork?!" The others stand in the shadows, watching anxiously to see how much more Mickey Lemur can take: how long until the button pops off the pants of patience? When will he finally punch Little Gyulay so they can all beat up Mickey together?

Insidious provocations become an everyday show. But why only him? They make the requirement for membership a blood pact because they know Mickey can't stand the sight of blood. They approach him with a pocketknife pretending that this is the only way for him to regain his prestige. They seem to promise: we get a glass of water, slit our fingers, recite the oath, drink the bloody water together, and you're the king again! Mickey knows where the idea originated from: Freddy Takács is so talented in thinking up, organising and carrying out such merciless psychological torture.

Mickey Lemur has now changed places with Little Gyulay on the power ladder. He has been demoted to Little Gyulay's former position, and he has disappeared. He hopes they all get some unknown, painful disease.

Mickey catches Gyulay in the hall next to the toilet. A sly, cowardly smile stretches across Gyulay's face, that disgusting smile that says, we're still friends, but if you mess with me you're finished.

"I'll tell on you," he whined when he realised his situation was serious, and backed up against the wall. Mickey Lemur pretended like he wanted to punch Gyulay, but instead he kicked him in the shins. Gyulay wriggled on the ground silently, waiting for the pain to reach his brain. And then he started to wail, really loud, calling for help: a teacher, a pal, whoever. Mickey whacked him so hard with his backpack full of books that Gyulay's head bumped against the wall.

The end of break bell drowned out the sound of his cries. Mickey Lemur thought he was late to class, but the classroom was only quiet because Mr Kozma had come in to announce the date of the masquerade party.

Teacher Charlotte talked about moraines while Gyulay passed notes with Freddy. Freddy eyed Mickey disgustedly, and Mickey started to shake his foot under the desk. During the review session at the end of class Teacher Charlotte called on Mickey.

"A moraine is a kind of dispersed drift residue."

The bell rang, and Mickey went out into the hall where the dark angel of justice, by the name of Frederick Takács, was waiting for him.

In fifth grade Kőszegi joins our class. He is an eminent student with no sense of humour. He memorises everything. No problem, he won't make too many waves. But Herendi also becomes a member of the class. Herendi is on the kayak team, walks women home from parties and shows us dirty pictures in the boys' room. He has no idea how the traditional system of power works here, and he doesn't give a jack's ass. He has a hooked nose, his hair hangs in his face, he knows "what's shakin'". He grows a beard over the summer. His older brother is a really cool guy. Calls the cops "buffaloes" and has KILLER tattooed on his arm. Herendi can eat the entire gang for breakfast. He cancels out any reminders that I was once the Big Chief around here. Yes, I was a heartbreaker. I was Superman on 24-hour duty. To put the cherry on top of my humiliation, the doctor prescribes glasses for me, my parents forbid the mere mention of the subject of buying cowboy trousers (I try to stretch my sweatpants into bell-bottoms), and somehow the news gets out that I wear a retainer at night, which is partly true, and partly not true, because when Mum leaves the room I spit it out of my mouth and throw it under the bed.

One after the other, Herendi picks up all the girls. He knows how to do the twist and says, "Hi, baby, you wanna rock around the clock?"

I made the final, fatal mistake of signing up for the kayak team. I was on the team for one day. I swished the grey water of the Danube around with the oars while sitting in my practice canoe tied to the jetty. A flock of crows circled above the boathouse. Every once in a while they started cawing, but at the signal of an unseen hand they fell silent. The dressing rooms were dark and smelly. Ugly big guys sat on the rotten benches massaging their dicks.

The coach asked me to bring a paper that claims I can swim. He didn't know that I cannot show him such a paper. I walked alone to the entrance of Margaret Island. A black crow stood underneath a bush watching the joggers. I felt small and crow-like. I can maybe swim a couple of metres, but after that I sink. A jogger stopped on the path, picked up a stone and tried to make a dent in the crow, but the crow just watched, its head tilted to one side, as the stone ammunition landed in the grass nearby. It stared at the man querulously. Stupid people, hurting the birds, I thought, and went home.

After we all graduated school, Freddy Takács and I met again many years later by accident in some dingy flat on Ráday Street. The sun was just coming up. A plastic bag full of Bulgarian glue was thrown under the kitchen sink. We had sniffed it all up. There we were: Erika, prostitute and sister of our host, Freddy, who got one of his legs blown off by a gas explosion, and me, forty-eight kilos a college dropout. All three of us thought that the bag under the sink full of Bulgarian chemical genius had a much better effect than the Hungarian version of it. The previous night two neighbours, reliable alcoholics, came over to play cards. In a short round, Kuronya and Freddy Bak sought to humiliate their opponents: the home team beat the shit out of the visitors. What really happened was that they broke one opponent's little finger and gave the other one a bloody shiner. The two defeated players returned shortly with their liquor-head friends, but instead of fighting another battle they were singing the blues in each other's arms within a few minutes. The night I met up with Freddy they were all still lying on the floor practising death throes.

I asked Erika if I could feel her breasts. I was a little disturbed that Erika was a hooker, and she was a little flustered that I was a college student. I hadn't slept with a girl for months. Erika didn't know that Freddy had only one leg, and Freddy didn't know that Erika was a prostitute. Erika's brother slept under the sink with the girl who was my first love, the tattooed cross of reform school on his arm. I peed into the sink above them. Behind me, Peg-Leg was smooching the slut. I bent down and touched the breasts of my first love. Two different tits in two minutes. Well, I'm all set with breasts. I watched her, my snoring ex-love. Erika screamed and, knocking over several bottles of salt spirits, fled from the flat. Freddy sat on the floor in his underpants, the glue bag in one hand, his detached prosthetic leg in the other. I put a record on, Erika came back, and we fell asleep on the divan.

*

They backed me into the corner by the toilets. They wanted to see a one-on-one with Freddy. No-one else took part, they just laughed like hyenas. The outcome of the battle was to be in their favour, no doubt. They had been working out the whole scenario probably for weeks during kayak practice. Freddy was the one left standing up. He pressed me to the floor and signalled to Gyulay who shook with hate and fear as he punched me in the stomach.

My parents had no idea what was going on between Freddy and me. A few weeks before school was over for the summer Freddy announced at home that he wanted to invite Pete instead of me to go with him on the family's holiday to the sea. Our parents made desperate phone calls, held consultations, wanted peace talks, but they never got a word out of me. When Freddy and Pete came home from their holiday they told everyone how in Bulgaria the rule is that the women have to sunbathe naked.

While Freddy and Pete were lying at the feet of naked Bulgarian dames, Nagyvarga told us a big secret: pull the skin up and down on your wiener and it feels good. Aha, so that's the ecstasy I feel before falling asleep. I can't ask about it at home: the shiny softness that lifts you to unknown heights and lets you fall into sweet dreams when it's over.

The nightly rapture had no obvious connection with the philosophical problem of the existence of girls. Once Freddy Takács said that he was informed by a reliable source that you stick your willy in a girl and that's how you get babies.

Freddy and I had known each other since we were three.

"You're an idiot," I said, "but there's still time to grow out of it."

"You get kids from fucking," said Czakó, "the man sticks it in, squirts and that's it." I smacked him in the ear, and he left before I awarded him another on the other ear.

"You can sign up for one too," I told Szanisló, so he got up to follow Czakó.

I couldn't believe how the disgusting confabulation of someone's sick mind could blind these guys. I knew their innermost thoughts better than they did. My sane ideas were obviously in the minority. Freddy held on to his stick-your-willy-in-the-girl story fool-heartedly. Where did he get this crazy idea anyway? Sheesh! Even the thought of getting undressed in front of a girl was absurd!

"Okay, fine," he said, "then you tell us where babies come from if you're so smart."

"You get babies from kissing. Everybody knows that." The guys with simpler minds listened to my answer with respectful seriousness as I opened the flower of knowledge before their eyes. Even a few eighth graders came to me to find out the truth concerning this important question. I became the stubborn supporter of the Immaculate Conception and was not willing to take part in any more dialogue concerning the degrading idea of peeing into a girl to have a baby. I concentrated on proving the basis of my theories. Unfortunately, I had only a small number of followers adhering to the school of thought that the mouth is a reproductive organ and that the emotion of love can transform into a baby.

One day I happened upon the book called *The School of Love* by Dr Fritz Kahn. Though abstract and full of poetic metaphors, it still seemed to allude to the terrible idea that Daddy plus Mummy gets you little Tommy, and not from kissing either. Around the same time I was reading Fritz Kahn, Herendi stole some home-made porno pictures from his older brother. My prestige plunged into uncharted depths. I could never look into the eyes of grown-ups again. I shuddered constantly from humiliation, always thinking, maybe they really do *that* every night in bed?

And then there was the legendary passage in the book called *What about the Stork?* On page 101, the following words are written: "Well now, the penis fits perfectly into the vagina. If the mother and the father want to have a baby, the penis becomes hard, and . . ." I couldn't believe it. "Well now, the penis . . ." this is how they explain it: "Well now." Resistance is futile, the truth is out. Well now, the penis fits.

I took up a few hobbies: collecting old money, calendars, matchboxes and stamps. My new friend from our building, Nagyvarga, and I practised holding our breaths. We timed ourselves with a stopwatch and made bets in money. We never talked about the skin-pulling thing any more. I still didn't see any connection between the heavenly bedtime feeling and the brutal declaration of "well now, the penis fits perfectly". And even if it does fit perfectly – which I strongly doubt and what does that mean anyway, "*fits*"? – Mother Nature would be playing a very sick joke on humanity. I made a vow to protest against all this for the rest of my life.

When deciding to collect stamps, very important decisions must be made right at the very beginning already: should you collect foreign or Hungarian stamps, should you start collecting them from the end of the war or from the date of your birth? There are several themes to choose from: the flora of Nyasaland, or perhaps the Chalyuskin expedition complete with polar bears, or there is the Martyrs series . . . You start by buying a box of stamps à la Cat in the Bag. You get one hundred stamps. Check the edges of the stamps with a magnifying glass to make sure all the teeth are intact. Petrol shows any hidden flaws, like "windows". Windows occur when the stamp is detached from the envelope and in the process the top layer of the stamp gets damaged. Never forget, always soak it first. Then wait until it comes off by itself. Remove the wet stamp with tweezers, back facing up, on to the pink blotter. Don't rush the drying or it will wrinkle. Place the stamp between two blotters and then press it in a thick book. Put something heavy on to the book, like Dad's boots. Good Young Pioneers don't trade faulty, repaired or fake stamps, and don't mess up the collections of others. You can work towards collecting all the stamps of People's Democratic States or get a book of stamps to aid the flood victims.

I also have a lot of time left for other modes of entertainment, like plucking hairs from various parts of my body, biting my nails down as far as possible, turning my eyelids inside out, inserting large objects into my mouth (a corn cob sideways), cracking my knees, wiggling my ears, popping my knuckles, burping and farting at will, lighting farts, ripening farts, burps, saliva, tears and other bodily fluids in empty medicine bottles. I'm an expert at long-distance spitting and spitting up into the air, catching it in my mouth and spitting it up again. I can spit puddles; it takes about a half-hour, but I dry out completely. I practise grotesque faces in front of the mirror at home and then reproduce them in class when the teacher turns around: I can do cross-eyes, wheezing, ventriloquism. I see what happens when I leave my tongue out and wait for it to dry. I push my ears forward and tape them down: do they flap back? I attempt making an oath of silence, writing with my left hand, tying my shoes with my toes and putting out matches by inserting them in my mouth.

I wind my limbs around the arms and legs of a chair, stick my hands in my pockets and swing back and forth like that for hours. I drag myself around, writhing. Teacher Clara tells me to quit it, "you look like a snail crawling in its slime."

I draw a picture of Spartacus lowering himself off Mount Vesuvius on vine to catch the Roman legion off guard. Spartacus looks like Mickey Gyulay coming down the rope in gym class, his peach-fuzzy groin revealed from under his gym shorts. I draw battle scenes, comic strips, wildly romantic landscapes and stick-figure caricatures of teachers. I have the hardest time drawing the human hand. I try to draw the hand that is not drawing with the hand that is drawing. I can never draw it properly. On the paper my little finger always sticks straight out from my palm. I erase it, erase it again and finally, when the paper becomes a thin membrane, the hand is perfect. I put the picture in a gold-plated baroque frame. Great. I hang it on the wall, stare at it and then notice that my little finger is still perpendicular. My palm is okay, the rest of my fingers are okay too, but my pinky looks like it suffered a serious accident. There are some things that simply cannot be drawn properly. But sometimes an imperfect depiction can depict perfection. And anyway, a flat drawing can only *allude* to round reality: a two-dimensional pinky to a three-dimensional pinky. Actually, it's impossible to draw anything at all, and still, it is possible to draw anything. You can even draw something that doesn't exist. You can imagine and draw a non-existent, modified hand, a three-headed superintendent, a scooter with a sidecar, an underground airplane, you can imagine the past, the future, life on earth in a thousand years, imagine it and you've drawn it already! Similarly, you can never express anything properly in words, but still you can say things. You can say things that are almost possible, even things that are quite impossible, even things that are quite impossible, even things that you're not supposed to talk about because they are scary and disheartening, or even things that you should be denying and keeping quiet about. You can even talk about things there is no language for, or things that cannot be. Maybe that's the only thing that *can* be expressed. Maybe we should only talk about the impossible, the forbidden. That's what we must express at all costs: the non-existent, the negative, the nothingness that is not allowed but still envelops all. That's what you have to do: express unintelligible signs about the non-existent inexpressible, the helplessness, the knowledge of sure failure and the unutterable exertion of speaking. You *must* speak! Because if you don't, then it's all over for you. Learn to respect and love the all-conquering power of empty blabber.

[INN]

COMECON ISLANDS 2

KÁDÁR'S ISLE, ATOLL AND MAINLAND

VICTOR HATÁR

The Shot Hare

Hare Like
He flies before the volley, riddled through
As I, my Lord, being wounded, flee from You

On Film
A vast crowd gathers to observe the game
As you release the safety catch, take aim

Screen
The gamekeepers are cherubim; they ring
Us round in choirs, wildly signalling

The Kill
Your angels too forget their customed hymns:
From lofty tribunes rise their mingled screams

Three
I leapt three Himalayas, but I found
None of Your vaunted mercy, no safe ground

I Fear
My ears pinned back, I strain hare-ears to hear
(The hare's own shadow knows enough of fear)

Report
The firing stills my terror. "Brave wee chap!
His glossy coat would make a winter cap
To crown the Milky Way." The hammers tap,

They nail me up, but I'm not quite done in:
My skin may yet suffice to save my skin.

[GS]

Vampire

once in the course of my stealthy expeditions, my capacious cloaked circumambulations, I happened on a heart-rendingly beautiful Neck of Improbable Length

my eyes glued to it I lapped up this vision of the Neck and like a drunk mathematician calculated the three possible uses to which I could put it

the first. I would kiss it until it choked and she expired in my Kisses Appropriate to Long Necks

the second. As we adhered to one another in the course of the kiss I would sink my teeth in and bite through Longstem

the third. Instead of kissing her to death or biting her in two I would hold her at arm's length, strangle her and visually enjoy the long death agonies of Longstem

in the end I chose the fourth course. I married her

ever since then, day and night, I have lived under the spell of this Neck of Improbable Length. I can never exhaust my appetite for its contours

often it happens that I cling to her in such a mad ecstasy of love that I forget to listen to what she is saying and I don't understand her. Then she gets very angry:

You're not listening to what I am saying. What did I say? You pay no attention to me . . .

Silently I hear out the buzz of her accusations but my ears are tuned to her neck now rather than her throat and –

say it now! say it now! once more! – I cry. And she repeats her accusations gurgling and cackling under my kisses (by the way) partly (since it is through my sensuous parts I have proceeded part by part along her and tasted all the flavours of her neck), partly through my kiss-sensors I have sought out her jugular. Now! Now! the thought has flashed through my fangs, now I ought to cut short her life, to put an end to her struggles. Now! Now! . . . but she dropped her fourfold blonde portcullis over my eyes and I found myself in a golden cage. As Odysseus clung to the ram that saved his life, so she battened her arms and legs around me in a brainstorm of embraces; though I was practically there, her carotid pulsing between my canines – too late. I had the perfect opportunity and missed it.

Instead,
scorpion fashion, I injected my stinging tail into
her from below, and once I was sure that I could penetrate no deeper I released my paralysing position. I ordered the flooding of her cavities and marshalled an ejaculation

she gave herself up to death by ecstasy and obediently accommodated her pelvic rhythm to our mutual dying. When we woke from our corpses there were three of us; but only in an emblematic sense, heralding only a pair of twins, otherwise there might have been a whole army of them like a set of organ pipes. And beside me on the pillow there still stretched the long slender junoesque Neck

– You obstinate, you roughneck! – I continued gently, twisting the rough word into her neckverse, just as I had always sharpened my knowledge of vernacular rhetoric on her. You Neck! You've got a "neck": even without your ornaments you have an Ornamental Neck!

– And you, you're all tongue: leave me alone! You cling to me like a necklace . . . !

I don't remember her face, I never saw it. I carried the majestic vision of the Neck with me into my cinerarium which is cast in the form of Isis the Earth Mother, and I mingled my dust with hers in the jar – eternal peace measured to its precise length.

[GS]

Identifications

monkey monkey monkey monkey
    locked away in monkey shape
myself am locked up under one key
    inside a solitary ape
consciousness self-knowledge cannot
    worm however hard it tries
out of its monkey skin and phizzog,
    monkey fur, face, ear and eyes.

spider will remain a spider,
    catfish gawp as catfish do,
you'll not cut yourself from inside or
    shed your skin by slicing through!
ants are ants and have to stick it
    gladly though they'd flee the heap
walk two-legged through the wicket,
    or sprout avian wings and cheep –

on your neighbour's skull go knocking:
    its chitin armour will not give!
friend! my body needs defrocking!
    one must change if one's to live!
How keen we are to swap our tallies
    with any likeness! Oh our dust
might yet be human, though our bellies
    heave with the old toad of lust

life gulps, grasps, slobbers, croaks and jostles:
    all gut! a thousand mortal tussles!
and from disgust's amphibian roe
    the glooms of pantheism grow.

[GS]

GYÖRGY SOMLYÓ

A Fragment from a Play

Strophe

He always had to be a "Jew" here
Now an accepted Jew
And then a Jew tolerated
A Jew generously allowed in now and then
If not a Jew banned
A Jew spared
Or a good-for-the-shitheap Jew
Still a Jew loved despite everything
Or a Jew it's embarrassing-to-like
A Jew liked enviously
A Jew liked condescendingly
A Jew liked guiltily
A Jew liked with sincere condolence
But a Jew liked by yours sincerely
Sometimes a Jew granted the favour
Of appreciation qua Jew
On occasion even honoured as befits a Jew
(And so forth and so on)
(Pass it along)

Epode

Except by the weaker sex
Usually stronger than the stronger
And naturally those relations (when they occur)
Develop from the first on another stage
Under the trap door out of sight of Good Society
Out of body-to-body soul-to-soul
In that Eden

From which we were so stormily driven
No sooner than it had bloomed on Earth
Though given some luck between lightning and thunder
And thunder and lightning
Managing to find our way back
(Only to be driven forth again and again)
Yet those rare moments . . .
Beneath those Trees as yet untouched . . .

Antistrophe

And elsewhere?
Elsewhere? . . . One or another kind of vocalisation – someone
A sort of Jederman or Nemo Nobody
Each in some way – or another – or another – whatever suits
S'il vous plaît or M'sieur or Salut Georges
One among Many – and here and there what's more even among the
  Many the One
Even better than he thought himself to be sometimes
Maybe even what he actually was sometimes – actually is
By definition – which is however truly rare
We know – Elsewhere too.

Envoi

(Prince, I'm not complaining)
(Not really complaining)
(I just want to say – in case I've never said it)
One way or another, or another as long as it lasts
No matter where you're born
Life usually passes

[JK]

MIKLÓS MÉSZÖLY

Exact Tales on the Way

The yellowed notebook that I brought along to read on the way turned up after a funeral and was sent on to me some days ago from Kolozsvár. Outside it is still raining. Authentic October rain, almost final. The water seeps beneath the compartment window, forming puddles on the narrow ledge. In the notebook entries made in green and blue ink alternate. The green letters are less faded. For years I believed that this uncle was called Gábor and it is only now, from his diary, that I find his name was Ernő. I read a little, then stop. A young man is sitting opposite me. His shoes are double-soled, his fingers stubby, with bulging pinkish cuticles. There is a red stamp stuck on the window-pane, from the transport series. A red Parliament Square, a sightseeing bus. Uncle Ernő went on a trip around the world in 1911, and visited a brothel in Cairo. "The girls are very handsome," he writes, "but they use couches carved of stone for the purposes of love." We are delayed at a station. At the corner of a wooden warehouse hangs a wire guard globe and a five-hundred-watt bulb in it, shimmering through the rain in an arc several yards wide. Beneath the eaves, a fire-house, buckets, a ladder. The young man sits huddled. He is wearing a well-cut dark blue suit and a bow tie. Seems his feet are smelly. The smell does not go with his fashionable clothes, rather with his cuticles. A motor train hoots in the distance but does not pass us. We rattle on. The young man plucks up his courage and in a rush begins to speak.

"Excuse me . . . do you know where we are?"

"No . . . I've never travelled along this line before."

"You haven't? Neither have I," he says, his eyes lighting up. Then he turns cautious again. "I'm afraid I'll miss my stop."

"So am I . . . We'll ask, when the time comes."

Later, he addresses me again. He still seems a little awkward. He picks at a spot on his trousers, licks his handkerchief and goes on rubbing at it with that. He works at some enterprise headquarters or other, he doesn't tell me which or where. He spends a couple of days in the country every week, checking orders, doing quality control –

whatever that means, it is not quite clear to me. For this he gets a basic salary of three thousand two hundred forints.

"And when I'm travelling, my accommodation is always taken care of beforehand. There's never any trouble over lodgings. There's always a room."

He laughs.

"And then there's the per diem. But that always gets spent, somehow. It's only that I'm sick and tired of it all, it's wearying . . . No food for the imagination."

He spins his lighter absent-mindedly.

"Where do you live?" I ask.

"I have a flat in Budapest."

"Do you live with your parents?"

"That wouldn't do at all!"

"Are you married?"

He laughs again.

"That's all I need!"

He kicks my foot by accident, glances down, brushes a little ash off his trousers.

"Smoke?"

I shake my head. The notebook begins to slide off my knees; he pushes it back.

"It's nicer to sit at home at this time of the year than travel . . . I knew where I'd be allotted at the beginning of the week."

"And is it better to know beforehand?"

"Much better. If I arrive on Friday, say, all I have to do on Saturday is prepare the conference, then there's time for fun. Sunday sleep and a man's fit by Monday. Unless there was a headshot."

"A headshot?"

A woman has a couple of hens beneath her seat; with wild clucking, the covered basket overturns.

"This isn't a smoking compartment!" she shouts indignantly.

The young man goes out into the corridor to smoke beside the toilets, turns and smiles back at me. I'm not going to do much reading. I'll continue at the hotel. On one of the pages I find a detailed drawing, a hansom-cab with large wheels and a hood, bedecked with flowers. Beneath it, the printed characters read: "Ilka's carriage, after the memorable opening night in December". The young man comes back, sits down.

"You really haven't heard that before? Headshot . . . I thought you knew it."

"I didn't. But I worked out meanwhile what it means."

"Or Grand Maxi . . . that's another way of saying it. It's just a fad." He stares at my hands for some time. "I did my military service in these parts . . . two years. I know all the girls. When I meet up with my mates we always have a good time. I wrote them that I was coming this way."

"You said you were a stranger here."

He looks at me embarrassedly.

"Well, it isn't Paris, that's for sure. Of course it's different if you've got a car . . . I could save up for one, but I'd rather not. In the train I can sleep at least, watch the scenery. Nice scenery, worth more than having to concentrate on driving. And the breathalysing. That's an extra mortal danger."

"What are you saving up for then?"

"Nothing. The money just goes. Under four thousand it does not make sense. For a flat, maybe . . . but I've already got one. Two rooms and all mod cons." He laughs again. "I don't let the wife work. She isn't too happy about these trips either . . . Women aren't, as a rule, but there's no other way to earn a bit on the side. Five thousand all in all, say, which means she can sit at home without worrying. But she'd really prefer to have me home nights, dinner together, play with the kids and so to bed, with her. But you can't have it both ways. And military service isn't as bad as they say either. The mates . . . they count an awful lot. No woman could mean the same to a man."

He turns around, glances back with a cynical expression.

"Those hens stink."

"Do they? I haven't noticed."

"You've got to be kidding."

As he crosses his legs, he nudges my knees, brushes a speck of dust off his trousers.

"Won't you have a smoke? It's all right to smoke outside."

I shake my head. I get up instead and look out of the window. The pane of glass reflects the scene behind me: the compartment, the basket of hens. The young man looks me over assiduously, from my legs up. When I sit back down again there is still something of that persistent gaze left in his eyes. Then he is all helpless ungainliness again. A good ten minutes and the train begins to slow down.

"There'll be someone meeting you, won't there?"

"I think so."

"I'll walk you to your hotel, if you like."

"Thank you, but I don't know where I'll be . . ."

He turns at the sound of clucking. Almost everybody in the compartment gets off.

"Can you really not smell them? They're terribly smelly, those hens . . ."

"It could be something else you're smelling?"

"Could be," he smiles.

My suitcase is small and light, I tell him I can manage by myself. He picks it up and puts it down immediately.

"You're right, it really isn't heavy."

His voice is matter-of-fact, not at all impertinent. He does not help me on with my coat either, pushes politely ahead with his briefcase, calls back from the doorway:

"Follow me . . . I always go to the best places."

The station is quite dark, the rain has stopped but there is a wind blowing. For some minutes I lose sight of the young man, and cannot see the person supposedly sent to meet me. The station empties quickly. I begin to walk hesitatingly after the crowd. We turn into a winding, deserted street. The young man reappears, takes the suitcase from my hand.

"Let's have a glass of wine together."

"Thank you, but I have to get up early in the morning."

"Albanian cognac isn't so bad . . . it's all the rage now."

On the other side of the street a woman hugs her coat tighter around her, chilly, obviously, looking for someone.

"I think she's waiting for me," I say, pointing towards her.

He shrugs his shoulders, puts the suitcase down beside a puddle.

"If that's the way you want it," he says, and holds out his hand.

I automatically tell him my name and hold out my hand. He stares at me, a little surprised. He wants to be rid of me as soon as possible, knocks over the suitcase in his haste but does not pick it up. After a couple of steps he turns back.

"We might run into each other in the street, you know, even though you're glad to see the back of me!"

I find some sheets of toilet paper in my pocket, wipe the suitcase clean and cross the street.

"You're not waiting for a lecturer from Budapest, are you?"

The woman does not reply. Her eyes are set close to each other, which somehow makes her nose look pointed, sharp.

"No . . . I'm waiting for my husband."

"Well, that's not me then," I say, laughing.

"Where do you want to go?"

"To either of the hotels . . . Perhaps the Sió?"

She takes hold of my coat, eyeing the cloth. She seems a little friendlier.

"I'll walk you there."

"Is it far?" I ask.

"No . . . no, it isn't. A half-hour's walk."

The banks of the Seine, the Eiffel Tower on her printed scarf. She tries to fall in step with me, taking now shorter, now longer strides.

"I've been waiting for my husband for two days," she says. "And it's been raining all the while. It only stopped an hour ago."

"It was pouring when we left Budapest."

"That's different. I always listen to the weather forecast; they tell you what the weather's like in Budapest but they never say what the weather's like here. My husband sometimes asks and I can't tell him. And my daughter wants to be a meteorologist."

"How old is she?"

"Eleven. She likes that new kind of dance music . . . She has a Polish penfriend, a boy. They exchange scores. We always know what the weather's like in Cracow. The child likes to know."

A car approaches from the opposite direction, its headlights catching us, and immediately she falls silent. She does not speak until it is dark again.

"He comes home for the weekend . . . He says he stays in lodgings, but I haven't seen the room yet."

"Where do you work?"

"Here, in the factory . . . We couldn't get along, on his income. Luckily I've got a good job, one thousand four hundred forints. There's the child, and the flat to keep up . . . She has lunch in school. How do I know he lives, up in the city!"

"It can't be easy. There are great distances . . . a lot of rushing around."

"There are great distances here too."

"One's glad to get home, in the evenings."

"Not alone, though."

"What are you going to do now, then?"

"Go home. I can't stand the waiting, even if it isn't raining. I can't stand stations. Does your husband travel too?"

"No . . . Not much."

"That's good. Or isn't it?"

As she waits for me to answer we come to a little square. She takes hold of my arm.

"Do meteorologists travel a lot?"

"I don't know . . . I don't think so."

I'd like to say something, like there's weather everywhere, you don't have to travel for the weather, but I know it would sound silly, a little forced. She points out the hotel to me.

"Why, it was quite close."

"There are distances here too," she says. "This town's big enough, for us."

I thank her for accompanying me but she does not reply. I am alone in the empty square. Opposite the hotel is a church, with a painted statue before it, one of the apostles, if I'm not mistaken. I'm too tired to go over to it and check. The hotel is a modern building which seems a little ostentatious with its neon lighting. At the reception desk I begin by giving the name of the colleague I am standing in for but they cannot find it on the reservation list.

"It doesn't matter . . . go on up," says the reception clerk, and hands me a key. "There are two ladies in occupation already."

"Is there no single room available?"

"Single bed's what you should have said . . . But you'll find a spare bed will do just as well."

And he exchanges a significant glance with another young man in uniform. Somehow they seem to remain silent a shade too long. There are just the three of us in the lobby. There is still a strong smell of new plastic, textiles and fresh paint.

"Will you take the room, then?" he asks.

There is a sudden noise. A miniature black dog is coming down the stairs, freezes, stares, then rushes out through the half-open door. I cannot suppress my laughter.

"Is it yours?"

He can barely suppress an oath and all at once you can hear the dialect in his voice.

"Of course not! One of our high-and-mighty guests must have sneaked it in!"

He marches off angrily after the dog while the young man and I start up the stairs. He tries to take my handbag as well as suitcase and blushes when I do not let go of it. Otherwise all his movements are well-rehearsed; his inexperience is in keeping with the smell of fresh paint, textiles and plastic.

"I see there is a lift . . ."

"Yes. It is being repaired at the moment," he replies.

There are potted palms, flowers, modern curtains, smoking lounges all along the corridors; the carpets are flush with the walls. I slow down.

"I wonder which room the dog came from."

"I have no idea," he says, surprised.

"Did it make you angry too, just now?"

"Yes . . . we only opened three days ago."

He hurries ahead, opens the door. Does not accept a tip.

"I like dogs," he says, and hurries away.

The room is pleasantly warm; I find myself suddenly sleepy. The beds of my room-mates are still unoccupied. The room has a balcony opening out on to the square. I step out for a look around. The square is still deserted. I do not see the dog either. The church stands out in bold relief against the sky like on a gaudy postcard; beside it stands the presbytery or whatever and a tall plane tree with a few accented leaves. Then the painted statue. From the balcony I can see the neon installations above the entrance. A gravelled, narrow awning with a jumble of pipes, wires and metal boxes. All open and uncovered: a precise and naked tangle. From the strong light down below only vague, tinted half-light reaches up here. One of the boxes hums softly; there is lemon peel and paper bags amid the wires. I go back into the room and go to bed without looking around much. I can ask my room-mates where the lecture is to take place when they get in; it is usually people who have come for the same conference that are made to share a room. But for a long time no-one comes. I fall asleep. Around two o'clock someone tiptoes in, glances around cautiously, absent-mindedly throws the blanket I have kicked off back on. Walks to the door, opens it a crack so as to have a little light to see by. Tactfully does not switch on the overhead lights. Undresses and slips into the bed next to mine. The beds are placed in such a way that our heads are not more than ten centimetres apart. A little later I fall asleep again, and an hour later the scene is repeated. Someone tiptoes in, looks around, leaves the door open, undresses. Holds her panties up to the light, chewing on her nails all the while.

In the morning I am first to awake. I turn over cautiously but not too considerately. They have to wake up too. My neighbour is fat, with very porous skin. She crawls out of bed puffy-faced, looks at me:

"You the new room-mate?" She has a mannish deep voice. "Come for the conference?"

At that, the other woman turns her head; she is at least ten years younger than either of us. She sits up in her lace nylon nightgown, pretty by provincial standards, and rubs her armpits.

"Why did you get up so early?" she asks.

"I'm the lecturer."

"The lecturer . . . ?"

The young woman lies down again, goes on rubbing her armpit.

"You just go on back to sleep, we were up until two o'clock last night. There was an announcement that we'd be starting an hour later today."

"That's good. I want to buy some peppers this morning," says the other.

"This morning?"

"When else? Where I come from, there's been a shortage of them, these last six weeks. And we're a mining district, mind you, with our own supermarket. But when I wanted peppers, they looked at me as though I were a foreigner."

The younger one appreciates the joke, jumps up and down on the bed, laughing.

"Can you get yellow peppers in Budapest, Mrs . . . ?"

I tell them I'd much rather we called each other by our first names. The one in the nylon nightgown is Vera, the deep-voiced one is Irma.

"There are plenty, and cheap . . ."

Irma sits back on the bed, takes the chamber-pot out of the dressing-table and puts it back.

"What are you looking for?" I ask.

"Good thing you can pickle them," she says. "I'll get at least five kilos. If someone comes in late, it'll be me with the peppers. Don't look my way, will you?"

"All right, I won't. But five kilos . . . that'll make quite a package . . ."

"I'm going to shop around for shoes," says Vera. "You can get much better shoes here."

Irma makes a disconsolate gesture.

"Shoes! You don't know what you're talking about." She has her hands under the sheet now, looking for something. "I have to get back tonight. My husband went on a two-day shoot, he'll be bringing back pheasants. That's all they ever shoot, pheasants, and I don't even like them."

"But they're good. How do you cook them?"

"In a paprika sauce."

"Try roasting them for a change, larded with bacon . . . And boar?"

She shrugs again.

"I hate it. My husband hates it too. But when he brings back a boar, I roast it."

"I braise it in red wine . . . with mustard and pepper."

Vera gets up, pulls off her nightgown, ties it around her waist.

"Where are my panties?" she asks aloud, but it is more of a rhetorical question.

Irma looks at Vera attentively. There is a cross-shaped scar on her bottom.

"I hate the taste of wine in food," she announces. "I hate cooking."

"Cooking game is fine. I love it."

"It's easy for you . . . but try cooking on a brushwood stove! Not that it matters now, we're moving to Kőszeg soon."

"How come?"

I get up, Irma follows suit. Now there are three of us coming and going in the room. Vera shows us her shoes.

"How do you like these heels?"

"Nice . . . but don't these shoes pinch your feet?"

"Not much . . . a little."

Her nightgown is slipping down, she pulls it back in place. Keeps looking at the shoes. Irma is standing by the balcony door. Fresh, moist air is streaming in. There is a loud crash from the corridor, something must have broken. She walks over to the washbasin.

"Two more years and we'll be moving to Kőszeg. Retiring. And I'll have a gas cooker."

"Why don't you get one now?"

"For two years?"

The washbasin is placed so high it is impossible to wash feet or any other parts in it. Irma gives up on washing. Vera stands up on a chair, squats over the basin, and leaves the chair in place for me. She pats the basin.

"Can you imagine how many times this is going to be broken? There's sure to be some who'll try and sit in it."

"Why did they put it so high?"

There is a pipe running diagonally across the ceiling, thick as a chimney, plastered over, but it really is a pipe, I heard it gurgle in the night. It is probably a drainpipe. It has already begun to leak. We look at the wall, searching for damp spots, Vera finds some fresh ones. There is a modern writing-desk beside the washstand, it keeps getting splashed, it is already covered with spots. Vera is furious.

"Couldn't they have put in a shower? Or a little vestibule?"

"Kid, they've only just built the place," says Irma.

The furnishings really aren't too comfortable, though the effect is pleasant. The wardrobe, the floor-lamp and the walls are all in tone, and the curtain was chosen to harmonise with them. But the room is overheated, stupefyingly so. We open the balcony door a little wider. Irma and Vera sit down to write postcards.

"Are you staying?" I ask.

"We promised Márta we'd wait for her here," says Vera.

"All right. I'm going down to have breakfast."

The corridor is empty. A tall woman comes walking towards me with a folder and some notebooks in her hands. Her legs are conspicuously thick, swollen out of shape, appearing to be squashed into the high-laced boots. I guess that she must be Márta, but do not speak to her, just turn back for a second look as she passes. It so happens that she too picks that moment to turn around.

"Are you in Room 27?" she asks.

"Yes. Vera and Irma are waiting for you."

Her face breaks into a smile.

"Did Vera find her panties?" she asks.

"I think she's got them on," I reply, laughing.

"Good . . . Last night she got a little fuddled and was going to spend the night in our room."

In the lobby I find the day clerk. He hasn't heard about the dog. I am surprised and a little annoyed that his colleague has not told him about it. I try to go into the restaurant but the doors are closed. In the end I go to the café next door. I learn that it too opened only a couple of days ago. I come upon an acquaintance from Sopron, Erzsi; she is here for the conference too. She jumps up when she catches sight of me. She is plump, but not as fat as Irma. Her hair is freshly done, she spent yesterday morning at the hairdresser's.

"It bores me to go, at home," she says, "but when you're away, it's different. When you're away you can afford to indulge yourself. For once in my life I'll be taken for a lady."

They have only just switched on the espresso machine; there are only a few customers in the café, it is still early. The furnishings are pathetically overbright, glossy, there are flowers on the tables. At this time of the day, in the morning, even the waitresses seem friendlier, less impersonal. We smile at each other; Erzsi and I have not met for over a year.

"How are you all?"

She pushes the flowers aside, takes my hand.

"My mother broke her arm – you can't have heard about that. Something always happens. I do admire my mother – she's always cooking, but they don't want me to move out. The only time I spent apart from them was the six weeks I was married for. My flat is standing empty, central heating, electric cooker, you know, I let that deaf colleague of mine stay there for a while. And those incessant phone calls – where was I, what was I doing? Should I say no to them now? They're used to having me around, and I'll be forty soon. I think that's what broke up my marriage."

She falls silent.

"God knows. Perhaps it would have broken up anyway."

I want to fix my hair, at last she lets go of my hand.

"I have to watch my weight," she says, "but in the mornings I allow myself a roll. Come on, let's share something. If I eat a pair of frankfurters I put on about half a pound but if I have just one, it'll be a treat and perhaps not so fattening."

We eat our frankfurters; she looks up.

"Are you going to be giving a long talk?"

"No . . . not too long."

"That's good. We're all worn out . . . we were up until late last night, carousing. We even sang in the streets, but luckily there was no policeman around to stop us." She laughs. "What could he have done with so many tipsy women, anyway? Nursery school teachers – women are always treated differently, have you noticed? I wouldn't mind seeing a male nursery school teacher one of these days. But that subject is taboo. And then, with a nationwide conference . . . What can a country copper do anyway?"

The girl behind the counter interrupts us.

"Will the lecturer from Budapest go to the hotel . . . there is a car waiting for her outside!"

I pay quickly, say goodbye.

"We'll be seeing each other again soon, then."

"Sure. Just keep it short!"

She kisses me, hard. She uses East German Kalodent toothpaste.

We are going to the municipal community centre. As it is just a step away from the hotel I find the courtesy of being driven there a trifle extravagant, but the two young girls sitting beside me appear to be enjoying the ride.

"Where are you from?" I ask.

"From the asylum for the deaf and dumb," they say.

"Do you work here?"

"Yes, in the office . . ." They exchange glances. "But we aren't deaf!"

"I guessed as much." They are sharing something from a paper bag, throwing handfuls of whatever it is into their mouths, I cannot tell what. "What on earth is it that you're eating?" I finally ask, leaning closer for a better look. They burst out laughing. "Chocolate wafers . . . but we sat on the bag by mistake and squashed them and now they're just crumbs." They do not rest until I agree to have a taste, shake a handful of crumbs into my palm. They are sad when the car stops. The lobby is already full of people waiting for us, milling round in a cluster, administrative staff, nursery teachers, locals, country people. There are hardly any men. The first few minutes are spent in introductions, I do not catch any of the names. They are all in actual fact taken up with each other, with some mix-up in organisation, I cannot follow the comments. Through a dusty tall window I look out on to a yellow wall with an artistic spot of damp dribbling down it. Someone sticks a cigarette between my fingers, but she is pulled away. I do not feel like smoking. A new round of introductions, several people kiss me on the cheek. I put the cigarette unobtrusively on a window sill. A little further back, aside, stands a young man in a black suit, claret shirt and yellow tie. He walks over to the flower-stand, flicks the air-root of a philodendron lightly. A member of the administrative staff shoves a huge sheaf of paper – the programme of the conference ending today – into my hands. I flip the pages, curious about preceding lectures. In the meantime I take advantage of the opportunity of being left alone and open the door of the auditorium. A stage with draperies, brand-new furniture, concealed lights, a table up on the stage, two bottles of mineral water, glasses. Around it, chairs with Op-art covers. Facing the stage, a huge gallery. I am a little disconcerted. There are wires along the walls; a young man assures me that there will be a microphone at my disposal. Four people come looking for me, I am to go to the office. "What office?" "Never you mind!" We hurry up a service staircase. The office is full of smoke, stifling, people are sitting on tables. We are given coffee, biscuits, apricot brandy. The young man in the claret shirt is there. As far as I can tell he is not speaking to anyone, he tops up his coffee with apricot brandy. The telephone rings. "A trunk call! They want the lecturer from the ministry!" A short woman in glasses takes the receiver, a batik scarf around her neck. For a moment the room falls silent, then everyone begins to speak again. They are arguing about the subject of my lecture. "You are a stand-in after all . . . What would you like to talk about?" By the time we have come to an agreement, the medical secretary suggests something different. The trunk call is over, we all fall silent again. The woman from the ministry decides I should stick to the subject given in the programme. "Right . . . how long should it be? Forty-five minutes?" "No, that's too long . . . I need time to close the conference," she says. "There's always a rush on Saturdays. They all have families waiting, back home." "Whatever you wish . . . just give a signal when you want me to stop." We begin to crowd towards the auditorium. At the door someone hands me another glass of brandy. I drink it quickly. Shudder. Go up on stage. Only the first six rows are occupied, half of the participants did not show up today. I begin haltingly, try to concentrate. In the gallery, two children are reading magazines, you can hear the paper rustling from below. Irma arrives a good ten minutes late with the peppers. I see a familiar face, a face I know from Budapest, we had met at an exhibition opening. Renata something, I think. Vera is here too. Erzsébet is sitting in the first row holding a roll wrapped in tissue paper. At first I touch upon general problems, then go on to questions of minor detail. "The slackening of family ties, which is a worldwide phenomenon, means a particularly supplementary role for nursery school teachers . . ." I list concrete, illustrative cases, educational techniques. And watch the local bosses' faces; no-one makes a sign, though I have been speaking for over thirty minutes. I add another eight and finish. There is much clapping; Irma drops her bag of peppers but only a few roll away. I make way for the woman with the green scarf. "You were great," come the whispers from behind. "Are you coming to the Asylum, after . . . ?" "Where?" I ask, also in a whisper. The woman from the ministry is trying to keep it short, but loses the thread of what she is trying to say, ties and reties her scarf as she speaks. She too gets a round of applause. In the back rows some people stand up, then sit back down again. Someone from the county closes the conference, a burly giant of a man. His speech is articulate, didactic, he bridges over the pauses using the same suggestive smile. We clap for a long time, standing. Then everyone mills round again. I stay in my seat. The secretary signals to me to come to the office. Renata walks up from behind, hugs me tempestuously. "Do you recognise me?" "Of course." "It was a wonderful six days," she says, speaking quickly. "It's just that we're all worn out. It's a pity you didn't come sooner. Do you know what's next on the agenda?" "No, I really . . . perhaps the Asylum . . . ?" "What?" she says, clutching her necklace. She looks around irresolutely. Leans closer. "We have to get together in Budapest . . . There's a new crowd . . . poets, painters, a couple of engineers and chemists . . ." She laughs. "They've served over forty years in prison between them, and not one of them is a reactionary!" Irma joins us, we look at her peppers. "That was a very good speech," she says. "I understood everything even though I missed the beginning." Then the man from the county comes over to congratulate me. "Will there be something over at the Asylum, do you know?" I ask. He wipes his forehead, sniffs at his handkerchief. "I'm afraid I don't. It is quite by chance that I made it here at all – I am expected at the court of arbitration and conciliation." Renata makes a face and moves away, Irma stops to chat. A young, slender woman takes my arm, excuses herself for interrupting. "Have you had any experience with deaf-mutes?" "No . . . have you?" "I thought you were going to lecture there too." "Why, are we to go over to the Asylum after all?" "Please wait here while I find out . . ." And threads her way persistently through the crowd. I go out into the lobby, where I learn that we are to visit a model nursery school nearby. "Why do you look so surprised?" asks the secretary. There is a cataract beginning on one of her eyes. "It's just that I thought we were going to the Asylum . . ." "There was never any question of that," she says and hurries off in the direction of the toilets. Everyone has put on their coats, Irma is squatting behind the counter, wrapping her bag of peppers in a Women's Day poster. We troop out into the street tumultuously, blocking the road. "Where are we to go now?" cries Vera. "The nursery school?" I hold out my hands, palms up, to show her that I don't know. "Did you find them?" "What?" she says uncomprehending. I don't want to say the word out loud, shrug. "Márta was afraid that you'd lost them . . ." "My panties?" Then we hear the clapping – coming from a woman with a starched kerchief from the nursery school. The secretary leads me over to her, introduces us. "I've heard of you," she says, and hugs me. Suddenly I realise there is something missing. My umbrella. The secretary offers to fetch it for me, but I refuse. "You won't be able to find it, I'm an expert at losing things." "All right, we'll be on our way then," says the woman in the starched kerchief. "First street to your left, you can't miss it . . ." And we smile again. The lobby is empty. It is hard to believe that there was such a tumult here a few minutes ago. Absent-mindedly I begin to read an article pinned up on a bulletin-board. I hear steps. The young man in the yellow necktie is coming down the stairs, treading softly, but the lobby still reverberates with the sound of his footsteps. He stops beside me, stiffly polite. "Aren't you coming to the model nursery school?" I ask. He shakes his head, traces precise, figurative signs with his hand in the air. That is when I realise he is a deaf-mute. "At first we were to go to the Asylum . . ." I say awkwardly. For a moment he is silent, then answers with his hands, as if he were certain that I understood sign language. We stand, ill at ease. At last he bows and walks up another staircase. He watches from the landing as I walk out with my umbrella. There is no-one waiting for me outside.

Towards five o'clock I dash out to the station. Vera and Irma had taken an earlier train. It is raining again. A strong wind is blowing. I trudge along the street I walked along the previous evening with the meteorologist-to-be's mother. Uncle Ernő is interested in the weather too. He describes at length the haze-free air of Egypt in his diary, the fluctuations of temperature. They had even been to see the Sahara. "The pyramids," he writes, "made no particular impression on me. They are not so much monumental as coarsely made, rough-hewn. But the Sphinx was a unique experience. The idea of having it stare out into the desert is unique." At the station I find the information booth closed. There is a slip of paper outside with the words: "The cloakroom is opposite." I walk over to it. A thickset man is leaning on the counter, not looking anybody in the face, and this somehow makes him look less intelligent. At first he does not seem to hear me. "Can I change trains for Szilas from here?" "If they issue you a ticket you can. Go to the booking office." "Why . . . can I or can't I? Aren't you sure?" "Yes! You can change trains." He is annoyed at my asking again to make sure, wipes the counter with a cloth and leans on it again. The ticket is issued without a word. There is a rubber bandage around the cashier's wrist and a bit of sponge around her finger. The life-and-accident insurance stamp falls off my ticket for the second time. "Never mind, it isn't all that important . . ." I say, sticking my head in at the window. "But I've already charged you forty fillérs for it!" And wets the stamp for the third time. Finally she taps it with the handle of the rubber stamp, but still it refuses to stick. "Don't hold up the line!" people shout from the end of the queue. Everyone is drenched, irritable, the stamp falls to the floor. I leave it there. I hurry out to the platform. I ask directions from several ticket inspectors, in vain; in the end a fireman leads me to the right platform, leading the way between two sets of carriages. The engine is already in place, two coaches, this'll be the train for Budapest. There is no heating yet, the carriages are dark. I sit down, shivering, in an empty compartment. On the platform beside ours stands a train that is lit up. There are many children, a man in shirtsleeves, his braces cutting into the flesh of his shoulders, a handkerchief stuck beneath one of the braces. An elderly couple is eating a chicken from a shoebox, putting the bones on the lid. A little girl sitting opposite keeps reaching out for the bones, the woman pulls the lid out of her reach, smiling. They give the child half a gherkin. Beside them two angular women are knitting engrossed, a peasant skirt rolled up into a sausage hangs down from above their heads. In my compartment the radiator begins to rattle; outside a cloud of steam rises, whipped and torn by the wind. The lighted-up carriages begin to move. As the last car passes us the cloud of steam hangs in the air for a moment longer, then is caught up and snatched away. That is when I catch sight of them. Renata and at least ten others, standing with their suitcases on the other side of the tracks. It takes them some time to recognise me in the dark behind the unlighted window. "How come . . . that you're here already?" Renata runs ahead; she seems to be a little tipsy. "What a piece of junk! It'll fall apart by the time we reach Pest!" Some of the others catch up with her, all wearing identical black wellies, shiny black, like freshly dried shellac. Then they charge the steps. There are plenty of empty compartments but they all flock into mine. At last everyone is seated, on suitcases, crushed against each other, grateful that I saved them a place. Renata pulls out an opened bottle of plum brandy from her bag and they hand it round. "There's plenty where that came from, girls!" My neighbour breathes into my face, sucking her teeth. "Are you coming to Budapest too?" In the hubbub of voices she doesn't catch my reply, everyone is talking all at once. "No . . . I'm going to visit my aunt first." "Who?" Someone cries out, sharply: "Jesus, there's no heating in here!" They all fall silent, as though total silence were necessary to be able to feel the cold. "Every hole'll be frozen over in here," says Renata. My neighbour shrugs. "You were lucky you didn't come to the restaurant. In the end they dragged us off to the Asylum." "So you did go, after all," I say, a little envious. Meanwhile, the train pulls out of the station, unnoticed. It takes some time for the noise to abate. Some of them fall asleep. A couple begin to play a game: relating a story – some kind of police communiqué – in various ways. For a while I try to pay attention, then fall asleep. I wake up at Dombóvár. The others say we have been standing for a good half-hour; they uncoupled our engine but first shunted us on to a siding. It is unpleasantly cold. We cannot see the station, just a stack of barrels. Later, a shunter comes to a stop beside us, they are firing it now. There are hardly any new passengers. They are all waiting for the express in the warmth of the railway restaurant, most likely. We stay where we are. There is a general feeling – engendered by Renata – that it is better not to move so at least we'll stay together, in one compartment. Every time they open the boiler door our faces are sharply lit by the ruddy glow. Someone pulls down the window, five heads lean out all at once. I am crushed into a corner, surrounded by hips and thighs, a wired bra presses against my mouth. I slip down in my seat. There is some light filtering in between two armpits. I can just make out the opposite seat. Renata is staring ahead of her, limply, emptily, her face framed by the armpits. I reach out towards her with my umbrella, she catches hold of the tip, startled. Her face comes to life, her eyes begin to focus. "Do you know Attila Bódi?" she asks. "Bódi? . . . No . . . Never heard of him." In the dark I lose sight of Renata's face. I would like to adjust my suspender-belt but I cannot reach it. I try to concentrate on the slight pain the fastener is causing me. Not really a pain at all – something akin to what a point of intersection might feel. But it serves to isolate me a little. And I begin to doze again. I wake up with a start at the sound of shrill laughter and a loud rumble. "Why, would you know how to handle deaf-mutes?" asks my neighbour, leaning into my face. Renata looks out of the window, standing up on her seat. "That's the express for Pécs, girls! Coming to the restaurant?" Then squats down all of a sudden, presses her hand to her stomach and sits back down again. All of a sudden I feel I have somehow lost my bearings. Everyone is jumping up, stretching, voices raised in excitement resound in the corridor. We are shunted on to another track and coupled to the express. This impatient haste seems almost ludicrous; it is as if they were trying to rectify an error instead of us. At all events we are all adrift outside, except Renata. At the last moment she stayed behind, with two others, we do not know why. Renata likes to play-act, they say, but perhaps this time it's simply that she's getting her period. We elbow our way through packed compartments. The restaurant is crowded too; the crew table is the only one left untaken. Here we learn that on its way down from Pest this morning the train ran over a cow at Rétszilas. The cow was thrown across the engine-housing, everything was blood all over, and this shocked the driver to the extent that he was unable to continue. In the end an old steam-engine was coupled on to the train and took it to Pécs. They've got the right engine recoupled now but so far have not been able to make up for the time lost. I begin to worry about catching my train to Szilas. Erzsi and her crowd order tea and bacon with scrambled eggs. It turns out there is no tea to be had, they did not take enough water on board at Pécs. "Surely, there's enough water to make tea with?" The waiter smiles. "The water at Pécs is very bad. Even the newspapers have written about it." His reply irritates them, all their happy good humour is gone. They all order mineral water, ostentatiously, and cancel the scrambled eggs. They begin relating detailed accounts of hushed-up scandals. "They know the ropes, kid. They can foist anything they want on you . . ." "What about the wine-bottle scandal, then? They got half a decilitre out of every bottle . . ." "Who did?" "How do you mean, who? *Them*." The subject came up at the right moment, they can give vent to their irritation. "Why, you ever hear anyone say *WE*? Only the bosses ever say *WE*." In the end none of them leaves a tip. On our way back we run into the ticket inspector, and I ask him about changing trains to Szilas again. He reassures me that the passenger train to Szilas will wait for us at Alsó-Varasd. When we walk into the compartment we find Renata and the two others huddled up with their heads together; Renata is reading them Attila Bódi poems from a notebook. I am surprised at the hushed, reverent awe with which they are listening to her. We all sit down in silence, all turning our eyes away, looking somewhere into the distance. "Who is this Bódi?" asks Erzsi quietly. Renata does not answer, goes on turning the pages, absorbed. "He's a fantastic person," she says later. "We should visit his studio sometime. You've never seen such a hovel in your life . . . And on top of it all there are four kids and a hermaphrodite dog." This makes them all laugh a little. "A what? . . . I never even knew there was such a thing." "I didn't know either . . . that was my first time too," says Renata. "They examined it several times at the Veterinary College." While we dig out my suitcase we make a date to visit him together. I dare not admit that I am just as interested in the hermaphroditic dog. Then I say goodbye to everyone, kiss them all in turn. The train is just slowing down as I walk along the corridor and reach the door. Someone else is getting down too, from the carriage next to ours, but jumps back at the last moment.

[EMol]

SÁNDOR KÁNYÁDI

I Shall Die

The way I die
will be such that even my last
gasp will be first
picked up then played back
on tape by
someone who re-
plays it a few times
toning it down till
it's more acceptable
or just wipes it
Better to leave him with
that hint of a smile
of course without bitterness
that's what he was like
with the hint of a smile
says that someone without
a sigh the someone whose stif–
ling hand I have felt
at my throat
through the whole of my wretched life

[GG/CW]

History Lesson

history – I tried to
explain it to the stones
they were silent

then I turned to the trees
the leaves kept nodding at me

then I tried the garden
it gave me a gentle smile

history consists
it said of four seasons
spring summer
autumn and winter

now winter is drawing near

[GG/CW]

ADÁM BODOR

The Sinistra District

I (COLONEL BORCAN'S UMBRELLA)

Two weeks before he died, Colonel Borcan took me with him on reconnaissance to one of the barren heights in the Dobrin forest sector. Keep your eyes open, he said, especially on the rowans with their clusters of little orange-red berries all over the roadside scrub, to see if the waxwings have yet arrived. It was mid-autumn: the brush was buzzing with unfamiliar sounds.

Such patrols by the forest commissioner begin with a visit each morning to the bear farm, where he sized up the livestock, and on the way home, while ambling along some mountain ridge, breathing in the intoxicating silence of the nature reserve and tuning his ears to the babbling of brooks from deep in the valleys below, he would formulate a report on what he had seen. Now, however, making his way along all but impassable trails by following markers left by the mountain infantrymen, he was headed straight for a secret vista. Word had it that the waxwings had indeed arrived and that, in their tracks, so too had the fever that visited this forested region each winter. In the Sinistra district, who knows why, it was called the Tungusic flu.

A rest area assembled from rocks and insulated with moss awaited Colonel Borcan up top. On nearing it he dropped his leather umbrella – the sort used by the mountain infantry – on the grass, whereupon he loosened his greatcoat and found himself a comfortable spot to sit down. He removed his cap, too, anchoring it by tossing a few rocks mottled with lichen on to it. Bareheaded, hair fluttering in the wind, earlobes shivering, he sat there for hours on end with his eyes glued to binoculars directed towards the eastern horizon.

This secret vista consisted of a rocky crag that jutted out, just so, beyond the pines. This formed part of the crest of Pop Ivan, from where one could see far across the border, to the bluish rolling hills of the Ruthenian forest country. Dark smoke rose from behind the furthest of those hills, perhaps as far off as the open country. A purplish curtain draped the horizon to the east, as if night were already coming on, but this faded with the rising sun. When, hours later, the valley filled with the opalescent lights of afternoon, the forest commissioner packed away his binoculars and picked up his hat: the reconnaissance had come to an end.

Whether he had in fact caught a glimpse of what he sought on the slopes across the way, of the waxwing or some other sign of the Tungusic flu approaching from bush to bush, was to remain his secret for ever; nor did I ever figure out why he had taken me – a simple harvester of wild fruits, stranger that I was – along that day to the Ukrainian border.

On the way home, once we were down below, he asked if I'd seen a waxwing. Reckon I did, came my reply, two, maybe three, whereupon Colonel Borcan announced that he would then put in an inoculation order.

We were already near the barracks when he again dropped his umbrella on the grass and once more removed his binoculars from their case; the colonel, I should add, was the only member of the mountain infantry who roamed those dank forests both summer and winter with an umbrella under his arm. The stranger they called the Red Rooster happened just then to be walking along the edge of the blanched autumn meadow beyond the stream. Feet hardly touching the ground, he swaggered along the baulk of turf that marked the border between forest and field; his red hair and beard seemed ablaze against the black pines. Colonel Borcan followed the Red Rooster with the binoculars until he disappeared into a swarm of lustrous yellow birch leaves. Then he spoke to me, in a hushed, almost intimate tone.

"Say, Andrei, by any chance was a little package mistakenly left with you recently?" Gathering from my nonplussed stare that I barely understood what he was getting at, he added, "A little something for me, that's all. Let's say a freshly caught fish."

Although the question was odd, as was his disheartened expression when I replied that I had no package for him, no doubt I would have forgotten the entire matter. Except that not long after, that stranger, the Red Rooster, called on me at the fruit depot. A plastic bag all fogged up inside swung from his hand, and glistening at the bottom of this bag in a little water was a fish. Now this bag and its contents would rightly have been the forest commissioner's. By that time, however, Colonel Borcan was no longer alive.

*

Most residents of Sinistra have dark brown or black hair, blondes being awfully rare and redheads practically non-existent. There was one exception, as far as redheads were concerned: Bebe Tescovina, the young daughter of the canteen manager. Everyone thereabouts knew Bebe by her hair, which, being orange-red like rowan berries, shone from afar. Since folks around there weren't in the habit of dyeing their hair, if some other redhead turned up everyone knew at once that it could only be a stranger passing through.

The Red Rooster seemed to be a simple rambler, cutting across the slopes as he did with easy steps, his hair and beard suddenly lighting up here and there against the black pine forest like a flaming rose bush laden with hips. Indeed he arrived in mid-autumn, when the rose hips were ripening under the bite of early frosts. One morning the tracks of foreign-made rubber boots appeared on those rimy trails: his boots.

He was a slight, wispy fellow who spoke Ukrainian, Romanian, Hungarian and even Zips, a German dialect of the region, but none of them well. Most probably he didn't have a decent command of a single language spoken in those parts. Even his way of walking, a self-assured swagger, wasn't the way people around there walked. Besides, he spent all his time outside, as if to leave no doubt that the only reason he rambled along the Sinistra River was to gaze in awe at the mist-shrouded mountaintops.

In the vicinity of Dobrin, where this stranger paid his respects most every day, the Sinistra branched off into various smaller streams, and steep valleys cut deeply into the ascending face of Pop Ivan. Winding their way along the water-worn ravines up to the mountain's rocky ridge were steel rods wrapped in barbed wire, concrete posts, watchtowers and gullies filled with traps: the border ran along this ridge, which also marked the divide between two watersheds. The web of fences, ditches and other obstacles opened only a crack, in a draughty mountain pass where an old dirt road somersaulted into the hills on the other side, which were bathed in the foreign lights of the north.

The road at that point was blocked off by a blue and yellow crossing gate beside which stood a little guardhouse and a threadbare camp tent filled with shivering soldiers. Although this was the only operating border station in the Sinistra district, the gate was lifted just once a week, for a few hours on Thursday mornings. The soldiers on patrol marked the occasion by nosing around each other's side of the border for a while in the name of brotherhood in arms. Meanwhile, those two or three civilian vehicles that had a permit from the regional authorities to travel the route would cross the border.

The Red-headed Rambler, whose hair, dress and unconcerned, stately posture gave him away as a foreigner even at a distance, nonetheless did not first show up on a Thursday but on a Saturday. Masons dismantling the forest chapel came upon his tracks one morning, and that afternoon, Géza Kökény, a nightwatchman who spent his insomniac days in a watchtower at the edge of the village, spotted the stranger descending the slopes of Pop Ivan. Like the wind, the red-headed fellow seemed to walk freely about the hedgerows and the barbed-wire entanglements. Down below he was asked on several occasions for identification, but the infantrymen always found his papers to be in order, although they presumably were forged.

He had brown rubber boots and a grey felt jacket of the sort worn on the far side of Pop Ivan with numerous green corduroy patches, and he was hatless, as it were, which is to say that his narrow-brimmed hat, ornamented with kestrel feathers, dangled on his back from a long band. Fluttering from the top of his head was a crest of red hair, while a rakish beard parted down the middle ornamented his chin.

From the very start, on glimpsing the fellow, the nightwatchman who was also on lookout by day dubbed him the Red Rooster; since no-one knew his name, this simple but telling appellation stuck. A mottled calfskin knapsack ornamented with metal fittings and brass clasps hung from his shoulder, and a semi-transparent plastic bag swung from his right hand. Wriggling about inside this bag, like some silver-bellied fish, was a shiny platter. Sometimes he would approach those at work in forest or field and offer it for sale, whereas surely he must have known that folks hereabouts weren't given to using platters. For a while everyone was taking guesses at just what in fact the fellow was up to: poking about to ascertain the purchasing habits of the locals, was he? Or to see how friendly they were? The mountain infantrymen hassled him for a day and a half or so, asking to see his papers again and again. But then, it seems, they were told to let up: they didn't so much as look at him twice. After all, no-one with such a resplendent appearance, no matter how much they might wish to, could possibly hire themselves out as an agent or spy.

Each and every morning the lower reaches of the forest were tinged pearl-grey with hoarfrost or sheathed by a film of passing night-time snow, so the trail of footprints that regularly took shape from Pop Ivan towards Dobrin was visible even from a distance on those downy hills. The stranger was sometimes accompanied on his wanderings by a whole flock of waxwings. This bird moves into the valleys of the Sinistra as a harbinger of the numbing winter winds from the north. Meandering about on the blanched meadows with the birds swirling above his head, the stranger, it seemed, had not come from the Ukraine at all, but had arrived on the domestic landscape straight out of some old picture book.

The waxwing, by the way, was not well liked around there. The locals chased them with stones, and those really on the ball simply spat at them, for it was believed that where these birds appeared in flocks, they would be followed in short order by the Tungusic flu, the very fever that, in the end, did Colonel Borcan in as well.

The colonel, poor man, looked me up again – something he didn't do too often – only days before his death. Practically begging, he grilled me once more about that certain package.

"Come on, Andrei, tell it to me straight. Didn't anyone leave a plastic bag by your place? There's a fish inside, nothing else. It's okay if you ate it, but tell me at least."

Although I swore I was telling the truth, he left with a brooding look of suspicion and resentment, and we never did meet again. Before long, Nikifor Tescovina, the canteen manager in the nature reserve, spread the news that the forest commissioner had disappeared. Bear wardens and colonels alike drank at the canteen, so he knew all there was to know. So it was Nikifor Tescovina, once again, who announced that Colonel Borcan had been found on a bare mountaintop – unfortunately not in time, for a bird had already built a nest in the colonel's gaping mouth. Later, someone – a poacher dressed in a mountain-infantry uniform, no doubt – had nailed the corpse to the ground by thrusting bayonets through the hands and securing the legs among the rocks with bands, to keep the griffins from tearing away the flesh.

The Red Rooster looked me up afterwards at what was then my workplace, the fruit depot; blueberries, blackberries and mushrooms were my business. I even lived there, in the storage building – in one of its rooms, that is, among tubs, buckets and aromatic barrels. I recall the incident quite well, for it was the same day a new harvester, Elvira Spiridon, came by with her load. Elvira, who was the wife of the mountain dweller Severin Spiridon and who, there's no harm in adding, later became my lover, introduced herself by bringing a basket full of blackberries and a satchel of parasol mushrooms.

A few hundred bears were kept at the Dobrin nature reserve, and, as they loved parasols and blackberries, their feed was supplied by the fruit depot I managed.

I noticed that Elvira Spiridon – this ordinarily restless quivering tendril, fiery snake, red-hot titmouse – was now limping on one foot. All at once I found myself thinking: If only a thorn had punctured the sole of that foot, why, it would be my job to remove it. It may have been a ridiculous wish all right, but Heaven heard it. While I emptied the basket of blackberries into a barrel and spread the mushroom caps about on a sieve, Elvira Spiridon sat on the threshold, and, with the bronze loops of her colossal earrings flashing, she proceeded to my delight to remove the sandal strap from her ankle. I didn't hesitate at all: kneeling before her, I placed her foot in my lap and, with my very own hands, unwrapped the white felt rag that was her sock. Her stubby little foot was still brown from stacking hay that summer, and a purple web of veins spilled fragrantly over the surface. Her sole was almost pink, somewhat tender and moist, as if she tiptoed everywhere, and lurking in it was not a thorn at all but the silvery-golden prickle of a thistle. Naturally I pulled it out with my teeth. Allowing it to glitter for a moment on the tip of my fingernail, I spat at it before wiping it discreetly onto the underside of my shirt. All the while I clutched Elvira Spiridon's foot in my other hand. If anyone were to have caught a glimpse of the scene, they would no doubt have thought I was just then introducing myself to her.

Sure enough, this someone was in fact loitering nearby. Without so much as a rustle, a silhouette complete with coloured edges suddenly appeared before the threshold. The Red Rooster. Of course it couldn't have been anyone but him: the studs and clasps on the broad knapsack strap that passed over his chest and on the leather satchel that hung from his waist gave off a blinding glare. In his right hand was a plastic bag; wriggling about in a bit of murky water inside this bag, like a platter, was a silver-bellied fish.

"Listen me, Andrei," he said. 'This take you to Colonel Borcan. Until the sun sets."

"All right," I agreed, embarrassed by the proximity of Elvira Spiridon. "Put it down over there."

By then Colonel Borcan was no longer alive, but this was none of the stranger's business. I tossed the plastic bag, fish and all, into an empty barrel, and no sooner had the stranger left than I hastened after

Elvira Spiridon, who along with her glittering earrings faded away in fear into the marshy meadow, one foot still bare, the sandal dangling from her hand. My compliments full on deaf ears: she, too, it seemed, had lost heart at our unexpected encounter with the Red Rooster.

Back then it so happened that my attentions were focused on that old battle horse, Aranka Westin. As far as I could tell from various subtle cues, she was as interested in me as I was in her. Indeed I often daydreamed that one night while her boyfriend, the barber with whom she lived, was making the rounds at the barracks, cutting the hair of the mountain infantrymen, Aranka Westin would dash out of the village in a flimsy shift or, perhaps, completely naked and make her way along the backwater straight to the fruit depot where I lived. She too worked for the mountain infantry, as a seamstress, so, sometimes even late in the afternoon, I'd call on her using frayed collars or danglings buttons as a pretext.

This is exactly what happened the evening after the Red Rooster's visit. I'd awakened to the sound of wild geese, which had been driven towards the Sinistra peaks by the autumn smoke that now covered the open country to the east. The frosty nights would have been dead silent but for the thunderous cackling of these passing birds. Their strangled squeals, like the occasional sound of the gatekeeper's clarinet, wormed their way down chimneys and groped about in ash-laden stoves until the crack of dawn. So it was that these nerve-piercing, yowling cries invariably awoke me to my solitude, and to thoughts of Aranka Westin.

Deep within the village yards, behind the grating-like silhouette of the leafless plum trees, light still emanated that evening from behind Aranka Westin's window. I tore a button off my jacket. Stealthily passing over a few fences, before long I found myself tapping at her window. She reached for the jacket and, while stitching, asked, "What the hell was that red stranger doing up by you?"

"You mean the Rooster? Oh, I don't remember – nothing really. He wondered if I could recommend a good privy."

"Now, Andrei, don't you get mixed up in anything. Everyone knows he left a plastic bag with you. There's a silver platter inside, real nice."

So irritated was I by the whole affair that on my way back home to the fruit depot, I took the fish, which was still writhing about in that barrel, to the outhouse at the far end of the yard and dropped it through the hole. I wanted to keep my mouth shut about the whole thing including the Red Rooster's visit; for I had no desire to wind up in some shady business that would get me banned from the area. Years earlier I'd been secretly informed that my adopted son, Béla Bundasian, was living in internal exile on a nature reserve not too far away, so I'd gone up there looking for him. Hoping to pick up his scent, I'd hired myself out as a fruit harvester. It would have been a shame to let down my guard now and ruin everything; why, I'd already got to the level of harvest co-ordinator at the depot.

Something was up, indeed: at dawn the following day the Red Rooster looked me up again. He looked terribly unkempt – mud-stained up to his thighs, hair matted down, thoroughly bathed in sweat – as he made his way hastily across the meadow, which was overgrown with weeds and grass. Why, his hair didn't even have that tell-tale fiery look, not now; instead, his skin, not to mention the tips of his nose and ears, glowed, in fact flared, with both terror and rage.

"For Christ's sake, Andrei," he hissed, "why didn't you tell me Colonel Borcan was dead?"

Why, indeed. I shrugged: because.

He was looking for the fish, and as soon as he realised I hadn't eaten the thing and where it could now be found, he ran off to scoop it out of the muck. He scrubbed it clean in the stream, wrapped it in a burdock leaf, tucked it into his mottled calfskin knapsack and left. The Red Rooster disappeared for ever from Dobrin.

A new forest commissioner, Izolda Mavrodin, arrived to replace Colonel Borcan as commander of the mountain infantry. My life changed somewhat. One blustery spring day, I, too, disappeared.

Many years later, with a Greek passport in my pocket, I rolled about the roads of the Sinistra district in my sparkling new, four-wheel drive, metallic-green Suzuki jeep and spent hardly a day back in Dobrin. I arrived via Baba Rotunda Pass, thinking I'd see how my one-time lover, Elvira Spiridon, was getting on in those fields of thyme or, more precisely, on the upper floor of the log cabin she'd lived in with her husband, Severin Spiridon, in a roadside clearing. But there was nothing where their lot had once been; nothing, that is, but a heap of petrified dark-blue cinders pummelled by rain and ice and surrounded by tender yellow blades of grass and freshly sprouting nettle and saffron. Most probably their grave.

It was late afternoon. The cloud of woe, a colossal, orange-red cumulus bank, lit up the eastern horizon. Lately, a passing cloud of this sort, its imposing creamy towers submerging into the purple veils of the coming night, had invariably reminded me of the past. This saddened me a bit. Bowing my head, I left the jeep by the roadside and walked past some familiar nooks and crannies marking the edge of the forest.

Winding through the clearing before me were two close-fitting parallel bands that glimmered in the reflected light of the clouds. Bands of ice? Or, who could say, maybe glass? Yes, my own former ski tracks wound their way over the radiant springtime grass far into the darkness of the forest, etched into the ground during that final winter I'd spent there, in the pass. Anyone who has spent much time skiing through a forest is well aware that if you pass over your own tracks a few times, the snow gets packed down underneath, sometimes melts just a little, then freezes over and over again. Even once such a double track melts away, its impression, which in silvery light resembles a ribbon of silk, only fades entirely in early summer. Some never do.

That last winter I had skied every day towards the meandering subterranean streams of the Kolinda forest, which bubble up to the surface here and there. A few unauthorised recluses hid from the mountain infantry in the dark underground lairs and caves through which such streams run. Neither when called upon nor when begged to do so were they willing to emerge. At first I was ordered to set traps for them, jaw traps made of iron; then, in the end, we simply filled the entrances with cement. And so for weeks I skied around the area with sacks of cement on my back, always on the same tracks. Under my weight – cement is heavy, mind you – the snow crystallised, like diamonds.

I was almost lost in reveries of my former life when I found two red hairpieces hanging from a pine branch by a clearing. Swinging to and fro in the wind, they looked as if they'd just burst into flames under that strangely luminescent cloud of woe. Skewering the hairpieces with a twig, I examined them closely: one was a head wig and the other, judging by its shape, was a beard. In a dark corner by the clearing lay a young man, stretched out on last year's dank fallen leaves, snoring loudly and dreaming as kaleidoscopic flies buzzed about him. At his side, a mottled calfskin knapsack; beside him, an empty bottle tipped over. He closely resembled someone I'd seen before. I hurried away.

As a foreigner, I had to register my arrival before taking a room at the Dobrin inn. But once darkness came on – after I'd had a drop or two, that is – I snuck outside and spent the night with my former girlfriend, Aranka Westin. It was she who informed me that Colonel Borcan – who'd received a posthumous death sentence – had been chums with a Polish border guard of the same rank. Anyway, they must have been cooking up some scheme: the Pole always smuggled his messages, if not actual dollars, to Colonel Borcan in the belly of a fish.

I didn't want to hear another thing about it.

Being an essential part of the story, however, this much should be added: although no little time had passed, we rubbed knuckles once again under cover of darkness. There I was lolling beside her, feeling my heartbeat; I was musing about whether I might be able to stay at least one more day. Which is when a clarinet-like caterwaul suddenly intervened from above: the wild geese announcing their presence among the clouds above Dobrin. They'd become regular visitors, it seemed. As could be discerned unmistakably through the night-time silence, the geese were coming from the south, from the Kolinda forest; on reaching Dobrin, they turned suddenly north, towards Pop Ivan. I sensed them down to my fingertips, I swear: there's not a sound more disquieting than theirs.

So when the mountain infantrymen came to fetch me around dawn and informed me that since I'd secretly left my designated lodgings they would revoke my residence permit and ban me for ever from the Sinistra district, I'd already been alert for a long time, waiting for morning, waiting to be done with the place for ever.

2 (ANDREI'S DOG TAG)

One spring day I arrived by bicycle at the Baba Rotunda Pass, from where I first glimpsed those imposing peaks at the foot of which I would later all but forget my life up to that point. The Sinistra basin reposed before me with its long, sharply angled shadows in the orange light of afternoon. Stands of willows loomed at the bottom of the valley by the bends in the river, and a sparse row of houses snaked along the far bank. Shingled roofs glistened on distant, sunbathed slopes, and, furthest away, the icy peaks of Pop Ivan and Dobrin shimmered above black, forested collars of pine. Behind them, that expanse of glassy green foreignness, the northern sky.

There were no more roads from there. The nature reserve near which I planned to lay low was presumably under the steep walls opposite. Somewhere deep in that wilderness lived Béla Bundasian, my adopted son. I'd been searching for him for years.

The main road, once it wound its way down from the pass, followed the railway embankment for a while, then the double track suddenly disappeared into a tunnel at whose entrance the watchman was playing his clarinet. Further on, towards the village, the embankment once again ran up alongside the road, and before long a local, narrow-gauge railway found its way there, too. Bicycling along, I arrived at the terminal of the Sinistra branch railway almost simultaneously with the train.

A shabby one-storey building stood by the end of the tracks. Hanging from the eaves was a painted wooden board bearing the name of the village: DOBRIN. That was not all: someone had painted the following, in mud, on the wall directly below: CITY. It was spring, towards evening, when I arrived in Dobrin City.

Having propped my bike against a railing, I waited for the mass of silent travellers to pass by. Some wore rubber boots; others, sandals. If someone seemed agreeable, I'd strike up a conversation. It was my first time in Dobrin.

Smoke stirred above the station, wood smoke: the trains around there burned wood, and a few clouds even crept upward along the main street as if pulled along by the passengers walking home. Leaning against the wall of the loading platform across the road was an olive-brown man who, blinking incessantly, was eyeing the spaces that opened up in the dispersing crowd. He wore a sleeveless, dirty white undershirt, stained army trousers and sandals on his bare feet. I did not intend to greet him, but once the travellers had dispersed, he jumped off the ramp and ran directly over to me across the now empty space.

"I take it," he said in a soft, oily voice, "you're looking for a place to stay."

"Something like that."

"Because I know a place."

This is how I met Nikifor Tescovina. His name was obvious from the start, for he wore it on a little tin plate dangling conspicuously on a chain around his neck. For his part, not only wasn't he interested in my name, but he fended off a handshake as well. Let's not force the issue of just who you are, he said, until Colonel Borcan calls on you in person. The forest commissioner would decide my name, among other things, for he commanded the mountain infantry in Dobrin.

"And if you hadn't noticed, people here don't get about on bikes.

You won't be needing yours any more, either. Leave it here, someone will take it."

He was always one step ahead of me as we ambled through the village, which stretched out over the bottom of the valley. Sometimes he walked into a puddle to wash off the dust that got into his sandals. For him summer had already arrived, yet hardly had the sun disappeared for the day behind the peaks to the west when the puddles were encircled by cuticles of ice. A narrow, weasel-shaped patch of snow glistened on the steep mountainside above the village, whence there came a cool evening breeze permeated by the odour of pine buds. Cut power lines dangled in this breeze around the utility poles along the main street of Dobrin City.

"Everything around here is the mountain infantry's," Nikifor Tescovina explained in that same soft, oily voice. "Including the place where you'll live. Around here, they take care of people."

"Until now I saw them only in pictures," I replied, as softly as possible, "but I've heard the mountain infantrymen are decent, proper folk."

"That they are. And make sure to tell them you lost your papers. Colonel Puiu Borcan will pretend he believes it, too."

"Come to think of it, my papers," I said with a start. "I stashed them in the frame of my bike, under the seat. I wouldn't mind going back to get them."

"Oh, leave it. Your bike's gone by now, anyway. Forget they ever existed."

Towards the end of the village, a stream of rushing white torrents passed under a covered wooden bridge. On its bank sat a dwarf soaking his feet. Before long, Nikifor Tescovina left the road and headed into an alley that soon narrowed to a footpath. This footpath made its way along a backwater whose banks were soggy and overgrown with weeds and which passed between the village yards to a meadow. Looming at the far end of this meadow, beside some pines, willows and black alders, was a building made of coloured stones and with a dented roof. From the looks of things it had been a water mill, but the stream or the river had veered away, leaving it alone on the meadow. Birds nested in the broken windows as nightfall shimmered on the kaleidoscopic bladelike cracks of the shingled roof. The one-time furnishings, from axles to grindstones, had been removed; the meadow's evening fragrance wafted gently through huge, gaping holes in the wall.

Nikifor Tescovina passed through the hollow space between those walls straight to the first floor and stopped before a wide-open, rickety door. In a corner of the room beyond, which seemed to have been a storage space of sorts, perhaps for tools, was a berth of fresh pine branches.

"This," said Nikifor Tescovina, "is where you can lie low. No-one will ask you a thing."

"How did you know I was coming?"

"Since you set foot in the Sinistra district, Colonel Borcan has known your every move. This region attracts sorts like you. Those who follow the Sinistra upstream don't stop till they reach Dobrin."

"Whew, that's good to hear. So the colonel also knows I'm just a simple wayfarer."

"Of course he knows. By the way, simple wayfarer, what is it you aim to do? You seem like a versatile fellow."

"Well, I'm at home in the forest and know my trees, not to mention my shrubs. Let's say I know a thing or two about mushrooms and fruit: I've worked at food markets before. If need be, I can work in a timber yard or even as a bark stripper. Why, if it comes down to it I could even set traps."

"Not bad. I'll have a word with the colonel. But until he comes by in person, please don't leave this place. Don't even step outside, I mean."

"And if nature calls, in a big way, where might you allow me to go?"

"Best if you just stick your backside out the window."

Nikifor Tescovina raised a palm to his forehead: his way of saying good-bye. By the time he reached the far end of the meadow, where the village fences began, dusk had already swallowed him up. Leaning on the damaged window sill, I stared in his direction until, with a great swishing of wings, an owl flew outside from behind me.

Days passed before Nikifor Tescovina deigned to show himself again. Each morning I found a little bag hanging on the bolt of the front door; inside it there was always a bottle of water, a few congealed boiled potatoes, onions, a handful of prunes and a few hazelnuts. Those days of boiled potatoes and prunes quickly melted into one as surely as the mists that wafted fleetingly over the valley; from that point on, for a long time I had no idea whether it was Monday, Wednesday or Saturday. The passing of time was signalled by the changing shape of the snow patches on the mountainside above Dobrin.

But then, one morning, there he was again, Nikifor Tescovina, seated on the threshold beside the dangling bag of provisions.

"I'm glad to see you've been sleeping so well," he said. "Though I've come by often, I let you be. Let the man get his rest, I reckoned. But Colonel Puiu Borcan and I got to talking about you meanwhile."

"You don't mean to say he has time to deal with me?"

"Why, of course. He's the forest commissioner up here in Dobrin, right? He wants to see you, so he's going to come by soon. It looks like you can stay."

"If you've really arranged things, I'll repay you somehow. I'd like to make a go of it here. Something tells me this is where my life is going to come full circle."

"That could well be. Colonel Borcan likes the way you think. He reckons that if you were serious about that wild-fruit idea of yours, it might be worth giving it a try. The harvested fruit could be stored in barrels and tubs here at the mill."

"My thoughts exactly."

"And you could get a whole lot of shut-eye. The scent of fermenting fruit really puts a man to sleep."

"Well then, can you tell me how the area is for blackberries? It's mainly them and blueberries I had in mind, you know."

"I'm not sure. Frankly, it all depends on what the bears want. What you harvest will be theirs. A hundred, maybe a hundred and fifty, of them are kept here in the reserve. Yet another reason Colonel Borcan liked your idea."

For days I leaned out the window gazing at the mountain peaks, whose countenances seemed headstrong one day, capricious the next. Thus I awaited Colonel Borcan. But for three weeks on end, only the shadows cast by clouds and flocks of crows made their way across the meadow that stretched away between Dobrin City and the Sinistra River. Spring rain came from the west, from Sinistra, and when the clouds collided with the steep cliffs of Mount Dobrin, they would loiter for days amid the icy peaks. Light clouds occasionally descended on the peaks from all sides, assuming en masse the shape of the mountain range like a veil draped over a sculpture. When they lifted after several days Mount Dobrin appeared once more, glistening white, even as spring had taken hold all around. Sometimes Nikifor Tescovina happened to come by towards evening with my daily bag of provisions, and whenever this happened we would sit on the sun-warmed window sill taking in the scent of ivy as it wafted up from the stream.

"As you can see, you enjoy our complete confidence," Nikifor Tescovina kept saying. "Just you see, hardly anyone will ask where you are from. And don't you go telling anyone, either. If someone takes to badgering you with questions, why then, you should lie."

"Hm. So be it. Hopefully I'll get a feel for it. I'll say something different to everyone."

"I see you're getting to know the ropes. As for your name, forget it, just like that. I mean, if you so much as happen to hear your name hissing nearby, don't even blink an eye. React to everything with a poker face."

A thick, opaque darkness descended on Dobrin after sunset; above the black silhouette of the houses light could be seen only in the distant windows of the barracks. Signals occasionally flashed from the watchtowers of the mountain infantry. Thunderbolts from Mount Dobrin loomed amid the night-time clouds, and their faraway murmur interwove with the hooting of owls down in the groves. The misty yellow light of dawn invariably found me leaning out the window.

One day Nikifor Tescovina brought along his little girl. Even from afar the child's short red hair glistened through the fog like ripe rowan berries in autumn. They were near the mill by the time I noticed that the father had his daughter on a lead. A stone's throw from the entrance, he tied her to a boundary demarcation stake. Nikifor Tescovina entered the building alone.

That day he brought a bottle of methylated spirits, too, along with a tin mug and charcoal in a pot drilled full of tiny holes. He explained that, to render the liquid drinkable, it had to be filtered through charcoal into another vessel. In the absence of charcoal, he said, tinder fungus or blueberries would also do the trick.

"At first it'll make you puke, but you'll get used to it."

"No doubt."

Already he'd begun to pour the liquid over the charcoal, holding the mug underneath and watching for the first drops.

"Soon you can get down to work. The colonel has already ordered the tubs and buckets. He's also taken on the fruit-harvesting women. They'll be swarming all over you, but you watch out for yourself. Like I said before, keep that poker face no matter what."

"I've done pretty well at self-discipline lately."

"Then make sure you keep your collar up if you cross paths with a fellow by the name of Géza Kökény. He'll tell you he's not just any old bloke, that his bust stands on the bank of the Sinistra. Well, don't you believe him."

"I won't even listen to him."

"That's it. There, by the way, is my little girl, Bebe." With this he extended an open palm towards the meadow, where the red-haired child tied to the stake sat in the grass. "You'll get to know her. She's just eight, but from what I can tell, she wants to run away from me."

"Don't you let her."

"She's fallen in love with Géza Hutira."

"I don't know the man. Must be an alias."

"Hm, who knows. He's the meteorologist in the reserve. About your age, a good fifty. But his hair reaches the ground. My little girl's heart is his."

I'd already been staying in the abandoned water mill among voles, bats and barn owls for four, five, maybe six weeks when Colonel Puiu Borcan finally called on me in person. He came by with my new name. That day winter returned for a couple of hours to the forests of the Sinistra district. An icy cloud descended even upon the blossoming meadow, a shimmering glassy mush veiled the knolls along the stream, and snowy mountainside clearings shone upon the village. I glimpsed two figures approaching through drifting wisps of fog – one was my benefactor, Nikifor Tescovina. The other, a baggy-faced, big-eared man wearing an officer's greatcoat, adjusted his cap on his forehead as he approached. A big black umbrella swung from his hand. Although icy drops of vapour from the passing storm still permeated the air, the umbrella was closed, its sodden black fabric drooping like the wings of a sleeping bat. A huge pair of binoculars swung from the neck of the forest commissioner.

Later, once I earned a measure of his respect, I, too, had the opportunity to peer through those binoculars. On one occasion I accompanied him up into the forest, and while he went into a thicket to relieve himself, he entrusted me with his umbrella and binoculars. It being Revolution Day, I knew the mountain infantrymen were playing badminton down by the stream with the Dobrin railway workers. To this day I recall how that tiny, snow-white birdie flickered back and forth two or three metres off the ground, above the tall, swaying, untrodden grass.

Anyhow, that first day Colonel Borcan, with those binoculars around his neck and the limp umbrella in his hand, came to a halt on the threshold. His expression was woeful and damp. The light of the distant snowy mountain clearings glistened through his earlobes, tufts of hair frizzed out from underneath his cap, and drops of the recent freezing rain still clung to the stubble on his chin.

"So you're the one."

"Me."

"And what's your name?"

"I dunno. Lost my papers."

"Fine, then. All's in order."

From his pocket he removed a shimmering little tin tag that dangled from a watch chain. On it, freshly engraved: Andrei Bodor. My alias. He personally put it around my neck, clasped the loose ends below my nape with tweezers, and no sooner had he done so than the metal began warming my skin. Andrei – now that part of my new name I especially liked.

3 (ARANKA WESTIN'S WINDOW)

For weeks, months, maybe years I'd been living in the Sinistra district under the alias Andrei Bodor when a trackman's job opened up with the narrow-gauge forest railway. Tin-sheathed freight cars and scrapped miners' trolleys were used on this line to transport fruit, horse carcasses and other food to the bears on the nature reserve. There, behind the reserve's fences, far from the world, lived my adopted son, Béla Bundasian, who was the reason I'd moved to this mountainous region of the north. So as soon as I heard that trackman Augustin Konnert had been found in several pieces one morning beside the tracks, I applied for his post at once.

Probably I wasn't the only one who'd applied, but in no time I was summoned to the barracks for an interview. While waiting in the hallway I met up with Dobrin's resident barber, who had just been expelled from the district. That day marked the beginning of my long friendship with Aranka Westin.

It was around then that the wild-fruit depot in Dobrin had been closed down, and although I was immediately let go from my post as harvest co-ordinator, I continued to live in the storage building, sleeping in a pantry among barrels and tubs. The depot was situated in an abandoned water mill on a meadow along a backwater of the Sinistra; the stream had long before broken away from the mill during a spring flood, leaving the stone building isolated on the meadow in the company of some pines, rowans, willows and black alders. The place was marked by a tall yellow post that could be seen from afar even on overcast days, so that the fruit-harvesting women arriving from the nearby mountains could find their way there in a swirling mist.

On the morning of that memorable day, a narrow slip of paper torn from a bag fluttered from that now superfluously towering yellow post. Looming on it, in hastily scrawled letters, were these words: "Make haste, Andrei, to the office." The message was for me, written in the hand of none other than Colonel Coca Mavrodin, the new mountain infantry commander in Dobrin. I recognised her writing from the backward N's and S's. The unknown messenger must have pinned the note to the post in the early hours: tracks made by someone who had groped about in rubber boots covered the rimy soil around it. Autumn was coming to a close.

Taking a shortcut along the footpath through the meadow, which flanked the willows along the stream, I didn't encounter a soul. Only the bust of Géza Kökény appeared from beyond the yards, through the fabric of tree branches now almost bare of their leaves. Dobrin stretched out beyond the stream and, even past the village, practically on the mountainside itself, stood the barracks of the mountain infantry, whose buildings loomed grey at the bottom of the precipice like huge piles of fallen boulders. Behind them, in one of the valleys that extended to the border, lived Béla Bundasian, my adopted son.

It's a simple, everyday story, this tale of ours. My adopted son, Béla Bundasian, did not return home one time from Moldavia, where he went regularly to buy sheet-music paper from the black marketeers at the bazaar. From that point on, I never saw him again. After his disappearance, say for a week or two, it seemed conceivable that he was once again whiling away his time with that hot-blooded gal, his sweetheart, Cornelia Illafeld. She lived somewhere right in the middle of the Carpathians, near a mountain tunnel. But since he hadn't shown up even weeks later, and hadn't so much as given a signal of life, it was safe to assume he'd got mixed up in something or other.

That is just what had happened. He'd got mixed up in something, all right. Indeed, one and a half years later it became clear that Béla Bundasian had been resettled somewhere in the vicinity of the Ukrainian border, that he was living in a nature reserve in the Sinistra district. All this I learned from an anonymous well-wisher by way of words etched with a needle onto a coin, a twenty, which the person – maybe some well-meaning official, who knows – had dropped through my letter box.

Such news is far from being cause for celebration, perhaps, but I was delirious with joy. I gave up my job with the head office at the food market, where I had been working as an inspector and, sometimes, a mushroom authority. Then I travelled north, hoping to land a job at some mountain village along the Sinistra River. All the while I followed my nose, and finally – years having passed, of course – I ended up precisely there, in the vicinity of the nature reserve in question: dank, draughty Dobrin.

Harvesting wild fruit and mushrooms was a sure way of getting by even in the leanest of times, for one could always fill up one's own bag in addition to the government-issue pack basket. Blueberries, blackberries and chanterelles are, of course, much appreciated by many people. To dispel any confusion, I should make it clear that it wasn't some big canning factory we supplied but the nearby nature reserve, where bears were kept in the ruins of a chapel and in abandoned, caved-in mines. By way of dropped hints and wily enquiries, I determined that Béla Bundasian was living in the house of the meteorologist Géza Hutira, above the tree line in the snow-capped peaks. He had nothing to do, I was told. Sometimes, as a favour of sorts, he would go outside and note the position of the weathercocks perched out on the cliffs or take readings from the instruments scattered here and there on the high plateau. He never came in to the village, so I awaited a twist of fate that might somehow or other allow us to meet up once again.

Despite my prudence, the region's previous forest commissioner, Colonel Puiu Borcan, was unwilling to sign a pass that would have allowed me to go harvesting in the reserve. As if he had seen right through my plans. But one day Puiu Borcan failed to return from one of his patrols. For a while people thought perhaps he would reappear. But when a solitary black umbrella flew over Dobrin City, steered by the wind like some giant bat – only he, mind you, the commander of the mountain infantry, used such an umbrealla on his patrols – everyone knew the colonel was no more.

Colonel Puiu Borcan was succeeded as commander of the mountain infantry at Dobrin by a woman, Izolda Mavrodin, who went by the nickname Coca. She was a slender creature, quiet, diaphanous, like a dragonfly. Whenever she wanted to see me, she'd send a note, just a few short words scrawled with a piece of charcoal and ragged at that, invariably torn from a paper bag. What's more, recognising her messages was easy: her N's and S's were always backwards. As I headed down the footpath towards the barracks, such brown strips of paper fluttered here and there on dry stalks and leafless twigs. "They've waiting for you, Andrei, very important business."

Coca Mavrodin had summoned others to the office as well. The lobby was full of resin-scented lumberjacks, forest rangers and the like. This is how it happened that, while awaiting my turn, I met up with the barber of Dobrin, Vili Dunka. As if no longer in the mood to (or allowed to) recognise anyone at all, he was just leaving the office with angry, disdainful, hurried steps. But I went after him. We'd been known to chum up over a drink or two.

He was no more pleased to see me than anyone else. He explained that he was in a hurry, for he had to leave the village, the whole Sinistra district, in fact, on the first available train. That morning he'd been summoned to the barracks, allowed to bring a travel bag, a change of underclothes and some personal effects. He was heading straight for the station. The barber's shop had closed in Dobrin City, as had the bar; all establishments where people tended to chit-chat while lingering about had been shut down. To prove the veracity of his story, he pulled out the free rail ticket he'd been given to travel to his designated new abode.

"And what does Aranka Westin have to say about this?" I asked.

"Nothing. It doesn't apply to her; she'll go on patching up officers' overcoats. She'll stay here, naturally."

The woman in question sewed for the barracks, and until that day she and Vili Dunka had lived together.

"I ask because you no doubt realise," I said, continuing my initial line of thought, "that you'll be away for many years. Perhaps you won't ever come back."

"Uh-huh, that's how things look. I'm ready for anything."

"And I don't know if you ever noticed, but I've always had an eye for Aranka Westin. Now that you're off, I'll do all I can to fill your shoes."

"Yeah, that crossed my mind, too. Well, it's simple: I just won't think about you two."

"I'm saying this now because I'm an upfront sort of fellow. I wouldn't want it to look as if I'm doing anything behind your back. No, I wouldn't want you to end up thinking anything bad."

"I've forgotten you two already. Most of my things are still there, with her, so feel free to use anything that's to your liking. My undershirts, slippers, underwear, still there – we're about the same size. All I'm taking with me are scissors, straight razors and a couple of shaving brushes, not to mention shaving cream. My barber supplies, you know. Everything else is yours."

"You're a decent chap."

"What the hell am I supposed to do?"

"Then again, who knows what's going to happen with me? As you see, they called me in here, too."

"But you don't have your travel bag with you. You can stay. At least for a while."

"I hope so. And that's why I'll take the liberty of asking if you might give me some advice. How should I behave towards her? What are her habits, her feminine whims?"

"Damn it, man. You just worry about her big white shanks, not her whims. Okay, let's just say that if she's busy sewing, don't even think of bothering with her. For her, duty always comes first. And now I've got to be off, if you don't mind. All the best."

"Thanks. Take care of yourself, huh?"

And with that, Vili Dunka, the former barber of Dobrin, headed off. From the hallway window I watched him cut across the yard with its glistening puddles and wait by the porter's booth for the officer on duty to let him out. Finally, his path on the other side of the solid fence was apparent only by sparrows taking flight. Vili Dunka disappeared along the road to the station, and that was the last anyone ever heard of him.

It was late afternoon by the time I was called in for the interview. Seated in the forest commissioner's chair was the coroner, Colonel Titus Tomoioaga, who asked me to excuse Coca Mavrodin, as she happened to be occupied at the moment. However, he assured me, she was reviewing my application for the trackman's job. But there was a small problem – namely that my files had been lost while being taken to the records office. Until they turned up, a few reliable persons would be asked for their opinions of me. And who was to say, she might just employ me as a courier of sorts, if not necessarily as a trackman. Yes, she was in need of someone to take messages into the nature reserve.

It seemed she wanted to send me to the very place I'd been banned from until then. After waiting for so many years, perhaps I would finally meet Béla Bundasian again. Feigning indifference, I stared listlessly ahead, as if the whole thing was not my cup of tea. And, after so long, I couldn't even bring myself to be too happy. Besides, to be honest, my thoughts were still on Vili Dunka waiting at the station, the free ticket in his pocket. The sounding of the short whistle would mean he had left. It would be nice to try on his slippers that very night.

Being late autumn, night was already coming on as I left the barracks and walked along the unpeopled roads of the village, the dogs barking and the mist swirling. More than a few years had passed since the power lines had been cut, so most houses cowered every night in mute darkness. But even now, so early, hurricane lamps and tallow candles glowed faintly here and there. A window shone dimly, like daybreak, from deep inside the yard of the seamstress, Aranka Westin.

For quite a while I peered through the cracks and crevices in the curtain, watching her grope about like a widow. There she sat in the flickering candlelight, patching heavy felt uniforms. A thick woollen shawl, folded into a triangle, covered her back; its tip reached her bottom, the two wings nestling on those thighs Vili Dunka had called shanks. She seemed a bit cold; perhaps she hadn't had the time to light a fire that day.

I went out back to the woodshed, bundled a few logs in my arms and grabbed some kindling, too, before returning. Without knocking I opened the door by pressing the handle down with my knee. Aranka Westin looked up at once, but then promptly lowered her head; she flashed me another glance or two as I clumsily closed the door, again using my knee. Assuming her eyes were indeed sharp, and seamstresses surely have sharp eyes, she might have noticed the trousers trembling around my leg; perhaps she thought this was from the draught. At least five years had passed since I'd been with a woman.

I waited for the first encouraging sign – for the furrows on her chin to subside or for her toes to relax invitingly in her slippers. But most of all, I waited for her finally to drop the officer's cloak she was busily equipping with new pockets of grey felt. This little venture of mine was a sure thing, I knew, and now I also knew this: I mustn't make a move as long as the sewing continued.

[PO]

ZSOLT LÁNG

from *A Transylvanian Bestiary: Birds of the Air*

THE GREY RAVEN

It was not just that, as yet, there was no name for a plate – nor was there one for the mind. There did not exist enough of either for it to be worth christening them: a poking finger seemed enough should they happen to come under discussion.

Baron Sapré had a plate too, but he could take pride, first and foremost, in his mind, since he had acquired his plates, indeed all his tableware, the many cattle of his household, his properties, his rank and his power as well with his mind. The peoples of the surrounding area called the richly fabled deviousness of his mind sorcery; he himself, they thought, had sold his soul to the devil, and in return had received the occult science of wizardry and evil machinations. All that had stood on the site of his cloud-wreathed castle a few years before, in the recollections of those who dwelled down below, were capriciously fissured rocks, the ruins of an ancient fortress. Then, in a single stormy night, the new snowy-white stone fortress, its towers roofed with copper and its windows dazzling back the rays of the sun, had descended from the heavens, and flat, rounded stones, big as the broad hats of the Germans, had hailed down to pave the winding road leading up to the castle, while the baron, who likewise plopped down here out of nowhere, had been able to drive up to it in his leather-trimmed coach with the massive wheels, his silver-helmeted foot soldiers padding behind the coach, along with his baggage-waggons and his host of serving people, and the weather-cocked chimneys of the castle had begun to smoke. A grey raven that had never been seen before also made its appearance around the castle, blighting the dreams of folk with its muffled nocturnal croaking. In vain did Máté Kovács Nagy, headman of the village of Zsombok, have poisoned bait hung from the boughs of the oak trees; neither the black venom milked from the throats of snakes nor the toxic salt ground from the rocks made a difference. In the end, the village headman spread the rumour that the baron fed the bird off his own thigh, and that was why it would not touch any other nourishment.

The baron rarely moved outside his castle, yet he still knew about all that happened far and wide. But it was idle to see any wizardry in the matter. Zsombok Castle towered high above the lower peaks; in fine weather the entire country could be seen, from the Eastern Carpathians to the Western ranges, from the Fogaras alps in the south to Mount Crystal in the north. And he kept himself informed about what he could not see through the sounds carried up as a supplication from care-worn hearts, because at nightfall, when the daytime commotion was stilled down in the valleys, sounds soared up to the castle on high: conversations, cries, the rumbling of carts and carriages, the ringing of iron and steel, the knelling of a bell, the whinnying of horses, the shrilling of Turkish pipes and children, the cries of women in labour, the protestations and curses of menfolk eddied and seethed around the towers.

Although tears were still pouring in a stream down his face, and his body and soul were racked by sobbing, the cogs in his brain were spinning like mill-wheels, though these wheels were doing no grinding but piecing things together. In his brain, in a fleeting moment, a thousand possibilities were checked out against one another, and he, like the Persian inventor of the game of chess, was clear that, through successive doublings, it takes but a single grain of wheat placed on the first square for a whole sea of grain to shower on to the last square.

He thrust the blunt end of his lumpish index finger to the back of his throat in an attempt to scoop from himself the waves of acute nausea that were welling up, time and time again, from grief. He started to cough, and his scrawny body clattered like a sheet of iron. Then silence supervened, and the room filled with the noises of the outside, along with the light of dawn. Sapré, rising from his armchair and shuffling across to the window, flopped on to the crenellated stone parapet and looked out.

He heard the rumbling of his carriage on the paved road to Vidrány, heard the see-saw drone of the outbursts of fury that kept erupting from George Vidrányi's drunken cronies, and the blaring "come-in-do" boomed out by the host who met him at the door. I would like to take your daughter for my wife – the sound of his own timid voice from the past struck his ear . . .

Vidrányi goggled with bloodshot eyes, his vacant gaze gaping inanely at his guest; then, draining in one draught the goblet in his hand, he turned back towards the house, where his cronies were out-bellowing one another in their demands for a fresh barrel to be tapped. To indulge the throat, every whim, prank, revelry and, above all, merry jest. But this capped it all! He erupted into laughter, dashed his wine goblet to the ground, slapped his knee, doubled up, staggered around, trampling underfoot the yellow irises that bordered the path. Vidrányi's head was incessantly full of foolishness; a vile morality resided within him, and his conduct was informed by boorish habits. He slapped Sapré on the shoulder, then coarsely snatched at him between his legs, invited him in, saying there was room for him too. Pulling down the flap of his breeches, he began to urinate, directing the yellow arc into a mouse hole. By the time he had emptied his bladder, he had also regained his voice.

"Xenia, Xenia!" he shouted the girl's name, "your suitor has arrived!"

Sapré turned pale, his teeth chattered, his knees gave way as, all-atremble, he cast stealthy glances towards the house. He would flee in panic before the gaze of females, sensing that they were stripping him bare in order to make a laughing stock of his skinny body. Vidrányi started to reel his way back into the house; Sapré pulled himself together and crept dizzily in exactly the opposite direction, into the cover of the hazel bushes beside the lake. He threw himself down on a tree stump and burst into tears. And as he now heard that morning's sobbing from his window, the waves of humiliation seemed to wrench it from his puny chest with a magnet, and the bitter sobbing struck up again, so it was impossible to make out the painful voices of the past from those of the present.

Darkness shrouded the valley. Only above the towers did there remain a trace of light to splash the grey raven, now stealing on to the scene, with a white lustre. Sapré wiped away his tears and directed his gaze attentively upwards. He could interpret the bird's flight, the quivers of its wing pinions, the number of wing beats, the curve of its tail – a wisp of air swirled aside here, a barely perceptible eddy there, amplifying in a train of links to whip up a storm whose inundations would batter shores teeming with life. Such knowledge is important to anyone who plots the events of the future. The grains of sand trickle down in the hourglass and, however sharp the mind may be, cannot be prevailed upon to move contrariwise; yet the flux of the grains may be arrested by precisely inscribing the path of a single grain of sand, and time will be at a standstill in that obstructed trajectory. Human deeds are not regulated by divine foresight. God may be mighty, but He is unable to attend to the details; He does not keep track of the billions of aerial molecules. Only a human mind is capable of foreseeing the future, chequered as it is with nationwide misfortunes or insignificant adventures.

Over against the dipping sun rose the Moon. Sapré recovered his composure. He called for his valet, washed himself, asked for food. He gave out orders: the horses were to be harnessed, they were off to Count István at Gyulafehérvár.

Make haste, make haste, was heard over and over again from the carriage. By lunchtime they reached István, who stared at his guest with tiny, alarmed eyes. The last time an unexpected traveller had shown up out of the blue at his dining pavilion, with news that the Turks were pillaging in the countryside around Alvinc, he had taken such fright that he drained the vinegar cruet instead of his goblet of wine. Thereafter he quailed at every casual visitor, and had it been up to him, he would have received no-one; he protected himself from stealthy newsmongers with tripwires carrying bells. Only death did he fear more. His residence was full of mollycoddled soothsayers who, fearing the consequences of unfulfilled prognostications, flew the coop with panicky swiftness, only for their places to be taken by their ever newer fellows, dubious and sly of mind one and all. The chambers of the future cannot be decked out with alarm bells.

It was precisely about the future that Sapré wished to speak to him in person: right now it swarms as busily as a beehive, but if you fail to act the hive will empty in a trice.

But István had become snagged on the hook of speech:

"Speak up," he bawled, cupping the flap of his ear with the gesture of the hard of hearing.

"I wish to protect you from the machinations of malicious schemers."

"What awaits me?"

"Death."

"Tell me more, more!"

"You must act. The coming night our prince, Sigismund, will breathe the last of his restless spirit. Count Balthazar, who had been intriguing at the Holy Roman Emperor's court some twenty years now, is just waiting for this moment, and he will be back as soon as he receives the news, with the Emperor's appointment in the bag and a small regiment behind him. And you know what his first step will be? To silence the most eminent. Power-drunk scum always start with that. The heads of five nobles will tumble on the yellow dust in the marketplace of Fehérvár, and, to make the murderer's joy still sweeter, the last will be yours, István!"

A chill ran through the count. He blenched and clutched at his neck to search for his pulse; maybe it was already all up with him. After the chill, his blood began to boil; rage and unbridled hatred chased one another in hot pursuit around his seething innards, he smashed to smithereens whatever came into his hands. Finally he hunched his head between his shoulders in alarm and, blinking pathetically, turned to Sapré. The baron had no wish to anticipate events recklessly: should morning bring a black-flagged messenger from the princely court, that would be the time to break the seal on the edict carrying the future's secret.

On this, the guest withdrew to recuperate from the strains of his long journey. Paying no heed to the household hubbub around him, the usual comings and goings of those who live from one day to the next, he preferred to sleep by day rather than by night. Night-time was the busy part of the day for a child of the Moon. His imagination, as if it were the pallid stuff of light, streamed out into space to feel and spy out the tracks of the snails, which show him the paths that are without hazard to the point where he can launch out with assurance, like the vagrant Tartar horde, into the pitch-black of nights. Everything that happens in the world below Sun and Moon is subject not merely to the necessary influence of the heavenly bodies but also to that still more vital Power which governs the paths of the planets and stars, and strews the open spaces of the universe with vortical traps. Anyone who knows the location of these passages can gain a presentiment of the true intention of this Power, and he will always stay one step ahead of the game.

That day an emissary arrived at Prince Sigismund's with an ornate gift. The casket contains a sumptuous goblet: in it wine turns to honey, but that honey is poison, insidiously lethal poison. Averroës, the Arab sage, was dispatched from this earthly shadow-world in this manner, and renegade Moorish alchemists have concocted the treacherous potion ever since. The Andalusian beaker, the first grain of wheat, the first move . . .

* * *

Try as he might to conspire, the hard-of-hearing Count István's secret instructions carried far, and the agitated reports of his horsed messengers could be made out even a mile off; so loud were they bellowed it was as if their bearers were being poked with red-hot irons. As a result, Sapré got wind in good time of the insolent, meddlesome, ignoble intentions of the count's steward, who feared for his position. The night after the storm, he again sat out beside his coach, took out his letters and waited. A few minutes had barely gone by when the grey raven showed up with a noiseless beating of wings. Sapré attached the rolled-up documents below the wings, then the courier flew back to Zsombok Castle, where Domine Valentine, the baron's valet, awaited his instructions.

As soon as the storm had blown itself out, George Vidrányi had also set off in order to clear himself before the count, for relations with him had never been hostile. When news of what István was accusing him of had reached his ears, he sobered up for a moment from his years of sottishness and, on recovering his senses, suddenly grew sick of the eternal debauchery. He felt complete relief when it occurred to him to make the journey, seeing it as a form of spiritual and bodily pilgrimage. Of course, he was accompanied by the same cronies as had been revelling in his house, and by the second day of the journey he no longer had any recollection of his rehabilitated state. They headed first for Fehérvár but, on gaining intelligence of István's halting-places, broke off their journey and wended their way up towards Szatmár. Three carts trundled after them with their provisions, twice that many with the wine casks.

Xenia, against her will, was likewise travelling in the carousing cavalcade as it meandered across the country. She did not so much as glance outside her carriage, which in truth was no more than a hastily converted baggage-waggon with cushioning. When they drove up to the house of the Caspar Nagys the first evening, her father had to resort to the same force in ordering her to step down as in setting her on to the carriage at the start. She rushed up to the guest room, refused to touch her food and lay fully clothed in bed, pulling the eiderdown over her head. She did not fall asleep. Since she was a tot, the one thing on her mind had been how she would kill her father. Whether in her own room or in some forgotten recess of the house, she fantasised constantly about this; like finger sucking, it became an obsession, holding her in its thrall in the same way as did wine-drinking, or sweet talk to women and beasts, her father and his cronies.

The fourth night she fell asleep and, for perhaps the first time in her life, had a dream. Stone birds came down from the sky and flocked on the ground: on fields, courtyards, house-roofs and roads. She was scared of them but could go nowhere, could not even move a step.

Then, as if by chance, she touched one of them, and at this mere throb of a fingertip the stone bird came to life and flew off.

On awakening, still under the influence of the dream, she decided to escape back home. She crept out to the courtyard and, by the first faint glimmer of dawn, spotted an already saddled horse that had been left loose. She led it out of the courtyard, going in front with stealthy steps; even the horse's shoe clopped just the once, and nobody started up. The servants were sprawled unconscious, in a drunken stupor, on the ground. She levered herself on to the saddle by mounting an ant's nest. She had never ridden a horse before, but the animal was an old, experienced, full-blooded steed, not skittish, and she left the reins hanging slackly to let it take her wherever it pleased, on the surmise that the horse would also want to be back home. Once they got there, she would set fire to the house, which was a perpetual haunt for strangers, hulking men who filled every available room to overflowing, with the result that more building-work had to be done to accommodate them and the old, brown-burnished dining table of sweet-smelling yew-wood had to be replaced. The sun bobbed up, as if to betoken the already flickering flames. She winced at the blinding light, and through the wincing something stirred within her body. A bird started to flap inside her; it spread its wings and beat them, like a cockerel fleeing from the knife. Racked by cramps, she stooped over the horse's neck, even drew her knees up; in this precarious balance, she was jolted onwards. The horse, as if sensing the pain gnawing at its passenger and paying sympathetic heed to what was going on inside her, slowed right down. The bird flapped ever more violently; the girl screwed up her eyes in pain. At that moment a shadow flitted past in front of the steed's legs. The animal reared up with a snort, and its rider fell senseless to the ground.

When she recovered from her swoon and opened her eyes, a bird was circling high up in the broad daylight of the firmament. Lying on her back, she gazed at the lazy, entrancing orbits. Her heart was barely beating. She could feel the dampness seeping through her dress. Her skirt had become bloodied, as had the ground beneath. She scratched dust into the palm of her hand and sprinkled it over the blood on account of the flies. She looked for the horse, but it was nowhere to be seen. The sky too had emptied. Silence reigned in the thicket at the edge of the forest. She instinctively guessed at something, clambered to her feet and, with an expertise that she may have witnessed among the serving girls, tearing a strip from the frothy cambric of her underskirt, she prepared her first menstrual towel. She felt light and free. She would feel the same sense of relief when she was later to see blood spilling from the writhing bodies of the beheaded, as if every tormenting vision were ebbing away along with the blood.

She felt ill at ease wandering through the forest. Around her were fragrant wild strawberries, at the foot of every tree sprang a different-tasting source of water, and yet she still went hungry and thirsty. She started at the rustling of leaves in the breeze, the clinking of pebbles on the bottoms of streams, the mysterious patterns of sunlight filtering through the sieve of the leafy tree boughs, the cobwebs that stuck to her face. Yet for a fraction of a second she was overwhelmed by a sense of familiarity that she had never experienced before – a profound, all-pervasive feeling, such a pity it was so fleeting. At twilight she began to shiver and long for warmth. She was scared to death by a pair of eyes glinting amid the foliage of a bush, and since she no longer had the strength to flee, she burst into a frantic scream. She collapsed, as if she had slammed into a wall of hard rock; her breathing snagged, her heart paused in its beating, her skin grew pallid as the moon. Then, through the naked walls of terror, she heard the calls of her father's men.

* * *

The fog dispersed so suddenly it might never have been there. The west tower of the tortoise-shaped fortress pierced the red disc of the sun. Evening had come.

As the sky shone out, all at once silence fell in the square. A headless body was readily discernible, writhing on the scaffold, with blood spouting in all directions from the unstopped neck. The body then slumped senseless; the wild gush of blood also abated and silently trickled down from the planks into a swelling puddle in the dust. Every dog in the town scrambled there, lapping up the blood; snarling and baring their fangs, at times they snapped at one another.

The Sun's disc did not budge, seemingly stuck on the tower's flagpole or standing on tiptoe to see out the final scenes of the bloody drama. Then, on the opposite side, in the firmament above the scaffold, another scaffold arose at a vast height, a shadow of the earthly one, perhaps, yet looking the more real none the less, because, despite the outlines of distant peaks looming bluely behind the gentle hilltops, it belied the palpable high ground. And upon that heavenly scaffold a black figure of terror, hiding its face with a hood, as is the executioners' custom, rocked a gigantic axe, adjusting the axe-blade to the block as it dangled its free arm with death-presaging deliberation.

A bad sign, the thought flashed through István's mind, and even his coughing fits abated: his eyes staring, mouth gaping, he might have been the victim of a stroke. And to put the finishing touch to this horror, the aide standing next to him, who, following his master's gaze, had also looked up at the sky, saw the arrival of some sort of storm cloud in the phenomenon and speculated that the rain would wash out the market-place entertainments that customarily ensued after executions, and with a dismissive gesture of disappointment shouted up: The devil take you!

Xenia looked down on the purpling platform from quite near at hand, on the stone stairs at the foot of Skinners' Bastion. She gradually recognised her father's garments, saw the big, melancholy head roll away in a spiral to come to rest, after a little juddering, in the middle of the scaffold. The eyes blinked oddly, not together, and the lips mouthed with a frightful twitching. The executioner's assistant, slipping as he tried to stop the rolling head with his foot and only regaining his balance by swiftly flailing his arms, uttered an oath as he picked up Vidrányi's head by the hair to sling it into the basket. Xenia grasped at this point that the body could not be reassembled. She smiled to herself. The feeling of cold, gnawing hatred spilled out of her, spilled out like a clot of blood. She glanced instinctively up to the sky, where the familiar bird was now circling.

Only the next day was Prince István able to recover his speech, pronouncing judgement over the property of those who had been executed. Half of it could be kept by the heirs, the other part was to pass to the prince's treasury. Not a severe nor vengeful judgement. Kristóf's widow curtsied gratefully, but the girl, George Vidrányi's sole heir, was not to be found.

She had vanished.

The great bird circled above the square before gliding down before the castellan's house to alight on the shoulder of a tiny, fragile man. The little man started to caper; he danced like someone who cannot contain himself for joy. Then, quite unexpectedly, he dropped to his knees and sprawled flat on his face in the dust. The grey bird whisked off, but the man stayed prone in this peculiar pose for a while further. He was muttering something to himself that was inaudible, though the dust before his mouth could be seen to be stirring. He fell silent and cocked his head to one side, because he sensed that he was being watched. Their gazes met. Xenia took such fright that her innards tightened to a knot; she clutched her head and quickly turned into a narrow alley. Among the swirling scraps of the day's confused events she saw clearly before her the gypsy woman repeating incessantly, over and over again: the bird above, the serpent below.

THE HUMAN-HEADED PARROT

Count Boldizsár loved venturing into foreign lands and, mixing with seafarers, had even travelled overseas, but while he was away his relatives moved into his castles, pillaged his cellars and closets, stuffed their bellies with his droves and herds, scraped the bottoms off his plates and dishes. His steward, whose job it should have been to conserve and multiply the goods and chattels entrusted to his care, colluded with the relatives (two layabout brothers-in-law) and led the way in the pillaging, putting the count's property at the mercy of his own and the relatives' rapacity, covetousness and villainy.

Of course, Count Boldizsár had no need to look to his neighbours for a bit of knavery, malice or slyness, for he was a thoroughgoing scoundrel himself, a swindler slippery as an eel, whose repertoire of chicanery had been considerably expanded in the course of his long peregrinations. A nice little family!

How might he shift the winds from the unfavourable quarter from which they were now blowing?

He had one strange little chap, a talking bird acquired on his travels at a bazaar, a human-headed parrot. The deuced creature had barely grown two spans in height, so that virtually its entire length was taken up by a full-sized man's face. From a distance he looked like a waddling human head, especially when he shuffled across the courtyard to visit the hen coops. Then anybody might have supposed he was some kind of wood elf, hobgoblin or bloated domestic dwarf. He grimaced expressively with his human features as if he had genuine feelings; in the place of a beak gaped a regular human mouth, while in the mouth were rows of teeth (and when he talked a lot a rancid mouth-odour enveloped him), notwithstanding which his body was covered with conventional feathers (with pungent reminiscences of his escapades among the hens), and it was underpinned and carried by two *bona fide* bird legs. He was partial to hens; nothing pleased him more than to amuse himself all day long in their company. By imitating the hissing of a snake, he had managed to reduce the cockerel, that vain and stupid princeling, to a quivering wreck in under two days, after which he had taken over the rule of the roost, covering the hens and eating up the corn before them.

For all that he was a lazy creature, he could learn anything with ease; he knew long passages from the Bible by heart and could spout them fluently. Many priests envied his superb memory, no less the ingenious rhetoric with which he delivered his commentaries; nor did those exegeses lack intellect, or indeed the noble tendentiousness of morality, in the view of more cultivated minds.

People came from far and wide to see and listen to him. A golden ducat had to be plunked down first, but then the count would already have flung open the door to the parrot's separate quarters. There were no other furnishings in the room apart from an armchair and a table, and upon the table an open-doored cage, woven from white canes of osier, and inside that – the bird. The visitor would sit down, then ask something, while the bird would respond with a will. Neither the past nor the future was a mystery to him. His sentences avoided quibbling or vague generalisation; they were so explicit that even a half-wit could understand what had to be done or what could be reckoned on.

The rumours of his soothsaying prowess brought one client after another to the door, while Count Boldizsár was as happy as a huckster. His relatives ate their hearts out afresh, racking their brains over how they might lay hands on the new asset, the bountiful cornucopia that could be emptied in revelries without the least scrap of effort.

Yet nobody thought to ask the bird about when the flow of golden ducats would leave off.

* * *

False prophets can easily arise in the midst of a people that buries itself in self-lacerating moping, especially if that people is characterised by as much superstitious belief and childish credulity as the Székelys.

We never had a king of our own, they started to say. Then they hit upon one such who, laughable as he was, nobody laughed about.

They convoked an assembly, the gist of which was that the Székely nation, by the grace of God, elected the human-headed creature as its king. For them to flee their abject and sorry plight by going over to some king or another, to someone who might have a human form but in whom dwelt the soul of a wolf – that had happened before. But from this day on they would entertain no presumptuous hopes: the castle of Székelyrises was being built; there would be no Székelyruesit.

They picked those who were best cut out for the task of fetching the bird that knew the secrets of the future, having first liberated him from shameful bondage. Did that sound like a bird? No, not a bird, but a heavenly apparition, whom they had appointed twice over. *Nonnisi mutato habitu* – Fine feathers make fine birds, indeed. It was no chance that his face reminded them of their apostle: had he not foretold their early release from this earthly purgatory; and the fact that he had wings was also a sign of heavenly grace. To delay action after that was tantamount to infidelity. They even had a crown, one they had received from Byzantium, what is more, and kept hidden as a holy relic down the centuries.

The stately procession got under way. The steeds too were the handsomest creatures, fully a match for the equestrian stone figure on the hillside at Zsombok; the horsemen – the shapeliest Székely youths, chests swollen with pride, as though they had already successfully completed their mission. They passed under arches decked out with flowers, girls on tiptoe offered goblets of wine, the sun shone, spring foliage glistened on the tree boughs, the air was clear, the distant mountain peaks, still capped with snow, stood out sharply. Fortune was also on their side, because a chatterbox of a woman had already blabbed out where they might easily find the bird. Yet they became so immersed in the celebration that, in the end, they were left empty-handed. When they came to their senses from their inebriation and grasped their situation, they burst into tears, each and every one: so much for the king, so much for glory. They wandered round in a daze for a while longer, clueless as to which track they should follow, whom they might ask. They did not even dare look one another in the eye but just ambled along in silence, entrusting themselves to their horses. It is told that they went into hiding among the Turks, but in truth, crossing paths with the vagrant Tartar horde, perhaps deliberately seeking an end, they found death from the blades of swords that know no mercy.

It had been a Friday when Sapré reached István, and Sunday when the Lords who had gathered for the bison hunt murdered Kótai. And it was Friday again when István entered Gyulafehérvár.

The Andalusian beaker, in which wine turns to honey, though the honey is poison, a lethal potion with no antidote, revealed its provenance and its occult properties only half a hundred off three centuries later. The real criminal misled everybody; he was the instigator of events, he pulled all the strings. Not once did the new prince, Count István, notice what strings were being jerked left, right and centre. What a busy puppet! After having George Vidrányi and the other rebels executed on Szatmár's main square, he set off a search for the architect of the plot, head of the rebellion, the ringleader, Count Balthazar. Balthazar, minion of the Roman Emperor of the Germans. Who might he be? He supposed that Balthazar, in the Magyar tongue, was Boldizsár . . .

One morning, as Count Boldizsár was stretching himself, having just woken from his sleep, the human-headed bird waddled in (he almost never used his wings) and hopped up on the bed. For once it was he who asked the question first:

"Have you heard that your head will be cut off soon?"

"Who would do that?"

"That hard-of-hearing and so gullible lord, István – who, in his foolish naivety, will see black as white, if others say so – now considers he has found the leader of the rebellion in you. There is only one count around here called Boldizsár. The Walloon infantrymen will be coming for you the day after tomorrow."

Hitherto Boldizsár had sought out his bird on just a single question: where he might find a fortune, and how he should multiply it. Even now nothing else interested him, yet the damned bird kept prattling on incessantly about blood and executions, lopped-off heads and a girl who was also bleeding. He had had enough of it.

He locked it in its cage, then packed it off with one of his young fellows to Fehérvár, to appear before the new prince, saying that maybe he would be more interested in what that philandering devil of a wise-owl was blathering on about.

Before setting out on the long journey, the young envoy paid a visit on his intended, thinking to bid her farewell. He spent the night with her, and as they were parting he blurted out the nature of the consignment he was travelling with. The next day, the maiden, who was keeping more than one iron in the fire, blabbed on to the stalwarts who buckled her bed what she had heard that night. The stalwarts carried the news to their brothers-in-law, and the brothers-in-law immediately galloped off after the bird. They lay in wait for the envoy at the edge of a forest, gave him a sound beating around the head with their maces, and were soon trotting back with the canvas-covered cage. They thought the bird, the most prolific gold mine in the country, was now in their hands. But the snow-white cage was empty.

Count Boldizsár had extricated himself from innumerable tricky situations, but this time he completely lost his composure and became so bereft of his wits that, to the very end, he kept on reiterating the same confused story about a double who had carried out everything of which he was suspected; a parrot who knew about this, and had very likely played an active part in the machinations, since he was the devil's brood, there was no disputing it; so that the one they should be submitting to the axe here could only be the parrot; it ought to be produced, even if only from under the ground. The hard-of-hearing prince could make little sense of this farrago, which would anyway have overstepped the bounds of his patience. Only one person would have been able to penetrate his deafness, but he stayed in the background. The prince, left to his own devices, superstitiously rejoiced that here, at last, was somebody whom he could have beheaded without compunction. Until now he had vainly tried to cure the twinges of conscience that he felt on account of the Vidrányis with a tea made from the florescence of the castor-oil plant; the cure seemed merely to rekindle the pangs, and, what is more, he was continually having to urinate. Perhaps his internal problems would now subside! Death to the evil, power-crazed maniac! Death to the country's foe, death to the scheming Count Balthazar!

[TW]

SÁNDOR CSOÓRI

Barbarian Prayer

Wrinkled, unrelaxing stone,
rock of mother-daylight, take
the back again into your womb.
Being born was the first error;
the world was what I wanted to be:
lion and tree-root in one,
loving animal and laughing snow,
consciousness of the wind, of heights
pouring their dark ink-blot down –
and here I am cloud-foundered man,
king of a solitary way,
being of a cindery star,
and what I join within myself
splits me at once, because it goes
quickly and only sharpens yearning . . .
Wrinkled, unrelaxing stone,
rock of mother-daylight, I
stand at the entrance to your womb.

[EMor]

ATTILA BARTIS

Engelhard, or the Story of Photography

In the spring of nineteen-seventy-three, a shepherd named Ágoston Szöcske sheared precisely one hundred kilos of black wool off the backs of the Sáromberke famous sheep belonging to the parish priest. In the days following, the raw wool was washed, combed and stuffed into five sacks, then taken up to the presbytery loft. Naphthalene (against moths) and nails from a dead horse's hoof (against thieves) were placed at the bottom of all five sacks, so no-one could seriously think that the wool could come to harm.

After morning mass Father Ignác Vass got up on his bicycle, rode to the end of the village and told the Gypsies who made adobe bricks that they could set to work the next day: the hundred kilos of wool were ready and waiting for them. Beautiful and black, as they had asked.

"Moths got last year's wool, and the year before's was stolen. There'll be no church fence out of this year's either, Father, you'll see," said the Gypsies, though it was barely drizzling at the time.

And by six o'clock that evening, the River Maros had swept away all nine piles of bricks, the tents, the cart, the copper cauldron with the supper; at half past six it had added the stage of the culture centre and a hundred and fifty Thonet chairs, the public people's library, the complete works of Lenin were floating on the water, and the Maros was just warming to the job, it took the Electrolux radios, the Opera and Diamant television sets with the Sunday-night music programme, it took the glass fishes off the tops of the television sets, and the hen-houses, the agricultural engineer's Dacia car, the apple trees, the combine harvester, the road, the postmistress with the undelivered Easter greeting-cards, the reports off the policeman's desk, then it took the policeman as well, and it did not stop there, though the people of Sáromberke would have been content with less, but the Maros decided that it would take the seven o'clock mass as well, and the thirty-three black sheep, and Ottokár Prohászka's admonitions to youth together with Father Ignác Vass's Ukraine-brand bicycle, it was carrying all of these things but would have those five dratted sacks as well, so it started out from the presbytery kitchen up to the attic. The priest was sitting up in the attic beside the trapdoor, and when the water reached the seventh stair he burst into tears, took hold of the sacks and threw all hundred kilos of wool down into the kitchen for the Maros to take away.

Early next morning in Meggyesfalva, an old woman named Aranka Vájár peeped out of the window in her loft and decided it would be worth her while to risk her life. First she threw down the nutting stick with the hook at the tip, then, hoisting up her skirts, she too slipped down the ladder to the yard where the water was only knee-high. She gathered in the spoils so nimbly and deftly as if this had been her occupation since she was a child. First she pulled the postmistress's bag off the cherry tree, for that seemed the most promising catch, then she harvested two blankets off the pear tree, a potted plant (artificial) and a volume of Lenin from the roof of the lean-to kitchen, a set of underwear from the currant bush, three perfectly well-preserved devotional pictures from the Stations of the Cross series, and she was beginning to think her luck was running out when she caught sight of five large sacks floating past the hydrangeas, all in a row.

While the wool was drying Aranka considered the subsequent fate of the spoils. In the end she decided that the wisest thing to do would be to go to Vásárhely and make it up with my grandmother, whose house she cleaned and with whom she had recently had a disagreement about a set of silver cutlery which had inexplicably got lost; in a word, they would have a cup of coffee together – she'd bring the coffee, just so Grandmother would see she meant to be taken seriously – and then this business of the wool could be solved as well.

There was not much left of the roads, they were using tracked armoured vehicles to get bread to the villages, and Aranka could not have imagined a better time to make peace with my grandmother. She pleaded with the Romanian soldiers so insistently that they finally sat her up on one of the tanks and took her into Vásárhely.

While the coffee was brewing Grandmother lent credence to Aranka's tale concerning the set of silver cutlery and involving a cast of thirteen people; she begged her pardon for defaming her character, then disclosed her most recent secret: the remedy for malignant tumours.

One part oats, two parts black radishes, two parts aloe, two parts toasted apple-seeds, and three parts acacia honey, but for anyone who did not like oats, rye would do just as well.

"There's money to be made out of this, Mrs Gheraszim, you mark my words. A great deal of money," said Aranka, wishing to worm her way into my grandmother's heart. And when she was halfway there, in other words had one foot securely planted in the gold mine, she made mention of a certain black lamb, whose fleece was known to reduce high blood pressure. By the time they had drunk the coffee, all hundred kilos of wool had come into the possession of my family in exchange for four Maria Theresa guilders.

"Get rid of this filth this instant," Grandmother commanded Mother as soon as she realised that the deal she had made was no better than the last one, when she had exchanged a string of genuine pearls for ivory-looking plastic. So the wool stayed in our bed-linen drawer and the moths feasted on it, as Aranka had skimped on the naphthalene.

For some reason no-one wanted to buy the wherewithal to make woven material from us in those days. Then, a year later, a rag-and-bone man appeared in our street, he did not even have a horse, but pulled his cart himself, shouting, "Old clo! Rag and bone! Any ol' irons!" and he rang our bell too, three times, because Mother did not dare open the door.

We feared rag-and-bone merchants like hell-fire. At the first ring of the bell we already knew that we would let them in at the third, and if everything went well, they would not swindle us, just give us a good price for something beyond price. Give us, say, five hundred for the small mirror, a fair price that, you had to admit, but then they'd be taking all that was left over from the Christmas of nineteen-forty-four along with the mirror, and that of course came to more than five hundred, didn't it?

Well, there he stood, yet another rag-and-bone man, in the middle of the room, but this one was not interested in the antique furniture, nor in the silver plates, nor the paintings, he did not even take a proper look at them, but suddenly closed his eyes so he could concentrate better, then softly said:

"Something smells of the Maros here."

We were startled. He did not at all look like a rag-and-bone man.

"My wife's hair smelled the same, when her body was washed up, poor soul," he said, and then we weren't so frightened any more, but my mother opened the chest into which we had stuffed the wool of the thirty-three accursed lambs, which would have covered the entire costs of a church fence. At first the rag-and-bone man just ran his hand over the coal-black wool, then he took a handful, buried his face into it and burst into tears. He cried like a child.

"Take it! Take it all," my mother said, and she took out all five sacks from the bottom of the chest, then sat down beside him to help him pack away the wool. I stood in the doorway and watched my mother and the strange man sitting side by side silently, their eyes wet with tears, filling huge sacks with the scent of a dead woman's hair.

I too helped carry down the sacks to the cart. The rag-and-bone man wanted to give us ten metres of Bohemian upholstery fabric in exchange, but my mother would not accept anything.

"Then let me at least give the little boy something, madam," said the man, and from a huge pile of junk pulled out a peculiar-shaped pigskin case containing a Pioneer-brand Soviet camera.

The viewfinder of the Pioneer camera was like an inverted telescope. So for years I looked at everything that was too close through this lens. Mr Csipkés chasing after the pig with an axe and catching up with it; Mrs Müller, who took a chair to sit before her door every morning and rubbed at the KZ number tattooed on her forearm until noon; the postman who, being playful by nature, sometimes brought Mrs Muller a new Koh-i-noor rubber; in other words, whatever there was to see in the yard of that house I looked at through the viewfinder of that camera, just to be on the safe side.

I only forgot about the camera once, and that was when four men dressed in black came to take away a muddled tale from nineteen-ten to seventy-seven without paying for it; true, they were not rag-and-bone men. They were in a great hurry to reach the cold room with my grandmother, though they could at least have waited until my mother had a proper cry after it turned out that aloe with oats was as much use against cancer of the larynx as black wool against high blood pressure.

But the working hours of the undertakers allowed exactly three minutes of waiting during the removal of a body. Placing the body in the coffin: one and a half minutes; crying of the next of kin: three minutes; receipt of tip, conveyance of the body to the hearse: one minute each; six and a half minutes altogether, plus saying goodbye brings it up to seven minutes, also.

If I had had the courage to bring out the camera during those seven minutes, then the undertakers would have believed that I really did want to photograph them, and they would have smiled at me, from the heart, as only an undertaker can smile at a child, and I would have thrown my camera into their faces, which of course is an empty dream, a vain hope because that is not the way it happened, but at least then the story of photography would have ended as beautifully as it had begun.

Envoi:

Prince! There never was an Engelhard. Or if there was, he was not a photographer. Or if he was, we never knew each other. Or if we did, he did not leave me anything. Or if he did, then it was nothing but these seven minutes.

[EMol]

GÁBOR GÖRGEY

from *Interview*

1

I'm fine, thanks.
Teeth
in good shape.
Some hair, yes. I hope
it stays on, who knows.
Yes, family.
Naturally – why, don't I look
like a man who loves life?
It's brushed me, twice.
Vitality, and style.
Size 12. Yes, a little large.
I've quit, finally.
I wouldn't know.
This and that.
Here and there.
Lots.
Have a smoke? Coffee?
Any other questions, Miss?

2

Visions? Haven't any.
Shoving on step by
step through some
inimical stubborn
jungly stuff as sly
and tricky as a rogue beast,
clawing it out of the ground
down to the bone
I make what I can of it.
In childhood, once upon a time,
I had visions, lots of them,
poetic, the real thing.
But it stopped, just like that,

when I started writing poems.
Visions. What I get's the old shaft.

[. . .]

16
What I admire?
Concentration of soul
giving you the strength,
for example, to burn yourself alive.
And the iron calm
of the citizen in me
listening to the 8 a.m. news
and cracking the second
soft-boiled egg,
so essential for his existence.

17
It's a big, fat hypothesis, of course.
But well-constructed, even
a Martian could see that.
I admit there are other
palatable hypotheses, but
I'm not about to kowtow
grovelling in the dust
with the rest of them
every time the tribe's adored totem-face
stares at me.
My backbone's no thrilling conductor
of cultural currents –
in fact I'm turned off:
because these days it's not just
connoisseurs of the primitive
but conquerors too who
ooze goodwill.

[. . .]

22
Nice to hear that, Miss.
I do make a point
of shaving close, yes.
It brings in this sort
of mini-success among others.
But after razoring it clean,
deep-rubbing my wincing face –
how the lotion bites –
behind its contented grin
a bit of that endless rope of pearls
stringing out through the earth
exposes itself:
the *Homo sapiens* mandible.

23
Yes, memory's the problem.
What I don't recall just
isn't. Life after death
will only be perfect
(I mean, refined from earethly dross)
if they can sublimate my
dematerialised matter
out of all recollection.
If, however, from the ranks of tremulant souls
I can't pick my mother out
– because the memory's gone –
let me ask you, Miss, where's the point in it?

24
Happiness?
Listen, all it takes
with this grace-contraption
is losing that one single
screw
and my ramshackle residence
of light and shadows
tumbles down.
Happiness, it seems, is merely
a malfunction in the rhythm
of horror.

25

I do.
Naturally I do.
If I didn't I couldn't.
But since I can,
I have to,
and if I have to,
I certainly
can.

[JK]

ÁGNES GERGELY

London

With Héda, 1968

"No need to speak quietly here.
There are no hidden microphones."
We were just five minutes from the British
Museum, in that deeply
intellectual quarter where
even bits of pastry find their way
in among books, and you can forget
that you were robbed of your own books
during the war. After the war
they wandered off down damp passages
of sub- and co-let habitations.
"No need to speak quietly here."
Here everything is marble
and self-confidence. On the ground floor
the bust of Rameses II beams
down the main corridor like
inarticulate destiny. Everything
is whole. Instead of Latin high spirits
or German orderliness, a post-imperial
integrity persists like a pale
emerging shadow. "There are
no hidden microphones here." What for?
The painters' stinking paving stones
and the poets' dreamless, disorderly
quarter have long absorbed the night curse
of the prostitute screaming "Plague!"
whose half-dead infant is as much a part
of the Whole as the library,
the market, attendants and politicians.
It is the same old cage of words,
you are perfectly free to speak the truth.
No need to speak quietly here,

nor loudly either. No-one will hear you.
Your words are inaudible in Ithaca.
You may read the brilliantly documented
account of the voyage on the boat.

[GS]

DEZSŐ TANDORI

An Otherwise Unoccupied Swimming Pool in 1965; A String of Similes

As if in an unoccupied swimming pool where only
maintenance men, mechanics, street sweepers,
idle ticket collectors, snack-bar attendants hang out,
only office underlings, possibly
the management itself; and one or two amateurs like me
who got there who knows how and who
don't talk to each other, at best we're collectively
objects of indifference to the specialist staff,
bored as it is even with the professionals; as if
all alone in the morning at the deep-water end of
such an unoccupied practice pool, I were practising
the racing dive, something I've been
unable to master for nearly thirty years.
And so it's as if this wouldn't be me,
as if I'd consequently be practising with somebody,
so I'm again and again for a moment completely
alone, as among sycamore leaves and a tide of
spittle, other insignificant filth,
chucked-up bugs, my head pops up after
one of a number of by now perhaps not
entirely unsuccessful dives; but quality
won't cut any ice here, besides the whole thing's
just a string of similes. As if someone
would want to repudiate existence, but I'd
be insisting, as a father taking his such-and-such
son to practise the racing dive. Or other things.

[BB]

1976711/*b*

The wind is blowing, the wind I one time troubled over
so intensely; and now I'm glad of it, since it recalls
the time of those long-gone struggles
when it still blew riotously through my hair,

and that was important. As if now I were
catching at the trees; it's never possible
to look back even at a leaf-size wind. I'm able
to look at what is, at things that occur

so many times that they can't be themselves
once only. What am I to do with the leaves,
the wind, the looking; and, when it touched me

for the first time, with what the wind began
to do; and whether indeed it touched me; this one
blows now from a time that never will catch up with me.

[BB]

OTTÓ ORBÁN

The Father of the People

Which monarch-cum-deity had fewer restraints or more power?
His was the way, the truth and the life, but chiefly the death;
his world was as simple as Russian roulette,
the red ball, obedience: the black, execution . . .
A brief generation, to see his fallen statues' living original –
the short-assed, vengeful, industrious genius of organisation,
who dickered with his penknife in a functioning watch,
but failed to grasp the ideal in whose name he murdered.
Divinity requires a godlike imagination,
a pinch of poetry to go with the hard-line of strategy –
conscience and soul are not merely words in a spectrum,
sooner or later the lie starts to rot in the firm-looking binding,
and, chronically sneezing, time, the monumental mason, carves on
 the tombstone
of common memory: Xerxes; Capone; the once fearful name of the
 emperor.

[GS]

A Roman Considers the Christians

May the gods forgive me, but I really can't abide them.
Their idea is a great one, but look at them all:
a bunch of quarrelsome eggheads picking their noses,
who, under the spell of their thesis, would if they could
be hard-line dictators, all for the sake of tolerance naturally,
who'd not kill with weapons but with murderous disdain,
while breeding their own sloppy aristocracy,
along with other oppressive, life-hating state institutions . . .
So, let me embellish this with a gesture – a fig for them all!
Just one little problem: the starved lion bawling in the arena . . .
There are plenty with vision, but they are the ones prepared to be
 eaten

in dust clouds of water-cannon, where out of the screaming and
bloodshed
something emerges . . . the same thing? the worse? or the better?
the gods only know, if they know, what lies in the future . . .

[GS]

The Spirit of the Age

I saw a beggar. Recognised him. Knew him instinctively. "You have a damned nerve," I cried and shook his shoulders in cold fury. "You dare to poke your nose in here! Aren't you the liar who told us this would be positively the last struggle? Wasn't it you who promised every poet a redhead or red way ahead – to each according to his need?" I stood there for a long time screaming furiously . . . eventually he raised his hooded head and I saw he had no eyes. His hollow sockets were a keyhole opening on to a smooth and endless plain where fire and smoke mingled, and invisible feet pounded over a few exposed bones. It might have been cavalry or fugitives. There was the dreadful constant sound of something grinding. I couldn't tell whether it was a loose axle or a human cry, or if it was the earth scratching its bloody surface in the eternal drought that follows tears of suffering. Then he addressed me in a flat exhausted voice as if talking down a microphone. "You think yourself a seer because you've been disappointed. And in your infinite wisdom you bawl at me like some cheap whore. You come back with your dowry, your naive ideas, your bloody revolution! Bring back God, the family, tradition, and kick me out! But are we not one person? And isn't your imagination the whole problem? The wheel of time remains indifferent, you are the squirrel in the cage rushing round on the wheel which like a lathe turns out the centuries." He fell quiet and the wind dispersed him and nothing remained of him except the cooling ground where he had sat, and fire and smoke and dust.

[GS]

A Nice Little War

Of course a war would quickly solve our problems; Behemoth would answer: no more bald heads, no more surplus value, no New Left, no question of sex, no community project . . . The fever of youth could take a cold bath. Or one of fire. Why not? Imagine! the sea of swollen flame would stop before the cellar stairs. Imagine! those who have nothing would not be ruined by their losses . . . it would be their turn at last . . . the southern hemisphere would remain . . . Brasilia . . . this way madness lies. And not just because of the flattened steelworks or the mountains of corpses. We sought God and found ourselves; our limits; I am as I am because ultimately I cannot be anyone else. A clean sheet then? Inscribed with blood? If one could lean over the balcony of the stars this perhaps would prove our masterpiece: the pattern that dictates the passing of time. However, excessive objectivity disgusts me. It is precisely the smell of the earth that is divine in me; those I saw ploughing with wooden shares and tractors; the taut ocean begins to hum, and round it the reference points of the face of infinity . . . trees, potholes along the road, a centipede . . . as far as the world is concerned poetry is a matter of detail. I learned this during the storming of the city, the lesson took less than half an hour. At first we heard only the breathing. The wheezing of an enormous pair of lungs some distance off. Then we understood it was our lack of air pumping the live bellows in our chests. A vast silence followed. The sense of dizziness at having survived. An iron door. A gallery above. Mortar between clumsy stones. Later the silent film: coats covered in brick dust swaying at the resurrection ball . . . eyes drinking light like lidless mirrors . . . Could I look into another mirror now? The conquest of the world left me behind to act as messenger. The news burned up my lips as they were muttering: NO.

[GS]

GYÖRGY PETRI

Gratitude

The idiotic silence of state holidays
is no different
from that of Catholic Sundays.
People in collective idleness
are even more repellent
than they are when purpose has harnessed them.

Today I will not
in my old ungrateful way
let gratuitous love decay in me.
In the vacuum of streets
what helps me to escape
is the memory of your face and thighs,
your warmth,
the fish-death smell of your groin.

You looked for a bathroom in vain.
The bed was uncomfortable
like a roof ridge.
The mattress smelt of insecticide,
the new scent of your body mingling with it.

I woke to a cannonade
(a round number of years ago
something happened). You were still asleep.
Your glasses, your patent-leather bag
on the floor, your dress on the window-catch
hung inside out – so practical.

One strap of your black slip
had slithered off.
And a gentle light was wavering
on the downs of your neck, on your collarbones,
as the cannon went on booming

and on a spring poking through
the armchair's cover
fine dust was trembling.

[GG/CW]

The Under-Secretary Makes a Statement

Four special government committees
and five professors of dialectics with them
have been meeting to study the mysterious
rising-power that is inherent in prices.
The hypothesis put forward by the committees
is that prices have a *randy nature*
and whenever they sight a crowd of housewives
sniffing about in jam-packed queues, they instantly
stiffen like furious Don Juans and rise
and no amount of soothing will bring them down –
entreaties only get them more worked up.
As for wages, they have staying power,
so don't go up, although they do stand fast.
The mysterious working committees have so far –
at a hundred and nine working dinners,
three hundred and thirty-seven working lunches
and two hundred and forty working snacks
(what a job it was to gobble that lot up) –
held discussions in thirty different suites
at a total cost of twenty million zlotys
exclusive of all *per die*—— allowances.

But the housewives are impatient –
so many old hags, grannies in particular,
endlessly moaning on about varicose veins
and seeing no further than their carrier bags:
"Meat – meat – meat – meat!" they howl
egging their husbands on to do likewise,
grandpas out on the streets shaking their crutches.
Even the babies wail.

We simply cannot
work, there's so much noise. So, housewives,
let us, for the last time, make this appeal
to your sober understandings: either you make
your husbands and babies belt up, or else
we cannot be held responsible
and might be driven to perform such deeds
as you would later on regret yourselves.

The key to the situation is in our hands
and we do not shrink from using it to lock up
whole peoples, if that is what necessity dictates.

[GG/CW]

On the 24th Anniversary of the Little October Revolution

Uncle Imre, Uncle Pista and Co
corrected the world's course just a tiny bit.
They were hanged or locked up.
(Uncles Mátyás and Ernő buggered off
to Moscow. And the rest of them shall be nameless.)
Then came the land of Prester John:
"We'll never die!"
The total number of corpses –
and that includes both residents and intruders –
is estimated at somewhere between three thousand
and thirty thousand.
The figure is hard to verify so long
after the event. Many vanished.
Many were made to vanish.
Some people are put on the rack
of forgetfulness.
Some people were put on the rack.
Reality always reckons without herself.
Would she get her sums wrong? Settle her accounts?
A unified and indivisible entity
she failed her eleven-plus

has never properly learned to count.
I say just two numbers:
56
68.
You can add them, subtract them,
divide or multiply.
Your innumerable doctrines, baseness is their basis,
have failed, are bankrupt.

[GG/CW]

To Be Said Over and Over Again

I glance down at my shoe and – there's the lace!
This can't be gaol then, can it, in that case.

[GG/CW]

Song

This is my home,
this is my home,
this is my home: the Wild East
beautiful
Comecon islands
swimming in light.

And the air:
it *is*!
It is just so!
Yes, it *is*! Yes,
it is just so!
(So far.)

The air in our country,
you can drink it in!
In our land you can
drink the air!
Oh this magnificent
air!

Wild East, bewitching East,
there is no getting used to you,
oh you
star-spangled
Comecon islands!

[GG/CW]

SZABOLCS VÁRADY

Quatrain

I stand in a hole between Will Be and Was
waiting for things to change but nothing does.
The dust will mount for ever. Rain? Unlikely.
Thunder perhaps. But not here, not precisely.

[GS]

Chairs above the Danube

Those two chairs were not really
all that ugly. Too bad the springs
protruded from them and the upholstery
was so hopelessly filthy.

But chairs they were, all the same. And right for that apartment.
So we carried them, mostly on our heads
from Orlay Street across the former
Francis Joseph, now Liberty, Bridge,
to Number 2 Ráday Street where P. lived
at the time (as some of his poems will show.)

A chair, not to say two, has
many uses. "Two Poets on a Bridge
with Chairs on their Heads" – one can imagine
a painting so entitled. I hope it would be
a down-to-earth painting and not one of those
transfigurations. Those two chairs –
and it's important to make this clear – were by no means
just halos around our heads. About halfway across the bridge –
and not for the purpose of proving anything –
we sat down on them. The springs protruded more prominently
    from
one – I don't recall which of us

got it. Doesn't matter, since what happened later
can hardly be explained by that. It was a pleasant
summer evening. We lit cigarettes,
enjoying this one might say
unusual form of cosiness.
The chairs later served
nicely for a while: at the P.s' they
were *the* chairs. But man wants something better
than what is: the chairs were sent to an upholsterer. Then the P.s
moved also, the first time, because they had to, the second,
because they hated their apartment. Nowadays
we meet less often at their place. Several things
brought this about: G. left A.
(P.'s wife) and then M. (B.'s wife)
broke off with me, and the other M. (G.'s wife)
divorced G. and married me (while the B.s
also separated) and P. attempted suicide and
has been living more or less in a sanatorium ever since,
not to mention the changes in the world situation,
so anyway: there's nothing left to sit on.

[WJS]

ISTVÁN CSUKÁS

Albatross with Shopping Bag

I waddle along like an albatross on the upwardly
sloping deck of Csatárka Street,
winter and summer, clutching my shopping
bag, in winter as it happens, the fences
either side like a ship's railings
beyond which drones the sea
with the infinite sky above,
but I look neither up nor to the side,
only forward, always fixedly forward,
my nose a scarlet compass point
that I must blindly follow, an explorer.
That's what I am, for in their minds
everyone can fly, all are great travellers!
And me especially, in the morning between
eleven and half past eleven, as I trudge
into the store, for it's not time that is important
but place, for the sea drones everywhere
wearing its immortal hat of sky with which we greet
the deity, good morning, good evening, and the time
between is ours, we can take it home with us.
My wings tucked into my striped sailor's vest,
I breathe through the trusty compass of my nose
sniffling a little, even a trifle snotty,
but have no need of any other compass
waddling for ever in a single direction,
the mortal one I always waddle in
here on earth, but where else is there? And,
as I waddle among you, bearing my albatross
shopping bag, I mutter a line of verse, "Milk,
a loaf, sliced ham, some brawn and yeast . . ."
All essential things, everything needful
for the long journey, for the last great voyage
when I shall discover the Land of Nothing,
as have so many other travellers before me,

none of whom have as yet succeeded in returning!
But I am merely practising for now,
developing muscles, developing the spirit,
getting my heart used to it, since that is precious,
and it really isn't as difficult as you'd think,
and getting the world too used to it, so it shouldn't
weep or drop false crocodile tears, for what
would happen if I chanced to return after all?
After three days, say. Now there's a tricky problem.
I think I will also have a sly go at flying,
so my entry into heaven shouldn't take me unawares,
so, standing on tiptoe, I launch myself off
from the pavement. It isn't quite right yet.
I have a quick shufti. Has anyone noticed?
I wouldn't like it generally known
before I was ready in case people laughed at me.
Let them laugh at the way I waddle round,
at my old shopping bag and my rubicund
nose, and, when it comes to the point, we shall see
who laughs last. In the meantime I can greet
the universe gaily with my immortal hat:
waving good morning, good evening to everyone!
And look here is the store, I have got there,
and I hide myself delighted among the loaded
shelves, snuffling and scenting, stroking
the image of the summer apple on the fruit tin,
picking at little pieces of cheese, thinking,
so much to do, no time to die yet, that can wait
till tomorrow. If indeed there is a tomorrow.
Is this what my birth was like? And do you think
death will be as simple, so easy come, easy gone?
We don't disappear piecemeal, by degrees, but wholesale,
a monumental lack giving one final yawn.

[GS]

ZSUZSA TAKÁCS

The Double

My worst recurring nightmare after our separation
was that I would see you at a table
outside a cheap café in the Octogon,
every time I left my students and walked home
I'd see you lounging there where in return
for some minor favour they buy you
a scone or a cheese roll.
Each time my heart stopped still:
the same physique, same shape of head and beard,
and – don't be angry – the same slightly
down-and-out posture, have they been starving you?
or are you begging for love?
and all the time you're wearing this horny expression.
I imagined it was you,
and forced myself to miss the bus,
watched you in secret, frightened of course
that I'd draw attention to myself by my behaviour,
that this other would misunderstand me,
since he surely wouldn't believe why I was doing this,
I'd be pleased to get away with
no worse than paying for his scone, or rather, yours,
since I spoke of him to myself in the second person.
But my fear was groundless,
for he never noticed me, or rather, you didn't,
and I was tortured by the thought I was no longer
attractive to men such as you,
it deeply wounded my self-respect.
And while I was thinking all this, you got into such
an awful situation, I almost cried out,
you had been given a slip of paper
and were to take it to the photo shop next door,
there must have been something rude written on it
for if the girl behind the counter refused you
you would be beaten up, and if she didn't

she would join the rank of your torturers;
but you must clearly have been hoping
that if you returned out of breath, you could
take your place among the card-players again
and though you had lost all your money
they'd give you credit (I also recognised
your passion for gambling).
So you waited for the note,
the first time they handed it down to you
from a height, then suddenly snatched it back
and dangled it under the table between the table legs,
and you made several grabs at it,
just like a dog after a bone, I was already
feeling ill, and you laughed willingly; your laughter
lashed me like a whip; it was how you used
to laugh at some sophisticated joke.
Meantime the spectators had changed about,
buses were coming and going.
Soon you had finished your errand
and returned with money. I recognised
neither your stained suit, nor your exotic tie
which showed monkeys swinging from a tree.
It would be an exaggeration to say I was crying
but I wept bitterly in my heart.
It was my cousin who disturbed this fantasy,
thinking I was waiting for a bus, not knowing
I was saying a final goodbye to you.
We got on the bus together and she asked me
what had happened. I said, my students had died,
it was my last journey on this route, it is autumn,
the trees are rotting, do I need to make myself clearer,
the gravestones are toppling,
no, she said, she understood.

[GS]

Refurbishment

Some slips and vests, the sticky blouses, jumpers
shrunk or stretched, that prickly woollen

waistcoat, a lot of unwanted stuff
picked up at sales, that skirt too easily creased,
soaked walking boots in which
my cracked heel used regularly to bleed,
paper tissues in a chequered pocket,
the blown pages of an Updike dropped in the bath,
inkstain, greasestain, heartstains
on discarded rags. "A prosodic approach to the translation
of Lorca", offprint in eighty-seven copies.
A white tie mourning with a dirty edge.
Second-rate authors, duplicate copies, prescriptions
not collected, an empty notebook with the word *DIARY*
silver-embossed on the cover, children's bathing towels.
A one-week luncheon voucher dated seventy-three
(each day I dined with someone else)
a dried ink cartridge, in which
is written the terrible truth:
farewell my youth.
I sit before the open doors
of the wardrobe, while workmen rip
the house apart, and twenty years spin by.
The inflatable paddling pool, stuck together now,
the Italian gymslip which fitted years ago,
and a hospital report (*ab. incompl.*) slips
from the silk pocket of a sun-bleached denim handbag,
my brows cloud thinking of that May morning.
Clods of earth are falling
like plaster in the renovated flat.
I sit entombed within myself, picking at
the musty grapes of autumns past.
And I can hear the neighbours arriving, but no-one
crosses the mountain of rubble. Dust flies, creeps
under doors. I might once have feared cockroaches
but their thousand feet are not so fearsome now.
I manage among the sounds of demolition.
Clothes unmade and yet already ruined
flap on the clothes line of the future.
I writhe in sweaty man-made fibres and sandals.
Undeveloped rolls of film make me laugh
with ever greater abandon.
Hoarded addresses, unrecognised telephone numbers

bulge in tomorrow's diary which slips behind
a drawer and I cannot find it again,
only paper bubbling from jammed drawers
I've tried to force open.
To have been dwarfs in Lilliput,
what is that to the millennia?
– Our lives, that's all.
                    Our one hand gropes about
our sentimental heart. Our laced-up feet, like Magritte shoes,
wait for permission to enter the secret gate.
Our eyes, cracked with use, drop the odd stone
or tear on stitched-up uncomplaining lips.
Wrinkled necks of silk hiss in the resurrected wind.
A sagging lacy breast lights like a butterfly
on an ancient bony shoulder. Their blood was fire in a bottle of scent.
I can still start over again, wrote the
hand, slowly drowning, on the sunworn horizon
of the fading shore.
                    The day was long ago.
                    If non-existence proves possible
under such fertile soil, I may forgive you.

[GS]

PÉTER ESTERHÁZY

Fraighaoters

So they've arrived! So they've arrived, the fraighaoters. Their bellows shiver the dawn – shattered, grizzled, frayed – the hush is fragile and empty. I saw my sisters' frightful faces! – raging! raging! – What, for the love of God, has happened, my dearests?

Through the thin crack of the window-slats, the frothy bridle-bits of hard-driven horses – stripling coachmen up on the box, it was them, they who were bellowing with rosy-chilled faces as, leaning forwards, they coyly commanded their horses. The reins twitched back and forth, the skimming of ice tinkled beneath the iron-tyred wheels. Here! here! – Mucky daybreak! The clock started ticktocking loudly, squeeze it between your thighs, yell my sisters, and stuff that confounded clock in your skirt. Right now, hush is what we need most.

The fraighaoters, they were lolling in the backs of the carts, unperturbed, weary, like lords or eminences. In bulky furs! Beside them, it is clear how scrawny all those wastrel driver lads are, their sparse scraps of hair are lamentable, their chequered peak-caps threadbare, their lugs stick out, their hands are frozen blue and livid. Their sallowness is called pallor. Well might their teeth flash as they swaggeringly swung their carts around the curves, chortling vociferously, but what is that compared with wolf-skin furs? Who should be squirming here?

The boles of the fraighaoters – objects, thus – were propped against soft corn husks, the air before their mouths steamed yellow by their breath, as if they were smoking cigars. Their faces are broad, bearded nearly all, but not unfriendly, not in the least! – from the distant forage-racks they exchange desultory laughs, terse and soundless. They understand one another, I can see that much. Their thighs are robust, the britches must be taut.

Our good dogs, baring their teeth, chafed on their perennial chains, but they frightened no-one: the lads did not provoke them, and the fraighaoters gave no irrevocable order. Possibly they slumped sulkily in their furs.

Your faces have budded, my sisters, but why the bloom of anger? – Why are you dragging me away like this, prising me from the window? – futile my clawing on tooth and nail – sharp, green flakes of paint – you little tadpole, why were they hissing? scram, you little tadpole! – and why did they leap back, terrified, at the noise the shutters made on bursting open in the scuffle? What light.

Now do you understand why your hearts flutter mysteriously on seeing its approach? A clear sound rose across the stillness, a limpid spot of colour refracted through a crystal, light poured into the depths of the eye that . . . An incredible rainbow, a well-nigh fanciful freshness, caressed my eyes. The light drives a wedge into me, the lustrous horses, the mist, the voice, the rustling, the frozen sludge, the circle of bleak barns. Sweethearts, why are you flattening yourselves to the wall? Be joyous, there's no need for these airs, the terror.

A majestic figure, a strapping fraighaoter, at this point lifted himself to one knee in his cart and, on a nod from him, his coachman, startled, halts the team, all yellow the harness; the guv'nor is now upright, legs astride, proudly his servant winks back at him, and he points up here, up here, at our room – a glance was flashed at me, and the cockleshell in which my heart had been slumbering burst in its radiance.

The horses whinnied, clopped restlessly, the icy courtyard is pulverised. Dawn: all kinds of traces; who knows. The body shivers, my sisses' whimpering gives me an insane strength, stroppiness, fear, a sensation of unconfinedness, exultation, gripped me – stray traces of vapour on the windowpane, thin nightshirt clutched together at the belly, creasing and squeezing, yes, he is looking at me, his fur coat dangles like a bell. *Voilà votre mort, monsieur!* I shouted out spiritedly.

On the porch our mother – dear Mother, yelling at the hounds as if at her unruly whelps, at us. In our room murky again, a keen, frantic murk – wretch, wretched dimwit, my sisters chanted: they had got back into bed and were feigning sleep.

No use my begging to be allowed to lie down between you, poor, drowsy girls, the drowsiness, they were shamming that; I wanted to hug them but couldn't. I wanted to hug you but couldn't. I hated you, with one and the same heart, and I hated the space that invests our room . . . – Our room! Oh, how many the awakenings of a morning on the boiling, soft bellies of my sisters! Not mine: if I finger that, muscle I feel, and bone, muscle, bone. My sisses are fair, those I love are fair, I spy on them in amazement, their twirls in front of our mirrors, their grumpy titivations – face-powder sifting down like dust on burdock leaves – and then, once alone, a finger draws tracks on the pane, knotty, scribbled scrawls. Sometimes I would be allowed to tug up the zips on their backs, I feared I would pinch their alabaster skin. By the evening their faces would be drained of colour, they would sit wordless, silent, on the edges of their beds, hands drooping limply in their laps. That was when I would kneel before them, undo the ribbons, undo their features, undo their looks, lay my head on their weary laps and from there caress their backs in circles, higher and higher, reaching up, then, panting, snuggle down next to them, rub their goose-fleshed arms – my siblings! – their hands smelled of onions and perfume, and finally their hair, the curly ringlets frazzled by then – mane and hair – stretched straight back, sleek, with a dubious sheen, expediently bound with a skimpy bright red, yellow or black rubber band from a preservative jar; that too I would undo and root fondlingly in their hair. Puppets, they just tolerated it impassively. I would undress them, their clothes clinging stickily to their bodies – would warm their beds for them with my own body, they would embrace each other and close their eyes. Another day come to a happy end, I would say to myself; little Sophie, little Sophie, they would whisper, and fall asleep as if they had dropped dead. By the morning, though, their tummies would be boiling and fluffy, and on awakening my cheek would again be toasting on their navels. Silver the music of their growling stomachs.

Woe betide you, curs! In-buckling mail corselets, horse-demise. By the spring grass and naked lady will grow over you, and dog's tooth violet. <text corrupted>, what's that noise? Stagbeetlethunder-clapping, I replied. In the doorway, and light anew, our mother as flux, her fair, plump body gleamed rosily, to love is good: love being difficult, I rushed to her, hugged her passionately, bored my head between her bosoms – exaggerations, she herself, the cherry-red lipsticks, the thick, greasy make-up paints, heady lavender waters, I have only to look at her to feel that I am rich and no harm can befall me. Her fingers are yellowed with nicotine, her arms freckled, the skin on her heels is hard as rock. I am fat just as the moon is silvery, she says.

Oh, my chuckabiddy, she sighed, and a tear trickled down her broad face, my make-up will be smudged, she immediately sniffed angrily, dress in your Sunday best, put on your pearly necklet and, above all, slip on a fresh pair of knickers, you little fiend! Good, that is a fine answer.

How we admire Mother's plain speaking, the simplicity and verve with which her utterances blaze a trail to their obscure goal, how well I understand her at these times! Wash, she said, the rest will take care of itself, and with that, for her, my education was completed. There was a time when we went down to the village – to call on the Countess, that's all our mother ever called her, the Countess, indeed a clever, much-travelled, worldly-wise lady, she had even been to Bratislava, Subotica and Pest – I pity people who are terrified by just a single century or whose affections do not run beyond a country's confines; as a result, she had a splendid feel for tying her comments, in an altogether natural manner, to the day's eventualities so that they related to us personally, especially me, for my instruction, my edification.

Let me look at you, she said the first time, clutching my face in her cool, firm hands, you have a cute face, a cute little face. Those unforgettable excursions! The crusty bread, the creaking picnic hamper: noises, tablecloth on the grass, white, green – green – The sky, the sea: a dense living stratum in which life swarms and races on . . . I am lost in wonder at the seagull's miraculous form and how it flies. How was this flying craft made? My slender sisters were resplendent in the sun, twirling their silk parasols, we're going to pick mushrooms, they giggled, I screwed my eyes up and felt dizzy from all the intense light, we're going to pick mushrooms; long, deadly drifting midst quivering August shadows – and not infrequently, on the spur of the moment, we would snatch off our frilly garments to take a dip in the brook, and while we cavorted, completely transforming ourselves at will, by the second, from tomboyish to tame – the Countess, she in her high-necked, summer, summer, close black dress, constantly stood sentinel over us, so to speak, the wrinkled smile around her lips showed she was well aware of her role, and sometimes that may have pained her. The Countess! On the bank, a wolfram helmet, filled with measures of honey and pitch. My sisters would become peevish and start talking finely and movingly about boredom – that man finds nothing so intolerable as to be in a state of complete rest, without passion, without occupation, without diversion, without effort. Then he faces his nullity, loneliness, inadequacy, *dependence*, helplessness, emptiness. At once there wells up from the depths of his soul boredom, gloom, depression, chagrin, resentment, despair.

A cute little face you have – I feared no-one – I did not know what fear was – nothing is as precious as what you are in others, and what others are in you – On high, all is one! On high, all is one! They taught me deportment too, my sisses unspooled a red silk ribbon in the garden and I had to walk along it, as on a narrow dyke beset on both sides by treacherous waves, while they shouted ecstatically, the Countess too, bravo, Sophiekins, take a look at that, what an elegant little butt, watch that imp strutting her stuff!

The rapturous tumult grew ever wilder, we whirled and danced, then flushed of face – dance and dance – and if I ended up in Mother's big, soft arms, as a conciliatory gesture, one might say, since I had pledged as much to the Countess, she would hug me emotionally, sweetie-pie, how lithe you are. But I, in turn, placed my hand on her waist, just look, on her eddying, full waist, placed my hand on her back, her broad, regal back, placed my hand on her belly, her soft, rounded belly, placed my hand between her breasts, between her massive, marble breasts – oh, no – oh, no, Mother, you are wrong, and it surprises me that you are wrong, your flesh is lustrous and radiant, I envy you, because all I feel in myself, all about, is muscle, as if I were a chewy piece of meat – muscle, bone – confine, confine, you are great, and I love you – now, now, my pet, you said that nicely and with youthful ardour, immaturely, my tummy is paunchy, anyone can see that, my waist is flabby, my breasts sag, my back is blubbery, and let's not even talk about my behind. Mother!

I put on my swishy white Sunday best, though it was no Sunday, no, that it wasn't, and cool, white silk knickers. That hush! My sisses were no longer feigning sleep, they got dressed – at other times how much prattling, giggling, panting, gasping and grappling. They tore me off a strip when I began flouncing around as a lark – just wait, they hissed threateningly – but why so out of sorts, pussums? Aren't those who have turned up the ones about whom so many colourful words were spoken, dreams woven? Aren't . . . My sisters pounced on me and ripped me apart – we're sick of that pious cant. Just you wait. I should not yet regard as wisdom what is merely melancholy, indifference, disillusionment . . . My sisters kneeling on my skinny arms – curses, curses.

There is but one mother. On our mother a silver-fringed scarlet peignoir, the broad Chinese belt, silk slippers, felt over-boots, the ravishing rainbow aigrette in her jet-black hair, bedazzlement, persistent wind, the tiny glass pendants of Viennese chandeliers clinking together – zephyr, breeze, breath.

Aren't you afraid, Sophiekins? Oh, Mother, if I were now to hazard an answer with all the tactlessness of my sincerity, I hazard I would say, no, I don't understand your question, for how indeed could one fear what exists, isn't what is not far more fearsome <the nothingness that is; what isn't is>, shush, shush, be quiet, silly, naughty girl, be quiet. A dipping-tolling tickle on our lips, rainbow aigrette, a peal of laughter and fireworks again. *Ah tais-toi, je ne veux plus!* my sister cries, Mother is kissing me.

Suddenly a strident voice, hard to say offhand whence it came, from outdoors, indoors, behind the door or wherever, a derisive, squeaky snickering, yet a deep voice – so not, then, fine, fine and dandy that there isn't, no fear, the little missie wouldn't dream of it, why indeed would a calf not go straightaway to the slaughter – there's no fear – though was it not the little missie who just said that what isn't is far more fearsome – Craven sigh of relief, so it is you, Lamebrain, you giving us such a fright, as if we did not have plenty enough as it is, watch that sharp tongue of yours or I'll clout you one on that neckless neck, pip-squeak!

Who's this, Mother? A hapless wastrel – you might have seen him in the cart, cringing there at the feet of your fraighaoter, though he hardly stuck out of his poke, it's true – for sure, a piglet they're just lugging to the river – He believes in nothing. He says the stars are bare rocks, a lamp is not a lamp; a table not a table, a child not a child. – Unmanageable sprog. Maryonka, precious, I see that, as usual, in your heart of hearts you would have rid of me, said the one whom our precious mother has just called Fool, and out of the embrace of the shadows stepped Knight.

A quick scream then, how hideous, my stomach knots in a retch, hand clapped to gaping mouth – too late – Yes, Knight nodded, yes, Princess – Tiny manikin in a blue sailor's blouse, soiled plimsolls – trailing, tatty laces, shabby trews of greyish-blue duck – his head sprouts from his shoulders, a white puffball – on his right knee, an unsightly bump, as if he had a hunch there.

My dismay spawns silence. Self-evidently, spoke sad Knight, giving his leg a shake like a clown whose leg has no bone in it. Self-evidently, Princess, I am troubled by a stubborn injury.

You poor thing, I said, as is customary and I meant it sincerely – why pity? why pain? – the skin on Knight's lofty brow furrowed in a double arch, rising in tandem with the eyebrows, his parchment face, his weary face, his gaunt face, his face – He laughed – his bad teeth dully – My Princess, you pity me?, a worthless outlaw, shiftless pig in a poke to whom the Lord God granted more brains and less talent or power than was necessary, little girl! but it is not me who is scrubbed clean, excited and decked out – cheap necklace on a dark, hard morning, scrubbed clean, excited and decked out – Self-evidently; yet my doughty guv'nor, blessed be his name for now, is seated out there, in the grimy kitchen, dunking in the remnants of his bacon and eggs – You! – you would do well to consider upon whom you squander your earthly anguish, not on such an unworthy dolt, save it, an asset!, for yourself, just see, sobbing is not only useful but sweet too. Sweet . . . What does it mean to be a worm? sombrely to himself –

Poor, soft-headed, addle-brained, half-witted little thing, our mother howls, – Oh, spoke Knight flower dawn – Shut your trap for once, thus our mother, and then the little girl, me: dear stranger, I don't understand what you are saying, and if I did, which I cannot even imagine, not why, yet I saw you and see you, I saw you, I know it now, at the bottom of a forage-rack, curled up by a huge fraighaoter's boot, I see you now, reviled in body and covetous, all that makes you bitter and accusing . . .

Fiddlesticks, little girl, your immaturity makes you reckless, you are still a mere child, inexperienced, whence your courage to dispense advice – Whence your courage to observe? – peevish fractiousness little man. I blushed, maybe, but also smiled, I knew I could not be wrong – something inside me that wanted to speak for itself, no credit to me, and Knight fell silent, no, my dear, you are bitter and accusing, you are therefore in error, you do not perceive man's goodness, the world's illustriousness, the brilliance in which everyone is resplendent – Mangy curs, we bleed on pillows, we are magnificent. Only then clumsy and immortal – Not me. I seek not to blame you but be your support, with all the strength of my youth, don't ask why, what characterises strength is precisely that it is in surplus, weakness is what suffices, the former is overflowing, ebullience, turbulence . . .

So that's the way you'd have it, then, just so, that much, what I get, then, is the intention, would that be my present? this overspill, the frothy dribble on the side of a copper kettle, what would be left, impersonally, for anyone?! – Don't speak like that, good fellow, don't think me presumptuous for believing you may have need of me, Knight stamped angrily – I too by now uncertainly, accept me, sir, as your friend, accept my little hand, here, we may thus seal our friendship. Knight suddenly grew solemn, acerbity and superciliousness at which, I must confess, I took fright, for I had never thought I could be that important, teach me, the man said, what true purity is: not that bloodlessness detached from things but the impulse that pervades all beauty. Reveal what true love is: not the sterile dread of sin but that bold resolve with which all people, shoulder to shoulder, brace against the gates of life . . . whereupon he offered his hand to shake and, shy of the touch, so did I, but before my fingers could reach his, he nimbly snatched his own away – Silly goose! he exclaimed tearfully. Enough of this childishness, said our mother simply – precious stupid Knight, stupid clever Knight.

What, for heaven's sake, Maryonka, is this racket?! – the fraighaoter! – his face concealed by gloom, a secret play of light and dark, what a light the kitchen's stark and stinking kerosene lamps, like two spotlights, drew his figure into – lightning-struck there – the silhouette began to radiate, light, light, light, light and energy all about from the quivering, flaming edges, oh, yes, the fraighaoter is a fine man indeed – His massive thighs set astride – His bulky oaken trunk – The bison neck and the ruddy, doughty – Muscular head, yes, I see, I see, it is he and – and Me! Me! Me! – I am his partner, I am his, I became giddy from what I saw and from what I thought, Mother, who had been shielding me with her warm body, vanished from my side, poor Knight melted into thin air, his puny body disconcertedly humping off, I became giddy from the new lucidity – Knight! – about which we had spoken, the world's lucidity, only I exist, with the fraighaoter and this lucidity.

The foot stumbles in stiff reverence, the little girl hauls herself up there, on the cold stone, the apple basket has been upset, the winter apples cannoning all about, so many earthly globes, brown stains will be left in their place. Is this the frog? My belly is cold – the puniest or even a rigid object can explode with all-shattering force, or assume a miraculously active nature, should the match it seeks and awaits be granted. I must detach myself resolutely from emotions!!!

Tip-top, take it from me, top class, just be rather careful, fresh as today's newly picked strawberries – What strawberries, blathering crone – I'll give you a boot up the Khyber, what do you want with strawberries in the dead of winter? Or some hothouse speciality, sensual witch? *Mulier amicta sole!* Come here, woman clothed with sun, make it lively and sit down here – our mother's fluttering laughter, I love hearing it: as if a flock of birds were setting off on a journey or unaccountably just launching itself up in the air, tell her, Maryonka, to take a seat here in the kitchen, to just wait, and just take a seat. Be seated, *mulier amicta sole!*

This new, sweet, hard morning came and went. Lord, have mercy upon me, Lord, have mercy upon me. I pressed my cold back to the chimney-corner bench, a brisk shower of sparks over the cooking-range, large pots being shoved this way and that. The kitchen filled up with people, with silvery smoke – the coachmen more from the fringes, Knight with downcast eyes, the fraighaoters sitting round the shapeless wooden table, drinking our tipple from our pewter tankards, begging your pardons, good sirs, my sisters, comely and wholesome, apologised, alas, the vintage went to pot, the sun was not kind to us, so what use are sweat and industry then, and we also had our share of trouble with the vine-pests.

How fortunate, cousins, that at your disposal, Knight in an undertone, you had specialist manuals that my sterling guv'nors, in their goodness, at the beginning of time – Yup, huh, indeed it was, the fraighaoters nodded with a laugh, truly indeed. Strong men, a whiff of bacon and sweat spills from their shirts, fair, Knight nodded to my enthusiastic blushing face, you are right, girl, fair because they do not rely on others, they judge themselves by their own standards, fair because all facts are fair – all that is! Put so, that cannot be, since fair is possible when there can be foul. The foul is what is missing, said Knight. It was good having him by me, half leaning his weedy little body against me; he drew his knees up, involuntarily stroking them. Yes.

In a rapture of russet wines, amid a thousand roses, the clock races tinglingly on into the dream of night, our mother, my sisters in the fraighaoters' hard laps, scooped up by their great paws – the mood is pleasant, Mother is covering the fraighaoter with her body, but I know everything, nothing is hidden from me. So I suppose. I wait.

Something began to stand out against the kitchen clamour, the noise of guffaws and the crackling fire, a distant, wrong tone, a prolonged howl, then a short, sharp whimper – everybody abundantly here, the dogs' yapping swelled to a furious pitch – those are our komondors – what's that?, Mother slipped out of the embrace, what's that? We locals exchanged glances, we could read the anxiety from one another's eyes. Fraighaoters unstirring – what's that?, Mother repeated – Plucky, plucky woman – Pluck! did I hear right? I hear the word *pluck*, what's that you're mumbling, Fool?, asked the fraighaoter casually. A quavering reply, plucky woman, lor', what will become of us . . . All right, Fool, we relish it when you speak, and when so, we relish your being our living conscience, we relish your being witty and entertaining, and that you don't spare us when you sting and scourge, *courage de luxe!*, you see, you can afford to be moral, and that delights us with all our heart, perhaps it is not a vain hope to suppose that a mite of eternity will be shed from you on to us – we relish your . . . whatsit, your stiff-necked obstinacy – not that we are unaware of what you upbraid us for, we are aware, but everything has its place, you were born for this, we for that – our visages are as if pierced by a thousand tiny black needles; it would not be fortunate, however, if we were to catch you being ungrateful, after all, you are here with us, cowering in your sack, we make the rounds from house to house together, any firewood, any coal, you yell out along with us – and one has to eat – raise the curtain! whatever one may do, there is no other choice, one must either believe, deny or doubt – one must have deeper motives and judge everything accordingly but go on speaking like an ordinary person – we run heedlessly into the abyss after putting something in front of us to stop us from seeing it – denying, believing and wisely doubting are to men what running is to horses.

All right then, sweetheart, we understand one other, and we are not unduly disgusted, he placed a hairy, black paw, like a beloved brother, on Knight's shoulder – don't! touch! me! – in a shriek; the fraighaoter nodded indifferently: I am bored. Give me my cloak, please.

Knight inwardly obeisance – the only thing that consoles us for our miseries is diversion, and yet it is the greatest of our miseries. For it is that above all which prevents us thinking about ourselves and leads us imperceptibly to destruction. But for that we should be bored, and boredom would drive us to seek some more solid means of escape. But diversion passes our time and brings us imperceptibly to our death. Being unable to cure death, wretchedness and ignorance, men have decided, in order to be happy, not to think about such things.

Just jabber on, gammy gawker, but mark you well, I won't see harm done to man and progress – Man is great even in his lust, he has managed to produce such a remarkable system from it and make it the image of true charity – Maryonka! – a fraighaoter's cry!

The dogs fell silent. What are you doing, you scoundrels? What do you mean what? What indeed? Done, as though they were in darkness, by young lads, fraighaoters, what indeed . . . what indeed . . . Teasingly, they produced a scrap of bacon rind, we fed them; blue, the bacon rind was blue. Murderers! our mother screamed, sordid – now, now, the fraighaoters squirmed uneasily, our mother's face a red blotch, her brow inverted, her eyes clouded, she too has had a lot to drink, the men nervously gathered their things together to leave, calm down, Maryonka – I laughed too, they grabbed up my fay sisses and our mother, amid hooting and screeching, ran off with them like great sacks of flour, doors slammed – block cracked, lifted – all had waited for this, colourful din, for this, colossal racket.

Me too. Things are happening too fast. Void, indeed – oh, oh, little sister, Knight mocked, we were sitting there alone, like children left to our own devices: always. Does it hurt? – I asked him, and placed my hand on his fishy-boned knee. Knight blushed, a fiery heat suffused me too. I became infinitesimally small, compliant, pliable, like an infant – Knight's crestfallen, prematurely aged, bitter face, unable all the same to conceal the purity – the beauty that shines out here to one who recognises it – I was giddy, my thighs were giddy, my muscles all giddy, I took wing within myself: I am potentiality! – but then I began to shrivel, a rotten, sickening, uncertain feeling it was – to my bone, further – We reached a confine, ouch, I screamed and clutched his knee fiercely, beyond, on from there too, through, further in, deep, deep – I love you.

God grant that I may always hear and be able to make others feel, with an almost joyous intoxication, the endless music of things. Love alone is capable of mobilising the existing. Still, light, white, plane, leaves, wind: that is us – And unexpectedly, fear – Loathing and shuddering. Let's make our getaway! I cried.

Getaway? Get away to where? And above all, *from whom*? Come off it, Sophiekins . . . Intolerable weakness, I started shaking him, do something, you rotter, I shrieked – He hushed me, of course, well of course we'll make a getaway, leave them all in the lurch, or set ourselves up in the woods, our woods, they say a few young shavers from the manor have already set themselves up, we'll kit ourselves out with cudgels, crabsticks, arrows and rocks, we'll dig trenches, we'll take bread and bacon with us, and . . . and, Knight fell silent – Excuse me.

I am weak-kneed – Who's talking of wining? Perseverance is all – I was very early initiated into the thought that to conquer means to conquer in an infinite sense, which in a finite sense means to suffer. Kicked sore. It's not solving problems that is difficult but how we pose them – What is truer will find the light of day, and what is for the better will come to pass.

That is what I think, Knight, I sense with a shudder that there is room in my heart for both love and hatred. Knight! I love you. I hate you – Justice is on your side, Princess, the future does not belong to the "tired", nor even the hedonists, but to the enthusiasts, purifying themselves in arduous struggle and attaining ever more exalted heights, for whom tomorrow is important.

Mute, Mute – What man could enjoy the friendship of the King of England, the King of Poland and the Queen of Sweden and believe that he would one day nowhere find refuge and sanctuary? – Mute – You know it is right that what is just should be obeyed, it is necessary that what is strongest should be obeyed. Justice without might is helpless, might without justice is tyrannical. Justice without might is gainsaid, because there are always evil men about; might without justice is condemned. We must therefore combine justice and might, and for this end make what is just strong, or what is strong just. Justice is subject to dispute, might is easily recognised and is not disputed. So we cannot give might to justice, because might has gainsaid justice and has declared that it is she herself who is just. And thus, being unable to make what is just strong, we have made what is strong just.

Who then is the deceiver, the senses or education?

Man is naturally credulous, incredulous, timid, bold. Description of man: dependence, desire for independence, needs. Man's condition: inconstancy, boredom, anxiety – The eternal silence of these infinite spaces fills me with dread . . . There is only one kind of solitude . . . My sweet, my sweet.

I am afraid.

A shout as if from our sisters – the stars are mere rock – I sped, I flung open the first door in the corridor – beds pushed together, a broad, ravaged terrain, bodies with oddly protruding limbs – my God, what on earth is this? – my face icy – what's up? – perchance it wasn't you who called? perchance not your fervent voices, choked with sobbing, from afar? – scram! my sisters shouted, and our mother, pressed to the wall, the fraighaoter's linen shirt dangling round his knees, gestures, off with you, Sophiekins, be snappy about it.

The fraighaoter bawls, by no means may she be off either! – how is everyone moving here? what is this rhythm, cramping and twitching? – how are they talking here? – how do they draw breath here? – what's that? what's that? – our mother, object, slumped to the floor as the fraighaoter stepped away from her, panicked retreat, my sisses' faces buried crimsonly in their pillows, the fraighaoter got entangled in his breeks, tumbled headlong, cussing brazenly – drags me with him, object, me too – sweeps me off – Fool! help!

My legs uselessly together – like a butter pat being hit with a mallet, that is how I dissolved – it hurts, the fraighaoter hurts brutally – heavy smell of onions into me – as if I were tearing apart, as if my bowels were being torn out, as if my heart were being torn from my ribs, as if my ribs were being split open – my thighs slippery warmth – my skinny thighs growing ever skinnier, my God, what radiance was spoken of, just, just black blood.

Knight, raging, rushed at the fraighaoter, who swung out behind, swatting him aside, like a bear with hounds, down, boy, just carry on striking my back, driving in the wedge, drive it do, cunning Fool. Knight clambered to his feet, he is standing, by tipping my head back we see one other, I can't bear to recall a thing – He weeps, blubbing plaintively, I can't! I can't! Do it! No! He soon whips out the bluish bacon rind from his pocket, chews and chews, like a little animal – frantic careering round and round – Froth on his lips – He expired.

I am covered up; I heard our mother moaning one more time, no wailing, Maryonka, there now, the fraighaoter's voice is agreeably deep and calm, come on, it really is better this way . . . within the family . . . there now . . . bring meat! Maryonka, meat, bring meat!

Me, perhaps I stand to the centre. Perhaps it's evening. Perhaps twilight. One thing is sure: it's getting late. I am alone. I am throbbing. Outside, flames flicker in the dark with ominous flashes; the barn is on fire. A working hell without witnesses. Our hopes, the stars, stiffen in death. The windows smashed, empty frames swaying to and fro, the wind driving in billows of black ashes. The fire is still burning in the stove, though. The kitchen table is overturned, chicken bones strewn all around. There's no dog for the bones. My thighs have stuck to the blanket, I am freezing from within, I am an open wound, I stink, reek of sewers, I am undone, carry me away, Lord, even to a loneliness whither I would never have dared go of my own accord.

All right. I scrabble up, put water in a badly worn pot to warm. I tug the washbasin out from under the bed, it scrapes on the floorboards. I scratch protractedly at the enamel with my nails . . . I scour it with sand, I scour it with sand.

A carriage wheels round, them, they troop in, a swirling, laughing throng. I feel mildly nauseous, what will become of us? They cut into one another's words, the animals! they've set the barn alight! To hell with it, Mother laughs, it was empty anyway. They are still a little drunk or very weary. Their faces dusty, like burdock leaves. My precious ones, I say in an undertone.

They twitter and laugh like machines. I managed to find some salt, our mother calls out. So, my good sisters clown, smart dame that you are, then, what is the price of quick-wittedness, with something sensuous on top? No, no, you heartless creatures, all you need know is where! What, when, where . . . I had to put a little coachman lad in his place . . . And milady Mother put him in his place?! As you can see . . .

They think, that lot, they think they are everything, that anything goes. No. I swear!, so my sisses, I gave his nuts such a good mauling, the lousy fraighaoter went green – with both hands! bawling his head off, he was about to slam me, I said it's the latest fad in Paris . . . That didn't work for me, because he took to it from the very first. Maybe he had a scrotal hernia anyway, poor thing! Poor, poor thing – I think Mother and the others are going to get on well in life. Finally, my sisses declare: And we didn't come! No! Those clodhoppers think so, but no, *I didn't come*, they'll believe anything.

Winter's advancing. A lonely wolf made its way down to the village. They turn towards me, all right, then, Sophiekins, we are content with you, we saw your heart's in the right place, and for starters, especially now it's ended, they laugh, Fool will do, and we don't even have to worry about his nasty machinations any more.

I was in love with him, I say. So it was like that, then, the slender maidens exclaim, like that, you were in love with him, that's what you're saying, she loves him, they exchange incredulous glances, she's in love with a fraighaoter's fool . . . You're insane! Didn't you see who they were?! Didn't you see what they did?! You'd take up with people like them?! Feckless, toe-rag traitor, they come at me threateningly, draw daggers, get yours, Sophie, you must die, traitors must die. I am about to say my prayers, my sisses collapse in hoots of laughter on to their beds, on to the stained yellow butterfly coverlets, rolling about as they grapple, gasping for breath, their teeth glinting. Oh, you!

Mother brought warm water and a mug of milk. Lay the table, you lot. Make your beds. Stoke up the fire in the stove. Slacken the dogs' leashes and let them run free.

There is none. I sit in the washbasin. I scratch, like the enamel before, the flecks of blood. My own blood, this. Rinsing doesn't hurt. We are over it again, my sisters pant rapturously. Over it, over it, my darlings, Mother says, stroking my head with her heavy, ageing hand, over it, and we have salt, potatoes and petersilie. We break into heartfelt laughter.

[TW]

The novel contains quotations, whether reproduced accurately or in distorted form, from the works of Pierre Teilhard de Chardin, Søren Kierkegaard, Blaise Pascal, János Pilinszky, Rainer Maria Rilke and Géza Szöcs. "Fraighaoters" is imagined to have an Irish brogue, pronounced roughly "fray-orters".

PÁL ZÁVADA

from *Jadviga's Pillow*

1 "THE NATURAL LAW OF MATRIMONY"

Zachinam tuto knyizhechku.[1] I, András Osztatní, am starting this little notebook on the 5th day of the month of February, 1915, just one day before my wedding.

Restless and fevered with anticipation, I cannot sleep, and so I will now take out my notebook, which I bought at Binder's for the sum of one crown 40. (The minute I laid eyes on it, I was taken with the soft lilac lines on the sheets, and the indigo-coloured cloth binding, and I made up my mind to use it as a Diary as soon as I could call myself a married man.) The clock has just struck midnight, and so I can now set down that today, it being the 6th day of the month of February, 1915, I will lead Mária Jadviga Palkovits to the altar as my bride.

Gyakovaty pana Bohu,[2] may the Good Lord be praised that I have lived to see this day.

I will confess that at this point I put down my pen, clasped my hands together and, bowing my head, offered thanks for my good fortune, after which I stretched my limbs (nearly toppling the inkstand into the bargain), for if the truth be known, I have worked them hard today. However, the fatigue I feel is not heavy but light, and the anticipation, too, has ceased straining on my nerves, and courses through me like blood.

We finished the preparations in good time. *Zabijachka hotova,*[3] two piglets are in the pan, properly scored for baking, and with it patés by the tubful, well combined, 3 sheep, skinned and jointed, plus 50 pairs of hens and 60 ducks, all plucked, and the cakes laid out on 6 large tables, at least, and everything securely under lock and key in the cellar and the pantry. The 5 barrels of wine from Solt Vadkert were brought in yesterday. The *pálinka* is of our own distillation. There is plenty of it decanted into bottles, and I have also ordered 20 bottles of brown and green liqueurs from Komló Inn for the ladies.

The women will set to work at the crack of dawn, laying down the tablecloths at the Smallholders Club, bringing in the plates, and firing up the *kutkas*.[4] (Knowing Mamovka, she will insist on overseeing the preparations, as well as the cooking, though it'd progress just as well without her.) Hulina and Boszák will take the meat over on the dray, but Boszák will stay there, for I made him promise to devote his full attention to the stew, which he will make in 4 large kettles. I don't want a proper cook for *bárány paprikás*,[5] no matter how good. All I want is Boszák. The way he makes it, it's red and dark, like bull's blood, and not runny, like those low-grade meats in their greasy, watery sauces. His stew absorbs its own succulent pan juices, the colour of sour cherries, and it quivers like a foal's flank after a full gallop, that's how strong and hearty it is. It practically makes the plate into which they ladle out that steaming stew tremble.

Our relatives will come around at 3 in the afternoon, after which we will cross the garden and formally ask for Jadviga's hand in marriage. Needless to say, Mamovka and I clashed over this, too. We couldn't see eye to eye on who should be asked for Jadviga's hand. I didn't want my own mother to give Jadviga to me (especially after the vehemence with which she opposed my choice of a bride) but, for instance, the clergyman Szpevács's wife, my Jadviga's Judit mama. Or else, my godmother, *nyanyichka* Erzsa, she could be there to greet us. But when I saw that Jadviga had resigned herself to it, I let Mamovka have her way. Let it be as Mother wishes, I reflected, as if she'd ever let anyone sway her from her appointed course. Besides (or so I reasoned), though I have Apovka to thank for Jadviga, Mamovka gave her blessing to our nuptials, too.

But what am I saying? Who am I trying to fool? Her blessing?! There's no time to go into this thing now. Let it suffice to say, the first time I approached Mother, resolved though weak in the knees, after she heard me out she turned as red as pickled beet, and while her komondor growled menacingly, she advanced, huffing and puffing, backing me up against the wall. "*Cho? zhse koho? chsooo?!*" she repeated, first choking with rage, then screaming and yelling so hard, the windowpanes trembled, What's this? Who would I marry?! And also, that you will study, not marry, understand?! Though she was never one to curb her tongue, I have never seen her quite so incoherent with rage. We were practically at fisticuffs when the dog growled at me again, or so I thought, and I fled for the kitchen, and Mother slammed the door.

We didn't speak to each other for two weeks, but then I couldn't take it any more, and one night I said to her, "Let's talk it over . . ." She stopped me with a wave of the hand and snapped, "*Chobi vász chert zobrav, tak szi ju veznyi*," i.e., what does she care?[6] I was surprised that she had changed her mind like this, and elated, too, though she quickly added, Considering how I can't see or hear, she's got me so thoroughly hooked, she added. ("You let her lead you by the nose, son, didn't you?") And that I don't even care about the difference in our ages, and that her smell has made me lose what little sound sense I may have had. (To tell the truth, Mamovka used the word *szmrad* which, as we know, means "stink", because she's not used to Jadviga's lotions and perfumes. As far as I'm concerned, they make my head spin. Once on the way back from visiting her, I stopped in Vienna and bought some of the camphor ointment she uses, and I kept sniffing at it, sometimes until my head reeled, which went on and on until I could see her again, many months later.)

I wasn't offended by Mother's gruff manner though; I would have liked to hug her and thank her, but she rebuffed me, saying I should stop it, leave her alone. Still, I was happy, though once again, it was no thanks to me that Mamovka changed her mind in my favour. In this manner was the rosemary fragrance of our love born from the noxious brimstone fumes of Mother's curses and the camphor scent of my true intended.

But back to the wedding! The new carriage with the leather seats will be harnessed by early afternoon; we will mount the smaller one, which Gregor will drive with the ribboned French reins Apovka brought from Győr, and which he treasured like the light of his eyes. The big double seater will trail behind; it will contain Mamovka, Krszní Otyec and Krszná Mama[7] with my cousin Erka. Mother's house servant Zelenák can drive that, for all I care. (I gave him some proper clothing, seeing how Mamovka insists on this flea-ridden, pediculous Zelenák, so that she may have someone to order around, I expect. "Will you at least shave, for the love of God," I say to him. "What? *Zse cso?*"[8] Zelenák says, because he can be as deaf as a doornail when he wants, at which I say, "*O-ho-lyity!, rozumjetye?*"[9] and also, "Here, take this suit of clothes, they're your size!")

And thus I have been forced to make my own arrangements for my very own wedding, because my beloved Father, *moj milyí* Apovka, did not live to see it, while my poor Mamovka, try as she might to order a whole cackle of chicken-plucking women and hired hands around (not to mention the rest of us), was no mean encumberment to me. Now, too, it's a struggle every step of the way, may the good Lord forgive her, and me, too, into the bargain!

The truth is, she is infinitely more sour and forbidding since the loss of her daughter, for now it is but the two of us; my older sister Zsofka, who was a bride-to-be, we buried just four months before Apovka's death, in October, 1913, our poor unplucked lily-flower. She was the apple of Mamovka's eye, the daughter on whom she bestowed her name, and in whom she saw her former maiden self. It was for her she had planned a grand wedding like this, I know that, and not for me. And when my time would come, she thought it would be with somebody else.

She wanted me to marry the girl who was Zsofka's constant companion, and whom I would not offend for the world by setting down her name, the girl I did not want, whereas she always entertained certain hopes for me.

Incidentally, I saw her again three days ago at the Hromnyice Day ball, where she danced with my friend Pali Rosza the whole night, may the Lord be praised. It was there, at the Mária Day Smallholders' dance[10] and on her name day, that I first showed myself with Jadviga in public, and I was as proud as a peacock with my lovely bride, who was dancing as a maiden for the last time in her life.

This morning, I dashed over to the other house for Jadviga (it was built by Apovka for Zsofka, but now we are going to live in it). "Come along," I said to her, dragging her across the garden. I then opened the cellar with the long key and led my wonder-struck bride down the stairs to the oleanders wintering in the large cauldrons. "Pluck me a spray of rosemary," I said, "and stick it in my hat!" We laughed when she did this, and embraced, and then I said, "I had better be off, and so must you, lest someone should see us," even though it was not somebody else who did not want us to be seen together that day (or even custom, which is not especially strict on this point), but her.

If there was no separate bride's house and groom's house, she wanted to be spared, at least, for one more day, the ordeal of greeting a hoard of chicken- and cake-bearing relatives. Besides, she felt a cold coming on and preferred drawing the curtains in the new houses and inhaling a brew of herbal teas, and applying her camphorous ointments to fend off an attack of migraine on her big day. "Also," she said, "I need time to think, dear. I'm sure you understand."

"Oh," I said, stroking her, "there is nothing I wouldn't do for you," though I knew perfectly well that Mother wouldn't leave this, either, without comment. Mamovka Drahá! Mamo, Mother dear! If only the good Lord would soften her heart!

So it was this spray of rosemary that I have just put into my wedding-suit pocket (having read the other day in "A Practical Guide" that this is the way), and I also crumbled some between my fingers, because it smells so nice when I raise them to my nostrils. I will also take out the camphor ointment, possibly for the last time, so I can pine for its mistress, who will soon be mine for ever.

For this little notebook, and for myself, too (and for myself only), I will first set down how I won my Jadviga's hand in marriage, so that I may recall it until my dying day. I will write it down starting tomorrow, after I am a married man. Right now I am very tired.

*

8 February, 1915
The expenses and expenditures of my wedding were as follows: To the Smallholders Association, for rental of the Smallholders Hall, 30 zlati;[11] 1 fatted hen, 2 milk-loaves (50 zl.) and two carts of firewood for each trubatsh musician (Chmel with 16 boys). Drinks (all gone): 3 1/2 hectolitres of wine and 1/2 hltr. pálinka and liqueurs (60 zl.). Mamovka presented Jadviga with a gift kerchief and collar (25 zl.), plus 3 zlati for the bridal dance. We gave the best man a cart of firewood. The wedding invitations from Weiszmüller's printing shop, 160, cost 4 zl. This came to the sum total of 172 zlati, which doesn't include the rosewood for the fire.

I shall write more about my wedding (which went without a hitch, mostly), especially my wedding night, at a later date. (Actually, even though four nights have passed, it hasn't happened yet, not really, in its natural way, even though we have mutually assured each other of our amorous intentions – gentle stroking, etc. I haven't slept a wink for days, what with transports of ecstasy and extreme agitation vying for supremacy.)

*

9 February
I will now set our story down on paper, as promised, from the beginning, though our present situation, and most especially our nights – I would not forget any of it, not for the world. (Perhaps it could lead to understanding, or serve as a lesson.) But that will come by and by.

So then. Having harnessed Zephyr at the crack of dawn, I was soon out on the farm, saying I had to give Gregor his orders, whereas it is not Gregor at all who needs ordering, but me, for crying out loud, me, inside!

My Jadviga got up with me, an angelic smile on her face, whereas she couldn't have slept much either, and she gave me clean linen and *ranyajka*,[12] toasted bread in the stove (old Granny Blahov had fired it up by then), and spread duck fat on top. I stealthily pocketed my small notebook (I have pen and ink out on the farm), and we parted with a kiss.

I quickly gave Gregor his orders, dispatching him to do the harrowing, though he knows what he has got to do perfectly well, without me telling him. But hold on. Who am I trying to fool? If only this weren't a Diary! I can't send Gregor off anywhere, least of all to do the harrowing; I need *him* to tell me whether it is harrowing that's on the agenda today, or possibly something else.

I flung two sheaves of *kukuricsa*[13] husks on the embers, then I sat down at my old servant's table to write, moving it closer to the window. What I know I know mostly from Gregor anyway (who is steward of my estate), so it is only fitting that I should do my writing in this out-of-the-way nook, where he told me many a tale when I was a boy. He was Apovka's faithful servant since he was a boy himself. Grandfather had hired him, and though he never married, when this farm was left without dwellers, well on 20 years ago, Apovka put him here despite Mamovka's protests, who meant to put her field-hands here, women with all their kith and kin, because they flattered and badgered her (how it's such a lovely farm, and close to the village). But Apovka wouldn't be swayed, it's Gregor's as long as he lives, "*do szmrty*".[14]

My beloved father, György Osztatní, tripled his 30-hold inheritance and brought together a handsome homestead (not to mention Mamovka's 50 cadasters of land, which was cut off of the parental estate only at a later date, but part of which Mother managed herself, of her own volition, which Apovka observed with good humour). The other landowners referred to our estate as a real *bohatí majetok*,[15] and made fun of Father's name,[16] because he made the most of himself in the village, and from his own resources, mostly, because he didn't spend his life playing cards, cavorting all night and hunting, like Count Vaclavszky, for instance, next to us.

Yet Apovka could have made another life for himself had he, as Gregor says, not set his sights on his own aggrandisement and running around all the time, fleeing his home, but had settled for the schoolmaster and cantor's daughter, whom he must have seriously considered for a bride, and of whom I shall say more later; in short, had he not married Mamovka, whose inheritance of half of the mill my uncle, Godfather Jankó, bestowed on her right away, and whose parents promised – and paid – her a handsome yearly percentage from the income on the estate, which was left intact, and which just added fuel to the fire of Apovka's ambition to make himself a wealthier man than his neighbours.

Being a clever and competent farmer who attended gymnasium in Csaba (after which, having pestered his father until he gave his consent, he was sent away to study the art of husbandry and the German language), they soon wished to bring Apovka into local affairs. But he, preferring to dash about acquiring things, would rather sell somebody's wheat, or buy seed grain or machines, or purchase breeding animals, round up hired hands or even arrange marriages than work in a clerical job. Even so, he was repeatedly deputised to the local Chamber, the County or Budapest – wherever he was needed, but office of any sort he refused. They would have made him a magistrate, member of the County Assembly or a churchwarden, even president of the County Chamber, but he would have none of it. He refused to sit behind a desk or doze on a bench the whole day long, he said. He'll gladly offer his services short term, he said, but that he feels no inclination to do what he must. This was one side of the coin. The other was that Father preferred to look after his own aggrandisement, and never was he tempted by office.

It all began when my Father did a favour for a certain Benjamin Winkler, a German lawyer's apprentice who was unmarried at the time, and with whom he had boarded at the house of the hardware merchant Fehérvári during their school years. It transpired that once the widower Poldi Weisz (Fehérvári's older brother, a Jewish cloth merchant from the village) visited the family with his two daughters, one of whom, Mici (Aunt Mici to me), caught Béni Winkler's eye. However, because Uncle Poldi would not hear of a German marrying his daughter, even if he happened to be a lawyer, Father carried their letters and other missives for them in secret, finally bringing Winkler himself home with him, and arranging for them to meet. The meeting must have gone admirably, for Micike found herself with child, upon which the enamoured Winkler eloped with her and married her, ignoring the fact that his own parents had other plans for him and were expecting his return to Germany. ("You married a girl by the name of Mici Weisz?! *Gott im Himmel!*") But Aunt Mici gave birth to little Franci Winkler despite their protests, while the lawyer, as a token of his gratitude, recommended Father to his older brother in Velgast, in Mecklenburg, and subsequently (because he was instrumental in pacifying his father-in-law, old Poldi), once they were back home, introduced him to his circle of friends – county officials, merchants, bankers and contractors – who in turn employed Father as their business contact to the farmers of the district, while they served him in good stead as business and family relations, first throughout the country and, later, even beyond.

Still – though he had plenty of opportunity to do so – Father did not desert his native village, the reason for which must be sought, I suspect, in the person of Mária Ponyiczky. But even Gregor cannot say what brought a sudden end to their years of longing for each other, for, on the one hand, when their secret was revealed and Grandfather thundered and forbade his son to court the penniless headmaster's daughter ("*Cso kcses? Nye daju sznyov nyics!*"),[17] this would not have sufficed to sway my by then already headstrong father from his appointed path; on the other, one wonders how much damage the appearance of a certain young parish clerk might have caused who, they say, was probably transferred here only after Father, as Gregor relates, spent the night in desperate merrymaking to forget his sorrow, then, teeth clenched, and white as a sheet, he appeared at Mamovka's house during the Sunday meal, and without saying a single word to her, asked for the hand of the richest and haughtiest girl in the village (who, in her turn, had showed the door to many a wooer) in marriage. Not content with that, he demanded an immediate answer!

We will probably never know any of this for sure; we know only that it was on the same day that the devastated schoolmaster Ponyiczky, who had become a widower the year before, and who by then was regularly trailed by groups of mocking children on the street, accompanied his daughter to her wedding in the clerk's village; and it was on this day, too, that my father, György Osztatní, and my mother, Zsófia Racskó, held a wedding feast so fabulous that no-one has seen the likes of it, either before or since. Or so old Gregor says. The people of the entire village ate and drank to their heart's content. This was on the 7th day of May, in the year of Our Lord, 1886.

Within months, calamity struck in relentless waves, with just one gift of God shining forth from the dark relentlessness of fate, namely that Mária Ponyiczky, the schoolmaster's daughter, gave birth, though a bit before her time, to be sure, to a beautiful baby girl. However, sorrow and desperation left no room in her maternal breast for joy, for a year and a half after her mother's death she first lost her schoolmaster father, then her husband, and nearly her mind, too, into the bargain. The melancholy scribe of the prefecture who, as they say, wore his fate inscribed on his handsome, wide forehead, was reputed to have died of blood poisoning as a result of a wound. Not a year passed, and the young mother, who was forced to hire a wet-nurse and nanny (for she had no milk, nor the will to live), returned to her Maker, and there is no knowing whether she simply let her soul slip away from her, because she would not eat and never recovered from her confinement, or whether she drove it wilfully away, for there are those who say that she drank caustic soda.

I must stop now, because my wife is calling me to supper. I merely wish to comment that despite Mamovka's imprecations, Father first became the little orphan's legal guardian, then adopted her, and that she is called Mária Jadviga Palkovits, and she is my lawfully wedded wife.

*

Today, on the 10th day of February, Mamovka handed me, on bound paper sheets, the list that Ivka Kohut, my older sister's friend, had set down from dictation, and which is entitled "The list of Zsofka's dowry for her wedding".

"Take it," says Mother, "seeing how it was all left on my hands! I had it taken to your wife this morning. Nobody wants it any more. Have her count the things, and sign it, that you took it. It should have been Zsofka's by right!" And having said that, she slammed the door.

I go to my Jadviga's room. Her eyes are red from crying, but her face lights up when she sees me. She doesn't have to say anything. I know that what Mamovka gave her, she gave in order to humiliate her. Is it proper for her to take all this, she asks, and must she take it?

We did not sign anything, but I subsequently transferred the inventory to my notebook:

20 bed sheets
34 towels (30 for daily use, 4 with embroidered monograms)
10 tablecloths (3 damask, 2 store-bought, 5 homespun)
18 napkins (16 store-bought, various; 1 monogrammed, 1 big damask)
18 shirts, embroidered, 4 nightshirts, 1 striped shirt
11 white blouses, 4 white bodices
4 fustian underdrawers
8 blankets (4 white)
10 vests (6 white, 1 black, 2 pink, 1 with ribbons)
4 robes (3 for summer, 1 for winter)
12 underskirts (6 printed, 1 *noldová*, 5 store-bought)

8 skirts (2 silk, 2 printed and patterned, 4 *hárász*)
3 silk skirts with apron
13 aprons (2 hand-spun, with name, 1 *liszter*, 6 washable, 4 with tops)
3 flower-patterned silk frocks (1 patterned pink, 1 white with blue flowers, 1 *hárász*)
2 black frocks (1 plain silk, 1 repp)
1 white silk wedding gown
20 blouses (12 silk, 8 washable)
46 kerchiefs (16 silk, 8 *gaziros*, 3 broadcloth, 17 linen, 2 cotton flannel/fustian)
2 large shawls for the shoulder, dark brown silk with flowers
11 winter shawls (3 with plush fringes, 4 Berliners with plush fringes, 4 Berliners without fringes)
20 handkerchiefs
1 woollen sweater
3 winter overcoats (2 cloth, 1 plush)
10 pairs of shoes (3 pr suede, 1 pr white, 1 pr grey, 1 pr black, 1 pr beige, 1 pr snakeskin, 2 prs patent leather)
4 pairs of slippers (2 prs patent leather, 1 pr velvet, 1 pr with white roses)
6 pairs of stockings (3 prs silk, 3 prs ribble)
cotton flannel/fustian cloth for 3 blouses, *kazan* cloth for 1 blouse, chiffon cloth for 1 blouse, white lace cloth for 4 skirts
10 pillows each with 2 kg goose feathers
12 pillow cases (8 damask, 4 *kanevász*)
3 comforters/eiderdowns with 8 kg goose down each
3 mattresses with 7 kg goose down each

She will also take as her dowry;

2 veneered wardrobes
1 expandable table
1 mirror with stand
2 veneered beds
2 straw mattresses, store-bought
1 bedcover for a double bed
1 beige bedcover for a single bed
1 silk pillow case which Zsofka made herself

Of the above, the bedlinen and furniture were already in our possession. But Mamovka gave me this inventory sheet all the same, lest we forget, my Jadviga said, that we are living and sleeping in Zsofka's things, not to mention the clothes Mamovka gave Jadviga earlier, without telling her they were from the dowry. She especially said nothing about the wedding gown, whereas had she been able to refuse it, Jadviga would have had one made, because this was not to her taste. She also put away the silk pillow case, because she only uses the white embroidered pillow that came from her mother.

On the 11th of February, 1915, I bought, with my own money, parts for the Kühne seeder Mamovka and I own jointly: 3 pairs hinges for 42 fillérs, 100 nails, 9 seed funnels for the seeder from the tinsmith Strbka for 1 crown 80 fillérs, 25 screws for 10 fillérs, for a total of 2.42 crowns.

I do not have time to write about anything else now. Also, I do not understand anything, Jadviga most especially. Sometimes I feel like I am losing my mind. Poor Zephyr, for no reason I drove him so hard in front of the buggy today, he was foaming at the mouth. Then it rained, and I was drenched to the bone.

*

The following also happened yesterday. I must note it down, because tripping over that peacock is not all that happened.

The truth is when, as wet as I was, I unharnessed the horse and left the stable with the traces and wet blanket, I couldn't see a thing. Still, when (after flinging the stuff down angrily by the shed door) I kicked that poor stupid creature with all my might, I suddenly thought: She's just like this peacock. And also: Get out of my sight! And that my wife is just like you! And with that, I kicked it against the wall. I break out in a cold sweat, just thinking about it. It hawked, shook itself and, without looking at me, strutted away, swinging softly to and fro. And that's not all, because I don't know why, but as that peacock marched past me, its head held proudly high, its large tail swaying – is the long-tailed one the hen or the little grey one, I wonder? – my anger doubled in upon itself, and I grabbed the wicker broom and flung it at its young. I hit the largest of the three chicks, and as I removed the broom from its fluttering wing as it lay on its side, something clouded my mind, and I trampled it to death with my booted foot. The peacock never looked back at its young, but I looked around, horrified, lest someone should see me, especially Mamovka, who has been trying, ever since she had sent away for this pair of peacocks years ago, to hatch a rare egg or two; and it is only recently that these three chicks finally came, with a hatcher. I swept the flattened chick on to a dustpan, took it round the back, and, loosening the top of the dungheap with a fork, I stashed it underneath. I felt such loathing, I nearly vomited, but the loathing I felt was directed at myself.

*

The 19th of February, 1915, Zsuzsanna Day.
At the break of dawn, I toss and turn in bed. I cannot sleep. My mouth tastes bitter, my body is taut and restless. The lark should sing for the first time today, but I listen in vain. Will spring ever come?

*

On the 21st of February, two weeks after our nuptials, Jadviga's confession, that one sentence. (I got up without a word, went to the window, and she came after me and put her arms around me. Freeing myself from her embrace, I paced up and down the room until the break of day. Only then did I ask the first question.) However, I can not write or talk about it.

*

The truth is, before I turned the wick up in order to act as the faithful chronicler of my troubled heart, I downed two glasses of *terkelyica schnapps*,[18] chasing them down with a bottle of ordinary dry wine from Vadkert, which I got earlier from the *komora*.[19] I must drink, for I am overwrought; besides, the wine will give me courage for writing down such intimacies. Jadviga is asleep. I am not.

I smell my palm . . . At other times, when my camphor-scented Jadviga's smile holds out hope, I smell rosemary on her skin as it peeks out from under her gown. But like this, towards dawn, after the physical and emotional torment, I detect the smell of dill on us both. (Sometimes Mamovka uses such inordinate amounts of dill in her cooking and baking that it makes me nauseous, and I am quite overcome with loathing, and at times I must even leave the table. But I say nothing.)

In order for me to write down Jadviga's confession, I must back up a little.

I should begin with our wedding night, for in Stralsund, we never progressed beyond kissing, and for a long time, even that meant only the touching of the lips, for she would not let me probe between her pearly teeth with my tongue until the night before we left for home. (Not to mention pressing my face against her breast, over her bodice, or cupping my hand over it, these were also forbidden.) Here at home, she usually brought up Mamovka as an excuse, saying she might come in at any time. But she never repulsed me outright; she just smiled and gently pushed me away, though she was always blushing and hot, her breath quickened, and her lips, too, quivered ever so slightly, with hardly perceptible, convulsive little spasms.

We could not escape the wedding feast and retire to our room until very late. The more hardy of our guests, my friends Pali Rosza, Szvetlik and the others, had a grand time, and towards dawn had the band play marches only, and kept kicking the wooden floor with their boots so it nearly collapsed under them, but then they persuaded the girls to join them again and danced to Slovak songs. It was at that point we left; we glanced at each other, and off we went. (I told only Miki Buchbinder, but not Mamovka, who was in the kitchen, out back.)

We ran to the house, which from now on would be our new home, hand in hand, and the icy air refreshed me. Not wishing to grow drowsy and weak and get a bad stomach, I drank in moderation throughout the night, and though I ate a hearty meal (especially Boszák's excellent stew), I was able to relieve myself before we sneaked away, and to reduce the painful bloating. (I have often wondered while passing wind at night, under the covers – because it's not like passing water, when you can relieve yourself, and that's that; with wind you must wait patiently for it to happen, not to mention the fact that you cannot stay in the jakes for hours! – in short, I have often asked myself what it would be like with two of us in bed? And would the bloating, which can be excruciatingly painful at times, stand in the way of the body's labour of love, for with its abdominal excitations, that likewise stimulates the bowels. And will that mean a disillusioning dash for the jakes? Or what?)

We did not immediately divest ourselves of our clothing (having changed at midnight, she was wearing her "bride's dress"), but leaning against the lukewarm stove, and each other, too, we talked in whispers about the wedding and how well it had turned out. (However, I had first kicked off my boots and turned the lamp down a bit.) Later, Jadviga slipped out to the dark kitchen and washed herself in the porcelain washbasin. I peeked, and though I could see nothing, she reprimanded me, so I turned down the bed in the meantime. She came back fully dressed, and after I had also rinsed the sweat from under my arms, what's more (something I normally did only when I took my regular bath), I hastily splashed water on my privates as well and came back to the bedroom, she was sitting on the ottoman as before. I kissed her then, and she suffered it, but I did not feel her arousal as I had done the last time. When I began to fumble with the buttons of her gown, she removed her hand. Go slowly, she whispered, and that she would rather do it herself, and the other side, that's yours, Ondrisko. And she pushed me away. She slipped then out of her clothes, I could hear, then she sat on the side of the bed in her nightgown. I pulled off my trousers, but after some hesitation, leaving my shirt and drawers on, I got in on the other side and touched her.

I leaned over her and embraced her, and since she was still partly sitting up, and me pushing her down, she finally relented. Instantly, this made me so aroused, my body was one huge convulsion. But soothing my more urgent gestures, for her part, she asked that we remain still and just lull each other in an embrace. I did not care. Light-headed with her smell, I snuggled up to her, and since this time I was not vehement, she let me. And though I liked this, besides which I am by disposition not a fighter, my palm started slipping up her cheek just the same, then her neck, then her arm, then from below, from the knee, carefully working its way upwards. But she stopped my hand, saying I should come closer instead. Inviting and repulsing me at the same time, I thought, at which I plucked up the courage to lie full length against her right side (she was lying on her back, and me on my left side); cautiously, I laid my throbbing member on her thigh, and – there is no denying it – when she felt this, it made her shiver, and she shied away, but later, as we lay there without moving, she did not object to my lying so close on top of her. Still, though we were kissing passionately, when I tried to raise her gown with my right hand, again she would not suffer it.

And so it went. Kissing and snuggling, breathing ecstatically – that was all right, but finding my way to her lap, that was out. "Let's throw off our clothes," I pleaded (having first discarded my shirt). After much persuasion, she let me pull her gown up over her head, but she hooked a finger into the hem of her silken drawers, that was out, and she made me promise that we'd lie quietly side by side, just the way we were. However, she could not prevent me from freeing myself of my own drawers, and I was in seventh heaven as I snuggled up naked to her thighs (to the extent that the leg of her drawers would allow as it slipped up), and her right breast, too, not to mention the moment when, presently, I could touch the left. I could stroke her everywhere then; except the waist of her drawers, she would not let me touch that, she would not let me near her lap, despite my fevered embraces, and I tried to force her thighs open with my knees to no avail.

Yet she was highly excited herself, I am sure of that, and not just me. She addressed unforgettable, endearing words to me, as I to her, but she asked me to be patient, etc., let's get used to each other first, let's be satisfied with what we have. But I, such is human nature, could hardly contain myself at this point, and when she felt my breath turning more and more uncontrollably vehement and me pressing against her thigh with all my might, she grabbed me round the waist, tightened her embrace and began rocking herself slowly back and forth, and me, too, and she whispered, panting, no, don't, take it easy, my dear! *takto, takto! yes!* and while I rolled her drawers down her hips with my trembling fingers, so I could press my erection against her bare skin at least, we ended up holding on to each other for dear life in a quickening rocking motion, until the juices of my passion trickled down her waist. The bed spun round with me, and my breathing came so heavy, it burned me inside, tears of joy and gratitude flooded my soul, though mixed with shame, to be sure, but as I lay panting on her shoulder, Jadviga calmed, hushed and soothed me as if I were a child, and whispered, *dobre*, it's all right, my dear, it's all right. *Dobre, Milyi moj, dobre*!

*

Today, it being the 1st of March, 1915, is my wife's 28th birthday. I have a necklace for her. I will give it to her this evening. If only we could give ourselves to each other, too, entirely tonight! For I yearn to be in my Jadviga's lap at long last; I yearn to relieve not only my body, which throbs with want of her, but since her obscure "confession", my soul, too, into the bargain, tormented to its utmost limits with doubt. Perhaps I will also find the certainty I must have, possibly reassuring, as I now hope, or even the kind which, though it will corroborate my worst fears, will mercifully put an end to this unbearable state of suspicion.

But this gives pause for reflection. Could the painful certainty be preferable to this nagging doubt? Could it offer relief? Or will the opposite happen, and our love, which has not yet matured into unreserved giving, yet, despite its struggles, is profound (and may grow still more profound in our laps) – could our love, I say, be undermined by the mounting grievances? I do not know. However, let the inevitable have its way; let it come, if for no other reason then because she is my wife, a fact I would rather not remind her of. My patience is at an end, husband and wife sharing a bed, every single daybreak with teeth clenched, and virgins still!

Could her heart be already harbouring stories unfamiliar to me?

*

Yesterday morning I threw down my pen with a sigh, for what I wrote did not get me anywhere (nor did my night with Jadviga), and I went, instead, to supervise the spring preparations in the fields. It is high time I concerned myself with matters of my farm, which I have been neglecting, alas, for far too long. I must take the reins in hand, and find a way to invest my funds, now that I am my own master, for the aggrandisement of my estate. A pity that the resourceful ideas which, in his time, for instance, teemed with such plenitude in Apovka's brain seem to evade me.

I know this because Mamovka would often upbraid Father with having left her, even as a month-old husband, to go take workers, recruited in our area, to Transdanubia, while on his way back he would stop in Pest to look into his various affairs, only to rush off, after a couple of days, to Germany, to see Ludwig, Béni Winkler's brother, who lived in Velgasi, where he'd been a visitor even before his marriage. Then one day he came back with a profitable plan for organising the transport of people who had their mind set on America, and who, for about 20 years thereafter, flooded out of the Great Plain in what seemed like endless numbers.

My Jadviga's fate as an orphan was also resolved through Apovka's contacts, though that came later. At first, according to Gregor's account, the child's life was no bed of roses, though Father provided for the wet-nurse Anka, and furthermore, covered all of the little girl's other expenses. But after the death of the unfortunate mother, Mária Ponyiczky, Anka had to take the poor little orphan girl home with her, along with her own, which would not have been undesirable, for in this way, Jadviga would have had a sister, at least, but they lived in want and misery, not to mention the fact that there was Anka's good-for-nothing husband and foul-tongued mother-in-law to contend with, whose abusive language towards her daughter-in-law – as Gregor related to me – was outdone only by Mamovka, who chastised my kind-hearted father, saying, what the *zrányik*[20] hell business did he have with other people's brats. (By the way, up to that time they had only one sickly little girl, unfit for life, who lived but a few short days, and only four years later was my sister Zsofka brought into the world, and me two years after her, in November, 1892.[21])

Seeing how things stood, Apovka then had Anka, with the two little girls, taken in as a domestic at the Reverend Szpevács's house, in the neighbouring village, where he not only provided for the orphan but also paid Anka's hire instead of the Reverend and his family, who in turn were bound to treat little Jadviga as if she were their own, and to look after her even when Anka was given a day off, to go home to her family. And may the Lord be blessed, this servant of the Almighty, and his kind-hearted wife, well-disposed towards children, kept not only to the letter of their written contract but showed the orphan sincere love and affection.

These details of the story I could pry out of Gregor, I recall, only during the summer before last, after Apovka and I travelled to Germany together for the last time, and where, in express obedience to my father's wishes, I became reacquainted with Jadviga in Stralsund, though this time, as a grown-up. However, before I could reveal to Apovka the emotions this encounter had stirred in my innermost heart, he was taken ill with an especially virulent and dangerous disease, which evaded precise diagnosis, and which, after two horrible leave-taking weeks, the most painful period of my young life, took him from us on 8th February, 1914, at the age of forty-nine. I conveyed the devastating news in a letter to Jadviga, who confessed her great affliction in a desperate letter of her own and who, now that Father was taken from us, thanked me, personally, for everything for which she owed her only benefactor, she said, nothing less than eternal gratitude, yet at the same time upbraiding me for failing to dispatch a telegram as soon as Father was taken ill, for she would have come home then, either to nurse him or to take her leave. Poor soul, how could I have written?

1 I shall now begin this small work.
2 Praise be the Lord, in the Slovak language.
3 The little beating is done, i.e. they have finished slaughtering the pig.
4 Places for the cauldrons, made of adobe
5 Mutton stew.
6 In short, the devil take the both of you, go marry her.
7 Godfather and Godmother.
8 What's that?
9 Shave yourself, un-der-stand?
10 Hromnyice is the Day of Mary and Candlemass, and it is her name day because she is Mrs András Osztatní, née Mária Jadviga Palkovics. (Otherwise, a dance like this is just like the Smallholders' livestock fair, except they don't have to listen to the tooting trubatsh brass.)

11 Gold.
12 Breakfast. But they also call it *frustyik*, from the German.
13 The dried stem of the corn. But maybe he didn't write it correctly, because the corn stem was thrown in the kiln only after the cows had chewed off the leaves, but that's called "zetke".
14 In short, he will stay until he dies. (In death, nothing remains, not even vowels: *Szmrty*.)
15 A real wealthy estate.
16 Though it was not funny. In our part of the world, Osztatni in Slovak means "Last" even today, even though the dictionary doesn't say this, it says, "the rest", i.e. what remains. A sort of remainder. Of course, it could be construed as funny: "Last Dregs" family. This could be done, I suppose.
17 Meaning, what were you thinking of? They won't give you anything with her! (Meaning, a dowry.)
18 Two shots of grappa brandy.
19 And the "*komora*", that's the pantry.
20 *Zrányik*, that's a sort of poxing.
21 In order to provide a clear picture of things: Of the marriage between György Osztatní (b. 1865) and Zsófia Racskó (b. 1867) who tied the knot on 7 May, 1886, the first Zsofka was born 2 June, 1887, and died soon after; the other Zsofka was born 22 March, 1890 and died 9 Oct., 1913. András Osztatní was born on 21 Nov., 1892.

[JS]

COMECON ISLANDS 3

THE CROSSING

ÁDÁM NÁDASDY

Useful Information about Angels

They have accepted and proclaimed with trumpets
the sweet condition of emasculation;
they're not to be rebuked, are cold, creative,
their loyalty exceeds one's expectation.

Their gowns are daring, their wings practical,
perhaps they're over-sensitive to smells,
that's why they like the heights: it suits them fine,
they need no more than light and decibels.

They're never thirsty: on returning home
they do not jostle round the civic taps –
does their flesh store water? have they no throats?
They tend to appear at moments of collapse

and make for me through creaking chains of bridges:
are loners and impertinent, chilled seagulls.
They circle greedily, they offer nothing,
are worse than me as fathers, and more regal.

[GS]

Ethology

The diet of the young is unrefined,
that's why their innards are in such a pother;
they understand those who respond in kind
and so they sick up everything twice over.

The caresses of the young are crude, poor souls;
the miracle goes wrong, their palms gush water.
In vain the razor blades fixed in their soles,
the grass beneath their feet erupts with laughter.

The carapace of the young is thin and fine
and underneath they're soft and pink, alas;
an X-ray session turns them on, like wine,
their liver is honey and their ribs are glass.

They live in closets, sweaty atriums,
make civilised and tiny drumming noises.
And then they start to run, to shake and run,
and sprinkle kerosene over my roses.

[GS]

ISTVÁN BAKA

Passing Through

Like someone rudely woken on a winter
morning on a bench at the station, under
a glass roof soaked through by the bloody sun,
who sits up stiffly in the freezing, un-
swept hall, looks round and finds it all too loud,
and can't see what he's doing in the crowd,
or what brought him to this unfamiliar
terminal in the provinces (who are
these people, where have they all sprung from? why
this shoving others aside, this rushing by?)
then a sprinkling of semi-conscious drunks
spills from the doorways, bums with penknives, ranks
of fur-coated babushkas, loiterers,
soldiers on leave, newsboys, wheel-tappers, porters,
sad office workers with worn leather cases,
kids selling towels, gypsies with brown faces
and bundles, skiving students, a lunatic
with empty paper bags whose party trick
is bursting them, some tired security toughs
with bulletproof jackets and Kalashnikovs,
unshaven old tramps and an under-age
mother, her child screeching into her ribcage,
streetwalkers, cops, street preachers afloat
on rhetoric . . . from what vast womb or throat
have all these people issued, and why do they
rush blindly at commands from the PA,
why this swarming, what train is it they want,
why do they labour and look so hesitant,
of all this he knows nothing, but watches amazed
as dawn drips blood-grey through that distant glazed
roof and he cannot now remember whether
it was some curse or mission swept him hither,
or where he comes from, nor can he begin
to guess the past his home is swimming in

like someone rudely woken on a winter
morning on a bench at the station under
a glass roof, so was I born, so cold the air,
so hard the wooden bench, not knowing where
and why, not even now, what deadly crime
I have been exiled for, how long the time
till death or pardon come, His will be done
and God decide, so that I may move on.

[GS]

ZSUZSA RAKOVSZKY

Decline and Fall

At last they will disappear, finally just go,
those cinemas and cigarettes named after terms
derived from military history or constitutional law.
The waterworks, machine-tool factories, firms
producing matchboxes that advise you to pursue
a prudent lifestyle, they will vanish too.
Local branches of the catering industry,
chipped teacups, tubular-plastic bar stools made for short
legs, flat drinks in bottles whose labels sport
sundiscs and oranges as if the real sun had bleached
them both, tables with marble effects and sticky
tops. They'll survive a while, persist like rime
in the coldest microclimate, in random patches,
but when they do eventually go it won't be time
but earth which swallows them, they will flake off
and soak away: anniversaries, occasions of formal
mourning, ersatz occasions that pass for normal:
Mothers' Day, Women's Day, Children's Day, Sports Day,
each with its posters scrubbed, peeling away
to reveal a flowering branch or dove, or a block of
numbers pasted across a girl's virginal face
(as if atoning for a *Playboy* playmate's vast
overthrusting bunny bosom pressing against lace),
all these will fade away, as will the products
of the Totalitarian-Classical, filthy terminals
and waiting rooms, provincial cultural halls
with monstrous frescoes and mosaics docked
of odd teeth, showing humanity gathered
in full-throated choirs, celebrating harvests,
or the manufacture of ball-bearings, breasts
heaving in joy at the redemption of leisure
by culture. Not everything has weathered
so well: where are the experiments with white mice
or ferro-concrete? Burst like a balloon,

a thousand pieces exploding in one vast bloom,
or stretching, shrivelling, curling in long flames
resembling, if in nothing else but this,
a contemporary Rome or Babylon's nemesis.
My mass-produced mirror, my pot of jelloid face cream,
my little brown jugs, will not grace a museum,
provide educational outings for family Sundays,
nor will my remains be preserved in an airtight case
or my colour-rinsed curls and protruding eyes
be twisted into a sheath – my speaking likeness
will not be hung on the wall to oversee the moral
welfare of a new generation; indeed, of the wall,
a prefab component of my industrial high-rise,
of that whole moon-grey incubator where each block
rots faster than the inner city's overblown baroque,
not a jot will remain. A few turn-of-the-century
public buildings, like slices of elephantine
wedding cake, blackened and growing green,
might yet survive, but their bills designed
for the propagation of an ornamental diction
and their six-foot streamers will have declined
and faded, their threadbare carpets rotted
to an ultimate state of dereliction,
and dehydrating yellow leaves of potted
palms perished in civic halls where council
employees, women in business suits, fill
forms, harangue, register marriages,
and rooms where we presented ourselves, signed up
for birth, death or divorce perhaps survive
preserved in memory's indifferent syrup
only while we who lived them are ourselves alive.

[GS]

Old Women of My Childhood

What else was there? The cocktail cabinet with pillar
base and marble top of raw-liver colour.
Cups thinning in light to a grey mist, a few
back numbers of a magazine called *New*

Age, silhouettes of greyhounds in an oval frame,
a souvenir glass, engraved with the name
of a German town. Their mode of being was curious:
imagine a cuckoo clock or ten-piece dinner service
salvaged for one's sole convenience from a wreck
and cast on a deserted beach among the bladderwrack
twixt goats and palm trees. Why furnish a room
with two tall facing mirrors? To reflect the gloom
of an unlit damp apartment, with neither kids nor maid?
Who'd use silver spoons for gruel, or provide
a pair of sugar tongs for a grain of rationed
sugar? What hope obliged them to preserve old-fashioned
gowns in the purgatory of the laundry chest?
Did they imagine themselves elegantly dressed
on promenades in fashionable parks, wearing one of those?
When did they realise that earnest suitors would not propose
to me in country residences while under the spell
of my dazzling rendition of *Für Elise*? Who can tell
what delusions they laboured under, the poor fools,
firmly convinced that fate would observe minimal rules
of etiquette, or how they contrived to maintain
their innocent beliefs. One might explain
away a dose of sickness or penury . . . but this?
Alice, grey-haired, meanders in a mist
of manners, still wearing her lacquered shoes;
having no clock-sense she's likely to confuse
the times of day; her dreams are like stiff dough.
(Better, perhaps, a dream world that you know
than a half-cock universe beyond control.)
Meanwhile the clocks chime on and hours unroll
as if time still existed and was somehow theirs
bringing a green–white froth of roseblight to squares
never referred to by new official names,
or twisting snow into apparitional white flames
to crown a bronze lion's monumental mane or shroud
the transmitting tower that sends time-signals out.
For one last time the broken blinds will clatter down,
patches on walls grow expansive, blotches of brown
skin on hands wear through, cigarette-paper-thin,
and watering eyes sink ever deeper in
a hutch of soft crushed bags. What else is there?

Only an over-exposed photograph, a white spectre
or candleflame in the foreground: outside, it might
be a winter evening, inside: electric light,
a festive tablecloth's sharp crease intrudes
into the picture and a fogged mirror broods
in circles. In clots of shadows which probably
dominate the background one might be able to see
among barely discernible patches a faint outline
sufficient (with a little imagination) to define
a chin, shoulder or an unknown hand whose grey
boundaries too are finally washed away.

[GS]

New Life

For keeps this time? Why not? The flat, it's true,
is crammed to the hilt with others' history,
but what if it is? Theirs will not be too

different from yours. Some potted greenery
brought in for winter . . . three, four months swim by
and you don't even notice the scenery:

crash-helmet on the wardrobe, the pleated sky
of a deep-blue fan pinned out against the wall
like a dead bat, on which two pochards fly

skeetering towards the shelf . . . Puffy, dropsical,
the doorpost is swollen about rusted locks
(flesh round a wedding ring). A faint pall

of dust on the lamp whose little brain box
reflects the light, fire's pallid baby sister.
Is this a kind of vision, or simply how it looks?

*

A couple of years, and you don't even think of moving.
Or you might, but know it's just not on. Your friend,
D, will not move either, but will still be striving

with vibrant Dostoevsky's soul, and spend
the next five hundred years hunched over the screen
of his word processor; nor will there be an end

of J, the musician, trailing his scores between
the ground floor and the third, not to mention the Pekes
inherited from his girlfriend, trembling, obscene,

up greasy wooden stairs. A's lousy TV freaks
her out, with its constant humming, heads and busts
of terrorists or commentators with El Greco physiques,

grey skulls aflame in interstellar gusts.
True, she might, if the neighbours got her riled,
eventually fix the doorbell, but the mower rusts

in the shed, and our famous "lawn" grows wild
in winter, every little weed in furious sprout,
as if the bio-clock were running a self-styled

republic, and had surreptitiously winkled out
an immaculate display of bleeding hearts,
a hard sell of bright shrubs in shameless rout,

crab apple, japonica, like common tarts
to strut against a swirling February mist,
the anaemic catkins' less effective arts.

Those straggling off-white hordes in the park insist
on being seagulls, stiff, triangular,
and not the soft white geese your eyes first promised,

winged spools, awkward in flight. How spectacular
the sun is when it shines . . . it casts a fleeting halo
of backlight about trees and grass which are

ideas of greenness but real ideas! And oh
how its thoughtful fingers search my rough tweed coat
for tiny bits of fluff that cling like snow . . .

*

Two, three years, there's no doubt now: unfazed
by sheer excess, by eighteen kinds of mustard,
I've found my favourite cereal, appraised

the various brands of bathsalts and adjusted
to being nun or nautch-girl, jewel or jade,
eternally fidgeting in Monday's busted

après-festive pallor, or busily parade
my maddening superiority like a sailor who's
been to Hades. I've earned my accolade

by pitting dark experience against the ingénue's
blank innocence. The bellows driving the high
clouds of my vanity might wear out or refuse

to work, but there'd be air enough for them to hover by
till I grew tired and the ever less spectacular
changes of season, or the rain-blurred years' spry

progress offered me a part more in the vernacular:
teacher or housewife, or – why ever not? –
a leader in the struggle for gay rights or the Popular

Front for the Liberation of Animals, with a pot
of paint at the ready, and a razor in my hand
to slash a bourgeois fur: this could be my lot

if a plain existence were denied to me. (And
why should it? Seagulls, fire and catkins
are plain enough, you won't miss them.) To aban-

don your life is a matter of sloughing skins:
the checkout girl at the grocer's, an Albanian
on the game, tries to recall her origins

as a Friesian fisherman, or a lady in Japan
with a little white dog at her heels . . . Always
there is something . . . Something beyond the span

of time or space, from which their combined rays
are simply deflected, as from bulletproof glass . . .
some tiny dense trapped particle, something one pays

like an unreturnable deposit, like a compass
pointing beyond endless dark . . . a needle in a haystack . . .
Is there such a thing? *Well, is there? Well? I* pass.

[GS]

PÉTER KÁNTOR

On Liberty

There has been so much talk about liberty already
and there will be so much more,
we keep repeating ourselves,
we quote our predecessors:
sometimes the natural man prevails,
sometimes it's the moral man who's triumphant,
but in either case, he is dragged around;
they keep mauling him, torturing him, placing him, broken,
on wheels, this pathetic beast.
Who said this?
and who couldn't say the same thing even today?
Who managed to forge these two into one happy soul?
What's more, who has succeeded, and when,
at living freely among free men
and having an undisturbed night's sleep
which would allow, meanwhile, others to have one too?
Who can say that he's sane
and his conscience spotless,
while he just stares out of his window
on a weekday morning?
And, yet, the natural man has long forgotten what's natural,
and morality's no more than a legal code and a trademark,
plus a few disturbing stubborn feelings,
whose roots, like those of a birth, disappear into the dark.
We are perfecting, polishing ourselves, Mr Diderot,
as we do with all our other household things,
we are resourceful like Ulysses,
though we have a premonition
that for every new liberty we gain
we pay, and are newly enslaved,
whenever we break down a barrier
we immediately erect a new one in its place,
something more shapely, perhaps, more attractive, more clever,
more enlightened, dear Mr Diderot.

There's no novelty at all in it.
But who has managed even a hundred steps to the curb
without resorting to violence and bad faith,
a hundred splendid steps that could be recommended to children?

So much talk under the bridge,
so much resolute work,
so much blood shed for liberty,
of liberty how many beautiful songs.

[MB]

On Truth

When truth is mentioned everyone suddenly looks up.
After all, it's the kind of thing one can't ignore.
Or, as a matter of fact, one can ignore it, and
when it comes up, everyone starts spectacularly yawning.
Maybe it's because of Master Mo-ci's words,
who in his time warned against grandiloquence.
If we talk ceaselessly about something unrealisable,
it's mere rattle, Mo-ci said. Then again, it's the kind
of thing one might want to possess all the same,
and would readily proclaim: My truths, our truths!
Well then, that's a basis one can build on. Although
it's not for certain, although we must build all the same.

[MB]

GYÖRGY SPIRÓ

Forest

They were travelling on a renowned local train, along the Moscow–Gorky line immortalised by one of the masterpieces of twentieth-century Russian fiction, a key piece of writing, entitled *Moscow–Petoushki*. The author was still alive at the time, he died ten years later, world-famous, of cancer of the larynx caused by drink. It was strange to see the names of stations familiar from this short novel in real life, to see that a station called Serp i Molot (Hammer and Sickle) really existed, that it was not simply the invention of the playful, sardonic author. They tried to guess, between themselves, what fantastic concoction the protagonist of the Yerofeyev piece could have been drinking at this very station, for it is about a person, recognisable by intimation as the author's alter ego, drinking throughout the journey and chanting the praises of self-destruction, which, it must be acknowledged, is the only acceptable, rational, normal form of behaviour in an abnormal environment.

But it was ominous, too, that an ordinary local train had become steeped in Russian literature. He suspected that he was about to lose his wife. He should not have accompanied her on this trip. He had no hopes left, he knew that his wife had fallen in love with someone else, they were on their way to him now, his wife insisted on his coming along, his getting to know the boy who was living with a girl who was four months pregnant with his child; they had taken a dacha on lease along the noted Moscow–Petoushki line, a couple of stops before Petoushki, it was cheaper than renting a room in Moscow. He had no idea of what his wife really wanted. Perhaps she wanted him to keep her from engaging in a fatal love affair, perhaps she wanted his benediction, but she wanted at all costs to draw him into this thing somehow, and he was too weak to say no, in other words he still believed that a miracle could happen.

So they sat in the train, it being early in the afternoon it was not too crowded, there wasn't really much to find fault with, not even to Western eyes, though by then he knew the choice had to be made and in principle he had already made it, he had chosen the Western point of view, even if there was not much philosophical and aesthetic depth to be derived from it.

Only people are important, his wife was in the habit of saying at the beginning of their relationship, and she lived accordingly, she adored exceptional people, whether they were friends or students, and the friends and students adored her in return; statistics alone will prove that the vast Russian expanse produces more exceptional people than their confined homeland, and their extraordinariness is made all the more glorious by their background, ill-omened as it has been for centuries, perhaps perennially so, glazing it with an heroic aura and enriching it with the sanctity of their predecessors, that is the way truly significant tradition works, and in truth anyone who is excellent there is very much so, more resolutely, more fiercely so, which is something that tends to get around, especially if the person has artistic talent besides; it was something he always envied the Russians; his language, a splendid language by the way, could not, for historical and political reasons, compete with the renown of the Russian language, not even with that of the lesser Slavic languages, the corroboration of this latter fact was a humiliation each time he encountered it; incidentally, he was as fond of exceptional people as his wife, and often boasted that they were his marriage portion, the extraordinary people he had collected for himself over the years from all over Eastern Europe, he had introduced a large number of them to his wife, and they did reciprocally adore each other, yet he must have had an intimation about the twists and turns of life and death even then, for it had been around that time that the sentence "You must not love your fellow man; die he must and solitude will be your end" slipped from his pen, he was surprised at himself for writing it, because he sensed there was something in it. As to his image of himself, he was convinced that he too was capable of loving deeply, yet he always kept a certain distance, there was always a kind of modest objectivity about his feelings, and his wife was the only person he loved unconditionally, whereas his wife, when she loved, loved indiscriminately and uncritically, for as long as it lasted.

His wife was excited and happy, she would soon be meeting her beloved.

And she was very beautiful, as beautiful as when she had fallen in love with him, her future husband.

And like when, after three years of marriage, she had fallen in love with a superannuated Bulgarian ballet dancer at the Bulgarian seaside, because she could talk to him in Russian.

It was the Russian language that his wife was in love with, as he soon realised and even managed to understand. Russian was his father-in-law's native tongue, and as a child his wife had gone to a nursery school where the teachers taught in Russian, for her father, upon returning home from the Soviet Union, was attached to the diplomatic service, and for this reason his daughter happened to be born in Peking and went to a Russian-language nursery school in Sofia. She did forget her Russian later on, and had to learn it all over again, and her accent was never again quite perfect, yet, because her father had died young, at the age of thirty-two, of cancer, and because she hardly remembered him, she compensated for her loss with a passion for Russian language and literature, and was inclined to fall in love with anyone whose native tongue was Russian. There had been the Russian painter who had married a Hungarian girl from Kecskemét, that was sometime during their fourth year, back home; she had brought him home to the flat, wife and all, and they had slept the three of them in the bedroom while he, the host, the husband, had slept on a foam-rubber mattress in the living room; the painter was a hefty, disgusting fellow who boasted he had killed a man once, and it was true, he had thrown a drunk who had set upon him out of a moving train, and the man had died, and he was acquitted because of insufficient evidence. Then this painter and his Hungarian wife defected to Paris, and the affair petered out.

But this was different. Not because his wife was going to live with her lover, whose girlfriend was expecting his baby, anything can happen in Russia, children grow up parentless and neglected, such is life under any great power, no, the difference was that this time he was going to lose her no matter how he conducted himself in that dacha, because the crux of the matter was that it had got to be final.

The point was not that his wife was having an affair, but that she wanted to leave her husband. She was through with something.

Until he met his wife, he had always thought he would never marry. He had a number of affairs of sorts; they were not really important. He had fallen in love a few times, had known torment and anguish, that's what these affairs were for. But his wife was the first woman with whom he felt you could spend a lifetime. What kind of life he imagined for himself was of course never made quite clear. Obviously he longed for a peaceful, middle-class, contemporarily rococo idyll, constant, sentimental family intimacy, a lot of friends, a couple of children, as befitted the age he lived in and from which he tried in vain to keep a rational-ironic distance. Another thing that misled him was that his wife and he shared the same thoughts. He did not realise in time that this was because it was he who had implanted most of his opinions into his wife's thinking: he had taught her while on teaching practice in her last year of secondary school; nor did he realise that by doing so he had unintentionally, in other words inadvertently, been forced into a father-role.

When he realised that his wife wanted at all costs to treat him like a father, he protested, fought against it tooth and nail. But his wife proved the stronger. Or perhaps it was the powerful and intense need for a father hidden deep in his wife that was stronger. And something else too, a dark, suicidal impulse which his wife feared yet craved: she was caught stealing once in a department store, though she had money on her; there was no scandal, the affair was hushed up, though it was the scandal that his wife wanted; and she wanted to die young, of cancer of the stomach like her father. And like one of her uncles, whom she did not know personally, but knew that he had died as the director of what became under his hands the best provincial theatre in Hungary, also of cancer of the stomach, before he turned forty. They often went to that theatre later on, and as a husband he felt that these visits were in some way a perverse mode of condolence. It was to this craving mingled with fear that he attributed his wife's voracious lust for life which accepted no bounds, neither in her enjoyment of it nor in her suffering from it; let it be short but all the more intense, be it a question of love, travel, artistic pleasure, human relations, work, smoking; and in this Russian culture, Russian literature especially, would have abetted her even if her father's first language had not been Russian, but being the child of the 1919 generation of communist Hungarian emigrants, it was. Only this way the turn things took seemed that much more inevitable – fateful, really.

As a teenager his wife had been a zealous leftist, that had been her way of identifying; at the time he met her, she had grown up and become anti-Soviet, and her fanaticism found its object in Russian literature.

His default is all the greater for having believed that a relationship with such a companion could last a lifetime.

He, a mature man, should have realised that his wife wanted to treat him at all costs like a father so as to have a figure of authority she could look up to and adore, to rebel against when the time came and so grow up at last, and if he had really wanted what was best for his wife, he should have notified her in this endeavour. After that business at the Bulgarian seaside he should have said: I adore you, but you'd better go your way, not because you wanted to deceive me, but because my native tongue will never be Russian. He did not say it, though it was then that their marriage began to go downhill and never picked up again.

That he found he had no desire to make love after that, neither with his wife nor with anyone else, may have been his way of paying penance. What he wished to atone for he never made clear, not even to himself. He was not a mature person after all, it was just his wife who wanted to see him that way, and because she wanted it very much, she won, as she usually did. Neither did he believe that continence may be a solution for him, to whom ascetism was not alien, perhaps he was pressed into ascetism, into workaholism, wanting to follow his ten-years-dead father's footsteps (and that was an indulgence too, a pleasure-seeking of sorts, which was something his father could hardly have known, but he knew, at least his profession was such that he should know), but it could not be a solution for another person in whom time for some reason passed faster.

What was it that he did not want to lose, really? A person whom he adored. A person whom he adored mostly for repeating back to him his own opinions, for bringing up his own arguments to support and encourage him in his weaker moments. Someone for whom he was the absolute, the ultimate authority. Perhaps this was the most important factor of his love. It was this image that he did not want to lose, the image of himself existing in his wife in the form of juvenile hero-worship. It is almost pathological, this unconditional devotion to his wife, and to crown it all he is accompanying her now without a word of protest, like a squire, like the henpecked husband that he is, to meet the man she has fallen in love with.

Perhaps he is accompanying her so he won't have to be the first to speak of divorce; let the events bring about what must happen, let him have no choice but to slink away after the insufferable humiliation he will be forced to endure. He must, he needs to be a victim in order to be able to continue his rococo-sentimental life in the confined, lap-warm sty that is his homeland, his living space, Western compared to the Russian expanse, where tensions are pleasantly reduced, and conflicts need never be fully resolved, overgrown as they are by the myriad tendrils of petty lies. Where, however, insanity does not make rational thinking impossible from the outset, and from where there is a chance of understanding, if not elaborating, both Eastern and the Western, the inevitably religious and the ruthlessly interest-orientated, heterogeneous self-images of man, both are surveyable from the tower overlooking the two areas, and that one could acquire true knowledge through the dramatic confrontation of the two.

They arrived, got off the Soviet jerkwater train, his wife possessed a roughly sketched map, they set off along the frozen, beaten-dirt track, it led them past shabby, dilapidated, once stylish wooden houses, it's a wonder they're still standing after so many years of Soviet rule, and they were there.

The boy was tall, slender, blond, a beautiful Ashkenazi, his eyes blazing with what a Russian Jew's eyes should blaze; his companion was pretty, insignificant, her belly nicely rounded; the dacha was a real dacha, built entirely of wood, the garden was neglected, in keeping with Soviet conditions; they started drinking at once, their hosts had prepared for company, they had even taken a foam-rubber mattress upstairs; in that part of the world visits are the staying kind and last several days; they drank vodka, Stolichnaya, at that time it was not in short supply, and it was not too expensive either, for this all happened during the peaceably stagnant Brezhnev era, when there was still time enough to experience love and sorrow, read thick books and ponder; after the first couple of shots the conversation naturally turned to Akhmatova and Mandelstam and Pasternak, as it must, these truly great poets in their afterlife sanctified everything, even an act of adultery shortly to take place, a tangle that would affect many, an unborn child among them. He watched his wife sitting beside him, spellbound by the boy's sophisticated Russian speech and by his knowing the life-work of all the best Russian poets by heart; a Russian speciality, this; in the absence of books everyone commits to memory the samizdat volumes lent to them for a couple of days, this is why the Russian poets favour strictly cadenced, rhymed forms to this day, like in ancient times, complying with the demand for verbalism; his wife's eyes shone with a radiance he first saw in them when he was teaching her Attila József; his wife was destined to fall in love with a priest every time, he realised as he sipped his Stolichnaya, and this he could peaceably ponder over, the others not seeming too eager to have him join in the conversation, though it was true that he gave no sign of wishing to do so either.

He felt that there was something unbearably obscene in bringing poetry into all this, it was virtually an exploitation of poetry, sinful prevarication, he did not have the strength to deliberate on whether poetry was not a party to this somehow, but, though the vodka was rapidly befuddling his mind, he did realise that the beautiful, slender

Ashkenazi boy was in this moment the high priest of the mind of the Russian people, while he had been the high priest of the mind of the Hungarian people at the time his wife had fallen in love with him.

It is obviously no mere chance that both are Jewish, bobbed the thought to the surface of his mind, there may be some kind of compensatory dread at work beneath his unconditional love of literature too. That literature had a religious function for Russians too did not surprise him; that it may function in a similar way in his own country gave him food for thought.

But what made him ponder above all was the realisation that he too was a priest of sorts, and that this profession was inherently erotic. He could have interpreted the rambling, even unrestrained conversation about the Russian poets differently, as an obligatory prelude, or as procrastination, the four of them in that dacha were actors in an unwritten Chekhov scene, but he did not after all appreciate the situation in quite such a primitive way; it did occur to him though that to long for such a mediator between God and man, to create him even if this is not the main point, even if the essence is more compelling than the making and receiving of confession, because it is instinctive, arises perhaps from the exclusively religious disposition of the female soul, for it is ordained mediators that they crave to make love with, but not with ordinary mortals, and the love-making is subject to the condition that the man furnish evidence of his sanctity. Which he did, reciting a mass of poems from memory. That the Ashkenazi boy was beautiful and slender and blond and blue-eyed, as befits a true-bred Aryan according to the Nazis' book, was of no consequence whatever, nor was the fact that he was no match for the boy in looks. It was the religion of a vast area triumphing over the religion of a confined area that was happening here, as world politics and world literature made abundantly clear; the beautiful, slender Ashkenazi Russian boy could be hunchbacked for all it mattered, and he could be the most good-looking Hungarian of them all, it would be of no help: the things he knew about her were all true, her father-complex, her thirst for the Russian language, and anything else; the only thing he had not known about her until now was that his wife was a woman, and what this entailed.

The pregnant girl, allegedly his wife's friend since it had been she whom his wife had met first, before meeting her beloved, gave no sign of having the slightest inkling of what was actually happening here; from time to time she would kindly and pleasantly draw him into the conversation, and he would reply courteously, as befitted a guest, thereby, he could feel deep down in the gut, causing disappointment to his wife, who would have loved to make a scene both in a Russian and in a non-Russian medium, or at least to prolong her present state of exhilaration, revelling in pent-up emotion; he could sense, too, that the beautiful, slender boy could not understand his patience, his peaceable drinking either; the boy did not know his wife yet, that was quite obvious, he had just fallen in love with her, and why shouldn't he have fallen in love with her, his wife was the kind of woman you had to fall in love with, it happened to a lot of his friends after their divorces, and the reason why nothing became of those relationships was that they were hampered by the ex-husband's, that is his, shadow; the beautiful, slender boy was young still and had not yet made close acquaintance with women in whom the transitory stages between the primitive and the most complex are almost entirely eliminated, as they were in his wife.

It felt strange, sitting there on the closed porch of the dacha, sipping his drink on a bench by the roughly hewn wooden table, different from the way he imagined it on their way here. He had prepared himself, helpless and cowardly, for a total and ignominious defeat, primarily for the dramatic exposure of his henpeckedness, but this did not happen after all, which, he could tell, surprised his wife as much as it surprised him, consequently, in her heart of hearts, she had been desiring her husband's public and preferably scandalous humiliation. Instead of which her husband achieved a state of enlightenment, in which the effect of the vodka taken on an empty stomach may have had some part, it may have been the vodka that made him so self-possessed, dispassionate like he had never been before in his life perhaps; what he felt was that, though the events threatened to disrupt his very existence, the life-strategy he had adopted up until then, it was the play of greater forces he was witnessing here, which at the worst could annihilate him in due course.

His tranquillity was not feigned, but there had to be something provocative, something derisive in it, and he could sense that they sensed it.

In company, at such times, something has to happen, the seating pattern is disrupted, as if by chance.

It turned out that there was not enough bread.

Oh dear, how could that have happened? Someone must go and buy some more bread.

But the shop beside the station is closed.

Then the beautiful, slender boy said there's sure to be someone at the post office still, we'll ask them for a hunk of bread.

This was a summons. Addressed not to the four-months-pregnant girl, nor to his wife, for this was not the way he wished to tear her away from the company.

All right, he said, let's go.

They put on their coats, stepped out of the house, the two women watched them walk out through the garden gate from the porch.

They set out towards the station. The cold was dry and bitter, as was usual in that part of the world, and the scenery with its old, tumble-down dachas could have been designed by his wife, enamoured of Russian culture.

My wife does not rebel against me because she wants to grow up, came unbidden into his mind at the sight of the disintegrating decor, on the contrary, she wants to remain a child, irresponsible, childless.

The landscape, shrouded in mist, seemed baleful somehow, or perhaps it was just he who wanted to see it that way, because finally there was nothing special about the scenery, it was just miserable, dilapidated, temporary.

They went to the shop first, which was of course quite pointless as the shop had been closed for some time. This made it clear to him that the beautiful, slender boy was embarrassed. He found this amusing, but without malice, after all, he was no exception, it had happened to him, and whenever he had seduced someone else's wife he too had always been at a loss as to how to behave towards the husband, his own wife being a case in point, he had been present at her wedding, a guest, a friend, laughing at the back with other friends, and six weeks later the young bride had moved in with him.

Then they made their way towards the post office. The boy hurried on ahead, he walked a couple of steps behind. The boy – though he was only the subtenant of the dacha, by favour of the owner's son (the owner was an officially sanctioned writer, and as such could easily afford a dacha) – wanted to prove that he was on home ground, he understood this and was almost sorry for the boy.

He soon dismissed this thought, however, knowing that the beautiful, slender boy already had a child somewhere, whom he never even saw, he was just a Russian who lived for the moment like all the rest, his days were made up of a series of brief affairs, he had no plans as to what to make of his life, nor would he ever have, his about-to-be seduced wife would soon be forsaken too, and the child that would be born in five months' time, he had no sense of responsibility for any other person, the age-old evil spell had worked on him, producing a total indifference towards others, if things are going hard with him, let the whole world blow up, his soul was pan-Slavic, even if he was a Jew.

This was what his wife had chosen. Yet in the first three, beauteous years of their marriage he had remoulded his wife's soul, had awakened in her a love of Hungarian literature, which she had had no real knowledge of up until then, his wife had grown to love Hungarian poets and writers, and was truly grateful, it is its literature that makes the Hungarian nation, in other respects it is just like any other nation, a little better, a little worse, but the same. Strange that he had effected a Hungarian war of independence within a two-member family. It seemed for a while that the war would be won. And now it appeared that the Hungarians would be losing again.

The boy rapped at the locked door of the post office for some time, while he stood at the bottom of the steps and waited. The door was opened at last and after a brief transaction it turned out that they had no bread to spare either, and the door closed.

The boy came down the steps disappointedly.

Never mind, he said.

This path here, said the boy, leads into the forest, it's one of our favourite walks, would you like to try it?

Poosty pasmotrim.

They set out along the path and at once reached the forest.

Tall pine trees lined the path, the snow that had melted into slush in the village still frosted the boughs, a light night wind was blowing, and the smaller branches knocked against each other, making a tinkling sound. It was music that they made. He had never heard anything like it before.

The boy had perhaps prepared, even planned for one of those Slavic, self-tormenting showdowns, the kind people usually find so blissfully enjoyable, but then did not speak after all, and he did not speak either, the music was too beautiful.

They walked slowly along the path, the great trees gleamed blindingly white in the moonlight that reflected off and on to them and tinkled.

The boy wanted perhaps to show him a Russian forest, as a testimony of his own human superiority, for there surely cannot be such great, frozen trees in Hungary, and he, the Russian Jew, is the rightful owner of this forest, while his guest, whose wife he will bed that very night, does not have the disposal of such a forest, such and so wondrous a transcendence, and so cannot compare with him humanly either; or perhaps he wanted less, perhaps he thought that the forest was his, and he would show it off, the marriage portion as it were; or perhaps he wanted something more human, wanted to share his property with he whom he was about to rob, offering up the forest in the stead of the woman; or perhaps, driven by a burdened conscience, he wanted to conciliate in advance him whose rights were to be violated; but the guest, who had never seen such great trees in his life before, did not think of the forest that enthralled him with its frozen beauty in terms of a Russian forest, but saw it instead simply as a forest, a phenomenon of the planet upon which living beings such as they, possessed of a fleeting awareness, reside temporarily. Or at least that was what his silence was about, and the boy must have sensed some part of it, for he continued to walk on in silence.

Then they stopped. The boy suggested that they turn back. They turned back. They walked on silently. They reached the dacha, went in, took off their coats, their *ushankas*, the women had made a griddle-cake of sorts out of potatoes and anything else they could find which served instead of bread, they ate and drank until dawn, getting drunker and drunker, every half an hour or so he declined the suggestion to go upstairs with his wife and turn in, at dawn his wife accompanied him to the station, and waited with him for the first train to Moscow, she could have got on the train, there was plenty of time, she could still have decided differently, he had no say in the matter by then, but his wife looked at him as if he were a stranger, it was a stranger she had accompanied to the station, an imperceptibly small ant from a distant, small region, she did not board the train, he rattled back to Moscow, witnessing her first retreating steps from the window.

That was when it happened; what was done could not be undone. The religion of the more spacious, more fatal land triumphed. That was when he had to wake up to the truth that he had reached adulthood, that his marriage with the woman he loved above all was over, that his European-sentimental-peacetime vision of the future was in pieces. Not that this was in any way a decision on his part, one doesn't really decide anything even when one solemnly resolves to do this or that, the rest comes later anyway, the senseless, pointless, passionate outbursts, the back-downs, the vain attempts, the futile sacrifices, the self-torture, all aimed at making a total wreck out of the other by way of retaliation, humiliating emotional tantrums to while away the time, and the like.

After she returned because her scholarship had expired and she lived as if in a dream, lying on her bed for months on end reading Russian novels, and they finally got a divorce and moved apart, for a while his wife seriously considered going back to the Soviet Union to live with that boy, or with someone else.

He tried to dissuade her, tried to protect her from the special kind of madness that is common in those parts and of which every variety is lethal; to a certain extent he did achieve his purpose, his wife did not go back, and he had at least satisfied his conscience.

It was only much later that he realised that her staying was not his doing after all, it was his wife who had accomplished this for herself and by herself, in the process of growing up. True that she had finally picked herself a family where infantile existence was permitted, the members all being artists, and where inner emotional turmoil was extroverted or camouflaged by the lavish entertainment of interesting and less interesting native and foreign friends and acquaintances arriving in hordes almost every other day, and by the continuous, endless sensation this multitude created, but, because he too sometimes moved in those circles, he could see that his wife had become one of the most adult persons there. Whether his wife was assisted in this by her religious passion for Russian culture, which the members of that large family always open to guests did not share, he no longer had the insight to tell. Perhaps she was. If someone has a private little world where they can retreat to in their hinder brain, a place that is their very own and no-one else's, it will protect them from life. This was something he knew from experience, it was his clamorous, restless fancy, squirming within his crocodile brain, that saved him from the monotonous sequence of day-to-day existence.

Then one day his ex-wife paid him a visit, he was living alone at the time; without taking off her coat she sat down in the armchair where she often used to sit back in the days they were still living together, I only dropped in for a minute, she said, putting the small ashtray she carried about with her everywhere on the armrest and chain-smoking, as was her custom, and they talked for three hours or so, or more precisely his wife talked and told him about the things she felt she owed him to tell. He listened, hardly put in a word, his wife had become an adult, thinking being, she knew everything one can know, was able to take a rational view of their shared past and her present situation among other things; he admired the person who sat in his former wife's armchair and was not in the least jealous of her current husband, he would have been afraid of living with such a person by then.

He was happy that he knew such a person, but had a sudden, strange premonition, their conversation was running a course that made him feel as if it might be the last. And at the end his wife apologised, and it was no good him telling her what he really thought, that there was nothing to apologise for. After his wife left, the flat where he had been living alone for years in the thrall of his memories became irrevocably empty, and he pondered for a long time why his former wife had begged his forgiveness so adamantly.

This happened two months before his former wife found with her own hands the tumour that the doctors had been unable to detect despite her complaints.

Time ran a rapid course in his former wife, and she died of the same cancer that had killed her father and uncle, though, in consequence of the progress of medical science, it took much longer; she suffered for six years and in that time was forsaken by everyone who loved her, friends, students, even he, her second husband; everyone except her new husband; from the heights she had fought her way to she reverted after the third operation to the level of a ten-year-old child and did not deviate from it, it was the only way she could bear what was happening to her, and perhaps she was right, she had to undergo surgery four or five times after that because of the metastases, in her more lucid moments she would say I'll be damned if I kick the bucket just to please you.

That forest, that forest may not have changed, but even if it's been cleared, if they've destroyed it root and branch like they destroy every living thing over there, it still exists somewhere, or it will grow again sometime, and the frozen branches will knock against each other.

[EMol]

LAJOS GRENDEL

The Story that Didn't Make the News

The news that armed men had occupied the cellar was brought to the knowledge of the chairman of the tenants' committee by the caretaker's wife at six o'clock in the evening. By then the caretaker had been negotiating with the commander of the troops for an hour and a half. The intruders had obviously got into the house in the morning, when they had only the pensioners and the unemployed to contend with. "All right, madam, compose yourself, we'll think of something," said the chairman of the tenants' committee, who was a university lecturer.

The news spread like wildfire but luckily did not create a panic. No-one knew where the armed men came from, nor what they wanted. Some suspected a military putsch, others the outbreak of civil war, but on the whole it seemed most likely that two rival gangs were about to settle old scores.

"Which would be preferable," commented the bachelor from the first floor, who had been a secret policeman under the communist regime, and whom some of the tenants still went in fear of. "A gang war is always better than civil war."

There was a lot to be said for this opinion. The chairman of the tenants' committee knew his duty at any rate. The awareness of his responsibility at once infused him with great courage. He called the police without delay.

"We are aware of the situation," they told him. "We have taken the necessary steps."

After this the chairman of the tenants' committee called an emergency meeting of the tenants for nine o'clock in the evening. The caretaker was also present at this, though the impression he gave was that of someone under the influence. True, this was the impression he most often gave. He was the only tenant who admitted to beating his children.

"There are a great many of them. A great many," he said, and his lips continued to work even when he had stopped speaking.

"What do they want?" someone asked.

"They want us to clear out," said the caretaker.

Several people broke in.

"But why?"

"Ask me another," said the pale and rattled caretaker, and his face registered all the misery that went with his job. "But there sure are a great many of them," he repeated dumbly.

However, the chairman of the tenants' committee did not lose his head. He assured those present that the police were on the job, all set to smoke out the armed intruders, and would intervene at a propitious moment. The atmosphere of the meeting changed. The tenants who up until then had definitely been alarmed regained their composure, and some of them were already beginning to make conjectures.

"Most likely it's the Hungarians who are behind it all," said one.

"No, no! It's the Jews for certain," said another.

"We killed off all the Jews in the war."

"Then it's got to be the Hungarians after all."

"Gentlemen, gentlemen!" placated the widow from the fourth floor, mother-in-law of a famous actor and who for this reason thought a great deal of herself, sometimes acknowledging her neighbours' greetings, sometimes cutting them dead, never anticipating their greetings. "Let's not make a political question out of banditry."

"Our fate is in the hands of our courageous police force," said the chairman of the tenants' committee, and broke up the meeting.

The remaining hours of the evening passed peacefully and quietly. Radio and television news bulletins included no disquieting news on home affairs. The government was in place. The armed men did not come up from the cellar. The chairman of the tenants' committee rang the bell of every flat, encouraged everyone to persevere and bade them goodnight. At the request of a number of tenants he called the police again.

"We wish to avoid unnecessary bloodshed," came from the other end of the line.

By midnight silence descended upon the neighbourhood, those with good nerves dropped off to sleep while the worriers stayed up for a while longer. It seemed certain that the police would surround the house under the cloak of darkness and ambush the intruders. There was no need to fear armed conflict as the tenants were unarmed. And besides, Christmas was coming, the feast of goodwill.

The armed men, bandits or not, did not conduct themselves inimically. True, they wanted to seize the house, but for the time being they were satisfied with the cellar. It would have been pointless and unwise to provoke them. It seemed increasingly obvious that two rival gangs were waging war against each other, so the situation was not desperate. It is best to remain neutral, in local feuds of that sort, and life goes on anyhow.

In the morning most of the tenants decided not to go to work and stayed at home. There was still no sign of police intervention. The chairman of the tenants' committee was beginning to lose patience. First he sent the caretaker down to the cellar to resume negotiations, then he telephoned the police again. The police, too, were running short of patience. They told the chairman of the tenants' committee to stop harassing them.

"What should I do, then?" asked the chairman, despairing.

"Bide your time."

In the meanwhile the caretaker reappeared, looking like a startled mouse.

"They insist on our leaving the house," he said miserably, reporting the failure of his mission. "If not, they'll turn off the heating."

"By what time are we supposed to leave the house?" someone asked.

"I forgot to ask," said the caretaker, and went back to the cellar. Presently he came back. "They did not specify."

A storm of indignation swept the corridor leading to the cellar steps, where fifteen or twenty people had gathered, the chairman of the tenants' committee among them.

"Let's storm the cellar," proposed a hot-headed young man, said to be a sportsman.

"That would be a very irresponsible thing to do," said the former secret policeman.

"How many of them are there?" someone asked.

"A great many. More than yesterday," replied the caretaker in a choking voice.

Luckily, the chairman of the tenants' committee did not let his emotions run away with him.

"You had all better sit tight and keep your heads," he said. "The police may be here any moment now."

The remaining hours of the day were spent in nerve-racking waiting. The tenants' committee was in continuous session in the chairman's flat, and co-opted the caretaker. The caretaker informed them – in strictest confidence – that the armed men down below were cooking goulash in a stew pot on an open fire, and from time to time sang marching songs. There were no women among them. The situation seemed grave but not desperate. The armed men had no intention of harming the tenants, and this indicated that they might not be bandits after all. One of the committee members surprised the meeting with the suggestion that the armed men could perhaps be persuaded to lay siege to another house if the chairman of the committee were to ask them nicely.

It was the caretaker who carried this message to the cellar in lieu of the chairman but was back in a short time, crestfallen. It was this house that they wanted, and no other. The chairman contacted the police again.

"Preparations for the operation are in progress," they replied.

In the meanwhile the armed men carried out their threat and turned off the heating.

Acting upon the proposal of the tenants' committee, approximately half of the tenants – the women and the children – temporarily left the building to take refuge in the homes of friends and acquaintances. The caretaker was once more sent down to the cellar to relay the departure of the women and the children, and present it as a compromise to the commander of the armed forces. The caretaker spent less than five minutes down below.

"They say it's not enough," he reported. "We all have to go. Or else they'll turn the electricity off tomorrow."

On hearing this piece of effrontery the despair and anger of the tenants reached its peak. The chairman of the tenants' committee cautioned against precipitous action and disorder, and others too were of the opinion that anger is a bad counsellor. The armed men obviously had substantial reasons for besieging the house. It seemed unlikely that they had come to rob or plunder. In any case, they had promised the caretaker that they would touch neither the furniture nor the furnishings.

According to the caretaker, their commander was a remarkably intelligent man of experience who spoke several foreign languages and even had a PhD. The armed men were not in uniform, were all well dressed and well fed, pleasant and cheerful chaps on the whole. There were no foreigners or Gypsies among them. The spirit of the troops in the cellar was fine, you might even say excellent, but most of all comradely. They were all patient, though determined.

The caretaker's account did much to appease the ruffled feathers of the tenants. At half past seven in the evening everyone retired to their unheated flats to watch the news on TV. Nothing out of the ordinary had happened on this day either. There was a fire in some remote corner of the world. In other places there were floods, and civil wars raged here and there. At home, peace and quiet reigned. Parliament was in session. The president of the republic received a foreign head of state, the foreign minister an ambassador. A referee was insulted during a basketball game. In the Zoo, the heating in the lionhouse was turned on. Employees of the State Railway elected a beauty queen.

After the news the committee assembled again to map out a course of action. The chairman called the police again, but all he got was the answering machine. The answering machine assured him that the police force was in place and occupied with the prevention of crime.

"Well, at least that's something," said one of the committee members.

The committee had just agreed not to give in to the threats of the armed men when the house was suddenly plunged in sepulchral darkness. The perfidy of the armed men caused general consternation. Moreover, the water was cut off at the mains.

"Something must have happened down there," said the caretaker in the dark, while the chairman went to fetch a candle from the kitchen. The caretaker stumbled down the cellar stairs to parley some more. There was nothing to be gained by his doing so, however, as the words of the commander – though spoken politely and pleasantly – soon made clear.

"They told me to tell you that they can't wait any longer."

The sportsman's blood was up again.

"And what is that piece of cheek supposed to mean?"

"It means that if we aren't out of here in an hour, they'll blow the house up."

The ultimatum of the armed men added fuel to the fire, and placed the chairman of the tenants' committee – whose authority had already been shaken by the dark, the cold, the inaction of the police, and the protracted negotiations – in a position where he had no choice but to take matters into his own hands, and this he was called upon to do, or to resign. After some hesitation, he chose the former.

Candles and floating wicks lighted the corridor leading to the cellar, as if it were All Souls' Day. At the bottom of the stairs a veteran with a sub-machine gun barred his way. But the chairman did not lose heart.

"I'm the chairman of the tenants' committee," he said. "I want to speak to your commander."

The commander sat on a crate in front of the boiler-room door in an unbuttoned winter coat, smoking a cigar. He looked tired but resolute. He could not offer the chairman of the tenants' committee a seat, or perhaps did not want to. He remained seated during the conversation, with three young bodyguards standing by to see he came to no harm. Through the half-open window the draught brought in flakes of snow.

"Why did you occupy the house?" asked the chairman.

"So that it should not fall into enemy hands," replied the commander.

"What are your intentions?"

"To join battle with the enemy."

The chairman of the tenants' committee politely and patiently gave voice to his incomprehension.

"I see no sign of the enemy. There are only peace-loving, well-intentioned citizens living in this house."

"I know," said the commander. "The enemy is over there," he said, pointing towards the neighbouring house.

"And what is going to happen now?"

"We are going to annihilate the enemy."

"But why?" asked the chairman, still uncomprehending.

"Because otherwise they'll annihilate us."

"Is there some kind of ideological dispute between you?"

"Nothing of the sort," smiled the commander.

"Financial then . . . ?"

"Not at all."

"There must be some reason for your being at war with each other."

"Of course. They're our enemies."

"That's not a reason," said the chairman.

"But it is! You couldn't find a more substantial reason, sir!"

The chairman of the tenants' committee saw that his efforts were in vain, he would not be able to drag an intelligible answer out of the commander. So, recklessly, he flung in his face:

"We are not going anywhere. This is our house."

"As you wish," said the commander, and turned his head. His bodyguards led the chairman of the tenants' committee away. He was greatly agitated, his eyes brimming with tears of frustration and anger. "We'll defend this house to our last breaths," he called back from the stairs.

But it would have been too much to expect heroics from the chairman of the tenants' committee. He had done what he could do, and everyone was saving their last breath for some later date. While he was parleying with the commander down below, the tenants had packed up their valuables and evacuated the house, assembling in front of the building. Only the mother-in-law of the famous actor stayed behind to wait for him.

"They charged me to tell you this was a decision reached by mutual agreement. Old Vojtek's the only one who chose to stay in the house."

"A courageous man," nodded the chairman of the tenants' committee.

"It's easy for him. He's going to die soon anyway," replied the woman.

Darkness descended upon the neighbouring houses as well. It was not difficult to guess that they too had been occupied by armed men. In the park enclosed by the houses, under frosted trees weighed down with snow and hoarfrost, a great crowd of people had gathered, as though a mass-meeting were in preparation. Mostly men, but the chairman saw a couple of older women, and even some inquisitive children. It was cold. A rumour spread that the police had closed off the neighbourhood, but that was shortly denied. The people did not talk much, and did not mingle, the tenants of each building forming separate groups, as if this had any sort of significance.

"They sent emissaries over to our lot from Number 7," the former secret policeman informed the chairman.

"How do you mean, our lot?" said the chairman indignantly.

A woman answered his question.

"Well, those who occupied our house . . . They're our lot now. They're defending our house from the enemy. That's the way the whole house sees it. Don't you?"

The chairman thought this over for some time.

"There's something in what you say," he said at last.

"Once the fighting begins, it is our duty to range ourselves with our lot against the enemy. It is the only ethical thing to do," continued the former secret policeman. "Of course, they may make peace and go away. That's why they're parleying now. We've got to be ready for any eventuality."

"And negotiations may drag on, for several days," said the chairman and moved away.

He left the perilous neighbourhood stealthily, practically unnoticed.

It crossed his mind that perhaps he ought to have resigned before leaving, but he did not have the heart to turn back. The tenants had given evidence of great patience, civic discipline and wisdom, from now on they would surely get along without him. Some of them would perhaps supply the troops with provisions, others, the hot-headed ones, would engage in the fighting. The way it usually happens.

[EMol]

LÁSZLÓ KRASZNAHORKAI

from *War and War*

LIKE A BURNING HOUSE

1

I no longer care if I die, said Korim, then, after a long silence, pointed to the nearby flooded quarry: *Are those swans?*

2

Seven children squatted in a semicircle surrounding him in the middle of the railway footbridge, almost pressing him against the barrier, just as they had done some half an hour earlier when they had first attacked him in order to rob him, exactly so in fact, except that by now none of them thought it worthwhile either to attack or to rob him, since it was obvious that, owing to certain unpredictable consequences, robbing or attacking him was possible but pointless because he really didn't seem to have anything worth taking, the only thing he did have appearing to be some mysterious burden, the existence of which, gradually, at a certain point in Korim's furious rambling monologue – which, "to tell you the truth," as they said, "was boring as shit" – became apparent, most acutely in fact, when he started talking about the loss of his head, at which point they did not stand up and leave him babbling like some halfwit, but remained where they were, in the positions they had originally intended to adopt, squatting immobile in a semicircle, because the evening had darkened around them, because the gloom descending silently on them in the industrial twilight numbed them, and because this frozen dumb condition had drawn their most intense attention, not to the figure of Korim, which had swum beyond them, but to the one remaining object: the rails below.

3

Nobody asked him to speak, only that he should hand over his money, but he didn't, saying he had none, and carried on speaking, hesitantly at first, then more fluently, and finally continuously and unstoppably, because the eyes of the seven children had plainly scared him, or, as he himself put it, his stomach had turned in fear, and, as he said, once his stomach was gripped by fear he absolutely had to speak, and furthermore, since the fear had not passed – after all, how could he know whether they were carrying weapons or not – he grew ever more absorbed in his speech, or rather he became ever more absorbed by the idea of telling them everything from beginning to end, of telling someone in any case, because, from the time that he had set out in secret, at the last possible moment, to embark on his "great journey", as he called it, he had not exchanged a word, not a single word, with anyone, considering it too dangerous, though there were few enough people he could engage in conversation in any case, since he hadn't so far met anybody sufficiently harmless, nobody, at least, of whom he was not wary, because in fact there really was nobody harmless enough, which meant he had to be wary of everyone, because, as he had said at the beginning, whoever it was he set eyes on it was the same thing he saw, someone, that is, who directly or indirectly was in contact with those who pursued him, someone related intimately or distantly, but most certainly related to those who, according to him, knew his every step, and it was the speed of his movements, as he later explained, that kept him "at least half a day" ahead of them, though these gains were specific to places and occasions: so he had not said a word to anyone, and only did so now because fear drove him, because it was only under the natural pressure of fear that he ventured into these most important areas of his life, venturing deeper and deeper still, offering them ever more profound glimpses of it in order to defeat them, to make them face him so that he might purge his assailants of the tendency to assail, so he should convince all seven of them that someone had not only given himself up to them, but, with his giving, had somehow outflanked them.

4

The air was full of the sharp, nauseous smell of tar that cut through everything, nor did the strong wind help because the wind, which had chilled them to the bone, merely intensified and whipped the smell up without being able to substitute anything else for it, the whole neighbourhood for several kilometres being thick with it, but here more than anywhere else, for it emanated directly from the Rákos railway yard, from that still visible point where the rails concentrated and began to fan out, ensuring that air and tar would be indistinguishable, making it very hard to tell what else, apart from soot and smoke, that smell – composed of the hundreds and thousands of trains that rumbled through, the filthy sleepers, the rubble and the metallic stench of the rails – comprised, and it wouldn't be just these but other, more obscure, almost indiscernible ingredients, ingredients without name, that would certainly have included the weight of human futility ferried here by hundreds and thousands of carriages, the scary and sickening view from the bridge of the power of a million wills bent to a single purpose and, just as certainly, the dreary spirit of desolation and industrial stagnation that had hovered about the place and settled on it decades ago, in all of which Korim was now endeavouring to locate himself, having originally determined simply to cross over to the far side as quickly, silently and inconspicuously as possible in order to escape into what he supposed to be the city centre, instead of which he was having, under present circumstances, to pull himself together at a cold and draughty point of the world and to hang on to whatever incidental detail he could make out, from his eye-level at any rate, whether this was barrier, kerb, asphalt or metal, or appeared the most significant, if only so that this footbridge, some hundred metres from the railway yard, might become a passage between the non-existing and the existing section of the world, forming therefore an important early episode, as he later put it, of his mad flight, an object which, had he not been detained, he would have rushed obliviously across.

5

It had begun suddenly, without preamble, without presentiment, preparation or rehearsal, at one specific moment on his forty-fourth birthday, that he was struck, agonisingly and immediately, by the consciousness of it, as suddenly and unexpectedly, he told them, as the appearance of the seven of them here, in the middle of the footbridge, on that day when he was sitting by a river at a spot where he would occasionally sit in any case, this time because he didn't feel like going home to an empty apartment on his birthday, and it really was extremely sudden, the way it struck him that, good heavens, he understood nothing, nothing at all about anything, for Christ's sake, nothing at all about the world, which was a most terrifying realisation, he said, especially in the way it came to him in all its banality, vulgarity, at a most sickening level of naivety, but this was the point, he said, the way that he at the age of forty-four had become aware of how utterly stupid he seemed to himself, how empty, how utterly blockheaded he had been in his understanding of the world these last forty-four years, whereas, as he realised there by the river, he had not only misunderstood it but had not understood anything about anything, the worst part being that for forty-four years he thought he had understood it, while in reality he had failed to do so; and this in fact was the worst thing of all on the night of his birthday when he sat alone by the river, worst because the fact that he now realised that he had not understood it did not mean that, hey, now he did understand it, because being aware of his lack of knowledge was not in itself some new form of knowledge that he could exchange for an old one, but one that presented itself as a terrifying puzzle the moment he thought about the world, as he most furiously did that evening, all but torturing himself in the effort to understand it and failing, because the puzzle seemed ever more complex, and he had begun to feel that the puzzle of the world that he was so desperate to understand, that he was torturing himself trying to understand, was really the puzzle of himself and the world at once, that they were one and the same thing, which was the conclusion he had so far reached, and had not yet given up on it, when, after a couple of days, he noticed that there was something the matter with his head.

6

By this time he had lived alone for years, he explained to the seven children, he too squatting and leaning against the barrier in the penetrating November wind on the footbridge, alone because his marriage had been wrecked by the Hermes business (he gestured with his hand as if to say he would explain about it later), after which he had "badly burned his fingers with a deeply passionate love affair" and decided: never, never again, would he even so much as get close to a woman, which did not mean, of course, that he led an entirely solitary life, because, as Korim elaborated, gazing at the children, there was the occasional woman on the occasional difficult night, but essentially he was alone, though there remained the various people he came into contact with in the course of his work at the records office, as well as the neighbours with whom he had to maintain neighbourly relations, the commuters he bumped into while commuting, the shoppers he met while shopping, the barflies he'd see in the bar and so forth, so that, after all, now he looked back at it, he was in regular contact with quite a lot of people, even if only on the most tenuous of terms, occupying the furthermost corner of the community, at least until they too started to melt away, which probably dated from the time that he was feeling increasingly compelled to regale those he met at the records office, on the staircase at home, in the street, at the store and in the bar with the regrettable news that he believed he was about to lose his head, because, once they understood that the loss was neither figurative nor symbolic but a genuine deprivation in the full physical sense of the word, that, to put it plainly, his head, alas, would actually be severed from his neck, they eventually fled from him as they might flee from a burning house, fleeing in their droves, and very soon every one of them had gone and he stood alone, very much like a burning house in fact: at first it being just the matter of a few people behaving in a more distant fashion, then his colleagues at the records offices ignoring him, not even returning his greeting, refusing to sit at the same table and finally crossing the street when they saw him, then people actually avoiding him in the street, and can you imagine, Korim asked the seven children, how painful this was? how it hurt me most, most than anything, he added, especially with what was happening to the vertebrae in his neck, and this was just when he most needed their support, he said, and while it was plain to see that he would have been pleased to explore this matter in the most intricate detail, it was equally obvious that it would have been wasted on the seven children because they would not have been able to respond in any way, being bored of the subject, particularly at the point when "the geezer started going on about losing his head", which meant "sod all" to them, as they would later tell their friends, and looked at one another while the oldest nodded in agreement with his younger companions as if to say, "Forget it, it's not worth it," after which they simply continued squatting, watching the confluence of rails as the occasional goods wagon rattled by below them, though one did ask how much longer they were going to stay there as it was all the same to him, and the blond kid next to the senior one consulted his watch and replied merely that he'd tell them when it was time, and until then he should shut the fuck up.

7

Had Korim known that they had already arrived at a decision, and specifically at this particular decision, had he in fact noted the meaningful gesture, nothing would have turned out as it did, but, since he hadn't noted it, he wasn't to know and, as a result, his perception of reality was incorrect, for to him it seemed that his current predicament – squatting on the ground with these children in the cold wind – was increasingly fraught with anxiety precisely because nothing was happening, nor was it made clear to him what they wanted, if indeed they wanted anything at all, and since there was no explanation forthcoming as to why they were refusing to let him go or just leave him there, he having succeeded in convincing them that the whole thing was pointless because he really had no money, he still felt that there should have been an explanation, and indeed had found one, albeit the wrong one as far as the seven children were concerned, he being aware of exactly how much money was sewn into the lining on the right side of his coat, so their immobility, their numbness, their failure to do anything, in fact the utter lack of any animation whatsoever, took on an ever greater, ever more terrifying significance, whereas, had he looked at it another way, he might have found it progressively more reassuring and less significant; which meant that he spent the first half of each moment preparing to spring to his feet and make a dash for it and the second half remaining precisely where he was, apparently content to stay there and keep talking, as if he had only just begun his story; in other words, he was equally disposed to escape and remain, though, as it happened, every time he had to make a decision he chose to remain, chiefly of course because he was scared, assuring them how happy he was to have found such sympathetic listeners and how good it all felt, because he had so much, it was extraordinary quite how much, to tell them, really and truly, because when you took time to think about it, "extra-ordinary" was absolutely the right word to describe the full details of his story, which he should describe so it would be clear to them, so they should know how it was on Wednesday, at what precise time he could not remember, but it was probably some thirty or forty hours ago, that the fateful day arrived, at which point he realised that he really did have to embark on his "great journey", at which point he understood that everything, from Hermes down to his solitary condition, was driving him in one direction, that he must already have started on the journey because it was all prepared and everything else had collapsed, which is to say that everything ahead of him had been prepared and everything behind him had collapsed, as tended to be the way with all such "great journeys", said Korim.

8

The only lamps burning were those at the top of the stairs, and the light they gave out fell in dingy cones which shuddered in the intermittent gusts of wind that assailed them because the other neon lights positioned in the thirty or so metres between them had all been broken, leaving them squatting in darkness, yet as aware of each other, of their precise positions, as of the enormous mass of dark sky above the smashed neon, the sky which might have glimpsed the reflection of its own enormous dark mass as it trembled with stars in the vista of railway yards spreading below it, had there been some relationship between the trembling stars and the twinkling dull red semaphore of lights sprinkled among the rails, which there wasn't since there was no common denominator, no interdependence between them, the only order and relationship existing within the discrete worlds of above and below, and indeed of anywhere, for the field of stars and the forest of signals stared as blankly at each other as does each and every form of being, blind in darkness and blind in radiance, as blind on earth as it is in heaven, if only so that a long dead symmetry among this vastness might appear in the lost glance of some higher being, at the centre of which, naturally, there would be a miniscule blind-spot: as with Korim . . . the footbridge . . . the seven kids.

9

A total dickhead, they told a local acquaintance the next day, a total dickhead in a league of his own, a twat they really should have got rid of because you never knew when he'd grass on you, 'cause he'd had a good look at everybody's face, they added to each other, and could have made a mental note of their clothes, their shoes and everything else they were wearing that late afternoon, so, yeh, that's right, they admitted the next day, they should have got rid of him, only it didn't occur to any of them at the time to do so, everyone being so relaxed and all, so laid-back, like a bunch of dopes on the footbridge while ordinary people carried on leading ordinary lives beneath them as they gazed at the darkening neighbourhood above the converging rails and waited for the signals for the six forty-eight in the distance so that they might rush down to the cuttings, taking up their positions behind the bushes in preparation for the usual ritual, but, as they remarked, none of them had imagined that the ritual might have ended in some other fashion, with a different outcome, that it might be completed entirely successfully, triumphally, smack on target, in other words with a death, in which case of course even a pathetic git like him would be an obvious danger because he might grass, they said, might get into a funk and, quite unexpectedly, grass on them to the cops, and the reason it worked out differently, as it did in fact, leaving them to think the thoughts they had just thought, was that they hadn't been concentrating, and can't have been, otherwise they'd have realised that this was precisely the kind of man who presented no danger because, later, he couldn't even remember what, if anything, had happened at about six forty-eight, as he had fallen ever deeper under the spell of his own fear, the fear that drove his narrative onwards, a narrative that, there was no denying, apart from a certain rhythm, lacked all sense of shape or indeed anything that might have drawn attention to his own person, except perhaps its copiousness, which was the result of him trying to tell them everything at once, in the way he himself experienced what had happened to him as a kind of simultaneity that he first noticed added up to a coherent whole that certain Wednesday morning some thirty or forty hours before, two hundred and twenty kilometres from here in a travel agent's, at the point when he arrived at the front of the queue and was about to ask the time of the next train from Budapest and the cost of the ticket, when, standing at the counter, he suddenly felt that *he should not ask that question here*, at the same moment recognising in the reflection in the glass over one of the posters over the counter, two employees of the District Psychiatric Unit, disguised as a pair of ordinary numbskulls, really, two of them, and behind him, at the entrance, a so-called nurse whose aggressive presence made his skin prickle and break into a sweat.

10

The men from the District Psychiatric Unit, said Korim, never explained to him what he had wanted to know, which was the reason he had attended the unit to start with, which was how, in effect, the whole system that held the skull in place, from the first cervical vertebra through to the ligaments (the rectus capitis), actually functioned, but they never explained it, because they couldn't, chiefly because they themselves had not an inkling, their minds being shrouded in a wholly impenetrable darkness that resulted in them first staring at him with a wild surmise, as if to indicate that the question itself, the mere asking of it, was so ludicrous that it provided direct and incontrovertible proof of his, Korim's, madness, then giving each other significant glances and little nods whose portent was (was it not?) perfectly clearly that they had dismissed the subject, the one natural consequence of which was that he made no further enquiries regarding the matter but, even while steadfastly bearing the enormous weight of the problem on his shoulders, tried to answer them himself by asking what that certain first cervical vertebra and the rectus capitis actually were and how (sighed Korim) they performed their crucial functions, how it was that his skull had simply been propped on the topmost vertebra of his spinal column, though when he thought about it at the time, or so he told them now, the idea of his skull being fixed to his spine by cerebro-spinal ligaments, which were the only things holding the lot together, was enough to send shivers down him when he pictured it as such, and still did send shivers down him since even a brief examination of his own skull demonstrated the patent truth that this arrangement was so sensitive, so brittle, so vulnerable, one of the most frail and delicate physical structures imaginable, that, he decided, it must follow that it was here, at this particular juncture, that his problems had begun and would end, for if the doctors were incapable of coming to any worthwhile conclusion after looking at his X-rays, and things had turned out as they had done, then, having immersed himself to some degree in medical details and self-examination, he had no hesitation in proclaiming that the pain he was in had its root cause here, in that lodging of tissue in bone, where vertebra met ligament, and that all attention should be focused on this point, on the ligaments, at which precise point he was not yet certain, but he was certain about the sensation that spread through his neck and back, week by week, month by month, increasing in intensity, knowing that the process had started and was proceeding irresistibly, and that this whole affair, if one considered it objectively, he said, would be bound to lead to the terminal decay of the union of skull and spine, culminating in a condition, *not to beat about the bush*, for why should one, said Korim pointing to his neck, whereby this frail piece of skin gave up and, inevitably, caused him to lose his head.

II

One, two, three, four, five, six, seven, eight, nine sets of rails could be distinguished from the vantage point of the footbridge, and the seven of them could do little but count them over and over again, concentrating their attention on the confluence of rails in the perceptibly deepening darkness, which was accentuated by the red lights of the signals while waiting for the six forty-eight to appear at last in the distance, for the tension that had suddenly appeared on everyone's hitherto relaxed countenance was occasioned by nothing more at this stage than the impending arrival of the six forty-eight, the sucker they had set out to mug having failed, after their first couple of attempts, to provide sufficient entertainment in the short period of their waiting, so that within fifteen minutes of having cornered him, even if they had wanted to, they would have remained incapable of listening to a single word more of the seamless and endless monologue that, even now, cornered as he was, flowed unstoppably from him, because he kept on and on regardless, as they explained the next day, and it would have been unbearable had they not ignored him, because, they added, if they had continued to pay attention to him they would have had to do him in if only to preserve their own sanity, and they had, unfortunately, ignored him for the sake of their sanity, even though this resulted in them missing the chance of neutralising him, for they really should have neutered him good and proper, or so they kept repeating to themselves, particularly since the seven of them would normally have been perfectly aware what failing to do this might cost them, a witness like him, who would never completely vanish in the crowd, not to mention the fact that they had begun to get a reputation in certain important places as "cut-throats", a reputation they had to protect, and killing him would not have been difficult, nor indeed a new proposition to them, and this way they would have been taking no chances.

12

What then befell him – Korim shook his head as if he still could not believe it – was, at the beginning, almost inconceivable, nigh unbearable, because even at first glance, following an initial survey of the complex nature of what was involved, a single honest appraisal told him that henceforth he had to abandon his "sick hierarchical view of the world", explode "the illusion of an orderly pyramid of facts" and liberate himself from an extraordinarily powerful and secure belief in what was now revealed as merely a kind of childish mirage, which is to say the indivisible unity and contiguity of phenomena and, beyond that, the unity's secure permanence and stability, and, within this permanence and stability, the overall coherence of its mechanism, that strictly governed interdependence of functioning parts which gave the whole system its sense of direction, development, pace and progress, in other words whatever suggested that the thing it embodied was attractive and self-sufficient, or, to put it another way, he now had to say No, an immediate and once-and-for-all No, to that entire mode of life, if only so that, much later, say after a hundred yards or so, he could correct some aspect of what he had originally termed his rejection of the hierarchical mode of thinking – though it was not the case that it was this particular order of things that he had elevated into a pyramidal structure that self-evidently needed correcting or rejecting in perpetuity as misleading or inappropriate, for no, strange, indeed extremely strange to say, he had lost nothing by the rejection, for what had actually happened on that certain night of his birthday could not be accounted loss but gain, or at least a first point gained, an advance in the direction of the all-but-inconceivable, all-but-unbearable – since in the gradual process of walking a hundred paces from the river to the point where the struggle began, and having been granted a glimpse of the terrible complexity ahead, he saw that while the world appeared not to exist, the totality of that-which-had-been-thought-about-it did in fact exist, and, furthermore, that it was only this, in its countless thousands of varieties, that did exist as such, that what existed was his identity as the sum of the countless thousand imaginings of the human spirit that was engaged in writing the world, in writing his identity, he said, in terms of pure word, the doing word, the Verb that brooded over the waters, or, to put it another way, he added, what became clear was that opinions were a waste of time, that it was a waste thinking that life was a matter of appropriate conditions and appropriate answers, because the task was not to choose but to accept, there being no obligation to choose between what was appropriate and what was inappropriate, only to accept that we are not obliged to do anything except to comprehend that the appropriateness of the one great universal process of thinking is not predicated on it being correct, for there was nothing to compare it with, nothing but its beauty, and it was its beauty that gave us confidence in its truth – and this, said Korim, was what struck him as he walked those hundred furiously thinking paces on the evening of his birthday: he understood the infinite significance of faith and was given a new insight into what the ancients had long known, which is that it was faith in its existence that had both created and maintained the world, the corollary of which was that it was the loss of his own faith that was now erasing it, the result of which realisation being, he said, that he experienced a sudden, utterly numbing, quite terrible feeling of opulence, because from that time on he knew that whatever had once existed, existed still and that, quite unexpectedly, he had stumbled on an ontological place of such gravity that he could see – oh but how, he sighed, how to begin – that Zeus, for instance, to take an arbitrary example, was still "there", now, in the present, just as all the other old gods of Olympus were "there", as was Yahweh and The Lord God of Hosts, and there alongside them, the ghosts of every nook and cranny, and that this meant they had nothing and yet everything to fear, for nothing ever disappeared without trace, for the absent had a structure as real as the structure of whatever existed, and so, in other words, you could bump into Allah, into the Prince of the Rebel Angels and into all the dead stars of the universe, which would of course include the barren, unpopulated earth with its godless laws of being, as well as the terrifying reality of Hell and pandemonium which was the domain of the demons, and that that was reality, said Korim: thousands upon thousands of worlds, each one different, majestic or fearsome; thousands upon thousands in their ranks, he continued, his voice rising, in a single absent relationship, and that was how it all appeared to him then, he explained, and it was then, when he had arrived thus far, continually reliving the infinite capacity of the process of becoming, that the trouble with his head first started, the predictable course of which process he had already outlined, and possibly it was the sheer opulence, the peculiar inexhaustibility of history and the gods that he found hard to bear, for ultimately he didn't know, to this very day it was not clear to him, precisely how the pain that started suddenly and simultaneously in his neck and his back, began: the forgetting, subject by subject, random, ungovernable and extraordinarily rapid, first of facts such as where he had put the key that he had only just now been holding in his hand, or what page he had got to in the book he had been reading the previous night, and, later, what had happened on Wednesday, three days ago, in the period between morning and evening, and after that, whatever was important, urgent, dull or insignificant, and, finally, even his mother's name, he said, the scent of apricots, whatever made familiar faces familiar, whether he had in fact completed tasks he had set himself to complete – in a word, he said, there was literally nothing that stayed in his head, the whole world had vanished, step by step, the disappearance itself having neither rhyme nor reason in its progress, as if what there was left was somehow sufficient, or as if there were always something of greater importance that a higher, incomprehensible force had decided he should forget.

[GS]

PÁL BÉKÉS

The Age of Discovery

AMERICA

We didn't have a garden, but the Gerhardts' apartment was in a building on Ilka Street, so they did. There were three chestnut trees, two stone boxes for flowers, a thick horizontal iron rod for carpet-cleaning and a shed for garden tools. Whenever I visited them, Gerhardt's mother told me: "This is a nice, neat middle-class building." I felt she was belittling our home, in fact, so I always retorted: "Ours is exactly the same as yours, except it hasn't got a garden." She didn't say anything but sent us to play. Gerhardt's mother was quite good-looking, but still I didn't like her.

The shed was in a corner of the small walled garden. Between it and the high brown brick wall there was a narrow passage that remained invisible from the windows. Gerhardt said we would dig right there. I asked why and he said so we could dig for treasure. I wanted to know why just there, and he said I was an idiot, the rest of the garden is paved over in concrete. Treasure can be hidden here just like anywhere else, so why not dig? He sounded really convincing. We began work immediately. He had two toy shovels, he handed me one and I broke it instantly. So he stole the sewing box from his grandmother's old Singer sewing machine. It was made of shining chrome-steel and seemed ideally designed for digging.

The soil was full of stones, so we proceeded slowly. We found some broken bricks and rusty barbed wire. On the second day the sewing box hit some metal and we got excited, but when we cleaned the dirt from our find, it turned out to be a tin. Sardines in oil.

On the third day Gerhardt announced that the work was over, that we weren't going to find any treasure here, so we had to move on. Well, that's the risk you take with treasure hunting – sometimes you win, sometimes you lose.

We were terribly sorry for all that work down the drain. We were staring at the deep hole sadly, it reached up to our hips when we stood in it. We were speculating that perhaps we could use it for something else. And suddenly he grinned and shouted: "I've got it! Sure! We'll dig a tunnel to America!" At first I didn't understand, but then he explained. The earth is round, America's on the other side, so if we dig the tunnel straight through the centre of the earth we'll end up there. Our hole is perfect for a beginning. I was extremely doubtful, and told him the earth is not round. But he was very persuasive. So, I told him OK, but first I was going to make sure, because I don't like tricks and I'm not willing to dig in vain.

I went home and asked my father. He confirmed that what Gerhardt said was true. I resented this as I thought he should have been on my side. He took me to see our neighbour, Mr Varkócsy, who had a globe. I was turning and scrutinising it all evening. I had to accept the truth that the earth is round, but I measured very exactly and discovered that the other side of the world is not America but the Pacific Ocean, and the closest body of land is a tiny dot in the water: the Mimicry Islands.

Next day I told Gerhardt what I had learned about the shape of the earth and he nodded, "Sure." But as for the Mimicry Islands business, he was firmly against it; he wasn't willing to give up his conviction: the other side of the earth is America. We made a bet on a big bar of white chocolate and said we'll see when we get through. We swore to keep our plan secret. I was pushing the tunnelling as much as I could as the following week I was to be sent to my aunt for a holiday and I wanted to find out the truth by then.

We were digging like mad. Gerhardt's mother was whining all the time, why are we so filthy? But we kept our oath and didn't reveal anything. In the evenings I revolved Mr Varkócsy's globe and kept asking the old man about America and the Mimicry Islands. He said America is big, everybody is rich, drives a car and beats up black people. Women have nylon stockings, men have Colt 45s, they all chew gum and want war. As for the Mimicry Islands, he was a bit uncertain but said that – judging from the name – it must be a disgusting place.

The hole was so deep, we both disappeared into it when we stood on each other's shoulders, but still we had the vague suspicion that most of our work was still ahead of us. We permanently changed our positions: the one on the bottom of the hole filled the chrome-steel sewing box and handed it up, while the other one took it and emptied it – there was hardly any space left between the blackened planks of the shed and the high brown brick wall.

We hadn't finished the tunnel when I had to go to my aunt for my holiday. Gerhardt told me he would continue with the tunnel alone. I begged him to wait for me, but he wouldn't listen. We parted in anger.

We met again at the opening ceremonies at school. White shirt, dark shorts, the director was giving his usual speech. We were standing near each other in the first line, unfortunately between two teachers. Still I couldn't endure it and whispered out of the corner of my mouth: "So?"

"I won," Gerhardt whispered back. "It's America on the other side."

"So you got through?!" I was so stunned I forgot everything and was immediately disciplined by both teachers.

"Sure." Gerhardt nodded silently, staring knowingly at the director. He was talking about discipline. I was hesitant to believe him and wanted to cross-examine him, but the national anthem prevented me.

After the ceremony I cornered him.

"So?"

"So what?"

"What is it like?"

"Nothing special. Just like here."

I asked if it was true that everybody is rich, drives a car and beats up black people. He said it was true. I asked if women have nylon stockings, men Colt 45s, if they all chew gum and want war.

"Sure," he nodded. "But otherwise it is just like here."

I was a bit suspicious.

"So pay up," he said. "I want the chocolate bar with the red label."

"I wanna walk through the tunnel and have a look at America too."

"You can't. It got buried. It caved in as soon as I got back."

Suddenly I understood everything. What a pig! He made the tunnel collapse on purpose! Now it was clear that he had got to the Mimicry Islands and he wanted to hide the truth! I told him my opinion really harshly. I hate it when anyone wants to dupe me. I told him to forget about the chocolate.

THE OCEANS

We found the washtub along the Rákos stream. It was during a botany field trip organised by Mrs Bátki, our teacher. We visited her apple orchard on the outskirts of Budapest. She said first we should pick the apples from her trees, then for an hour we could do whatever we wanted to, and after that we'd rush back to school so our parents wouldn't worry. Her apple orchard wasn't far from the tram terminal, and we finished picking apples very quickly as it was poor harvest. During our free time we went roaming along the stream and suddenly – wow! – a washtub. It was made of wood, its inside covered with sheet-iron.

"Just like a ship," Szász said.

"There's a hole in the bottom," I said, after inspecting it.

"It could be stopped up," he answered with an expert expression on his face.

We stuffed some cloth into the hole, and now the tub really looked like a ship.

"What about going?" he said.

"Where?"

"The Oceans."

(It was as if he said "To the tram terminal".)

"Why not?"

"But I'm captain."

Well, that's what I always hated about him. I protested, but he held firm. In the end he agreed I could be the helmsman as a ship needs one of those too. I accepted, but then I realised there was nothing to steer.

"And now? Where?" I asked at last, because even if we didn't have a helm, the helmsman is supposed to know which direction to go in.

"First we go down the Rákos, that takes us to the Danube, that runs into the sea and then to the Oceans."

It sounded fairly logical, but still I had some doubts.

"Is it going to be good?" I hesitated. "I mean the Oceans."

"Sure," he encouraged me.

He was talking about banana trees, waves as high as mountains with spray at the top, graceful, snow-white schooners in the harbours (I asked what a schooner was, he said a kind of a ship, I asked if it was like ours, he said yes), and he was talking about friendly natives with flower-garlands around their necks (I asked how he knew, he said from the TV, and I believed him as we didn't have a TV.)

I liked the banana trees the most. I hadn't eaten bananas yet, but my father had talked about them.

"Let's go," I urged him. "Right now."

We launched our vessel; we sat opposite each other and began the voyage. The hole with the cloth stuffed in it was right under my bottom. As soon as we left, the ship turned around. I put my hands in the water and tried to navigate it with paddling gestures. Szász was commanding: one-two, one-two. I protested: I am the helmsman and not an oarsman. He told me to shut up; it was his duty to suppress rebellion as the captain has power over death and life on a ship, in case I didn't know. But he helped me.

We moved along quite well; we were carried by the dirty water along the concrete embankments.

Suddenly I felt the cloth leaking and water seeping into the ship. I reported it to Szász immediately and suggested we look for a harbour. He said: "No way. We can't afford to lose time on our way to the Oceans." He told me to scoop out the water with my hands and he'd take over the steering.

First I scooped with one hand, then with both, but in vain. More and more water seeped into the ship. Szász commanded me to sit on the hole to stop the leak, but whatever I did the water got higher and higher until we were sitting in water. Soon our ship went out of control. It drifted into the middle of the stream and sank slowly. We gave up scooping. We realised our voyage had come to an end. Only an inch or two of the washtub was still above the water-line when our captain ordered us to abandon ship. I began preparations, but he didn't move. He said the captain must be the last to leave a sinking ship. I sat back and told him I would stand by him till the bitter end. He thanked me and we sank together, face to face.

The water was up to our necks when the washtub hit the bottom, but we didn't move. I could only see Szász's head sticking out of the stagnant water, and he only saw mine as we sat in the concrete stream bed with the washtub under us. I don't know how long we could have stayed like that, but then some disgusting carcass drifted by and we began flapping our arms and struggled ashore. Where once our proud ship had stood, now only the nauseating and loathsome carcass floated, decaying slowly.

We were covered with mud, with stinking water dripping from our hair when we turned back and walked along the Rákos through a cabbage field.

"What's the matter?" he asked with tears in his eyes.

"The banana trees . . ." I cried.

"That's only on TV." He wiped dirt, tears and snot from his face.

"The Oceans," I sobbed, shivering. "The banana trees!"

We were clomping through the cabbage field.

We got back in time for line-up.

[PB]

LÁSZLÓ DARVASI

Mr Stammer in São Paulo

A few days after they moved in the young couple had their baby. There was some celebrating, not more than such an old building can still tolerate, and perhaps not only tolerate, but secretly even enjoy, it has been so long since legitimate transgression of any kind last happened here. All the same, the morning after, the old man inspected the row of letter boxes, looking for their name.

They were called Tóth.

The old man stared moodily at the strip of paper pasted on the flimsy tin box, Tóth, Tóth, we really could have done with a better-sounding name.

In the end he shrugged his shoulders.

One can't help being called Tóth, after all.

Then they shuffled along to the shop together, as they did every day. They did not have far to walk to the grocery that took up the whole corner of a nearby block. They always went arm in arm, as they used to do on family outings when they spent the day rambling on the island or strolling beneath the plane trees of the park. But in the last few years they had taken to going everywhere together, clinging to each other so neither could come to harm when the other was not there. It was together or not at all. But only to the chemist's, the doctor's or the grocer's. A quarter-kilo of bread, a litre of milk, some sliced cold meat, that was what they bought, that was all they could afford, and it usually lasted them two days. They ate like the birds of St Francis of Assissi. They pecked at their food, chewed every mouthful ponderously, softened it, reduced it to pulp. They ate for the taste, for illusion's sake. A morsel of bread was to them a slice. Their meals-on-wheels were brought to them in a dinner-pail by a hefty woman whose name they did not know. This slatternly female had become the most important person in their lives. She had introduced herself the first time she came, had rattled off her name, but they had not caught it then and had never asked her since.

"Girlie," they would say to the stoutly built blonde woman in her thirties. The soup was always lukewarm by the time she got to them, but the vegetables were hot. Vegetables take longer to cool, especially if there is meat to go with them, roast for the most part, rib-roast, yes, meat takes longer to cool than gravy.

In their experience at least.

Sometimes the old woman would complain about the absence of pickles.

"And where's our apples? There used to be a dessert too, girlie. Iced teacakes or chocolate cake, even."

"Catering's centralised these days, Ma," said the blonde, shrugging her shoulders.

Sometimes even the old man found himself wanting to protest about a maggoty apple.

In their old age their shrivelled faces had become very similar.

Their noses had grown alike and they stared, blinking rapidly and often, with the same lustreless, watery, puckered eyes; their earlobes drooped, their hands were mottled and shaky, their brows deeply furrowed, and they walked with the same halting, tottery steps, as if co-ordinating their ominously growing weaknesses; they sniffled and gurgled and hawked in the same way and if the old woman had a pain somewhere, the old man at once developed shooting pains in his back or shoulders. They lived on each other's words. They never spoke of their dreams, they had woken for years to the same images, meaningless, or a thousand times dreamed.

In the beginning they often heard the baby crying.

"The little Tóth," the old man would say to himself.

"The little Tóth," the old woman once said over a plate of lukewarm peas. The baby cried a lot and loudly, and his choking sobs, like a disquietening piece of news, went the rounds of the house, bubbling up from the chinks in the wall and from hidden corners, coursing along the old pipes, carried by the beetles scuttling up chirping from the cracks in the floor, and if the Dormicum pill had not taken effect, the old man sometimes heard the cries continue till dawn. No-one raised any objection, not one of the tenants, of course they did not either, everyone knew it was hardest on the Tóths. The poor Tóths. And they, the two old people, lay on their damp bed at a distance from each other, for it was some years since they had last cuddled up together, and listened to the crying.

"He's crying," the old woman would say.

"He's crying," the old man said.

A few weeks later they were just setting out to go shopping

together, as usual, when the young man almost ran into them at the point where the piercing bright light streaming in from the courtyard slashes the murky gloom of the stairway. Tóth cast a quick glance at them and, muttering some sort of greeting, brushed against the old woman in passing.

She knew she ought not to, but the old woman called after him anyway.

"We haven't heard the baby much lately."

Tóth turned back.

"You haven't?"

He looked offended somehow.

"There's nothing wrong, is there?" asked the old woman.

There was a scar from an old dogbite under Tóth's eye. His thin, pale face gleamed in the gloom of the stairway, the smooth cheeks rarely needing a shave. He leaned forward slightly, as though drawn forward by his hairless chin. It all seemed quite unreal. Had he really spoken the words they believed him to have said, or had they been lip-reading and misunderstood something, or had they perhaps simply imagined the whole thing, both of them at the same instant – well, it wouldn't be so very surprising if even their hallucinations were the same after all these years.

"What did you say?" the old woman asked just to make sure, fumbling with the ends of her kerchief and shaking her tiny bird-like head. Tóth took a quick step upwards. He kicked the chalky parapet with the toe of his pointed shoe. Then trampled upon the bit of plaster that had fallen off the wall.

"You heard right," he said.

"What did you say?" asked the old man in turn.

"The baby died," repeated Tóth slowly, practically syllable by syllable, and this time they heard him clearly. Tóth stared at them, his face expressionless, at the two twitching, trembling birds' heads, then turned away for a moment and stared at the patches of saltpetre rot on the wall.

"Oh dear," said the old woman and, like in a trashy film, clutched her husband's shoulders with both hands.

It took all the old man's strength to hold her up.

"What do you mean, sir?!" he asked, poking at his glasses, and repeated, "What do you mean?"

"The baby died," he said for the third time.

He took another step upwards. Now he was standing right above them. He stared down at them as if he were looking into a deep dark well. He put his hands in his pockets, sniffed, and this made him seem even younger. He made a face.

"Dear God," the old woman shook her head.

Tóth suddenly took a step down and stared into their faces from close up. And, like a small boy, broke into a smile.

"I was only joking," he shrugged.

And set off at a run up the stairs.

The old man made an angry gesture as if to strike the young man, and almost fell down the stairs, dragging the old woman with him.

They did not go into the grocery. There was a squalid-looking playground two blocks from the shop; they sat there a while silently, stiff-necked, on a bench badly in need of a coat of paint beside a sand-pit dotted with dog-turds. Before they left the old woman stood up, stepped behind the old man and brushed the dandruff off his shoulders. It was growing dark by the time they got home. For a long time the old man pottered about the study crammed with books. With drooping lips he gazed at his shelves, at the huge oak writing desk covered with a fine film of dust.

"Magda, make me some coffee please," he suddenly said.

The old woman stared at him.

"Coffee, at this hour?"

"And bring me a shot of cognac before you go."

The old woman looked at her husband again, then shuffled over to the cabinet, running her eyes musingly over the dusty, unopened bottles. A few bottles of vintage Tokay, Villányi Cabernet, a bottle of honeysweet liqueur from Lisbon and an opened bottle of apricot brandy from Kecskemét.

"There is no cognac, Ferenc . . . We finished the bottle last summer."

The old man meditated, rubbing his chin.

"Then bring me some apricot brandy! There's got to be some of that left."

The old woman first took one glass out of the cabinet, stood pondering, then took another small glass from among the rest. She picked a Viennese handkerchief from the chiffonier, with a pattern of tulips and the Stephanskirche embroidered on it, and used it to wipe the glasses. She wiped them several times. Then she filled them carefully.

"Your health, Magda!"

"Your health, Ferenc!"

The old woman stuck her tongue into the glass and as soon as it touched the liquid and she could feel the taste, ran her tongue over her gums.

The drink burned her mouth and that was good.

"Serve the coffee in the Zsolnai service," croaked the old man.

The old woman went out into the kitchen, past being surprised now. The old man stood for a long time before the rickety bookshelf that touched the ceiling, reached up for a leather-bound Marcus Aurelius, leafed through it. He stared fixedly at an underlined sentence but did not read it, just stared ahead, unseeing. He dropped the book. Reached up at random for another. *The Forms of the Hungarian Soul*. Reached up for another. *A Journal of the Plague Year*. Then he came upon a Zrínyi.

A Miklós Zrinyí.

The old man frowned.

Then suddenly cried:

"São Paulo!"

The old woman stuck her head around the door that was open a crack.

"What did you say, Ferenc?"

"Have you any idea, Magda, what they are doing right now in São Paulo?"

The old woman took a step inside, shrugged her shoulders.

"How does São Paulo come into all this?" she asked hesitantly.

She stared at the wizened bird's head, at this little, dishevelled man. As though she had suddenly realised that the person she was looking at, whose lined face had again become hardened by the severity that used to terrify so many pupils, was in reality another man altogether.

"How could you know!" the old man grumbled.

"They are taking a siesta!" he shouted, rummaging in the over-stuffed drawer of the writing desk. In a moment he found the directory with the international dialling codes and, licking his fore-finger, began to turn the pages. His tremulous lips moved as he read the numbers. And he was already dialling. The old woman made no move to go, just stood astonished, an incredulous half-smile turning up the corners of her mouth. The line was dead, the old man shook his head irritably. He dialled again, unsure of the exact number of digits needed. Then suddenly the phone began to ring at the other end. The old man pressed down the cradle and smiled.

"Taking a siesta," he said.

He dialled again and once more the phone began to ring.

Rang once, and once again.

Then someone spoke at the other end.

"Hallo?"

It was a woman's voice, cross, breathless. Gasping for breath, choking almost. Like someone coming up from underwater at the last moment.

"Is that São Paulo?" asked the old man.

"What . . . do you . . . want?" panted the woman again.

"I'd like to speak to Mr Stammer," said the old man quickly.

"What Mr Stammer are you talking about?"

"My name is Gerlóczy and I'd like to speak to Mr Stammer."

The woman's voice lashed back, breathless still and sharp with irritation.

"Is this . . . some kind of a joke? It's . . . siesta time."

"This is Ferenc Gerlóczy speaking from Hungary, and I would like to speak to Mr Stammer . . . It's rather important."

In the kitchen the percolator began to bubble fiercely, but the old woman made no move to go. She just stared in amazement at her husband, who was speaking with São Paulo, wildly gesticulating with every sentence.

For her part, the panting woman in São Paulo was becoming more alert by the minute.

"There's no-one by the name of Stammer living here . . . Stop that," she suddenly said, aside.

"Are you quite sure?"

"Are you really . . . stop it . . . are you really calling from Hungary?"

"From Europe," the old man nodded.

A bad-tempered male voice jabbered at the woman.

But the woman retorted:

"They're calling from Hungary . . . Europe . . . Stupid."

The old man heard a rough curse from the background but the woman had begun speaking to him again.

"Are you sure you're not . . . calling from Rio?" she asked. "How can I be sure you're not speaking from Rio?"

"I am speaking from Budapest."

"And how come you speak Portuguese?"

"I am a teacher."

"A Portuguese teacher?"

"I learned it."

"How did you learn?"

"From books."

"And who is Mr Stammer?" The woman's voice had become quite

animated, her breathing was almost back to normal, and her irritation had been absorbed by incredulous wonder.

The old man concentrated.

"Mr Stammer . . . is my friend."

There was silence at the end of the line in São Paulo.

"Is Mr Stammer . . . Hungarian?" the woman asked suddenly.

"Naturally," said the old man.

"You know," said the woman, "I've never spoken to a Hungarian before."

"Well, there aren't too many of us," bantered the old man.

"You're quite old, aren't you?" asked the woman.

"I just . . . want to speak to Mr Stammer," said the old man.

"I'm very sorry," the woman explained, "we've been living here for ten years, and this has been our telephone number for ten years."

"I see," said the old man.

"I really am very sorry," said the woman.

They were silent again.

"Are you still there?" asked the old man.

"There's no-one by the name of Stammer living here," the woman sighed.

"Well, if there isn't, then there isn't. I shall look into the matter," said the old man, playing for time.

"Goodbye," said the woman.

"Goodbye."

The line went dead. The old man listened to the dialling tone for a little while longer, then slowly replaced the receiver. The old woman, who was still standing in the doorway, heaved a deep sigh.

"Who were you talking to, Ferenc?"

"A Brazilian woman," said the old man absent-mindedly.

"A Brazilian woman," mused the old woman. "And what would you be wanting, Ferenc, from a Brazilian woman?"

The old man shrugged his shoulders, smiling.

"And who is this Stammer?"

The old man's eyes were suspiciously bright, as if he were the worse for drink. He did not reply, just shrugged his shoulders again. Then he sniffed the air. At once the old woman turned and in a few minutes brought in the coffee. As her husband had demanded, she served it in the Zsolnai service, on a silver tray with birds engraved on it. The porcelain sparkled as if it were Sunday afternoon. The old woman poured a drop of coffee for herself as well. She watched the other sipping from his cup.

First brandy, then a Brazilian woman, now coffee.

Six months ago he had been rushed to St John's Hospital in an ambulance.

"What would Dr Hevesy say if he saw you now?"

"Dr Hevesy can go to hell!" rasped the old man.

"But Ferenc! . . . Really!"

The old woman pretended to be really offended.

This sudden, exorbitant intemperance was truly insupportable. Swearing too, he is surely not himself. She hadn't seen him like this for years. She cast a contemptuous glance over her shoulder and went into the next room, leaving her husband, who was sipping his coffee noisily, to his own devices. He walked up and down, muttering to himself, and every now and then broke into a wide smile.

All at once he heard the music.

The horns striking up playfully.

"Stravinsky," said the old man and pondered.

"The card game," he said after a while. "And ballet."

Then he shuffled into the other room to join the old woman.

And there his wife was, sitting at her dressing table, wagging her little bird's head and playing patience in the pale, diffused light of the small table lamp with the glass shade. Her grey hair fell loosely upon her shoulders, as in a cheap copperplate print. Yet she looked just like she had in the old days. The old man stood beside her. His wife glanced up and smiled at him. The old man cleared his throat and, like one wanting to make peace, remarked:

"On the other hand, Magda, the piece is about a poker game.

But it was as if she had not heard him.

"The king of spades goes here in the middle," she began to explain. "Then the seven of diamonds will come here on this six, the queen of spades goes here in the middle, on the king . . . are you paying attention, Ferenc?"

"Yes," the old man mumbled confusedly.

"Are you really paying attention?" His wife looked up at him like a stern little girl.

"I really am paying attention," the old man muttered with bad grace.

"Good. Now we'll rid ourselves of the queen of hearts, you see, which will free the jack of spades, so we can put him here in the middle . . . Are you really paying attention, Ferenc?"

"Yes."

"We'll put the seven of hearts on the eight, and set the king of clubs in the middle . . . Now we'll put the four of diamonds on the five of hearts, so as to free the ten of spades . . . So. Does that look right to you, Ferenc?"

"It does," said Ferenc, wagging his head.

The old woman heaved a deep sigh. And looked up at him, giving him a despairing, withering look.

"You're not paying attention, Ferike."

"I am," the old man protested uncertainly.

"Can one put a diamond on a heart?" the old woman asked, shaking her head theatrically.

"One can't?" asked the old man sourly.

"How could one?!" said the old woman irritably.

She sighed in resignation.

"Watch, Ferike. The five of hearts goes back on the ten of spades, and we put the two of hearts here in the middle."

Then the old woman stared at the cards for a long time.

"What do we do now?" asked the old man.

"I don't know," said the old woman, dispiritedly shrugging her shoulders. "That's the end of the game." She pointed at the position of the cards. "We deal again. This position is finished, there are no more moves to make."

The old man watched his wife shuffling the cards. She shuffled them quickly, her fingers quite nimble. Then the old man switched off the record player, the needle had reached the last groove. And as he turned he looked straight into the expectant eyes of the old woman. The old man could not have described exactly the expression that flitted across the thin, lined face. A tranquil, distant little smile, or perhaps the unfamiliar flush of a mischievous, provoking fever.

Then the old woman spoke.

"Are we done with joking, Ferenc?"

The old man smiled.

It was a bad smile.

Old, as if it did not belong to anybody.

"We are done with joking, Magda," he said then.

And watched the other laying out the cards for a new game.

[EMol]

SZILÁRD PODMANICZKY

Happy Birthday to You

I had yet to open my eyes. The eiderdown was sweltering and light; weights were chasing one another in my head, as if I were picking up the pulse of my own circulation. A dull ache had settled on the nape of my neck. If I opened my eyes, I knew I would feel dizzy. I tried to go back to sleep: an hour or two can be a huge bonus, sparing one the initial, most horrendous stage of sobering up, when nothing is where it should be, when even the faintest spark of strength has gone, when every movement takes five times as much energy and concentration, and it would be no surprise at all if, one of these days, at a time like this, the world were to split in two.

With the first move I made, to drink a glass of water perhaps and down an aspirin, a blast of cold air slipped under the bedclothes. I shuddered and shivered. Then a wave of heat surged through me, and I was drenched in sweat. I lifted the bedclothes a few times with my legs, the better to shiver and perspire, to sweat out the toxins. With each fresh wave of heat, I imagined the crumminess seeping out of me into the eiderdown, and when the bulk of that had been transferred I would jump out from under it.

I caught a whiff of a peculiar odour, a smell of musty whitewash and clothes; the floor radiated coldness.

We had been three days into celebrating my birthday; that's how it's been for years now, and if I can last it out, it really is like being born again.

I had left my flat along with others on the first night; we were all wide awake, bar the odd lapse, and traipsing from one place on to the next. After the third day, the very idea of the smell of fish-soup that had been left in my kitchen was scary. Eventually I'd pull myself together somewhere, maybe here, and go home. I couldn't take any more; last night in the rain I was already starting to see tiny, iridescent pixies in the light of the street lamps.

After a while I felt a bit better and opened my eyes a fraction. It was still dark in the room; I could hear the sound of a car, the headlights sweeping strips of brightness around the room through the cracks in the window blinds. I did not budge. More and more cars came by: must be getting on for dawn, I thought to myself. I was lying a couple of yards from the window. My eyes were rheumy and stung; the strips from the cars swam, as if there were a herd of zebra clattering around the walls. I'm used to living in a multi-storey house, and you don't often see that kind of thing there, I thought to myself, then right after that: where on earth could I be, another fine mess.

I was bracing myself to sit up and drink a glass of water when something flicked the back of my neck. As if I had dreamed it. I didn't move a muscle. The slight weight of the something lingered on my neck. It was as though some creature were trying to enter my head at precisely the point where the dull ache was throbbing. I gingerly drew back and turned over. I was lying in a twin bed, and there was somebody sleeping beside me; only the top of the head was showing, the hair spread in clumps on the pillow, and a long arm, the fingertips of which had slipped on to the nape of my neck.

I clambered out of bed. It was daybreak already, and it could have been no more than a few degrees above freezing in the room. I found my clothes at the foot of the bed and dressed, but I could not find my briefcase.

The place was unfamiliar, but that did not surprise me; I was used to that sort of thing by now and merely thought to myself: another fine mess . . .

I went out of the room and in the kitchen drank some water and rinsed my face. From the kitchen window I was able to look out on a yard in which stood piles of dry, chopped-up trees and beside them a smallish fruit tree – cherry, perhaps. The sky was overcast, and an autumn mist spilled down the bole of the tree. I stepped out into the yard to take a breath of fresh air. A man greeted me from next door, and I returned the greeting.

I went into the house to have a look for my briefcase and push off home. It grew lighter while I was searching. The somebody in the bed stirred, pulled down the bedclothes from over its head, but did not open its eyes. An old man. He was champing, trying to swallow his spittle. My fear suddenly pervaded the whole house. I had no idea how I had come to be there, or who the old man I had slept beside might be. I attempted to retrieve the last image from my memory, but I could no longer match even a day to what I did remember.

With a great effort, the old chap twisted halfway round in the bed and said something in a high-pitched voice, almost whistling and whining: "You've got here?"

I didn't know whether he was just talking to himself or I was expected to answer. I felt diabolical. I dithered a bit longer on account of my briefcase before deciding that it didn't matter, the main thing was to clear off. No sooner had I made up my mind, though, when a car drew up under the window and its headlights were switched off. I started to sweat again in my clammy, stinking clothes. I was so jumpy that I trembled all over. It was too late now to bolt from the house. I have to hide, I thought to myself. But the whole house comprised just two bare rooms; there was nowhere to go. I looked out of the window: it was not a police car. I calmed down a little at that, but the next instant there was a knock at the door. Having tidied my clothes and also my hair, there was nothing for it but to open the door. Good morning, said the man in the yellow overalls, a doctor's bag in one hand. Good morning, doctor, I replied, come in. How is the old fellow, he asked. Well, I said, but without waiting for an answer the doctor went straight into the room and pulled a chair across to the bed. You came yesterday, he asked. Something like that, yes, I said, and started slowly to feel my way into the role, or rather it occurred to me that I might scrape through if I were to get into the swim of it.

The doctor examined the motionless old man while I hung around in the doorway. He set the chair back in its place, packed up his bag, then on the way out paused by me. I suppose you don't want to have him admitted to hospital, he said, I've known him for thirty years and this is where he wants to die, in his own home. What's wrong with him, I asked. The doctor stared straight ahead. His internal organs, he said, he needs a special operation. That would allow him to hold out for a few more years, maybe even get him back on his feet. What do you think? I don't know, I replied. My hands were ice-cold. The operation would cost a million and a half, he said. Well, what can I say, I replied. You know best, he said, placing a hand on my shoulder, then made to go but lingered in the doorway: try to get some food down him, grated vegetables or fruit, and fluids. Who took care of him up till now, I asked. I did, and I'll look in again tomorrow, the doctor answered, and he departed. I heaved a sigh or two.

I turned towards the old man, who was puffing almost imperceptibly. It grew even brighter in the room. I searched through my pockets to see whether I had any money left on me: just a few tattered paper handkerchiefs. I rummaged through the drawers, the wardrobe and the dresser in the kitchen. I found no money, no briefcase, just a few utensils and a threadbare suit.

That's enough of that, I thought to myself, closing the front door after myself, then the garden gate, and set off down the muddy street. The occasional cyclists and pedestrians, having eyed one another, nodded silent acknowledgements. It was even colder on the street, with the wind going right through my clothes. I heard the sound of a bus around the corner and quickened my pace.

The names of two villages were displayed on the bus's signboard, neither previously known to me. I did not board, having no money on me after all, though I did exchange glances with the driver for a few seconds before he closed the door. I could not have explained why, or even if I could, but there was no way he was going to let me board without money. I gazed for a long time at the bus's wobbling stern. Then I set off after it.

I contemplated ringing a doorbell and asking for some money, to be sent back later. I resolved to do that. I looked around: no-one on the street, then I rang the bell on the wall of one of the larger houses. A dog scampered up to the fence and began sniffing mutely; it did not bark. No-one came. I pressed again. The dog snorted. I waited another minute, but still nothing.

The fumes from the bus were still swirling around in the dank air. I carried on after it. I was overcome by hunger and thirst, and I was freezing. The road climbed gently then swung round into a street market. I caught the smell of roasting meat from way off. In the market there were second-hand clothes and food for sale: loads of fruit and greens, and fresh-fry stalls. I searched through my pockets yet again, then thought what a pity it was I didn't have a wristwatch, I could get a thousand for it now. By one of the second-hand clothes stalls the idea of selling my jacket flitted across my mind, but just before I had buttoned it up to the neck so as not to freeze. I was simply loitering, but then it occurred to me that if I was going to steal anything, I would have to be snappy before I became conspicuous.

I half unbuttoned my jacket and made my way along the row of stallkeepers like someone who had business there. On one trestle stood piles of carrots and apples; the vendor was deep in discussion with her neighbour, before whose stall there was a small queue of customers for eggs. I lifted a few grubby carrots and apples, whisked them under my jacket, buttoned it back up and dodged past the queue.

The icy-cold carrots and apples pressed on my stomach; my hands were so cold they had lost all sensation. If I were to leave the village, I would freeze, so I had to stay there, and I longed, with every fibre in my body, to get myself under cover. Without much further ado, I set off back towards the old man's house.

It was strange how much at home I felt moving around that unfamiliar place. I let myself in, dumped the stuff from my jacket in the kitchen, then looked in on the old chap; he was lying there as before, but as I stepped closer my nose was assailed by the stench. He had shitted and wet the bed. I dithered for a while: this was unbearable, it had quite taken my appetite away. I thought the whole thing over afresh; my head was clear by now.

I chopped up some kindling in the yard, lit a fire in the kitchen range, put water on to heat. Within minutes warm air was wafting through the kitchen, so I opened the connecting door to the other room. Having washed with the hot water, I felt a great deal better. I turned the old man over on to my bed, wiped his arse, yanked the soiled sheet off his bed, shoved it into a bowl of steaming, soapy water, laid my own sheet under the old chap, then aired the room. Only at this point did I pause for a moment: how come the beds had been made for two? No matter, maybe it was the doctor, I thought to myself.

The walls soon warmed through, and I took the soiled sheet in the bowl of water out into the yard. I inspected my hands, and it struck me, for no particular reason, what a lot of things they had handled already. I rinsed the carrots and apples, peeled them and chopped them up on to a plate for the old man.

I sat him up in the bed; he did not open his eyes, though from time to time the whites of his eyeballs flashed, but I could only get a few morsels down him, and three sips of water. He swallowed mechanically; I had to hold his head tight so he would not choke, and told him in a loud voice what to do: Swallow! Chew! Sip!

I went back into the kitchen and slumped on to the chair; I was exhausted. I slowly nibbled up the carrots and apples, stoked the fire, took my jacket off, then tried to gather my wits in order to work out how I was going to get home. I was not going to set off that day – that I was sure of. And I also thought to myself that anyway the doctor would be coming the next morning, maybe I could trust him, tell him everything, scrounge some money and clear off.

The old man was sleeping peacefully in the bed; he was warm enough to have pulled the bedclothes down. I perched on the side of the bed, and all I could think of was that time should roll on and the doctor come as soon as possible. My eyelids were drooping, and I thought to myself that I could do with a spot of shut-eye, so I cautiously snuggled back next to the old man.

It must have been after noon when I woke, but I was no longer alarmed; I was partly reconciled to my position in that I had managed to gain some control over things, and I had a plan for deliverance.

Dusk was drawing in; the fire had burned down to embers, so I went out to chop some wood. The dull axe blade had trouble splitting the thick logs, and in the gloom I was fumbling in the earth in the hope of finding something on which to whet it when my hand hesitated. I sensed that someone was watching me. I raised my head. A shadowy figure was standing behind the garden gate. I tried to make it out in the twilight. Blow it, I thought to myself, I've overplayed my hand and come unstuck. Tossing the axe to the ground, I went over to the gate. After a few paces I could see that it was a woman, her oval face glistening in the light that was filtering out from the kitchen window. Good evening, I said. Good evening, she replied. May I come in, she asked. Of course, and I opened the gate.

In the kitchen I offered her a seat, then went to fetch another chair from the next room. She was mopping eyes alarmingly red from weeping. At first I thought she must be the old man's daughter, but because she did not seem to want to see him and did not even ask after him, I quickly dismissed that notion and trusted I would be able to carry on coolly playing the role of the son – at least until the morning.

The woman could hardly have been over forty, and if one discounted the overflowing tear ducts and a mouth puffed up from crying, I would go as far as to say she was pretty. She began by saying she didn't know where to begin. I listened to her for about an hour as it grew quite dark.

She was in a jam: everyone in the village looked on her as a city tart because she was pretty, and round there they hated outsiders; they were all supposed to marry someone from that village or, at worst, the next one over. Her husband drank like a fish; he had plenty of money, farming a few hundred acres with his workers, but he did little else except hit the bottle. She could not leave him, because he would go after her and kill her, he had sworn as much; either that or her husband's brothers would kill her, for what difference that made. She did not have the nerve to kill herself, and since I too was a stranger there, maybe I would understand.

I clutched my head in my hands. Somehow I felt unable to say that if only she would give me some money, I would not be seen for dust. That was clearly not going to solve her problem.

Come with me: bring some money from home, and we'll make ourselves scarce, I said. It's impossible, they'll be after me, she replied, and from the way she said it I sensed that it was too big a price to pay for my liberty, I ought not to take it upon myself.

We fell silent; she stopped crying. I did my best to help: what if she were to kill him, I said. That's impossible, I've already thought of that, it would be the end of me, she said. But maybe if you were to do it. At that my expression froze. Oh no, I responded, not that. I would pay you; he keeps loads of money at home, a million or so. I said nothing for a while. I can't do anything like that, I said. He's pegged out at home, out of his skull even as we speak. Come with me, please, I beg you, help me. She stood up, threw the door open and waited for me to go with her.

I didn't have the heart to leave the wretched woman to her own devices; I thought to myself, if I were to go and have a look-see, she might calm down, at least until tomorrow. I grabbed my jacket, and off we went.

Her husband was pegged out in the front room, his arms dangling from the settee, his mouth wide open. The woman studied me curiously to see what I would come up with. She glanced from me to the fat, dead-drunk pig to whom she had pledged fidelity . . .

And what if it were made to look like suicide, I whispered. I don't know; I don't know anything about that sort of thing, I'm all mixed up, she said. One could torch the house, let's say, I said, and I began spilling out ideas, each better than the last, but with a callousness that even I found surprising, as if I were just tossing them around in a brainstorming session. Torch the house, I said. Or bury him in the garden. That's not suicide, the woman said. True, I replied. Or stick him in his car and trundle it into a lake. There is a lake here, the woman said, just over a mile outside the village. Then what are you waiting for, I asked. Help me, she pleaded.

We went out into the garage, inspected the car, and I showed her how to set the accelerator, the gear and the clutch. But you have to do it, I said.

The car had not been used for years, the tyres were flat. I snatched the pump down from the wall and, though my head was reeling from it all, did not waste a moment. When I had finished on the first wheel, the woman gently grasped my neck and stroked my face. No, I said, you have to carry it through. She vanished while I was pumping the next tyre, and all at once it had come down to me: there was I, pumping up the tyres of the car of a total stranger, in a completely unknown place I had no idea how I had fetched up in, with the old chap croaking it back there, while here I was helping to send a lousy creep to his maker. I'll scarper before the woman gets back, I thought to myself. Except there was nowhere to scarper to; it was bitingly cold outside, and the fog was closing in, and she would follow me to the old man's house.

By the time the woman returned, I had filled all the tyres. In her hand was a bundle of money, which she stuffed into my jacket pocket. Eight hundred grand, she said. For fuck's sake, I yelled, get it through your head: No! The woman pulled down the garage door. Pipe down, they can hear you. Afterwards you can do whatever you want with me, she said. Oh no, not that, I said in a quieter voice, but the anger was undiminished, and I sensed that it was somehow alleviating my hangover. If I do whatever I want with you, that would leave you exactly where you were to begin with, I said. That rat also did whatever he wanted with you. The woman flinched, momentarily lost for words, then managed to riposte: But you're different.

I did not answer. I took the woman by the hand, and we went back into the front room, grabbed hold of her husband, lugged him to the car and stowed him on the back seat. From here on in it's up to you, I said, and left her there.

The old fellow was still lying peacefully on the bed, puffing faintly. I paced up and down. It suddenly occurred to me: the money. There it was in my pocket. Eight hundred thousand, I counted it out.

It was well into the night by now; outside all was still, the sky had cleared, and the temperature had dipped below freezing. I tossed a few more billets on the fire, got out the money, plonked down seven hundred thousand next to the old man, on the chair the doctor had used. I stuffed the remaining hundred thousand in my pocket, then started on my way.

On leaving the village, I started jogging to warm myself up. Every now and then I glanced back, so that if a car were coming I would have time to stop and thumb a lift. Nothing came, but after half a mile or so I grew weary, though I had warmed up. Then, all of a sudden, there was a flash of headlights on the road behind me, and my shadow was thrown a hundred yards ahead of me.

The car drew up alongside, and the passenger door opened. The woman was behind the wheel with her husband in the back, just as we had stowed him. Come on, give me a hand; I don't know what to do with him on my own, she gestured behind her. Leave me out of it, I said, so it beats me how, just a couple of seconds later, I came to be sitting in the car.

We turned off the road towards the lake; the reflected sky was glittering darkly on its surface. The car stopped in the wooded part of the reservoir, where a long slope led down to the water. With considerable difficulty, we heaved the man into the driver's seat and belted him in. The woman started the engine and set it in gear, while I fixed the accelerator pedal to slightly more than idling and wedged the clutch to the seat with a stick that could be yanked away through the rolled-down wing-window with a length of twine.

All set, I asked the woman. All set, she replied. I pressed the twine into her hand, and she yanked it without giving it a moment's thought. The car slowly trundled towards the lake. Then all at once the woman started racing after it. Hell's teeth, she shouted, I left my house key inside. She ripped the door open and clambered in: in the dark, I couldn't see what she was doing. The car was picking up speed all the while, and by the time it had reached the edge of the lake it must have been doing about twenty. Get out, I shouted after her. Just before hitting the water the car thumped against a hillock on the right-hand side and the door slammed; I raced after it. Even in the water it kept going before submerging. I ran up and down the bank; the water was icy cold. Come on now, come on, I urged the woman under my breath. The top of the car vanished completely under the water, the eddies swirled slowly outwards, and the lake grew calm again, with only the ripples surging towards the far bank to break its surface. One minute elapsed, then two. I could not bring myself to go in after her. On the contrary, I edged away step by step. On getting back to the road and setting off again in the dark, I thrust my hands in my pockets and had a feeling that somehow nothing had happened. And the further I went, the more I kept repeating that to myself: nothing, nothing at all. I don't even know who they are.

It was still night when I reached the next village, or maybe it was a town. There were even two taxis parked in the centre. I got into the first; a young lad was listening to the radio. They say the cold spell will let up tomorrow, he said. Good thing too, I responded, I've got a splitting head from this cold front. Where to, he asked. It'll be a fair drive, and then I named the town, pressing fifty thousand into his palm. Fair enough, he said, and I felt relieved.

He said nothing until we had left the village. Only then did he ask: Husband going home? And he guffawed. You got it, I said, on top of which I did two people in and saved someone's life. The lad's expression did not so much as flicker: That sort of thing happens round here, it's a prosperous area, and fortunes change hands easily. But if you give me another hundred grand, I never saw you. I've only got fifty, I said, and pulled it out. All right, he replied, then I'll say I only saw half of you – from the back, let's say. And he started to laugh his head off: A decent little caper at last. There was I thinking I would have to wait another week, he said. Though that one's a dead cert. Right? Get smashed out of my skull with my mates. That's when my birthday will be. Happy birthday to you, I said, and turned the radio up.

[TW]

KÁROLY BARI

Death of a Stag

1
From north to south, leaf-scented solitude,
stuttering of leaves, thunder of birds' wings beating
against the sky, what kind of king rattles
the fallen branches, abased to black bones?
the wind laments his flashing limbs, on his splintered
crown the smut of blood, the peal of littered leaves
greeted the flowers, flowers for the king,
leaf-scented solitude!

2
The trees' breathing grates
on clouds' brows, as though a storm were raging,
green fire were darting, crested, with tears of wild roses,
these leafy spears whisper without mercy,
impaling eagles, their shadows
full of pain, in their shadows with open-lipped wound adorned
lies the king, a dying stag, guarded by troubled silence.
Sparkling moments sleep in the forsaken house.

[DHo/EMol]

Winter Diary

Snow, fog, fingerprints
sprouting swans' feathers
on the windowpanes, the candles
walk the sills covered
with bristly carpets: the pine branches
in white wax dress suits,
flame flickers on the trays balanced upon their heads,
we still wait for someone, someone is coming now, will blaze up
before our door, like fiery hair: lightning

on the black soap of the sky, and pleads admittance,
tells memories of the light tying to his waist-belt
the dew-scalps of flowers, piercing together
our faces, saved from beneath the ice-harrow of the eaves,
like potsherds inscribed in cuneiform and whispers, grieve,
in the lake rising in place of the trundled-away night
burning hot, golden pitch bubbles, into it is cast
your heretic youth, the hands fumbling among the pearl-cargo of
brows
tremble, can youth have come to an end?
is the flying in the face of the storms' whetted breath
at an end? then why do I hear
the shrieking of imagination pressed against
the grindstone of fate? neon lights
strive hissing, boxed in, enclosed by the squares,
in the snow-saddle of lamp-maned streets
galloping round and round
consciousness balances
on vertebrae superimposed, escorting me handcuffed,
the clatter of heel irons, guards, guards,
from behind the shutters of their lips
they expel the manikins of spittle, show their teeth,
the blood-red fish-scales of days borne away: time
strews twilights among the onlookers,
is the march at an end? my tear-gloved eyes
are still black ice-fists, it is winter, it has always been winter since then,
through the walls gleam the snow-spokes of the wind, you stand
in your wide-open window, inevitably,
with unappeasable brow
protest, as they lead me away in chains before your eyes,
your touch burns away
the snow-buds sprouting on your velvet dress,
you send after me the flash
of the glowing red-hot knives
that sleep in your heart, send me a message,
your messages are cloud-wigged rains, leaves, dreams, the
petal-lamellas
of roses moulded by dew-hammers,
from the seaside cliff
a moon with earlocks of mist stares down
at the depths mounted in spray

as though it were an appraiser in a pawn-shop,
it too always brings a message from you,
it is with your message the snow
stealing beneath the door awaits my awakening:
radiance still our companion, still glides with us, still questions us,
we are sun-fires gasping, writhing before mirrors,
our gestures watch us,
it is winter, unbanishable winter,
at daybreak you sew shirts
for consciousness reproducing infinity, the dawns
slipping lightning-like through the eyes of the needles, the beds,
the jealous lovers
who, sharing pleasure, wrestle each other,
the pines shooting out from the mountain peaks flash,
the snowflakes tugging at the frosty topknots of the grasses, our fears,
the forests tie cloud-bands
around their silver hair
and flatten the parchment scroll
of silence before them, our lips are the footprints
of lightning-booted cries, I love you, I love you,
the hands of the trees move
as though they were writing.

[DHo/EMol]

GYŐZŐ FERENCZ

*The Party According to Ramsey's Principle**

How many people should be
Invited to the Ramsey party
So that among the guests there should
Be three at least who know or else
Not know each other?
Assume six people are invited.
One of them, say *John*, will know
Or else not know at least, say, three
Of the five others. If he knows three
And out of the three there are two
(*Mary* and *Paul*) who know each other
(Together with *John*) they form a quorum;
But if they do not know each other
(Only *John*) then, with the others,
They still constitute a quorum,
In so far as at least three
Don't know each other. And should four,
Say, know or else not know
Another person, eighteen guests
Are necessary. More than that
And only an approximate
Estimate is possible, but that
For now will make no difference.
The Ramsey Principle states clearly
That perfect disorder can't exist.
But how many parties must you have
And how many must I attend

* Frank Plumpton Ramsey (1904–1930), mathematician, philosopher, economist, made a lasting contribution to the field of combinatories; according to his theory, perfect disorder is impossible, the appearance of disorder depending on the size of the sample provided.

Or not attend that I may know
Or not know you. Either I will
Know your guests or not know them.
I know who knows me and I know
Who doesn't, but could we two form
A quorum, just the two of us
While not knowing how *John* gets on
(With *John*) or Mary (with *Mary*) or Paul (with *Paul*)
Or *you* (with *me*) or *I* (with *you*)?
Could we, and if so, how many of us,
Be guests at a Ramsey party
While examining our reflection
So helplessly in the hall mirror?

[GS]

FERENC SZIJJ

Bread-stickers (Sell-by date) / Monday

The way it looked from the great covered terrace,
the narrowest part of garden stretching below us
was a stage, all lights, dazzling, a frieze of hedges,
ornamental trees, a swing, but no corresponding plot,
no leading roles for leaf, bark, air or earth,
at most some minor creatures, birds acting birds,
the merest presence of ants in walk-on parts
simply passing to and fro with their usual persistence,
a definite hit we had only to sweep up after.

Or some living, carefully marked-out space
offering benign amplitude for our more-or-less
compulsory shared lives, an outdoor terrain, set round
nonetheless by an inner circle of columns, or vice versa
created for time – for family fevers, problems, anxieties,
for responsibility, and its curious infolding –
or for that which so many of us could finally still inhabit,
not a single step taken without extraordinary effort
that it should not be backwards, or nowhere here by now.

But for a child maybe it was a real garden,
a Hungarian summer no other time, listening
as he had learned so carefully to listen, to certain signs,
in fear that something was happening as he was playing,
a game, indeed, in which he arranged his affairs in vain,
and our affairs with them, we who owe him this much at least
because among the hustle and bustle, he feels a sort
of foreboding that something, defeat perhaps,
is about to happen. As happen it did, of course.

[GS]

FLÓRA IMRE

Psalm

I'm comforted by none at all
if you my lord won't comfort me
and nothing needs my hands or me
if you have not asked for me at all

yours it is to judge, my lord
to stop these quarrels and trials,
to stop this life and its trials
if life makes no sense, my lord

my lord, permit me to leave this place
permit me to make my way back
with hopes torn to rags on my back,
where pity, not justice, holds place

where neither humility rules nor pride
but mercy alone and peace, my lord,
open that eternal house, now, my lord
bring me to its threshold, let me step inside

[JK]

Snow Covers the Garden

snow covers the garden, the night is grey
we see mere nothings as in a mirror
calm have I always sought, and not terror
it's not the Blessed Virgin's Lenten way.

silence waste and peace to be found nowhere
the snow sifts down the trees stand bare and still
the signs we leave are signs of signs that will
say we are or were all the signs once there

the city looms a yellowed dome of light
shreds of a tattered sky go slipping past
what gleams above the snowy garden's night

wings of silence ever heavier wings
heavy portents that we too fall at last
thought I sought in calm just what dying brings

[JK]

MÓNIKA MESTERHÁZI

Echo (I Distance Myself)

How touched they were, and he himself how saddened,
how well he understood the situation,
and did I think his daughters, who had been
through similar things, might they perhaps regard
the deterrent example of my personal poems
as personal deterrent? What I think,
albeit at the wrong moment as usual,
is I've let the spirit of the age escape
in a dangerously user-friendly form,
I think the whole thing is a pack of lies,
that what I said bears only a passing likeness
and differs from me at certain crucial points
(I justify myself, as most do, by admitting
exaggerations meekly) – I think
that poetry is not a melancholy Sunday
but working weekdays, precise, to be endured.

[GS]

Sors Bona

They cling, mature, detach and have to go,
I cannot keep a single one by me
to justify this ceaseless ebb and flow.
There's no creation and no mystery
where I would be a tool to help it shape
its own unique selfhood-defining laws –
I was resolved, I wanted to escape,
and pay the awful ransom for the cause.
My cells receive freak signals from my brain
– a wrong command, or simply bad design? –
so I decided, I must break the chain,
this nonsense stops with me, end of the line.

I have no child in this scenario.
For twelve long years I've planned this very "no".

For twelve long years I've planned this sacrifice,
an eighteen-year-old, loveless and resigned.
I paid for lovelessness: love was the price
and noble phrases of the costly kind.
False certainties form part of what I paid,
and silences, the years I had to give,
uncertainties, as instinct was betrayed,
the ills of wanting something negative.
When I decided to renounce my claim,
others, in haste, just started to discuss
and face the facts. Besides, why should the same
reality apply to all of us?
My own stood guard between me and my bliss,
it was taboo-land, dark and feelingless.

Reality lay hidden, like a place
when hills stand guard around it. I was numbed
by consciousness (my hardest-ever case).
Future was one flash, where all one's life condenses.
My body wasn't sick: it ceased to be.
That "no" had crushed it when the teenage lass
rejected motherhood. But meanwhile she,
the young new woman, nearly missed the bus.
And where is now this eighteen-year-old child?
Her high uncompromising moral ground?
I wash my hands? How dare I then deride
her fate? I must be wiser, more profound
and look at it from this point of view.
And anyhow, there's nothing I can do.

I'm learning of my own self, cell by cell.
Shall I dissect myself to learn some more?
What pain, what heavy pressure may compel
me now to tell this, as never before.
I used to speak of it to seek attention,
– you see, my life does carry certain weight –
but now there are so few people to mention
who interest me. And why aggravate

one's life, if it was light in weight? Indeed,
genetics can be side-stepped. If we may
adopt young puppies, kittens, every breed,
then why not children? I stand in the way:
if I get round to it, what is it about?
(What makes me cling on to this roundabout?)

What's brought him here, this pigeon in a mess,
my helpless face is battered by its wing,
and if I hadn't whimpered, consciousness
would not have broken up my slumbering.
How did he come, I have to take good care,
has something moved towards a certain end,
where is it drifting, nowhere, anywhere?
Or will it follow a more happy trend?
She has lost her virginity, what more
is there to say: returning to the scene
she found it? Can I possibly withdraw
what I have written? What I have dreamed? Any
least moment of this time and what has been?
Have I more thirty years? More life-ways? How many?

[PZ]

KRISZTINA TÓTH

On the Nature of Pain

which, fundamentally, cannot be fathomed.
Some don't say anything, but – in a bad case –
just stare dementedly while rocking that way
and this way to an inner rhythm;

while others stand up, knock over a chair and leave un-
steadily, they don't turn around (in fact they
do, but not physically), and just their back stays,
caught in the picture frame, long after quivering;

they don't ask for a light, ignite themselves, or plan
some daring feat involving ropes and rails;
they walk across the bridge and just look down . . .

. . . How should I have reacted? Glacially still,
reached down into my bag and drawn
a gun on you, like in the films?

[DHi]

Metro Trains in Contrary Directions

You've got a good life now:
no more looking suspicious, rolling me round
inside your mouth, an unchewed morsel,
while all the grown-ups eat: now you're an angel.
The telephone won't interrupt you just when you're
giving your child an evening bath,
or any time, though you'll of course call me –
those steadily repeating stabs round midnight.
Nor will we meet by chance on buses:
the lovely serendipity
of strange occurrences is past, behind the smog-

filled sky the split-seconds will just move on;
you won't have extinguished the morning if
you don't go to the everyday bother of
draping the dark-red quilt over the glass door.
(I've left it there, it's pitch dark.)
Oh yeah – thanks for the title to the verse:
I'll be in touch as well, I will be there
in your engagement book, an eighth day with no name,
no business there and nowhere much to go.

[DHi]

File

"Hey, did it hurt? Hey, did you hear?"
I didn't. Lying back upon the couch, I gazed at
the coloured circles gleaming with the back-light:
like a church window, yellow, blue and red
stained glass: something I'd never seen in an apartment.
We had to rush – by five his mum was coming.
He hopped behind me, pants around his ankles.
I squatted in the bath; he stood at the tap.
Yeah, I love it too. The morning's when it's nicest.

I was just sixteen, sixteen more years elapsed,
Then, on bus seven one day, there he was.
"The stained-glass thing between the dining room and
the sitting room, you know? I guess you guys kept that up?"
"Be serious. That was just something Dad made.
He brought some coloured files home from the office
and put them in between the double windows . . .
. . . I get off here and take the metro. Cheers!"

Why do all wonders have to be exploded?
Santa Claus. Storks. And now comes this.

[DHi]

VIRÁG ERDŐS

A Lying Tale

Virág Erdős
is an idiomatic phrase from the south of Buda
like "bungee jumping",
people tend to say it when
they can't think of anything else to say.

Virág Erdős
is a natural disaster,
perpendicular,
twelve letters.

Virág Erdős
is a free gift
providing you are referring to
whatever you desire to refer to.

Virág Erdős
is a multi-purpose group of products:
it is in fact up to you what you do with her.

Virág Erdős
is an amphetamine derivative
the only hitch being that it is difficult to stop using it.

Virág Erdős
is a post-traumatic stress disorder,
the kind that might cause a man sitting in front of the TV, for example,
to think of something,
leap to his feet
and do something so . . . Pow!

Virág Erdős
is the ticket to a treasure trove that pays interest,
but you can say what you like to me
I'll trash the lot, no argument.

Virág Erdős
is a "freestyle T-shirt"
bearing the message
"NO".

Virág Erdős
is an ever more ardently protected species
like the Storkfinch, the Meadowchick and the Dwarfhawk:
to kill one, to catch one,
to disturb her natural habitat,
to collect her brood or her eggs
is expressly forbidden.

Virág Erdős
is the notorious doyenne of computer hackers,
but relax, they've tracked her down.

Virág Erdős
is a kind of "anthropological issue".

Virág Erdős
is a member of the Alliance Party
so it will not surprise you to know
that she guarantees you a secure long-term future.

Virág Erdős
is a Fiery Pokémon.

Virág Erdős
is a dangerous worm in your program
you just have to click on her
and you're in deep shit.

Virág Erdős
is a feral mutant
and I can't understand how they let her on to our TV screens.

Virág Erdős
is what is called an Xtreme Sport
in which you find a sponsor
then smash your head against a wall.

Virág Erdős
is a wholly new remix
the only problem is
elements of hip-hop are part of the package.

Virág Erdős:
no such brand name.

Virág Erdős
is one of the best-known Hungarian writers
but sadly she is dead,
or rather, not dead, it's just that
she always gets home very late.

Virág Erdős
is the *other* best-known Hungarian writer,
she writes texts for sweatshirts and wind-shields,
apparently, it was she who wrote:
"*I love Budapest*".

[GS]

Vision (Game Over)

"Woe, woe, woe" (Rev. 8.13)

The first angel is, I think, the Mirage 2000. The extent of its knowledge is enough to bring all heaven crashing about our ears . . . I am not a thrill seeker, but that's why I'd like to see it. I zip here and there about the sky, cast my eyes round and chill, while under me the bridges break up like pretzels.

The second angel is, I think, His Highness, Wacko Jacko. What I like about him is that he never ages. He's as old as my great-great-grandad, but he looks barely twenty. Of course there's a trick involved: music certainly helps. The trick is that he has been distilled into a quasi-essence. Even his colon is pure alchemical gold. When I think about it I can see this is the way the world works. Have fuck all to do with shit of any sort. Get rid of it.

The third angel is, I think, the Dobermann bitch. Not the flat-arse kind, but the other one. The most recent breed that comes with replaceable dentures that you can whip out at night, and slip into a little bag . . . and, should you feel an overwhelming desire to screw her for instance, you can bang away without worrying. She won't bite your neck while you're doing it.

The fourth angel is, I think, an electronic woman. Her advantage is that she has a meter on her back which will tell you exactly how effective your blows are. Of course you can do plenty of other things with her besides hitting her. She costs relatively little to run. You can plug her into the mains, and she is completely sterile.

The fifth angel is, I think, Testicle Baked in a Roll. In the Admiral Bar apparently they use male apes, but I have a suspicion they add a little something extra. I particularly like them slightly overdone.

The sixth angel is, I think, the new Renault Mégane. The gimmick is that it has no brakes. However much people jump up and down, there is no need to stop. And it makes no difference if you lose your temper. You can easily wash the blood off the grille.

The seventh angel is, I think, a fucked-up little yellow zombie. You attack it, thinking to beat it to a pulp, but it slips through your fingers again. *Zero credit* it proclaims with finality. It judders, ticks, waits a while longer, then turns off. And then the bastard produces a message that says you have no more lives left.

[GS]

PÉTER ZILAHY

News

Magic is a practical, purposeful activity. A concrete substitution: mumbo-jumbo instead of words, ritual instead of action, dolls instead of people. The primary consumers of magic are news programmes: they transform the world into numbers – dates, data, results, syzygies, body counts. In the news the planet spins under you like a treadmill; if you switch it off, you drop out of time. The news substitutes for time. As though things happened only for the oracle to read them out. In the news they always say the same thing; they say, this is how it is. If you have seen it once, there is nothing new it can tell you. The last time someone had any good news to tell was two thousand years ago. What is good in the news is like the commercial breaks in a film on the telly – a 30-second interval between two murders. Interrupting the action. It says, It's good to be alive, look how happy others are! You too can be happy! The Americans have perfected weather forecasts: a model presents a model of the earth, a map, and jabs at it with her pointer – here and there, this is going to happen. Voodoo. I switch on my subconscious; earthquake, hurricane, flood, volcano, they say, apocalypse now. Then they give reassurances that it's all just psychology. It always looks that way, but there is no need to worry. Why not? What is the difference between a state-sponsored and a commercial hell? One of them is superficial and runs more ads?

[TW]

Eternity

I wake up in a nuclear-powered submarine, we are executing a diversionary manoeuvre. Taking serious casualties, we dodge two barracudas and three seahorses. Sirens are howling endlessly. A soft-spoken officer briefs us. It transpires that we are responsible for the safety of a high-ranking Party official. A special assignment. We did not die for nothing. Looking at the sea, you might think we were in the West, it has simply everything in it. Brezhnev is swimming in the

Black Sea in a white bathing cap, flipper-shod scuba divers in train at a respectful distance, his personal physician in a rowing boat. Were he to sink, they would rescue and resuscitate him. And so it goes every day. And we die over and over again for the cause. That is eternity.

[TW]

ANNA T. SZABÓ

Hospital Window

The now. The melody of moments.
Exterior and interior voices.
The cool whisper of leaves at night.
Autumnal. Branch-flute. Leaf sighs.

Winds flutter. A bite of sky.
Mist. Dark damp. Bars of light.
Great birds, matted wings spread wide.
Ploughland clods. Sun in a void.

A beating pulse. Bones. Nerves.
Hollows deep as wells. Caves.
Roofs. Windows. House-walls.
Echo-emptiness. Cellar smells.

And yet desire for being, being . . .

The now. The out. The in. The nothing.

[CW/GG]

On Darkness

Where the heart was, a word is beating: Forget.
There was heat, though; you lay back in the grass
and felt the pulsations searing through your flesh,
under your eyelids, there, where the sun was;
a mirage burns into the retina
like the trace left by a touch upon your skin,
the grass, the sun, the feeling cold, the drying
and the smell over cooling water of the wind . . .
the word beats, stammers, forget it, let it drop
just as the warm, rough palm tenderly reaches,

unexpectedly, almost devoid of weight,
to touch the naked shoulder, while the beach
sinks into dusk, the water stirred by the wind,
a shivering body filling up with warmth . . .
you dare not move.
It's gone. Quite gone. The season
is changing – oh so slowly the sky revolves.
Snow falls on the water, forget, forget,
behind the eyes darkness without a flaw,
which does not warrant tears, it has not the weight.
But if you let it drop, you too will fall
beneath dark water cold as ice, oh such
a deep cold that there simply is no longer
sun enough to melt it with a touch.

[CW/GG]

ANDRÁS GEREVICH

Mediterranean

Our bed is rocking like the sea
beneath a ship. Your smell
is as unfamiliar as the harbour
to the tramp steamer.

I cling to you, water to skin.
The cells of my body are shoals
of excited fish and now the funnel
blares and the nets

are broken, the mesh has caught
on a reef. Sailors' arms
are glimmering in the regular
strobe of reflectors, the beams

of a squeaky, revolving
lighthouse. The gulls are ripping
the kraken to shreds: it chews
and digests its own body.

The ship splits in two,
the decks' tiny splinters pierce
the entire surface of the skin,
a pool of diesel spreads across the water.

[GS]

Seasons

On Sunday we escaped to play in the woods:
We ran, my head humming with birdsong,
Bees and bugs fizzed about my face,
We hid behind shrubs, behind tree trunks
To spy on strangers as they walked by.

The sun shone green through the swaying branches,
We played tag, pretended to be outlaws;
We clambered up rocks: I was harder
Than stone; quicker and slicker than snakes.
But sand got into my shoes, between my teeth.

I was up to my knees in dead leaves,
The mulch thick with ants, almost heaving
And crackling, as if the skulls of a whole flock
Of dead birds were crushed under the foliage –
I threw myself headlong although I was frightened.

Let darkness cover me, I could feel the damp earth
Beneath it, knew its raw stench. I was cold
And stood up, snow melted on my face and ran
Under my clothes. As it froze to my skin
It compressed me, snow covered me, my body was snow.

[GS]

POSTSCRIPT

TWO DEATHS

GYÖRGY PETRI

Credit Card

It's never a good idea
to rush things.
Annihilation included.
No good
ever comes of haste.
Therefore:
we stay alive.

In other words: we keep open
the purse of possibility.
We take death's million-pound note
and break it up
into the small change of life.

Or, not break it up exactly –
only present it.
For who on earth can give change
for such a fine, crisp deathnote?
But it's impressive. So
we can live on the never-never.

The General Bank of Death
guarantees everything
So our balance always stands
at moral zero.

[GG/CW]

OTTÓ ORBÁN

The Witching Time

from *Fifteen Songs*

"'Tis now the very witching time of night . . .
now could I drink hot blood"
Shakespeare – *Hamlet*

SONG OF THE BLAGGARD HOPE

Ever closer the grenade exploding by my operated skull,
Like birds my severed limbs fly off into the distance;
This is how I must clear life's debts in full
And pay for my being's culpable persistence.

The hot blood may still run laps through my veins,
Though what confronts me is a mile-high ice-escarpment –
Heartdeath and Braindeath wink across frozen sheets, the foxy dames:
Black-clad nurses both, from the death department.

SONG OF TIME'S RAISED FINGER

Where has it gone, that frenzied summer by the lake?
What has caught up with yesterday's high achiever?
Into what cubby-hole has the well-thumbed issue of last month's
Playmate
Disappeared with its exciting flash of beaver?

It's drought from here on in, nothing but constant drought,
Time points out with its admonitory finger.
What opens up ahead is a windy, cavernous mouth
Where all flames are blown out and no lights linger.

SONG OF DAILY DISASTER

Daily disaster is suffered by the body, this holed
Sack through which life pathetically dribbles,
If night at the end of the world decides to fold,
The vampire bats remain like tortured sybils,

And hell's small teeth in all those tiny grins
Bring you the news, flesh garnished with smoke and burning.
Whatever your lot was before, the night begins.
Bid fond farewell for ever now to morning.

SONG OF THE FLAME IN THE ICE

In the beginning flowers of darkening coal,
The coupling of cells out of which love arises.
The desired is human, blind, out of control,
And leads poor-fool-me to its booby prizes.

For it survives us, as idea survives mere neurochemistry,
Like a compound dissolved, in the new-born child's nerve-centre.
This is where things begin, where nothing is lost to eternity,
And thin flames dance on through the terminal winter.

SONG OF WARNING: DANGEROUS SIDE-EFFECTS

Your life hangs on such threads, can't count them all:
The myriad forms and manners of disaster
That may pronounce you dead are too many by far to call
Each individual terror your sole master.

Our youthful heedlessness keeps us alive,
This flood-fomenting, grassblade-shoving power,
Billy the Kid enters the card-sharps' dive,
Twists on eighteen and bankrupts the whole shower.

SONG OF THE ERA'S VIEW OF THE FUTURE

Our cherished ideals prophesying redemption, that if
  We worked together the world would improve, turned to ordure;
Our sad history, we thought, might take a more fortunate drift
  Should we desist from crucifying the Son of God, Our Saviour –

Forsaking *hominis lupus*, man would no longer call
  On limb-shredding bombs to render his victims harmless.
But night is coming, the moon has no belly at all,
  It is dark, there is nothing to see, it is utterly starless.

SONG OF SUCCESSIVE GENERATIONS

Looming through the mist the generations rise
  But I remain what I was, there's no new version;
My teachers, the years of war, filled all my skies,
  My skull carved by a scalpel-wielding surgeon.

There'll be no New World or Last Chance: No Dice.
  Our lewd brains nourish toxins of the spirit.
John Doe, executioner and sacrifice
  Go to the bubbling lime-pit, vanish in it.

SONG OF THE DIVAN AND THE OCEAN

The divan on which I spend the best part of my time,
  Serves as both table and sea-worthy appendage:
My head spins verses, dizzy from rhyme to rhyme.
  I patch my head with words like strips of bandage.

It's slower now than it was, the intellect creaks and groans –
  Ideas lumber forth in leaden-footed motion:
I notate the orchestral score of my seized-up bones
  And sink beneath the waves of the icy ocean.

SONG OF THE GREEN LEAF

Humanity's wormkind wriggle on the bough:
The green leaf chunters: jewboy, tinker, sambo!
The lads are not subtle thinkers, and have trouble in seeing how
Words may anticipate bullets or outshoot Rambo.

Successful parasites rot in office once they reach the top,
Use show trial and base instinct to keep their feet under the table
And should that fail they still have a secret multi-purpose prop:
The club with which Cain crushed in the skull of Abel.

SONG OF THE TASTE OF BITTERNESS

Up and down the bomb-shelter all day
Robbed me of childhood, nor did it make me fitter.
They brought me food in hospital on a tray
But suffering made the taste of it seem bitter.

Bitter the water I drank then and bitter the law
That supports the usurper and the interloper,
Bitter the fact that everything sticks in the craw
Drowned in the bloody vortex of *Mitteleuropa*.

SONG OF THE BODY'S TIREDNESS

Sixty-five years, then sixty-six: now death and despair
Fill up my poems gradually, by inches.
You can't fight metal-fatigue with fervent prayer
Nor with a dissolute choir of tits and finches.

Spring with its grass hairdo arrives, but not for me,
It's winter I get with its bald and frozen graces,
My song is headed for the cemetery
Of the common wordhoard's great wide-open spaces.

SONG OF THE CREATED WORLD

Do you hear me, ancient of days, old man?
   Is this the very acme of your creation?
This lightless cosmos with its enigmatic plan,
   Where supernovae ignite worlds by conflagration?

Myth is the dream of naked upright apes.
   No angels zip about in space. You're either baloney
Or you exist. Struggling and hobbling instinctively I traipse
   Towards my grave on foot, by Shank's pony.

[GS]

NOTES ON THE AUTHORS

ISTVÁN BAKA (1948–1995) was a poet, translator and editor. Having studied Hungarian and Russian, he taught in a secondary school in Szekszárd, his home town, and became the editor of a literary and arts journal for ten- to fourteen-year-olds. He published eight volumes of poems and two collections of short stories in addition to translating Russian poetry of the twentieth century.

KÁROLY BARI was born in 1952. A poet, translator and painter, his first volume of poems, published in 1970 when he was barely eighteen, attracted considerable attention. A Roma poet, he writes in Hungarian about the plight, the history and the traditions of his people, in a surrealistic style rooted in folk poetry. He has also collected, edited and illustrated Gypsy folk poetry and folk tales.

ATTILA BARTIS was born in Transylvania, Romania, in 1968 and has been living in Hungary since 1984. His publications include two novels and a collection of short stories. One of his books has appeared in German and another in Spanish translation; one of his plays has been in the repertory of the National Theatre, Budapest.

PÁL BÉKÉS was born in 1956. An author, playwright and translator, he studied English and comparative literature, taught in a secondary school and has been a full-time writer since 1981. He spent a year in the US as a Fulbright scholar, and in 2003 conducted a playwriting workshop in Australia. His publications include novels, collections of short stories and books for children; he has written successful plays for the stage and television and translated British and American fiction into Hungarian.

ÁDÁM BODOR was born in 1936 in Transylvania, Romania. Having spent years in jail as a juvenile "conspirator against the state", he was not admitted to university and instead studied Calvinist theology and worked as a church archivist. He published his first story in a Hungarian-language magazine in 1965 and his first book in 1969. Since 1982, he has lived in Hungary, where he is an editor in a Budapest publishing house. His short stories have won him many prizes and have been translated into numerous languages. In addition to nine volumes of fiction, he has published an autobiography.

SÁNDOR CSOÓRI, born in a small village in 1930, is a poet, essayist and screenwriter. He studied Russian but took no degree, and worked in editorial jobs and at a film studio. Like many others who came from simple village backgrounds, he began voicing his disillusionment with the socialist order but was allowed to get away with it as "a son of the people". His visionary-surrealistic poems speak of loss and loneliness in the big city. He was a founding member of the Hungarian Democratic Forum, the centre-right party that won the first free elections in 1990, and served for years as president of the World Federation of Hungarians. His decorations include the Herder Prize.

ISTVÁN CSUKÁS was born in 1936. Son of a village smith, he studied music and law but did not take a degree, working in various editorial positions before devoting himself to writing. His poetry reflects the experience of a first-generation intellectual, a village boy come to the metropolis. His collected poems were published in 1996. He has written several books for children as well as a popular series of puppet films for children's television.

LÁSZLÓ DARVASI was born in 1962. A poet, author and journalist, he has held various editorial positions in Szeged, his home town, and is now a contributing editor to a Budapest literary weekly. The author of a volume of poems, several novels and collections of short stories, most recently he has written pseudo-historical stories set in China.

VIRÁG ERDŐS, born in 1968, is a poet and author. She studied Hungarian literature at Eötvös University in Budapest, and has published two novels and four volumes of poems.

PÉTER ESTERHÁZY was born in 1950 into one of Europe's most famous families and spent his early childhood in a remote village to which they had been "relocated" by the Hungarian government. Having studied mathematics, he published his first volume of short stories in 1976. Today he is a leading figure in Hungarian post-modern fiction and perhaps the country's most popular author. His large oeuvre includes novels, novellas and essays, and his most recent book, *Harmonia Caelestis*, is a 700-page family saga-cum-childhood autobiography. Several of his books have appeared in other European languages and have earned him awards and prizes both in Hungary and abroad.

GYŐZŐ FERENCZ, born in 1954, is a poet and translator. He studied English at Eötvös University in Budapest, where he now teaches

British and American poetry, having previously worked as a secondary-school teacher and editor. He has published three volumes of poems, edited anthologies and translated many classic and modern British and American poets.

LÁSZLÓ GARACZI was born in 1956. A novelist, poet and playwright, he studied Hungarian, history and philosophy. In addition to volumes of poems and short stories, he has published a satirical postmodern novel about childhood in János Kádár's socialist Hungary; his most recent work is a volume of short sketches he calls "bagatelles".

ANDRÁS GEREVICH, born in 1976, is a poet. Having spent four years in Dublin as a child, he studied English in Budapest and in America on a Fulbright scholarship. He has published one volume of his own poems as well as a selection of translations of poems by Seamus Heaney.

ÁGNES GERGELY, a poet, novelist, essayist and translator, was born in 1933. Having worked as an iron turner, studied English and Hungarian, and taught in a secondary school, she became a producer for Hungarian Radio and, later, an editor on various literary magazines. She spent 1973–4 as a member of the International Writing Program at the University of Iowa. In addition to numerous volumes of poetry, she has published two novels, collections of essays and a book on W. B. Yeats, as well as translations of British and American poetry, including James Joyce and Dylan Thomas. She teaches postgraduate courses at Eötvös Loránd University, Budapest.

GÁBOR GÖRGEY, born in 1929, is a poet, novelist, playwright, translator and journalist. In 1951, he was "relocated" with his family from Budapest to a village. For the next forty years he wrote a regular column for a national daily, worked in film, theatre and television, and was the secretary of Hungarian PEN. In 2002–3 he served as Minister of Culture. His first collection of poems appeared in 1956; since then, he has published more than two dozen books, mostly fiction, and written twenty-three plays, some of which have been staged in Hungary and abroad.

LAJOS GRENDEL was born in 1948. A novelist, critic and member of the Hungarian minority in Slovakia, he lives in Bratislava, where he obtained a degree in Hungarian and English. He is the head of Kalligram, a publishing house for Hungarian literature in that city, and is the president of Slovak PEN. Of his fifteen books to date, nine are novels, while the rest consist of short stories and essays. He writes mostly about minority life and historical subjects; in one book he calls his country "Absurdistan".

VICTOR HATÁR, born in 1914, is a poet, novelist, playwright, philosopher, essayist and translator. Having taken a degree in architecture in 1938, he studied musical composition under Zoltán Kodály. In 1943, he was arrested and sentenced to death for conspiracy against the state; the following year, he escaped from a penal battalion, remaining in hiding until the end of World War II. In 1945, he began working for the UNRRA relief organisation; arrested for illegal border-crossing, he spent two and a half years in prison, where he started translating classical English fiction. He then fled to Britain, where he continued to write and publish in Hungarian, worked for the BBC and Radio Free Europe, and tutored diplomats in Hungarian language and culture for the Foreign Office. His works are now published in Hungary, but he continues to live in the UK.

GYULA ILLYÉS was a poet, author, playwright, essayist, diarist, translator and editor. Born in 1902 to a farm mechanic's family on a large estate, he joined a left-wing youth organisation and fought in Béla Kun's Red Army in 1919. To escape the ensuing terror, he fled to Paris, where he worked as a bookbinder and studied literature at the Sorbonne. Having befriended the Surrealist poets, he wrote his first poems in French but returned to Hungary in 1926, soon making a name for himself. He published his first volume of poetry in 1928. While working in the press section of the Hungarian National Bank, he travelled to Moscow as a guest of the first congress of Soviet writers; the experience opened his eyes to communist reality. Thought of by many as the last of Hungary's great poets committed to the cause of the nation, he was silenced in 1956 and only able to resume publishing in 1961. His awards included, among others, Commandeur de l'Ordre des Arts et des Lettres, and he was nominated several times for the Nobel Prize. He died in 1983.

FLÓRA IMRE, born in 1961, is a poet. Having studied Hungarian, Latin and ancient Greek, she teaches in a Budapest secondary school. She has published six volumes of poems, as well as translations of Latin poetry.

FERENC JUHÁSZ was born in 1928 into a stonemason's family. After studying Hungarian and philosophy, he became an editor and poet. Having become disillusioned with socialism and turning away from politics, he developed a visionary, mythic-symbolic style rooted in folk poetry. One of the most widely translated and travelled of contemporary Hungarian poets, he was shortlisted for the Nobel Prize in 1976.

PÉTER KÁNTOR, born in 1949, is a poet who, having studied English and Russian, has worked as poetry editor on a Budapest literary weekly. He spent a year in the US on a Fulbright scholarship and has published ten volumes of poems, poetry for children and an anthology of contemporary British poets that he edited and partly translated.

SÁNDOR KÁNYÁDI, born in 1929 in Transylvania, Romania, was the son of a Sekler peasant family. He studied Hungarian in Kolozsvár/Cluj, publishing his first poem in 1950 and his first volume of poetry in 1955. Until his retirement, he worked as an editor of literary magazines. When silenced as a poet in the 1980s, his poems appeared in Hungary, and he translated work by Romanian, German and French poets, as well as Saxon and Yiddish folk poetry of Transylvania. He has published more than a dozen volumes of poems. Among other decorations, he is a recipient of the Herder Prize.

IMRE KERTÉSZ, winner of the 2002 Nobel Prize for Literature "for writing that upholds the fragile experience of the individual against the barbaric arbitrariness of history", was born in 1929. A novelist, essayist and translator, he grew up in Budapest in a middle-class Jewish family. Caught in a random check of documents in 1944, he was deported to Buchenwald and, later, to Auschwitz. After the war, he worked in a factory and then in journalism, sustaining himself by writing libretti for musical comedies. His first novel, *Fateless*, based on his concentration-camp experience, could not be published for several years; with three other books it constitutes a loosely connected tetralogy about the Holocaust. He has also published short stories, a writer's diary, volumes of essays, "monologues and dialogues" and "meditations" about philosophical and moral subjects.

GYÖRGY KONRÁD, a novelist and essayist, was born in 1933 into a village hardware shopkeeper's family. Hiding to escape persecution as a Jew, he studied Hungarian, served as a national guard in the 1956 revolution and later became a social worker. His second novel was censored for years. In 1974 he co-authored, with the sociologist Iván Szelényi, a strongly regime-critical tract, *The Intellectuals on the Road to Class Power*, which was confiscated by the police. He became a leading figure of the democratic opposition, publishing his work in samizdat, for which he was often harrassed. In the mid-1970s and again in the '80s, he spent periods in Berlin, New York and Paris on scholarships, and from 1990 until 1993 he was president of International PEN. His books have appeared in English and most European languages, and his decorations include the Herder Prize, the Legion d'Honneur and the Charles Cross.

MIHÁLY KORNIS, born in 1949, is a novelist and playwright. Trained as a theatre director, his first successful work was the play *Halleluja!* (1981), a surrrealistic, grotesque comedy about family life and childhood in socialist times. One of his major subjects is the Jewish experience, which he best described in his novel *Sunbook* in a unique mixture of hilarious irony and powerful, provocative language.

LÁSZLÓ KRASZNAHORKAI, a novelist, was born in 1954. Though he studied law, he took no degree, instead working for years as an archivist in a publishing house. He has been a freelance writer since 1984 and now lives in seclusion in a village. His first novel, *Satan Tango* (1985), was hailed by critics and made into a seven-hour film by the director Béla Tarr; his second novel, *The Melancholy of Resistance*, was also filmed by Tarr. Both films won several prizes. He has written further novels as well as collections of essays and short stories. A visit to China in the 1980s had a lasting effect on his writing. His latest work is set in modern Japan.

ZSOLT LÁNG, born in 1958, is a novelist and editor living in Kolozsvár/Cluj-Napoca as a member of the large Hungarian minority in Transylvania, Romania. An engineer by training, he worked for a while as a secondary-school teacher, and has been on the staff of a Hungarian-language literary magazine since 1990. Out of his seven published volumes of fiction, four are novels, and three are collections of short stories; one has appeared in German, another in Bulgarian translation.

IVÁN MÁNDY, born in 1918, was a novelist and short-story writer who started publishing stories in 1937. From 1948 until 1957, he was unable to publish, so made his living by adapting classics and writing plays for children's radio, and as a "travelling lecturer" on Soviet and socialist literature in village cultural centres. The world of most of his succinct stories is a bleak district of Budapest where he spent his youth. In a hilarious novel he described the literary "underworld" of the Stalinist period, that of the penniless "rewriters", adapters and "travelling lecturers", of which he was one. The reductionist stories of his later years are close to poetry. He died in 1995.

SÁNDOR MÁRAI was born in 1900. A novelist, playwright, poet, diarist and journalist, he studied in Budapest and Germany, worked for various German and Hungarian papers before publishing his first book, a volume of poems. His two-volume autobiography, *Confessions of a Man of the Middle-Class*, made him a best-selling author. His novels, plays and diaries (which he kept from 1943 until his death) were highly successful. In 1948 he left Hungary, settling first in Italy and later in the US, pledging not to return until the last Soviet soldier had left his country, a moment he did not live to see. While abroad he continued to write and publish in Hungarian, although his books were pulped in his native land, only beginning to be published in 1990. Almost blind and penniless, he committed suicide in 1989.

MÓNIKA MESTERHÁZI, born in 1967, is a poet. Having studied Hungarian and English, she wrote her PhD dissertation on Northern Irish poetry. She taught for years in secondary schools and is now a freelance writer and translator. She has published three volumes of poems, as well as translations of British and American poetry and selections from the diaries and correspondence of Katherine Mansfield.

MIKLÓS MÉSZÖLY, born in 1921, was a novelist, essayist and playwright who studied law, fought in the war, spent time in a POW camp in Serbia, and worked as a journalist, editor and dramaturge at the Budapest State Puppet Theatre before becoming a full-time writer in 1956. His unusual reductionist narrative techniques, keen observation, dramatic atmospheres, and moral and literary ideas attracted many younger writers. *The Falcons*, a 1970 film by István Gaál based on one of his novellas, won major prizes at Cannes, Chicago and Adelaide. He died in 2001.

PÉTER NÁDAS was born in 1942. A novelist, essayist and playwright, he studied chemistry, photography and journalism, and worked for years as a journalist. He has spent long periods in Germany on scholarships. His first novel, *The End of a Family Story*, established him as a major writer. Short stories, plays and essays followed; his magnum opus, *The Book of Memories*, a novel in the form of three parallel memoirs, took him eleven years to write. Lately he has written, among many other things, an account of his resuscitation from clinical death following a severe heart attack. Most of his fiction has been translated into numerous languages.

ÁDÁM NÁDASDY, born in 1947, is a poet and linguist. He studied English and Italian, taught in a secondary school and, since 1972, has taught linguistics at the School of English and American Studies of Eötvös Loránd University, Budapest. He has published four volumes of poems, as well as a collection of essays on language. He has also re-translated a number of plays by Shakespeare published in classical translations, because he believes modern audiences should have access to more readable texts.

LÁSZLÓ NAGY was born in 1925 in western Hungary of peasant stock. He attended art school in 1946–9 and also attended the university in Budapest as a member of the People's College Movement but took no degree. He spent three years in Bulgaria on a state scholarship, returning to take up various editorships. His first book, *The Artilleryman and the Rye*, appeared while he was still in Bulgaria in 1951. His work is related to fellow rural-born writers such as Juhász and Csoóri. His early death at the age of 53 in 1978 marked an important loss to Hungarian literature.

ÁGNES NEMES NAGY, a poet, essayist and translator, was born in 1922. Having studied Hungarian, Latin and art history, she began publishing poems in the 1940s. In 1946, she started, together with her husband, the essayist and critic Balázs Lengyel, *Újhold* (*New Moon*), an important literary magazine, which was banned as "bourgeois" in 1948. Unable to publish until 1958, she taught in a secondary school, wrote poems for children and worked on translations. Besides volumes of poems, her oeuvre includes collections of essays on poets, poetry and translation, a travel diary of the US, and translations of poetry and plays. Her powerful objective verse has influenced many younger poets. The State of Israel awarded her the Yad Vashem medal for saving the lives of persecuted Jews. She died in 1991.

OTTÓ ORBÁN, born in 1936, lost his father in the Holocaust and was raised in a war orphanage, where he began to write poems, soon becoming a prodigy. Though he studied English and Hungarian, he did not take a degree. He began publishing in the 1960s. His strongly intellectual, sharply worded, ironic poems made him something of an *enfant terrible*. In 1976, he was a member of the International Writing Program at the University of Iowa, and in 1987 he taught poetry at the University of Minnesota, Minneapolis. Besides many volumes of poems, a prose account of his visit to India and collections of essays, he published a number of translations from British, American, French and Spanish poetry. Alan Ginsberg and Robert Lowell were major influences on his writing; he translated several of the Beat poets. He died in 2002.

ISTVÁN ÖRKÉNY, a novelist and playwright, was born in 1912. He studied pharmacology and spent time in London and Paris before World War II, publishing his first short stories in the mid-1930s. Having served in a Jewish forced-labour battalion, he spent three years in a Soviet POW camp. After returning home in 1946, he joined the Communist Party and wrote socialist-realist reportage and stories; the latter were severely criticised by the party's chief ideologue. Banned from publishing for his role in the 1956 revolution, he was only able to resume doing so after 1966. His keen sense of the grotesque, of social satire and of black humour made him very popular. His black comedy *The Tóth Family* and the tragicomedy *Catsplay* were shown successfully all over Europe and in the US, and are still frequently staged in Hungary. He died in 1979.

GÉZA OTTLIK, born in 1912, was a novelist and translator. Educated in cadet school, he studied mathematics and physics at university, publishing his first short story in 1931. An internationally known bridge player, he wrote several books about the game. He saved the lives of persecuted Jews during the last year of the war, among them the poet István Vas. He worked at Hungarian Radio in 1945–6 and was secretary of Hungarian PEN from 1945 until 1957. His collection of short stories, *Rooftops at Dawn*, appeared in 1957; his major novel, *School at the Frontier*, about life in a cadet school, had such an impact that, as a tribute, Péter Esterházy copied the entire 470-page text on to a single sheet of paper. He died in 1990.

LÁSZLÓ PARTI NAGY, born in 1953, is a poet, novelist and playwright who studied Hungarian and history and worked as a librarian and editor before becoming a freelance author. He often writes in a unique nonsense language, a mixture of distorted Communist Party lingo and primitive parlance, and in the platitudinous manner of poetasters and amateurs. His dramatic parodies have also been very successful.

GYÖRGY PETRI was born in 1943. A poet and translator, he studied Hungarian and philosophy. In the early 1980s, he joined the illegal democratic opposition, edited its underground journal, and either smuggled his work abroad or published it in samizdat. At first he believed in a radical, fundamentalist reform of socialism, but he soon discovered its absurdity and became, with his bitter, sardonic poems, the regime's most outspoken opponent. He was frequently followed, intimidated and harassed by the police. Publishing became possible for him again after 1985. He died in 2000.

JÁNOS PILINSZKY, born in 1921, was a poet raised in a deeply religious middle-class Roman Catholic environment. Though he studied Hungarian, Italian and art history, he did not complete a degree. In 1944 he was called up and sent to Germany; on his way back to Hungary after the war, he saw the recently liberated concentration camps, an experience that became fundamental to his work. Having published his first volume of poetry in 1946, he was silenced for years, so worked as a proofreader and wrote poems for children until 1957, when he was able to resume publishing. In addition to his relatively small poetic output, he wrote an oratorio about the concentration camps, as well as essays, criticism, meditations on religious and philosophical subjects, and "the novel of a dialogue": *Conversations with Sheryl Sutton*. He travelled a good deal and read at international poetry festivals. He died in 1981.

SZILÁRD PODMANICZKY, born in 1963, is a poet, author and journalist. Having studied to become a physics teacher, he became a writer instead. He is on the staff of a regional daily newspaper in the southern city of Szeged. Since publishing his first volume of fiction in 1993, he has published eight other volumes, mostly short fiction.

ZSUZSA RAKOVSZKY was born in 1950. A poet, novelist and translator, she studied Hungarian and English and worked as a librarian and publisher's reader before devoting herself to writing full-time. She has published four volumes of poems and a historical novel, *The Snake's Shadow*, which became a bestseller. She also has translated British and American poetry, essays and fiction.

GYÖRGY SOMLYÓ, born in 1920, is a poet, essayist, novelist, translator and anthologist. The son of Zoltán Somlyó, a noted poet in the first half of the last century, he studied in Budapest and at the Sorbonne, and held editorial and artistic positions in the theatre, in film and in radio in the 1940s and '50s. His large oeuvre, which has brought him Hungarian and international awards and prizes, consists of numerous volumes of poems, collections of essays, three novels, studies on contemporary poetry, its history, theory and major figures, and a great number of translations from French, British, American and Spanish poets. He was editor of *Arion*, a multi-lingual literary journal published in Budapest.

GYÖRGY SPIRÓ, born in 1946, is a novelist, playwright, essayist and Slavic scholar. He studied Hungarian, Russian and Serbo-Croat at Eötvös Loránd University, Budapest, worked as an editor, and was dramaturge and general manager of a theatre in Szolnok. Since 1981 he has taught Eastern European literature at Eötvös Loránd University. He has published four novels which deal with contemporary Eastern European subjects in historical settings, volumes of short stories, collections of essays and criticism, and a great many plays, some of which have been highly successful in Hungary and elsewhere in Europe. He has also translated plays.

ANNA T. SZABÓ, born in 1972, is a poet. Having studied Hungarian and English, she works as a freelance writer and translator. She has published four volumes of poems and translated British and American poetry, fiction and essays.

FERENC SZIJJ, born in 1958, is a poet and novelist who studied Hungarian and German at the Attila József University in Szeged, and worked as a librarian and as an editor on a literary journal. He has published five volumes, three of which contained poems, one of which was a collection of short fiction, and the last of which, published in 2001, was a fable for children. He presently lives in Germany on a scholarship.

ZSUZSA TAKÁCS, a poet and translator, was born in 1938. She studied Spanish and Italian, in 1963 teaching at the University of Havana, and was for many years head of the Spanish-language section at the University of Economics, Budapest. She has published ten volumes of poems, a collection of short stories, and numerous translations from Spanish, Catalan, French and British poets, as well as translating the complete poetry and selected prose of St John of the Cross.

DEZSŐ TANDORI, born in 1938, is a poet, author and translator. He studied Hungarian and German, worked for a few years as a teacher and has been freelance since 1971. In 1968 he published his first collection of poems, soon establishing himself as a major innovator in both poetry and prose. His texts, complete with typos, corrections and deletions, follow the seemingly arbitrary logic of the creative process. Over the years, he has created a sort of one-person performance at his readings. His huge oeuvre, ever experimental, consists of volumes of poetry, thrillers written under various pseudonyms, and books about his birds, teddy bears and button-football team, his drinking, his travels and his adventures as a horse-racing fan. He has also published essays, exhibited his drawings and translated an enormous number of English, American, German, Russian and Scandinavian poems and works of fiction.

SÁNDOR TAR, born in 1941, worked in a medical-instruments factory as a machine operator before starting to write prose in 1970. His often tragic but dispassionate stories, of which he has published seven volumes so far, deal with misfits, drifters and others down on their luck and scraping along in the margins of society.

KRISZTINA TÓTH, a poet, was born in 1967. Having studied Hungarian, she spent two years in Paris on a scholarship and worked for five years at the Institut Français, Budapest. Besides writing poems and translating contemporary French poetry, she designs, makes and restores stained-glass windows. She has published five volumes of poems.

SZABOLCS VÁRADY, a poet, translator and editor born in 1943, studied Hungarian, worked in publishing and began publishing poems in 1968. In 1988 he spent time in the US on a Fulbright scholarship. He has been poetry editor of *Holmi*, Hungary's most important literary monthly, since its inception in 1989. He has published two volumes of poems and translated many British and American poets and a play by Tom Stoppard, and has written the lyrics for numerous musical comedies. His recent books are a volume of three hundred limericks by Hungarian poets, including himself, and his collected poems.

ISTVÁN VAS, born in 1910, was a poet, essayist, translator and editor who belonged to the left-wing avant-garde before World War II. Called up in a Jewish forced-labour battalion, he managed to escape in 1944 and was saved by a friend. A Communist, he became disillusioned after the war and, having got into a controversy with leading Party ideologues, renounced his Party membership in 1950, a step that required considerable bravery. Forbidden to publish until 1956, he worked as an editor in a publishing house and translated English, American, French and German poetry, fiction and drama. His office became the focus for a circle of younger poets and writers. Beside his volumes of poems, he published a multi-volume semi-fictional autobiography, collections of essays and criticism, and translations. He died in 1991.

SÁNDOR WEÖRES, born in 1913, was a poet, playwright and

translator. His first poems appeared while he was still in secondary school. He studied law and literature, publishing his first book in 1934. Unable to publish between 1949 and 1957, he was dismissed from his job at a library; in those years he wrote for himself and published poems for children which became immensely popular; whole generations grew up reciting them with delight. His huge oeuvre consists of lyrical and epic poems, verse plays and translations from many languages. He was one of the most versatile of Hungarian poets and a virtuoso of language and form. A great tour de force of his, among many others, was *Psyché* (1972), the entire oeuvre, complete with juvenilia, correspondence and even a contemporary review, of an early nineteenth-century fictional Hungarian woman poet in love with an actual poet of the age, Erzsébet Lónyay. This work seemed so authentic that one academic critic reviewed it enthusiastically as an important discovery. He died in 1989.

PÁL ZÁVADA, born in 1954, is a novelist who studied sociology and worked for years as a sociologist researching the effects of Communist policy on his native village. He published a volume of short stories in 1996. Since 1992 he has been the fiction editor of *Holmi*, a Budapest literary monthly. His first novel, *Jadviga's Pillow*, became a bestseller and was turned into a successful film. His second, *Milota*, appeared in 2002. Both are set among the Slovak minority in Hungary, to which his family belongs.

PÉTER ZILAHY, born in 1970, is a poet, author and photographer who studied English, philosophy and cultural anthropology in Budapest, New York and Zurich. He published his first volume, a collection of poems, in 1993. His short stories are about trips to Sydney, New York, Cape Town and St Petersburg. His latest book, based on a Hungarian pictorial dictionary for children, appeared with his own photographs and was translated into eleven languages, as well as being adapted for radio and the stage.

NOTES ON THE TRANSLATORS

PAUL ASTON is an Englishman who spent some years in Hungary in the late 1960s and early '70s as a teacher of English. He was a language instructor in the English Department of Kossuth University in Debrecen.

BRUCE BERLIND, born in 1926, is a poet and was Professor of English at Colgate University, Hamilton, New York, from 1954 to 1988. Besides volumes of his own poems, he has published *Selected Poems of Ágnes Nemes Nagy* (1980), *Birds and Other Relations: Selected Poems of Dezső Tandori* (1986) and Gyula Illyés, *Charon's Ferry. Fifty Poems* (2000).

MICHAEL BLUMENTHAL, born in 1949, is an American poet, novelist and translator. Having studied at the State University of New York and Cornell, he worked for the National Endowments for the Arts and for the Humanities and Time-Life Books, taught creative writing at Harvard University, spent time in Budapest as a Fulbright lecturer, was an editor at the Central European University Press there, was a Fulbright lecturer in Berlin as well, and taught at the University of Haifa, Israel. He lives in Austin, Texas.

TONY CONNOR, born in 1930, is an English poet, writer and playwright, and a graduate of the University of Manchester. On a visit to Budapest in the 1960s he met a number of Hungarian poets and translated some of their work.

JÁNOS CSOKITS, born in 1928, is a poet. Having left Hungary in 1956, he lived in France, Germany, England and Andorra, eventually returning to his homeland. He worked for the BBC and Radio Free Europe, and has published an anthology of Hungarian poetry in French (1962), and several in Hungarian (1971, 1972, 1977), one in Budapest (1992). He is the author of one volume of poems (1988), a volume of János Pilinszky's poems in German translation (with Henning Paetzke), and *János Pilinszky: Selected Poems*, (with Ted Hughes [1976]).

GEORGE GÖMÖRI, born in 1934, is a poet, critic and translator. Having left Hungary in 1956, he studied at Oxford, and taught Polish and Hungarian literature at Cambridge until his recent retirement. He has published nine volumes of poems in Hungarian, translated

Polish poetry into Hungarian, and written many essays on Hungarian and Polish literature and Anglo-Hungarian cultural contacts. He co-translated (with James Atlas) *Attila József: Selected Poems and Texts* (1973); (with Tony Connor and Kenneth McRobbie) *László Nagy: Love of the Scorching Wind: Selected Poems* (1973); (with Clive Wilmer) *Miklós Radnóti: Forced March: Selected Poems* (1979); György Petri, *Night Song of the Personal Shadow: 20 Poems* and *György Petri: Eternal Monday. Selected Poems* (1991, 1999); and co-edited (with George Szirtes) *The Colonnade of Teeth: Modern Hungarian Poetry* (1996).

DAVID HILL was born in 1971. An English poet living in Budapest since 1998, he is on the staff of the *Budapest Business Journal*. He has published two volumes of poems and prepared translations from numerous contemporary Hungarian poets. He is the founder and co-host of The Bardroom, an English-language poetry and performance series in Budapest.

DANIEL HOFFMAN, the American poet, essayist and professor, was born in 1923 and served as Consultant on Poetry for the Library of Congress in 1973–4. He has translated numerous contemporary Hungarian poets, for which work Hungarian P.E.N. awarded him its Gold Medal.

TED HUGHES, born in 1930, befriended János Pilinszky and, with János Csokits, translated a volume of his poems, *Selected Poems* (1976). He died in 1998. The translation of Ferenc Juhász's poem published in this anthology was found among his papers.

JASCHA KESSLER, born in 1929, is a poet, author, critic, translator and retired Professor of English and modern literature at UCLA. His major translations from the Hungarian include: (with Charlotte Rogers): *The Magician's Garden: 24 Stories by Géza Csáth* (1980); *Under Gemini: A Prose Memoir and Selected Poetry by Miklós Radnóti* (1985); *The Face of Creation: Contemporary Hungarian Poetry* (1987); *Catullan Games: Poems by Sándor Rákos* (1989); and Ottó Orbán, *Our Bearings at Sea: A Novel in Poems* (2001).

RICHARD LOURIE is an American journalist, translator and author of books of fiction and non-fiction. He has also produced film and TV documentaries.

ESZTER MOLNÁR, born in 1956, spent five years in England as a child, and studied English and French at Eötvös University, Budapest. She has translated fiction by a great number of mostly contemporary Hungarian authors, but also some classics: Gyula Krúdy, Dezső Kosztolányi, Iván Mándy.

EDWIN MORGAN, a Scottish poet born in 1920, has translated a great many poems from the Hungarian; some are included in his *Rites of Passage: Selected Translations* (1976). He has also published *Sándor Weöres and Ferenc Juhász: Selected Poems* (Weöres translated by Morgan, 1970), and Attila József, *Sixty Poems* (2001).

ILDIKÓ NOÉMI NAGY, born in Canada in 1975, studied viola at the Liszt Ferenc Academy of Music, Budapest, and also took a degree in American literature at Eötvös Loránd University. Married to the author László Garaczi, she translated his novel, *Lemur, Who Are You?* (2000). She has also translated Hungarian works on art history and musicology.

PAUL OLCHVÁRY, born in the US in 1965, studied English and American literature at the State University of New York and Indiana University. From 1990, he lived for ten years in Hungary, teaching, writing and translating. He is senior copywriter at Princeton University Press. His translations include a novel by Lajos Grendel (1999), Károly Pap's *Azarel* (2000) and *The Letters of Ferenc Molnár to Lili Darvas* (2000).

IVAN SANDERS was born in Budapest in 1944. A translator and critic, he has lived in the US since 1956. He has a PhD in comparative literature from New York University. Recently retired as Professor of English from the State University of New York, he teaches Hungarian literature at Columbia University, New York. His translations include novels by Milán Füst, György Konrád and Péter Nádas.

WILLIAM JAY SMITH, the American poet, essayist and translator, was born in 1918. Co-founder of the Translation Center at Columbia University, New York, and editor of *Translation*, its journal, he was Consultant in Poetry at the Library of Congress from 1968 to 1970. His translations of scores of Hungarian poems have appeared in journals and anthologies. He edited and introduced *What You Have Almost Forgotten: Selected Poems* (in English translation) by Gyula Illyés (1999).

JUDITH SOLLOSY, born in 1946, is senior editor at Corvina Press, Budapest. Her major translations into English include fiction by Endre Ady, Géza Csáth, István Örkény, Péter Esterházy, Péter Nádas and Mihály Kornis.

GEORGE SZIRTES was born in Budapest in 1948 and came to England as a refugee in 1956. Trained as a painter, he became a writer in English. He has published twelve volumes of poems and about the same number of works in translation from the Hungarian; he is also the author or editor of numerous other books. Major translations include Imre Madách, *The Tragedy of Man*, a volume of poems by Zsuzsa Rakovszky, another by Ágnes Nemes Nagy, fiction by Sándor Márai and László Krasznahorkai, and a play by Victor Határ. He co-edited *The Lost Rider: The Corvina Book of Hungarian Verse* (1997). His awards include the Faber Prize for Poetry and the European Poetry Translation Prize.

ALBERT TEZLA, born in 1915, is an American scholar and translator who studied at the University of Chicago. He is Professor Emeritus of English at the University of Minnesota at Duluth. He edited *Ocean at the Window: Hungarian Prose and Poetry* since *1945* (1980), and his major translations include works by Iván Mándy, Sándor Márai, Miklós Mészöly, Lajos Nagy and others.

TIM WILKINSON was born in 1947. Since living and working in Budapest during the early 1970s, he has been translating from Hungarian, including many works on Hungary's history and culture, such as Eva Balázs's *Hungary and the Habsburgs 1765–1800* (1997) and Domokos Kosáry's *Hungary and International Politics in 1848–1849* (2003). More recently, his literary translations have included the prose of Imre Kertész (three novels will appear in the US in 2004) and other contemporary writers.

CLIVE WILMER was born in 1945. This English poet, translator and editor studied at King's College, Cambridge, but took no degree. He now teaches at Cambridge University. He has published five volumes of poems. His translations from the Hungarian, prepared in collaboration with the Hungarian poet George Gömöri, include *Forced March: Selected Poems of Miklós Radnóti* (1975, 2003), *Night Song of the Personal Shadow: Selected Poems by György Petri* (1991), and *Eternal Monday*, a new selection from Petri's poetry (1999). He has also translated Italian poetry.

PETER ZOLLMAN is a Hungarian translator living in England. Born in 1931, he studied physics in Budapest, fleeing to the UK in 1956 and working there as a physicist until his retirement. He has translated a great many Hungarian poets into English.